DESERT REMAINS

A GUS PARKER AND ALEX MILLS NOVEL

DESERT REMAINS

STEVEN COOPER

SEVENTH STREET BOOKS®
AN IMPRINT OF PROMETHEUS BOOKS

59 JOHN GLENN DRIVE • AMHERST, NY 14228
www.seventhstreetbooks.com

Published 2017 by Seventh Street Books®, an imprint of Prometheus Books

Cover image © Shutterstock
Cover design by Nicole Sommer-Lecht
Cover design © Prometheus Books

This is a work of fiction. Characters, organizations, products, locales, and events portrayed in this novel are either products of the author's imagination or used fictitiously.

Inquiries should be addressed to
Seventh Street Books
59 John Glenn Drive
Amherst, New York 14228
VOICE: 716–691–0133 • FAX: 716–691–0137
WWW.SEVENTHSTREETBOOKS.COM

21 20 19 18 17   5 4 3 2 1

Library of Congress Cataloging-in-Publication Data

Names: Cooper, Steven, 1961- author.
Title: Desert remains : a Gus Parker and Alex Mills novel / Steven Cooper.
Description: Amherst, NY : Seventh Street Books, an imprint of Prometheus Books, 2017.
Identifiers: LCCN 2017020340 (print) | LCCN 2017023972 (ebook) | ISBN 9781633883543 (ebook) | ISBN 9781633883536 (paperback)
Subjects: | BISAC: FICTION / Mystery & Detective / Police Procedural. | GSAFD: Mystery fiction.
Classification: LCC PS3603.O583 (ebook) | LCC PS3603.O583 D47 2017 (print) | DDC 813/.6—dc23
LC record available at https://lccn.loc.gov/2017020340

Printed in the United States of America

In Memory of

Dr. Alvan Fisher
And his son, Jeremy

Leanne Fisher Gitell
Ruth Kane Goldman

1

Her name is Elizabeth Spears.

She has blue eyes and short blond hair.

Her address is 9223 South Nightbird Trail. That's nearby in a section of Phoenix known as Ahwatukee. Many people don't like to say Ahwatukee because the word sounds kind of doltish, especially the accent on TOO-key, and the name is often met by nervous laughter and blushing faces as if it's the Native American word for "toilet," which it isn't. The translation is really quite lovely, romantic even. Ahwatukee comes from the ancient language of the Pima Indians, and it means "House of Dreams."

Elizabeth Spears is twenty-seven years old.

Her birthday was last month.

She's five feet six inches tall. Although it's hard to tell from this angle.

She is bejeweled. A string of shimmering stones clings to her wrist, likewise her neck, in hues of amber and gold, like the hues of the cave that shelters her.

Elizabeth Spears is an organ donor.

Homicide detective Alex Mills of the Phoenix Police Department hands the victim's driver's license to another investigator at the scene and now kneels beside the body. One. Two. Three. Four. He's counting the stab wounds. Careful not to contaminate or alter the scene, the crime techs are surrounding the body like a surgical team. He doesn't want to get in the way. There's blood everywhere. Five. Six. Seven. They all have a job to do. There are rubber gloves and flash photography.

Yellow tape and tweezers. Eight, nine, ten. Eleven. For all this commotion, he hears very little beyond his own counting. There is a stillness here in this barren cave in the middle of the desert, and Mills knows instinctively that stillness is all that there ever was and all that there ever will be. He understands this quiet reverence of the desert where winds blow in flawless circles, sometimes rising to the sky in pillars of swirling dust, sometimes hushed and invisible like the modesty of prayer.

It's five thirty. The sun won't set for two more hours. The slow unfolding of gold has just begun, as it always does, still yellowish now, still yellowish for a while, and then there will be the perpetual anointment of the desert, that timeless sanctification, that brings beauty to this desolate place. Tonight the beauty will be haunting when it collides with evil.

Mills rises slowly. When he turned forty a few years back, the new decade in life immediately yanked at his knees, greeting him with the ache and pain of every jump shot, every sprint, every hurdle he had ever performed in his quest for athletic excellence, which, he had promised himself, would compensate for his academic mediocrity. For the most part it had. And then one day, just one day out of nowhere, he started reading. Okay, that's not exactly true. One day he met an English major named Corinne Wiley who was as head over heels in love with literature as he was with her. Dickens was the fastest route to her heart. So was, God help him, Shakespeare. Corinne married a dentist, but Mills still loves a good book.

He studies the wall of the cave. Finally he gets a good view. Every responder had all but genuflected in front of that wall like sycophants at an art professor's opening. Mills understands the fascination; he feels it bubble in his blood. About an hour before, when he had first arrived at the crime scene, one of the other detectives, he thinks it was Chase, pointed at the wall and said, "What the fuck is that?"

"That ain't no petroglyph," the police photographer replied as he started to burst out shots, some with flash, others without.

"No shit," Chase barked. "Unless we got a new tribe that just arrived in the desert and started sacrificing people."

"For all we know it's illegal immigrants. I mean, hell, they're the newest tribe."

Mills knows who said that. It was Detective Morton Myers. Morton Myers is an English-only ton of lard who couldn't chase a tortoise from a crime scene if his next Double Whopper with cheese depended on it.

Mills soaks in the desecration of the cave. In the absence of a body it would be horrible vandalism. In the presence of a body it's horrifying. The killer left a portrait of the murder.

A rude carving, at least ten feet wide and five feet tall, depicts a man in a cowboy hat, perhaps a bandana as well, plunging a knife into the chest of a woman bent over his knee.

Alex Mills looks down at Elizabeth Spears and confirms that the chest wound on the wall matches a chest wound on her body. He looks back to the drawing. In it Elizabeth's eyes are wide with terror. Her mouth is twisted. The artwork is elementary at best. A fifth grader's rendition of bloody murder.

Mills steps away from the circle of dried blood around the body of Elizabeth Spears and takes a wider view of the scene: This cave, just below a hiking trail, just above a pebbly wash; this body exposed as if there were nothing to hide. Nearly open to the public. A vista in itself.

Elizabeth Spears could not have been dead for very long.

There is no evidence her body had been visited upon by carnivores. No signs at all that she had been taken for carrion.

A male jogger who is still out there somewhere talking to investigators discovered her body. Mills consults his notebook. Mark Green. That's his name, the jogger who found the body and then vomited several times before he could compose himself enough to dial 911.

"Is that your vomit?" Myers had asked him, pointing to the overlapping piles on the ground.

Mark Green nodded. "Yeah," he said. "Is it some kind of evidence?"

"It's evidence you got a weak stomach, heh-heh," the detective told him.

Myers needs a desk job desperately.

Detective Alex Mills needs some evidence desperately, some leads, the ah-hah moment, if you will. If there is evidence of a struggle it has been erased, presumably by a meticulous killer who wants the only version of the crime to be the version he has carved into the wall.

He has left behind no murder weapon.

He has left behind no carving tools.

He has left behind Elizabeth Spears, probably a hiker or a jogger, a young woman who's maybe a regular out here, who finds her solace here or her joy, who sees the desert as a gift to be taken, a gift to be used with pious respect. Or maybe this was her training ground, her proving ground.

Maybe the killer was not a man.

The calamitous crankology of maybes begins to rattle like pots and pans in Detective Alex Mills's sleuthish brain. And now he feels empowered by the crankology. The crankology is his real training ground; it is also his mojo.

Mojo, shmojo.

Mills can already hear the TV choppers fluttering above like big, beastly carcass seekers. He knows a swarm of reporters cannot be far behind. Timothy Chase, the scene investigator, has told a few officers to tape off the trailhead.

Mills looks again at the body of Elizabeth Spears and, as he always does when he is sent to a murder scene, begins to interview the victim.

Who are you? he asks. *What happened here?*

2

First he stares at the gallbladder. Then at the pancreas. He's not a big fan of the pancreas and here's why: it goes bad, you go bad. The pancreas has more potential to kill you than most other organs. Now he looks at the liver. Unless you're an alcoholic, your liver is most often unremarkable, a few benign hemangiomas notwithstanding. Then it's on to the left kidney: clear. He sees a tiny something or other on the right kidney, like a chickpea the size of a thumbtack. He doesn't say anything. He doesn't ever say anything. He's not supposed to say anything; instead he says, "Okay, Mrs. Golding, we're done. We'll have the report to your doctor in a few days. You may get dressed now."

Mrs. Golding, age fifty-four, 180 pounds, divorced, nonsmoker, allergic to penicillin and mushrooms (on the following medications: Lipitor, Boniva, Xanax, and Zoloft), history of cancer maternal side, history of heart disease paternal side, history of diabetes both sides, rises from the table with a wince. She is perfumed and powdered.

"Are you okay, Mrs. Golding?" he asks as he helps her down.

"I'm fine. Just a little sore from the table."

"I'm sorry."

"Did you see anything I need to worry about?"

He takes her arm and escorts her from the room. "The radiologist will look at the ultrasound and write up a report for your doctor."

"I know, I know. But did *you* see anything unusual? You must know when something looks different."

Ushering her into the changing room he says, "I'm not trained to interpret the test, Mrs. Golding."

"Thank you—what did you say your name was?"

"Gus."

"Thank you, Gus. I really hope I'll be okay."

He knows she'll be fine.

Gus Parker knows this because Gus Parker has a sixth sense. That is not to say that he sees dead people. That is not to say that he can always predict the future. He completely missed the Michael Jackson thing. He also missed his father's golf cart accident. His father is alive and well and still not talking to Gus, not because Gus missed the unfortunate afternoon when Warren Parker, distracted by the suddenly developed bust of Horace Michael's daughter, Rachel, drove his cart into a sand trap and broke an ankle and a wrist. His father is still not talking to him because Gus is the crazy son from the dark side of the world. One miss that still haunts him almost twenty years later: the 2000 presidential election. He didn't see the clusterfuck that was to become Florida.

Gus Parker describes himself as highly intuitive. Others who know him say he's a psychic. A reluctant psychic, maybe, but a psychic nonetheless. It doesn't exactly pay the rent because he doesn't exactly have a TV show, which is why he works here at Valley Imaging as a jack-of-all-organs, multi-certified in mammography, sonography, CT, MRI, you name it, except X-rays; he has a grudge against X-rays.

Call it intuitive or call it psychic, Gus is not at all surprised when he gets a call after Mrs. Golding's ultrasound from Beatrice Vossenheimer.

It went something like this:

"You still in, baby?"

"In?"

"Tonight . . . Eric Young."

"Where?"

"Books, Books & Beyond. Fashion Square."

"Oh, right. Of course."

"If you can't make it . . ." she chirps.

"No. Of course I can. I'll meet you at your place after work."

"I'll have dinner ready, Gus."

She disconnects.

Beatrice Vossenheimer is Gus Parker's only psychic friend. She's on a quest to expose the charlatans who invade the psychic circuit with shameful deception. She says they give people like her and Gus a bad name. Gus says if they make people happy, well, then, let them be. But she insists that people should not be parted from their money when they're being sold a lie. And Gus supposes she's right. After all, she's already exposed Candy Pellinger (best-selling author of *They Hover, They Hover: Part One* and *They Hover, They Hover: Part Two*), Andrew Bresbin (host of the syndicated *Andrew Bresbin Psychic Hour*), and Marjorie and Geraldo Quinones (stars of the reality TV show *Psychic Marriage*). These celebrity psychics and many others travel the country peddling their fallacious powers at bookstores, conferences, and conventions. They rent meeting rooms at hotels, and, for $79.99, they will connect you with your dead mother, father, son, daughter, canine, or feline. Beatrice, on a one-woman crusade to protect the name and integrity of authentic psychic power, is hunting the cretins down one by one, publishing her findings on her website, and hopefully one day in a book (a few publishers are interested); Gus has suggested *Psychic My Ass!* for a title. Though not a celebrity psychic, Beatrice is well enough known that she needs decoys at what she calls her "interventions." That's where Gus comes in.

Eric Young is holding court tonight at Books, Books & Beyond. He has a new book out.

"His fifth," Beatrice had told him.

Anybody else, Gus knows, and the motive would be envy. But Gus has never been in touch with another person's purity as he is with Beatrice's. It's as if he can hear the neurotransmitters in her brain radiating a constant hum of goodness. That is why sometimes when he listens to her, Gus feels as if he is listening to a poem.

He hurries to her house after work, stopping home briefly to shower and to feed a clinging Ivy, his indulged Golden Retriever. Beatrice lives in Paradise Valley or, as Gus says, Somewhere Over the Mountain, because only the squatting beast of Camelback separates them. For PV, it's a modest home, built into a rocky hillside, a ranch of white boxes and big glass. The curtains are sheer enough to reveal the stunning panorama of the neighborhood. There are always candles lit in Beatrice's home, little flickers of serenity, and shadows of the flames everywhere. This tiny woman lives somewhat like a sorcerer. She stands five feet, maximum. And her voice, commensurately tiny. She sounds like a finch. And she has told Gus, in her strange but beautiful vibrato, that he has always been a hawk.

Beatrice is wearing a little black skirt, black tights, and a red velvet riding jacket.

Her hair is in a bun.

At sixty, she's old enough to be Gus's—

"Aunt," she has warned him.

Beatrice brings a heaping bowl of salad to the table in the family room.

The television is on, which surprises Gus because Beatrice never watches TV. Though she does carry a certain torch for Alex Trebek.

"So you think this Eric Young guy is a faker?"

"Don't know," Beatrice replies. "I never go with prejudice. I go to find out."

"Of course."

"I made fajitas," she tells Gus.

"Yum," he says.

"What is CINCO DE MAYO?" she cries as she rises from the table to fetch the rest of the meal.

"That is the correct answer," Trebek tells the contestants.

Gus hears Beatrice clucking happily in the kitchen.

"Is Hannah joining us?" Gus asks.

"Of course," she says. "Now, shhh! Final Jeopardy."

He listens to the fajitas sizzle and the television music chiming while three contestants, all who look like they've been plucked off the prairie, puzzle over this:

Seth Grahame-Smith has introduced these classic horror characters to Jane Austen's *Pride and Prejudice*.

Beatrice returns with the plates. "What are zombies?" she says. And she is right.

"Congratulations," Gus says.

"Dig in," she tells him.

They're about three minutes into the fajitas when the TV sirens the beginning of the evening newscast.

"We have breaking news out of South Mountain tonight," the announcer says. "The dead body of a young hiker was found there this afternoon. Police say it's murder. Happy Friday, everybody. I'm Tyler Lore."

"South Mountain?" Beatrice says. "How awful." She lunges toward the sofa and grasps the remote. She flips through the channels as if she doesn't believe Tyler Lore.

One channel calls it, "A gruesome discovery."

Another channel calls it, "A gruesome discovery."

One channel, assumingly going out on a creative limb, calls it, "A grisly discovery."

And there is the channel that starts the news like this: "Hiking Horror. Do you know where your wife is tonight?"

"I didn't know you were such a news junkie, Beatrice," Gus says.

"I'm not. But I got a vibe. Let's watch."

Beatrice switches back to Tyler Lore who is talking to a reporter in the field.

"Well, Tyler," the reporter says. "Police tell us another hiker stumbled across the body this afternoon. They have not released the identity of the victim, and in a press conference late this afternoon, a public information sergeant would not comment on any suspects in the case. Let's listen."

Gus and Beatrice watch as the video plays.

"It's far too early in the investigation to identify any suspects," the sergeant tells the reporters.

"Any motive?" one of the reporters yells back.

"Uh, I can't speak to a motive," the sergeant replies.

"Can we see the crime scene?" another reporter asks.

"No," says the sergeant emphatically. "The scene will be sealed until further notice."

"Who's the lead detective?"

The sergeant indicates a man standing to his left. "Alex Mills is the case agent."

"Will he be making a statement?"

"No," the sergeant replies.

A new voice, the agitated voice of another reporter, asks, "What does the body look like?"

"What does the body look like? It looks like a dead body," the sergeant says. "Thanks for coming, everybody. We have nothing else to say at this time."

Gus recognizes the man standing to the left of the sergeant, smirking, it would seem, at the absurdity of the reporter's question. Gus knows Detective Alex Mills from several cases.

Last year it was the dead body at a horse ranch: a jilted lover.

The year before that it was a dead kid at the municipal pool: a lifeguard.

There were the dead children, five years ago, if memory serves him correct, at Phoenix Memorial: Nurse Patty Sanchez.

Gus Parker doesn't specialize in crime. He'd rather spend more time with clients. Or Ivy. But he's got a reputation. He's been hired by law enforcement agencies in Seattle, Minneapolis, Pittsburgh, Boston, New Haven, New York, London, Dublin, Prague, and, believe it or not, Riyadh, by the Saudi royal family themselves, who will deny it of course and made Gus sign some kind of document that threatened disembowelment or dismemberment (the translator wasn't Saudi's finest) should he ever disclose his work in the kingdom.

It's fine work if you can get it. It pays well. He slips in, slips out, relatively unnoticed. But the work is irregular, which is precisely how travel makes him feel, so the jet-setting psychic life is not something he really wants to rely upon to subsist. Not that he loves looking at spleens all day, but he loves the idea of seeing beyond the flesh.

Mills calls him Detective Psycho, but Gus doesn't mind because Mills, for some reason, believes every word Gus tells him.

"Beatrice, can you rewind the newscast?"

She lifts the remote and says, "Sure."

"There, freeze the shot."

They're looking again at the press conference. "You see that guy standing next to the sergeant?"

Beatrice narrows her eyes. "The guy on the left or right?"

"The left."

"Yes. Very handsome."

"He's the detective I've worked with." And then he asks, "Didn't you say you had a vibe about the murder?"

She shakes her head. "I had a vibe about a big story, that's all. Nothing specific about a murder. I just knew something big was happening."

Gus puts his hand out for the remote, and she passes it to him. He searches, then rewinds. "This is my favorite part," he tells Beatrice.

He hits Play. "What does the body look like?"

He hits Pause and laughs out loud. "What the hell does she think it looks like?"

Beatrice, always the beneficent one, says softly, "Maybe she's just a new reporter, Gus. Have some compassion."

"Do you see the look on Mills's face?"

"Not very compassionate," Beatrice says.

Gus is about to shut the TV off when he notices something. There is a woman on the screen. She's not a reporter. She's not a witness. She's in the video of the press conference, standing there behind Alex Mills, looking grave and aloof. It's an alluring combination on her face, but that's not what draws Gus Parker to this woman. Instead he sees a dangerous energy roiling toward her body, like a shock wave invisible to the naked eye but visible to him. First, it's the turbulence of desert heat rising from the pavement, shimmering like a mirage. Then it explodes outward, deadly rings of it, and Gus can see that if she doesn't get out of the way this woman will be consumed. Gus hits the remote and pauses the picture. That's it. That's it right there. This woman, whoever she is, is being watched by the killer right now. Right now. The killer has tuned in to study just how well the crime fighters appreciate his work; he has picked the woman out of the crowd, and Gus knows that he has chosen to stalk her. The killer is the shock wave creeping toward her. She's on his list.

Whoever she is.

Gus studies her. She must be one of Mills's colleagues, maybe a detective he hasn't met. She's standing beside one of the police officers, a brawny ex-Marine type. Gus tries to intuit how she fits or where she fits in the law enforcement hierarchy surrounding the sergeant, but he cannot. He's a bit distracted by her beauty. Her beauty is slightly off focus, slightly out of frame, given the camera's zoom into the sergeant, but Gus Parker can make out the intensity of those eyes, the passive-aggressive sensuality of her lips, a sort of flirtatious demand to be parted, a sort of stoic, guarded desire. She has black hair. A chiseled gully of a neck. Here he is unable to infer who she is but clearly able to intuit where her statute falls under the laws of attraction. *I am such an idiot*, he says to himself. *A fucking idiot.* The screen is frozen. Gus is frozen. Gus hopes it's not too late.

"Gus?"

Beatrice is standing over him. "What?" he says, startled.

"Can you help me with the plates? We have to leave in a few. Are you all right?"

Gus points out the woman in the video and describes his reading of her peril.

Beatrice peers at the screen again, really searches it for a clue. "You may be right, Gus. I'm picking up a vibe but nothing that specific."

"Really?" he asks, his face imploring.

"Really," she tells him, her eyes faraway.

"Should I call Mills?"

"Absolutely," she says.

"I don't know if I still have him in my contacts," he says as he digs his phone out of his pocket. He scrolls down to the M entries and is relieved to see the detective's name on the list. Next to the name there's a note: *Never returned book.* That's right. Detective Alex Mills is the guy who borrowed Gus's copy of *Great Expectations* and never brought it back.

The call goes right to voice mail.

"Hey, Detective, it's Gus Parker. You know, Detective Psycho. Look, I was watching that press conference from South Mountain just now. I've got to talk to you. This is important. I'm getting a vibe. And it's not a good one. Please call me whenever you get this. Oh, yes, and you owe me a book."

Beatrice and Gus finish cleaning the kitchen and leave for the bookstore.

3

Everyone showed up at South Mountain. Like a flash mob. Like a headache.

As if Detective Alex Mills had sent one of those annoying E-vites to the entire department.

Mills didn't really need any help, but he doesn't work well with the media, so it's just as well that others showed up to produce the dog and pony show. Dead body! No suspects! In broad daylight! Yeah, the body was found in broad daylight. We have no idea when she was killed. Doesn't matter. The media is a circus of hashtags and alliteration, teeming with "journalists" who'd rather read about the sisters Kardashian than *The Brothers Karamazov*. So, along came homicide sergeant Jacob Woods joined by Josh Grady, a public information sergeant who does all the talking, and the lovely frost queen Bridget Mulroney, one of the city's media relations hacks. She ducked her head into the cave.

"Good evening, Detective Mills," she said, her demureness implied.

He was on his hands and knees again studying Elizabeth Spears. He didn't look up. "What the hell are you doing here?"

"I'm here to handle the press so you don't have to," she told him.

"That was a rhetorical question," Mills said. "I know what your job is. But my department has Grady and Woods to handle the press. Who asked for the city?"

"It's a city park," she retorted. "I'll need some information."

"We don't have much."

"We don't need much," she said, tying the score. And then, "Ick, look at all that blood!"

"I'll be with you in a few."

She laughed. "Don't keep me waiting for long. The reporters are restless."

"Salivating, I'm sure."

Bridget Mulroney is a former TV reporter, herself, and one of the newest members of the city's PR team who most often tries to upstage the department's own public information officers; the officers normally don't complain because they're overall a jovial bunch who would, if given the chance, like to screw her. Bridget had a brief, if not notorious, career with a local television station before taking the media relations job with the city. Mills has come to understand that most reporters take similar jobs when their careers come grinding to a halt. Bridget's, by all accounts, came smashing to a halt like a wrecking ball. Something about sleeping with the station's general manager to save her job after she had been caught plagiarizing Stephen King for a story about a local prom. Her liaison with the GM lasted a few months until his wife found Bridget fellating him on the elevator between the executive offices and the newsroom. You would think the GM's wife might be okay with that, considering theirs was a Mormon marriage, but Bridget was fired. So was the GM. He now runs a franchise of doughnut shops. At least that's the story as Mills has heard it through the lard-fueled rumor mill around the station.

He felt her coming closer, inching this time across the threshold of the cave. "You can't come in here," Mills warned her. "You should know that. Wait outside."

She complied with his order but ignored his reprimand. When he turned to her, her jaw was defiant. "What the fuck is that supposed to mean?" she asked, pointing to the murderer's petroglyph.

"Not sure," Mills replied. "No word of it to the media, Bridget."

"What are you releasing?"

"Dead female. Found this afternoon. Twenty-seven years old. White. Presumably a jogger or hiker. Knife wounds. No weapon recovered." He brushed dirt from his uniform. "We think she's from the surrounding neighborhood. I'm sending Myers to the address on her license. We haven't identified next of kin."

"I think that'll give the sergeant enough to say. He's a man of few words, you know," she said with a wink.

Oh, please don't try to fuck *him*.

Mills didn't know Bridget Mulroney well, but what he did know he didn't like. A daddy's princess from a well-connected family, still playing dress up, still the debutante. She struts around on five-inch heels, damn noisy heels, and luxuriates in every second of being noticed. He's heard that she is batshit crazy (as if the elevator blowjob was not evidence enough), and he's never understood, save for Daddy's influence, how the woman has stayed employed.

"As far as I'm concerned, Bridget, what you saw in here you didn't see," he reminded her. "You don't repeat or report any more than I've told you. That's it. We're done."

Later he joined the formal semicircle of law enforcement flanking Woods and the department mouthpiece as the press fired questions. The tableau included Mills, Myers, Mulroney (an alliteration orgasm that even the press couldn't fake), and Chase. They all took turns rolling their eyes at the brazen stupidity of the questions. When one reporter asked, "What did the body look like?" Mills could actually feel the seismic wave of stifled laughter quake through the group.

The media was slow to disperse. Most of the photographers were waiting to get the money shot of the medical examiner's van, the official hearse of murder, driving the mystery of death from the scene. It was all very dramatic.

Turns out that Nightbird Trail address is a house Elizabeth Spears rented with a coworker. After the press conference Mills had sent Detective Myers to check. Myers is back now, clutching his notes in one hand and a Twinkie in the other. They're leaning against Mills's car in the South Mountain parking lot.

"The roommate says she hasn't seen the victim for a couple of days,"

Myers reports. "But she told me that's not unusual because she often stays with her boyfriend."

"Who does? The roommate, or Ms. Spears?"

"The roommate," Myers replies, slack-jawed. "Maybe both."

"Did you ask if our victim had a boyfriend?"

"No, sir. I did not. But I did get a phone number for the victim's parents," he tells Mills. "I didn't want to ask too many questions. I could tell she was nervous. And it was obvious she didn't see the news tonight."

"It's more or less your job to ask questions, Myers," Mills reminds him.

"You sent me over there to confirm where the victim lived."

"Oh, God, never mind."

"Fine," Myers mumbles. "You want me to find the address that goes with the parents' phone number?"

"I do," Mills says.

"No prob," Myers says, pushing a second Hostess cake into his mouth before he's finished chewing the first.

Notification, to Mills, is probably the only part of the investigation that he doesn't have the stomach for. Like most homicide detectives he knows, he can see rivers of blood and scrambled guts, severed limbs and bashed-in faces, and not miss a beat, but notification is cruel and raw every time, a nauseating cocktail of queasiness and dread as he walks that gauntlet to the door that shields the next of kin. And yet notification is possibly pivotal. If a family member is at the address, the family member will be told that Elizabeth Spears has expired and here's where it happened and when it happened and how it happened, at least according to our preliminary investigation, and please answer some questions before you completely fall apart. Then there will be an interview. It's that clinical. Mills feels as though he's done it a thousand times. If no family member is present, the search begins. For a boyfriend. Or a girlfriend. Or a coworker. Inevitably, they'll return to the Nightbird Trail address and search the house.

Mills fishes out his cell phone to call his wife. Sees a missed call. Doesn't recognize the caller. He tells his wife, Kelly, that he's working late.

"I saw the news," she says.

"Did you fall in love with me all over again?"

She laughs. "No. I fell in love with Myers. Is he single?"

"He's dating Halle Berry."

"Shut up," she says.

"Love you," he says.

"Always," she says and hangs up.

Myers is waiting by another cruiser, and he has the address.

"We'll take my car," Mills says.

"I'm going with you?"

"Yeah," Mills replies. "So long as everything is sealed off and we got enough officers to maintain the perimeter. I'm leaving Chase in charge."

Mills doesn't love the idea of Myers notifying the next of kin, finds it an odd job, a bad match of skills for a doughnut brain like Myers, but Mills is often surprised at how well Myers does this kind of work, despite the limitations in the frontal lobe. Perhaps that slack-jawed smile works to Myers's advantage. Perhaps it brings a comfort to the next of kin, a sort of paperboy simplicity to the delivery of bad news.

On the way through Scottsdale, Mills listens to his voice mail. When he hears Gus Parker's voice on the recording he tries not to betray his amusement to the curious Morton Myers. Detective Psycho. He doesn't know how Gus Parker does it, but Gus Parker can see through shit that no one else can see through. The guy doesn't really like to be called a psychic, but what else can explain the ability he has to generate leads, to see the world as only a detective could hope to see? Instinct? Luck? Witchcraft? He listens carefully to the message and is suddenly startled. A vibe about the press conference? What the hell does that mean? Parker's voice sounds urgent, imploring. Mills feels a rising sense of dread. This can't be good. He listens again. He analyzes the words. He meticulously combs over every sentence. He is trained to dissect, but in the end there isn't much to dissect here but a general sense of intrigue. Of course, Gus Parker specializes in intrigue. Intrigue pays his bills.

"What's up?" Myers asks.

"Nothing."

"Was that anything important?"

"Not sure."

Mills hits Call Back to dial Parker's number. He hangs up on the man's voice mail. He studies the twinkling desert ahead of him. Out there beyond the windshield is a dark landscape littered with strip malls and subdivisions. Somewhere there are mountains that used to be blacker than the night, but now the city glow makes them impossible to see. Somewhere there is a killer who has disappeared into the night, who remains darker than the night (such is the condition of humanity, he remembers reading in one of the classics), who, despite the trespass of urban light, may be impossible to find.

Mills doesn't like that hunch. And he thinks maybe he should make a deal with the polluted sky (shine your hazy light, I'll find the butcher) but then opts to borrow some illumination instead. So he redials Parker. Again there's no answer.

You don't need broad daylight to recognize a cookie-cutter neighborhood, even an affluent one such as this. Even at night you can make out a pattern of rooflines and windows, driveways and doorways. There are the left-hand versions, and the right-hand versions, and no imagination between them. In fact, there is little between them but concrete fences and thin dashes of land, the typical developer's dream of zero lot lines. They park in front of the Spears' home. Mills takes a deep breath.

"Let's go!" Myers says almost jubilantly.

Mills thinks about the proper pitch. About the open expression. About eye contact. He thinks about being them, the family, not the cop. The other detectives tell him he thinks too much. He tells them they don't think enough.

They approach the door. There is something very still here. Mills knows an empty house before he even rings the bell. It's not just the static darkness within or the strategic placement of a lone light on a timer; it's the absence of a pulse. A house always has a pulse.

He rings.

Myers peers through the glass window at the doorway.

No one comes to the door.

"Call their number," Mills says.

Dead silence from beyond the door. Then Myers says, "The phone is ringing."

"I can hear it," Mills tells him.

"No answer."

They hang there in silence for a few moments, a pair of prowling silhouettes, and then Mills says, "I'll come back in the morning."

"I can wait here 'til they come home," Myers tells him as they retreat from the house.

"I know you really want to do this, Morty. But you're not staying here."

"What about Scottsdale? We can have them watch the place and call us when they see activity."

"The family could be on vacation for all we know," Mills says.

Myers mumbles an unintelligible protest that Mills largely ignores because, as he gets behind the wheel, his phone vibrates. It's dispatch.

"I've got an officer at Fashion Square who's looking for you," the operator tells him. "Can I put you through?"

"Who is it?"

"It's Hall. Something about a trespass...."

"A trespass? I'm working a homicide for God's sake."

"Sorry, Detective."

Myers heaves himself into the passenger seat.

"I got Myers with me," Mills tells the operator. "I'll have him call."

"Thanks."

They disconnect.

"Call who?" Myers asks.

"I need you to get a hold of Hall and see what's going on at Fashion Square."

Myers nods, then says, "You think we should go back to South Mountain?"

He does and he doesn't. He thumbs through pages of notes. Did he capture everything with his own eyes? Did he record everything in his notes? Did he think as meticulously as the crime scene techs sifted? He has always had the capacity to do mental gymnastics. It comes naturally to him. He thrives on the acrobatics of the human mind, on the process of whirling the brain in a million directions and nailing the ultimate landing. The crime scene technicians meticulously mined for their version of gold. They combed and raked and dusted. And so did he. He's sure of it. Mostly. Besides if there's anyone more thorough than him, it's Timothy Chase, his scene investigator, and he'd left Chase behind.

"No. I don't think so, Myers. Just see what Hall wants and we'll call it a night."

4

Here's how it works:

Gus, who has no psychic fame and no desire for such, plants himself in the audience a good twenty minutes before an event begins. With an accomplice (usually Beatrice's secretary, Hannah), he begins to chat up a fictitious story about a dead mother or father, sometimes a brother; he discusses the death in detail as he and the accomplice wander the venue under the assumption that the fakers, themselves, plant informers in the room ahead of time to take notes. Then once the psychic takes the podium, Gus decides how he's going to deviate from the story in order to completely upend the faker's performance. The strategy works. It worked with Andrew Bresbin. And it worked with Candy Pellinger. Bresbin's TV show was canceled. And Pellinger is working as a dental hygienist in Akron, Ohio.

Tonight will be no different. Hannah meets them in the home-improvement section of the bookstore. She's doing an "extreme make-over" of her condo at the Biltmore. She's already lost a finger.

"Darling," she says to Gus, who kisses the woman on the cheek.

"Hannah, you look great," he tells her.

She twirls. "Do I really?"

Yeah, Gus thinks, for an eighty-two-year-old mother of twelve who still enjoys her liquor and her stash of "medicinal" marijuana, she really does look great. Hannah has a bald spot, but other than that her hair is nicely coiffed.

"What color is that?" Beatrice asks, pointing to the woman's head.

"Sherwin-Williams Tangerine Dream," the woman answers.

"Perfect," Beatrice says. "You two know what to do. Bye, dears."

When Beatrice retreats to a long aisle of tall shelves somewhere behind the religion section, Hannah turns to Gus and asks, "Who are we grieving tonight?"

"Roxy Paddington."

"Oh, I never liked her."

"She's not a real person, Hannah."

"I know that. But I don't like the thought of her. She's a family-wrecking whore, if you know what I mean."

Gus doesn't but can guess. He grabs her arm and escorts her to the center of the store where the event will take place. Once there, he and Hannah assume the role of strangers, circulating the painful story of Roxy Paddington's death.

"What was your aunt's name?" Hannah asks as they enter the seating area.

"Roxy."

"Excuse me? I'm a little hard of hearing."

"Roxy," Gus repeats loudly. "Roxy Paddington."

"Oh, that's what I thought you said. That's quite a name. Sounds like a movie star. Were you very close?"

"We were. She was my father's sister."

"Your father's sister."

"Yes. My aunt on my father's side," Gus explains. They made short half circles of mingling as they talked. "She moved in with us when my father was in the Persian Gulf. She became like a second mom to me."

"Wow, a second mom to you. No wonder you were close."

"She had beautiful red hair. All natural. You know, the red hair and freckles."

"Well, I just adore red hair," Hannah tells him. "Do you mind telling me how she died?"

Gus hesitates for dramatic effect. The crowd is large but not so large that Gus can't sense who might be incentivized to snatch pieces of his conversation. There are two of them. One, a large man with boulder shoulders dressed in black. The other, a pale-faced woman in pearls, about sixty; she could pass for a librarian, the shushing kind. Then, looking to the ceiling, Gus says, "Mountain biking. She went over the side of a cliff."

"Mountain biking!" Hannah shrieks, her hand to her heart. "How awful! To go over a cliff!"

"Yes. A cliff."

"I am so sorry."

"It was shocking."

"I bet," Hannah says with a conspiratorial pout.

As they take their seats, Gus's phone vibrates. It's the detective. *Damn it, I can't answer the phone now.*

He looks beyond the seating area and sees Beatrice now lurking in the Judaica section. She holds up a book. *The History of Israel: Golda Meir to Present.* He mutely forms the words *what the fuck.* She shrugs and pretends to read.

"I sure hope you get to talk to your aunt Roxy Paddington on your father's side," Hannah says.

Gus stifles a laugh. "Yes, me too. There will never be another Roxy Paddington."

About twenty minutes later, the store manager steps up to the podium and introduces Eric Young. "We consider ourselves very lucky to have Mr. Young with us tonight," the manager says to the audience. "And all of you are about to experience a very special night. Please give a warm welcome to internationally acclaimed psychic and author, Eric Young."

Gus tastes bile rising in his throat.

Young appears from behind a bookshelf, affecting the perfect entrance, a confident spring in his step, a few Hollywood nods to the audience, big open arms and a glittering smile. He's wearing all black. Of course.

He calls on a few people.

His formula never wavers. Gus saw him a few years ago at the Turning Pages bookstore in Tempe. He brought many people to tears there and sold out his books.

"I'm seeing the letter J," he tells a lady in the third row. "Is there a letter J?"

She shakes her head.

"No J. Wow, I really feel a J."

She says nothing.

"Maybe it's a K," he says. "Yeah, maybe I'm off a letter. That's why I don't play *Wheel of Fortune*."

The audience laughs at his faux deprecation.

"No, wait," the lady says. "I did have a neighbor named Janice. She died last year."

"Cancer?"

"Oh my God, yes."

"Breast cancer?"

"Uh, no. I think it was pancreatic."

"But cancer, right?"

"Right."

"You too were close?"

"No. Not really," the lady replies.

"And that's okay," Young assures her. "Janice wants you to know that that's okay. That even though you weren't close, she thinks you were a good neighbor."

The lady in the third row, small and round, just kind of looks at Young emptily. His smile fades, and he asks, "Honey, what's your name?"

"Barbara."

"Barbara, who did you come here to connect with tonight?"

"My husband."

"Your husband," Young repeats. "What was his name?"

"Bill."

"Bill. Bill. Bill. Let's see. . . . Was he a tall man?"

"Not really."

"Yeah, I'm seeing kind of an average-size guy. But for an average-size guy he certainly had a big heart, didn't he?"

Barbara begins to weep. A friend hands her a tissue. "He did. He really did," Barbara says. "A really big heart. That ironically failed him."

"It was a heart attack that killed him, wasn't it?" Young inquires.

She nods.

A few people in the audience gasp. They really do. Like they just saw Jesus perform a miracle.

"He had more than one?"

"How did you know?" Barbara begs.

He smiles like a game show host. "You know how I know. Let me tell you now, Barbara, that his heart is fine where he is now."

Now she truly sobs.

Shamelessly Young continues. "He has recovered on the other side. He is fine, and he is happy. He wants you to know that he misses you. That his heart, yes, his healthy, strong heart, is full of love for you."

Barbara dabs her eyes and blows Eric Young a kiss.

Young proceeds through a few more robberies of hapless souls in similar fashion and then surveys the room and says, "I'm seeing a great lady. A woman of strong character and conviction. She was very important to someone in this room. Does this ring a bell with anyone here?"

About six people, including Gus Parker, raise their hands.

"Well, I need to be more specific, because I am having a very specific vision that means something to only one person here tonight. There will be others, I promise you, before we're done tonight. But right now I am seeing a redhead. Maybe a feisty redhead. Maybe a woman who was a helper, a giver."

No one says anything.

"Nothing?" Young asks the crowd. "I know this as well as I know my own name that there is a redhead on the other side who wants to talk to someone in this room."

Gus raises his hand.

"Yes," Young says. "I knew I was dealing with a man. This woman, she wasn't your mother, was she?"

"No."

"But I'm feeling that she was like a mother."

Gus feigns a smile and nods.

"Not a friend of the family?"

"No," Gus replies.

"I think she was your aunt!"

"Wow!" Gus shudders. "You're right."

A quiet circle of applause.

Again, the phone. It's Alex Mills. For fuck's sake.

"What is your name, sir?"

"Joe."

"She died young, Joe," the psychic says.

"Well, not that young. But younger than most. She was sixty."

"And courageous," Young assures the group. "I'm seeing a woman who was courageous, who, at the age of sixty, did things most thirty-year-olds wouldn't do."

"You could say that."

"She traveled the world."

"I don't know about that," Gus says. "But she helped raise me when my dad was on the other side of the world."

"Right. That's what she's telling me now. I think she moved in with you and your mother."

"Yes."

"Extraordinary," Young says. "This is a wonderful but tragic story. Here we have this woman of great strength and many talents. But perhaps she was too adventurous."

"How do you mean?" Gus asks.

"Her death was an accident. That's what I'm sensing."

Gus nods. His eyes widen. He looks away for a sliver of a second to see Beatrice watching peripherally. She's shaking her head, disgusted.

"I don't know why I see a mountain. But I do."

Gus draws in a sharp breath.

"I don't think it was a car accident on that mountain. Or was it, Joe?"

Gus says, "No. It wasn't."

"But I'm seeing a cliff."

"Yes."

"Joe, this is really brilliant. Your aunt died doing something she loved. Didn't she?"

"She did. She was mountain biking when something happened and she went over a cliff."

The room buzzes with electricity.

"Joe. Joe. It's okay. We know what that something was. Your aunt is talking to us now." Young's eyes water up. "She is right there in the corner behind me, right up there. And she says a wild dog got in her way. She overcorrected, Joe, and went off the cliff."

"God," Gus says with a hearty exhale. "We always wanted to know. We thought my uncle did it."

Young shakes his head, looks perplexed. "Your uncle?"

"Yeah. He was with her on the ride. Never said anything about a dog. Always acted very mysterious about it."

Hannah kicks him, and he can hear her seethe with trapped laughter.

Young looks to the corner of the room behind him. He twists his mouth, juggles his hands, and then stands up straight and smiles. "Oh, Joe. No, don't you worry. She says there was no foul play. She says your uncle had gone way ahead on the trail. She wants you to know she's okay and that she—"

Beatrice bursts forward from Judaica.

"Stop right there," she cries.

Young looks to his left, then to his right. Then squarely at Beatrice.

"My name is Beatrice Vossenheimer," she tells the crowd. And there's rousing applause for her. Gus sees a small twinkle in her eye, and it's clear Beatrice enjoys the fanfare. "I'm here to tell you to save your money," Beatrice announces. "Mr. Young is a crook. That man Joe works for me. He made up the story about the aunt and the mountain bike, and he shared it with a companion before Mr. Young's appearance."

Gus can see how the crowd is arrested, the way the people shift back in their chairs. Two men approach Beatrice from the back. As soon as Gus sees them he stands up and steps into the aisle. He body blocks Beatrice. She continues to address the crowd. "Joe shared the story, and he shared it throughout this area of the bookstore. And it would seem that Eric Young had some plants in the audience who fed the information back to him before he took to the podium."

Young holds up his hands, warding off nothing in particular.

"Please, if the store manager is around. I think we need to remove this disruption from our event. I'm sorry, folks. I'm really sorry."

"No worries," Beatrice says to the crowd in a saccharine voice, "I am on my way. But be warned. He's not psychic if he's repeating a ruse. His books are lies. Read more about it on my blog."

Amid the bemused and confused attendees, Hannah stands up and extends a hand in Young's direction. "You, sir. I came here to see you."

While she speaks, Beatrice and Gus hand out business cards that provide the address to Beatrice's blog.

"What is it, my dear?" Young asks Hannah. Sweat is creating estuaries on his face.

"Can you please tell us who murdered that young lady at South Mountain?"

Again, the crowd is roused. To many of them news of a murder is a surprise.

"It just happened today," Hannah explains to the group. "I just saw it on the evening news."

"But . . ." Young stumbles.

"But what?"

"But I can't say that I knew of a murder."

"Well, can't you do your psychic thing and find out?" Hannah begs.

"I'm so sorry, my dear. It doesn't work that way. It really doesn't. I would need someone here who was close to the victim, who knew her." Then he turns to the rest of the crowd. "Ladies and gentlemen," he says, "I apologize for the unusual interruption, but that will be all for tonight."

A few people boo. They actually boo him as he bolts for the back of the bookstore.

"You know," Hannah calls after him, "you're a complete and utter douche bag."

Gus returns to gather Hannah and escorts her from the building.

"Well, I was just starting to have fun, you know," she tells him.

Beatrice is waiting outside by two police cruisers. "You two were brilliant. Absolutely brilliant."

"What's with the cops?" Gus asks.

She smiles coquettishly. "They're here to see me. Something about a disturbance."

"Tell me we're not getting arrested," Gus says.

An officer emerges from one of the cars. "No, sir, no arrests. We got a complaint. But we've got no grounds for an arrest. If you'll all just be on your ways, we'll call it a night," he says with a wink.

Beatrice winks back.

"Wait," Gus says. "You guys know Alex Mills?"

The officer laughs. "Of course. Everyone knows Alex."

"Okay, well, we've been playing phone tag all night. Can you get him on the radio or something?"

The officer looks suspicious. "What's this in reference to, sir?"

Gus hesitates. "Oh, never mind."

"Are you a friend of the detective?"

"Yeah, you could say that."

"You got an ID?" the officer asks.

"Oh, shit," Hannah says. "Don't go pissing off the police, Gus."

Gus hands the officer his driver's license.

"It's against policy for me to get someone on the radio for personal reasons," the cop explains. "Sorry."

"I understand," Gus says, taking the license back. "We'll be leaving now."

It's a beautiful Phoenix night. A breezy October evening. Not cold at all. Warm winds waltz around them. The air tastes good. They head for the car.

"Are you pleased?" Gus asks Beatrice.

"It went down like buttah," she drools.

"Personally, I feel bad for that poor slob," Hannah says. "He never knew what hit him."

Then they're interrupted by the officer who's quickly approaching, his shoes slapping the pavement. "Parker," he calls. "Detective Mills says you can meet him at Eli's. I have the address if you need it."

Hannah asks, "What's this all about?"

Beatrice whispers, "The murder at South Mountain."

Hannah says, "Oh, Lord, is Gus a suspect?"

Beatrice bellows a laugh, then catches herself. "Of course not."

"I have to bring one of these ladies home," Gus tells the officer.

"Nonsense," Hannah says. "I drove here. I'll take Beatrice."

The officer, who can't be more than twenty-five, eyes Gus with concern. Gus shrugs. "She has a license," he tells the cop.

The name Hall is engraved on the officer's badge.

"How long you been with the force?" Gus asks.

"Just a year," the guy says sheepishly.

"One of the best departments in the country," Gus says. "You should be proud, Officer Hall."

"Thank you."

And your girlfriend, no ... make that boyfriend, no ... make that wife; well, someone is cheating on you, Gus intuits. Right now, at this very moment, Officer Hall's significant other is being fucked by a third party. In such cases, Gus has learned, ignorance is bliss. A dental hygienist once stabbed him in incisor number nine and canine number eleven when he told her that her husband would be arrested for soliciting prostitutes on McDowell, a zone known for its cross-dressing hookers. "I thought you'd want to know," he begged, dabbing gurgles of blood from his chin. A few nights later there was a bust on McDowell that netted the arrest of thirty hookers and their johns. Gus could not have cared less, at that point, if one of the men apprehended was the hygienist's husband. So he didn't check. But he learned. Gus also learned long ago that psychics can't necessarily sense other psychics at first sight. Which is why Beatrice goes through all the histrionics like she has gone through tonight to weed out the fakes. Unlike most psychics, however, Gus is virtually powerless with duplicitous people. He has a blind spot with liars.

A car roars to life. It's Hannah in her Dodge Charger. One of the real ones. From the '60s. Beatrice blows him a kiss and one to the officer and jumps in. The two women are cackling fiendishly as Hannah peels out.

5

Alex Mills is not the most patient man. He knows this about himself. He doesn't suffer fools, has no time for small talk, does not believe in failure, and rejects mediocrity in all its forms. Even a bad cup of coffee makes him worry about humankind. He won't watch episodic TV unless it's on Netflix. The cop shows are all bullshit. Reality TV makes his blood boil. And yet, for all his struggles with reality, that is to say life on a daily basis and the general public with whom he shares Phoenix (particularly the douche bags), he loves his wife, he loves his son, he loves his small circle of friends, and he does battle every day against the loss of the man he emulated, or tried to—his time bomb of a father who exploded at the age of fifty-eight from a heart attack while prosecuting a former governor on corruption charges. Lyle Mills was the perfect man doing the perfect job with the kind of intensity Alex rarely found in others. Alex had no idea the intensity was killing him. No one did. At the time, Alex was a young rising star in the Phoenix PD, his gusty love for justice coming to him naturally, inherently, and the state of Arizona was even more fucked up than it is today, its politicians more brazen and criminal, and one prosecutor, Lyle Mills, more feared than anyone in the valley. Alex is not feared. He's respected. But people said he had the same temperament as his father. Today he's still doing the archeology of that temperament, digging for what was right and what was wrong. His father's uncompromising nature was both. With integrity came obstinacy. With courage and discipline came a void of compassion. With the fervor of ambition came the quiet clasp of death.

Sometimes (too often, his wife might say), particularly when he's exhausted as he is right now after staring into the eyes of a victim, after seeking out her family, Detective Alex Mills has no filter. And no patience. He's sitting now at Eli's, a diner about a block away from Fashion Square, drumming his fingers on the table and wondering where the fuck Gus Parker is. The place is manic with the clattering of dishes and the shouting of orders, and it smells defiantly of bacon. The waitresses are in polka dots. So is his headache. Mills stops drumming his fingers and cradles a cup of coffee with his hands. Decaf. Simmering. Waiting. The diner, itself, an amplification of every greasy notion America accepts as nourishment, for the body, for the soul, and the meek shall inherit, and so goes society. There he goes again, down that path. But he catches himself. And he grips the mug and releases a deep breath, a smile, and a Zen kind of decision to not give so much of a fuck. Often, telling the universe he doesn't give so much of a fuck yields the results he wants. That is his version of Zen, and, behold, there is Gus Parker, on cue, walking through the door.

Mills, affirmed, waves the man over. He laughs to himself how Parker, though the guy migrated here from SoCal years ago, will always look like the consummate surfer dude, with that disheveled head of hair, that golden skin, those beaded bracelets. Mills is shocked that Parker is actually wearing long pants and a shirt.

"I was told you'd be waiting for me here," Parker says, giving him a hearty handshake and a tap on the arm. He sits.

"I've waited less time for Godot."

"Who?"

"Beckett."

"Oh right. Of course," Gus says. "I'm sorry."

"Don't worry about it. But, this is unofficial, Gus. Totally off the record."

"No problem," the psychic assures him. "Good to see you, man. How are things? How's the wife?"

"Good and good," Mills tells him. "Everything's fine. How's everything in Psycho World?"

Parker laughs. "Predictable."

"Very funny," Mills says. "So you have a vision about this case?"

"Maybe. I was watching the press conference during dinner," Parker tells him. "I got a vibe on that woman. Who was she?"

"What woman?"

"The one standing with the sergeant. I figured she was one of your colleagues."

"Was she in uniform?"

"No," Parker replies.

A waitress comes by, and Parker orders hot tea. "Anything herbal."

Mills rests his chin in his hands and surveys an image of the press conference. There were several women at the scene, a few of them officers, a few of them techs, but only one woman flanked the sergeant. "I know who you're talking about," he announces. "Bridget Mulroney. She does PR for the city."

"Oh," the psychic says. "I've never seen her before."

"I don't think she was around when you and I last worked together."

"I think she's in trouble," Parker says.

Mills puts his cup down. "What do you mean?"

The waitress returns with Gus's tea. He tells her that'll be all and waits as she retreats. Then he leans in and whispers, "I got this vibe watching the press conference that the killer will be stalking that Mulroney woman."

"Really?" He knows the pitch in his voice betrays his doubt.

"Really, Mills," the psychic assures him. "I think we better have a talk with her."

Mills shifts in his chair. "You got to give me more than that, Parker. We can't just sit her down and give her some kind of vague warning. From what I hear, she's a bit of a loose cannon. She'll go right to the sergeant, and he'll be all over my ass."

"Tell him you want me in. He knows me."

"Look, Parker, if this is really about you looking for a payday, you should just say so. . . ."

Gus Parker, mellow, Enya-loving, stargazing, herbal psychic, does a full throttle, full body whiplash. "Huh? You think I'm looking for money? Dude, you're going to need me on this."

"You sure about that?"

Parker drops his jaw for a moment. His eyes pop out like light bulbs. "Yes," he says. "I'm sure. Sure as I am that your legal pad has more illustrations than notes. Am I right, Detective?" He doesn't wait for an answer. "And page after page is full of your scribblings of the murder scene. And that legal pad is sitting in the back seat of your car right now?"

"Stop it, Gus," Mills insists. "I get it. I'm sorry I said anything about a payday."

"And your notebook?"

Mills nods. "You're a genius," he says. "So, what's up with Mulroney? Is she going to die tonight or something?"

"No," the psychic says emphatically. "But he's watching her. He saw her at the press conference tonight, and I just sense that he has her on his radar. Nothing imminent. But I think she should be warned."

"Duly noted," Mills says. "If the killer's really going after Bridget, he'd better be wearing a cup. She's a ballbuster." Mills pays the check, and the men head out to the parking lot.

"Can you take me to the crime scene?" Gus asks him.

"Now?"

Gus laughs. "No, man. Tomorrow. How about lunchtime?"

"I don't know, Gus. Let me talk to the sergeant."

"Come on, Detective. Just take me over unofficially. It's a Saturday. Don't give the sergeant a chance to say no."

"I'll call you in the morning. I got to go find the victim's family first."

"I don't envy you."

Again, Mills thinks about how many times he has had to track down a victim's family. The scenes sort of flash by him in seconds like a career death reel, and all he can do is exhale because he realizes that somewhere in between those frames of sorrow he has really acquired a kind of emotional neuropathy. "You shouldn't," he says grimly to Gus.

"If you find them. Can you bring me something?"

"Bring you something?"

Gus tilts his head. "You know how it works. Get me something that belonged to her."

Mills stuffs his hands in his pockets. "That ought to make a good impression on her family."

"Hey, I'm trying to help you."

"I can't promise anything."

Mills turns to his car.

"I've never seen a murder in a cave before," Gus tells him.

Mills feels himself stiffen, senses a slight but building shiver up his spine. He looks back at Gus Parker. "No one said anything about a cave. Not during the press conference. And not since."

The psychic nods. "I know. The longer I am in your presence, Detective, the more I see. You've been drawing caves in your notepad."

Mills doesn't say anything else. He gets in his car and drives away. He doesn't know how he gets home, doesn't remember the drive at all. Doesn't remember the traffic, the stoplights, the intersections. The night itself had become a cave, yielding little in its darkness. He must have been dangerously lost in thought because here he is sitting in the driveway, staring at his garage door, thinking it should open on its own.

6

Gus Parker grew up in Seattle and never planned on leaving Seattle. That was until he heard from his dead uncle, Ivan. One night in a dream he saw Ivan diving from the heavens carrying in his hands a shimmering box the color of seafoam. The box was fastened in silver ribbon. Ivan had come with a gift, which seemed perfectly reasonable considering it was Gus's sixteenth birthday. He and Ivan had been very close. After all, they were so close in age, six years to be exact, given the late-in-life surprise for Grandma and Grandpa Lally. They had been practically raised as brothers. But a few months before Gus turned sixteen, his mother came to him, sat him down, and with tears rolling from her eyes told him some very bad news about a brain tumor.

"They can't operate, Gus," she said. "Ivan is not going to make it."

Gus remembers the feeling of an elevator in freefall. He had heard what his mother had said. He had been slammed out of his normal consciousness and had come back numb from the collision. The pain would catch up with him, but not until he actually went to visit his uncle in the hospital and sat there in the bed beside him. He would do that for days. Ivan would say, "I'm going to visit you after I die." And Gus would ask, "What the hell does that mean?" And Ivan would just unpeel the layer of tragedy off his face and stare at his nephew with an impish smile. Sometimes Gus would just bury his head in his uncle's chest, inhale the smell of Ivan, and weep. Ivan would hear the tears and mitigate them with laughter.

"I'm having a lot of delusions," Ivan told Gus. "I actually saw you graduating from high school. And we know that's never going to happen."

Gus was actually a very good student, an all-around everything kind of kid who was adored by just about everyone except that fuck of a math teacher, Mr. Brim. Still, Gus laughed at his uncle's joke; he laughed not so much at the content but at the intent. He found it seriously comic that a dying man with something like a piece of dried-up shit growing on his brain could conjure up shtick on his deathbed.

"And then there was that vision of you on a date with Barbara McAllister," Ivan said. "Another thing that's never going to happen."

"It may," Gus retorted.

"You are still a virgin, nephew."

"No I am not. I lost it before I turned fifteen."

"Your hand doesn't count."

His uncle died four months later.

But in the dream there was Ivan, looking as handsome as ever, muscular and statuesque, like Michelangelo's David with dark brown hair and a happier, more thriving face, diving to the earth with a gift in a box. "It will be there tomorrow for you," he told Gus. "Under the back porch."

Of course Gus rushed to the porch the following morning, feeling a bit foolish but determined, a bit misguided but equally hopeful, and, of course, there was no box and no ribbon and no evidence of Ivan.

His mother, who apparently had been watching from the kitchen window, opened the sliding door and said, "Gus, what in the world are you doing? Your breakfast is ready, and you're not even showered."

Meg Parker was a desperate housewife before desperate housewives became fashionable. She had been raised by a Stepford mother, and it was her destiny, it seemed, to mother in a detached but bemused sort of way. She indulged her children (there is Gus's sister, Nikki, as well, four years younger) but only so far; there were categories and compartments for affection, compassion, and even love. She had rules. She had lists. She allowed only two drawings per child on the refrigerator at any one time (that included awards, ribbons, and report cards). She allowed carbonated beverages only on Saturdays and only twelve ounces maximum per child. She dabbled in real estate. She used Avon products. She never slept late.

Gus looked at his mother and shrugged. "I was looking for my skateboard."

"What on earth would your skateboard be doing under the porch?" She stood there in her floor-length robe, one foot tapping the floor, her fingernails perfect as she gripped her waist with her hands.

"Sometimes I stash it there," he said meekly. "I don't know. I've looked everywhere else."

His mother rolled her eyes and turned away.

That's when it happened.

He saw his mother lose her grip on a shopping cart and go reeling backward, hitting the floor. He wasn't sure which aisle. But he thought it was probably near pickles and olives. Why was he seeing this? He had no idea. Was he half asleep? Good chance. Would she die? No, she would not die. But she'd slam her head pretty hard, and the people at Safeway would call paramedics, a crowd would form around her, and she'd be humiliated beyond belief.

Was this subconscious anger toward his mother? Likely. He loved her, but through his teen years he had come to understand and resent her limitations. He had come to hate her distance, her feigned interest, and her bony emotions.

But the least he could do was warn her. He entered the kitchen, sat at the table, took one gulp of OJ, and said, "Mom, are you heading to Safeway today?"

"Gus, it's Thursday. You know I always do food shopping on Thursday."

He bit into a bagel. "Right. Well, I think I just had a weird feeling about that."

She had been turned from him, standing at the sink, sorting dishes. Now she faced him, again with hands on hips. "What are you talking about?"

"I'd stay away from Safeway today, Mom."

"Did you see something on the news?"

"No," he replied. "I just saw this scene in my head where you get hurt."

"Finish your breakfast. I don't have time for this."

Later in the day, when Gus came home from school, he found his mother lying on the living room chaise, staring vacantly at the ceiling. Her head was in bandages.

In bandages!

"Mom?"

"Go away, Gus."

"What happened?"

"You know what happened. And I'm not sure what you're up to, but I want you to go away."

"Fine."

"But first make me a martini."

"You don't drink."

"I do now," she said, then barked, "straight up, no olive!"

Gus would have more visions and more hunches. Ivan would appear in more and more dreams, but Ivan would never come right out and say, "Yes, that is the gift I have given you." And, at first, Gus wasn't sure how to use the gift, or if he was even supposed to use the gift; Ivan once said, "Just use your instincts," and Gus had replied, "That's assuming I have any," and Ivan simply told him that he did. It would be years and hundreds of miles before someone would understand. Her name was Beatrice Vossenheimer.

Beatrice was really the first true friend he made after landing in Phoenix. She was a minor celebrity on the psychic circuit. That is to say she'd been on a few television shows, serious ones, like *60 Minutes*, to talk about the truth of psychic abilities, to separate fact from fiction, disavowing such atrocities as the psychic hotlines, the psychic chat rooms, and that idiot in Los Angeles who called himself the "Corpse Whisperer." Gus knew she was based in Phoenix and had a robust private practice. So when he arrived he made an appointment and asked for guidance. She told him, in her strange but beautiful vibrato, that he belonged in the valley, that he would do fine here, that life would be easier. That his family had simply misunderstood.

"They did more than misunderstand," he told Beatrice in her Paradise Valley home. "They basically banished me from Seattle."

He told her about the murder of Frankie McMahon, a twelve-year-old altar boy from Tacoma. His body was found on the shores of Puget Sound; his head had been bashed in by a rock. There were no suspects. The police were stumped. The investigation lasted sixteen months, and then it was closed. That was maybe a year after Ivan had left Gus with an intangible gift to see things, to sense things, to intuit the abstract. Meg Parker's injury, alone, at Safeway had not convinced Gus of anything absolute. No, he was still looking for the seafoam-colored box that he had seen in that dream. But he would finally understand that the box was really a collection of whispers from his dead uncle, an ongoing dialogue of sorts, that, at first, made him think he was going insane. He would hear Ivan, in Ivan's voice, whisper in his ear, "Doughnut," for example, and later that day his mother would come home with a box of Krispy Kremes. There was the time Ivan whispered, "Bob Dylan," and about five minutes later Gus turned on the radio and heard "Blowin' in the Wind." He told Beatrice about the time Ivan whispered, "Underwear," and Gus actually spoke back to his uncle and said, "Underwear? You gotta be kidding me," but later that day in the gym locker room three guys gave him a wedgie.

When he finally told his parents about the messages from Ivan, they dismissed it, called it a funny coincidence. The next morning his mother slapped his face and told him to never speak of Ivan that way again. When he persisted, the Parkers took him to a psychiatrist who gave him some medication for anxiety, which he shared with his friends. Instead of taking the pills orally, they would crush them into silky powder and snort them up their noses and melt into dreamy and blissful reverie. He stopped talking to his parents about the visions and kept going to the psychiatrist for the prescriptions. He made a lot of friends at school, among them the three boys who were prone to giving him wedgies. He'd trade the pills for wedgie exemptions. He even snorted the drugs with Cheryl Hamilton, a star cheerleader who had not given him the time of day until she learned about his stash of sedatives. She would become, eventually, his first fuck. So adults were right, after all. Drugs are bad. Just say no.

He had stopped talking to his parents about his visions, true, but he had not stopped seeing them. He saw good things like weddings and new houses and the sun headed for an otherwise dreary Seattle. He saw six days of sun, in fact, when the meteorologists had predicted more rain. He also saw bad things like mudslides, and earthquakes around the ring of fire. He saw children murdered in the jungle. He saw his sister, Nikki, mangled in a car accident and broke his silence. He warned them. They ignored him. Later he tore into the emergency room at Harborview Medical where his parents were holding vigil, his mother weeping tearlessly. He was on fire. "Is she okay?" he cried.

"She's in surgery," his mother whispered. "They tell us she'll survive. As will Mrs. Ferguson who was driving drunk with Nicole and Jane in the back seat."

"How's Jane?" he asked but already knew.

"Jane's dead," his father said.

Gus took a deep breath and started to bawl. He blamed them. "Why didn't you listen to me? Why don't you take me seriously?"

"Nothing could have prevented Jane's death," his mother seethed.

"No," Gus raged. "You have blood on your hands."

That was the last straw. His parents took turns smacking him. Right there in the ER. They smacked him hard, and no one bristled.

"You're meeting with Father Bryson next week," Warren Parker screamed into his son's face.

"Father Bryson?"

"Yes. You are a Catholic child," his mother screeched. "We won't have you playing with the occult."

He laughed. "Come on, I'm not a child. I'm almost seventeen. You can't make me go talk to a priest."

His father grabbed him by the chin. "As long as you're living in our house, you will do what we ask of you."

"Okay, Mr. Cleaver," Gus said, turning his back to them, leaving the ER.

There was nothing like this. Ever. As a kid he had told little lies to his parents and they had given him little punishments. But now here he was burdened with the truth and no one believed him. He could not deny it. If this was a gift, as Ivan would have him believe, he would rush to the store and return it. He asked Ivan why he would do this to him, but Ivan didn't answer. Gus stood outside of the hospital, shaking, trembling. Maybe he was going nuts. The sheer fact, the icy chill, that no one believed him turned him inside out. He was lost, alone, helpless; he might as well have been behind bars for a crime he did not commit.

Meeting with Father Bryson, the family priest at St. Catherine's, was perhaps the best and worst thing that ever happened to Gus Parker. The priest greeted him with a smile and patted Gus on the shoulder as he led him to his office. Gus was surprised to see real books on the shelves, not just the Bible and other religious stuff, but books he recognized like *Great Expectations* and *Moby Dick* and *The Godfather*, which surprised him the most. "I don't really have anything to confess," he told the priest.

"Which is why we're not in a confessional, Gus."

"Oh."

They sat.

"Your parents are very worried about you," Father Bryson said. "Worried about the demons inside of you."

Gus made a face, a disgusted, sneering face, in lieu of something more verbal like, "Shut the fuck up, Father."

"I want you to talk to me about these visions you're having, Gus," the priest asked him. "And I listen without prejudice. There may be a perfectly good explanation for all this."

Explanation. For. All. This.

He said nothing but listened to those words echo. He tossed them around in his head as he studied the crucifix on the wall behind Father Bryson.

Explanation. For. All. This.

Explanation. The smile of Frankie McMahon, an altar boy in all his innocence, toothy and fair-skinned.

For. All. This. The sheer terror of Frankie McMahon, running fast from someone. Running along the banks, out of breath, tears streaming down his face.

Explanation. Explanation. Explanation.

And then a man's hand clutching Frankie's shoulder, dragging him to the ground. A rock bashing his head. And the face of the man, fierce and furious. His eyes demonic and exalted at once. Blood spilled from Frankie's head. The man rolled the boy into the water and then spun around and raced off up a hill.

"Gus, I need you to talk to me."

"Oh? Well, I'm having a vision right now."

Father Bryson crossed his legs and smiled gently. "Would you like to share?"

"No," Gus said. "I would not."

The murderer gets into a car, speeds away. There he is speeding, swerving, clipping corners and then, finally, slowing, regaining composure behind the wheel, blending into traffic until he reaches St. Elizabeth's in Tacoma. The man gets out of the car, confident, orderly, his face betraying none of the evil his hands had just performed. Stoically, the killer approaches the church like a man approaching a confessional. Gus had only ever been to St. Elizabeth's once. After a sleepover at a cousin's, he was dragged along for Mass. He remembers little about that, but now he sees the church vividly and the man standing there with his eyes locked on the ominous steeple against a haunted sky. The killer's lips tremble. He whispers something to heaven, but he doesn't enter the church. Instead, he turns, walks into the rectory, and closes the door behind him.

"I think I have to leave," Gus told Father Bryson.

"But, my son, I don't think we've accomplished much."

"Maybe next time," Gus said as he rushed from the room.

He was shaking all over.

He ran to the nearest payphone and called 911.

"I know who killed the altar boy in Tacoma," he told the operator.

She kept him on the phone, asking him urgent questions, but everything was a blur until three police cruisers came whipping around corners, surrounding the payphone.

At first the cops didn't believe him. Why would they? They threatened to arrest him. They questioned him for hours. Then he led them to the scene and showed them the exact spot, a dimple of earth on the sloping hill, where the murder happened. Despite days of combing the banks, the cops had not identified the exact location where Frankie had been killed; his body could have floated from anywhere. Now they were there. And there was a rock. And bone fragments. And stains that even now, sixteen months after the crime, could harbor a microscopic wonderland of DNA.

Four weeks later Father Lawrence Richardson, the priest at St. Elizabeth's Catholic Church in Tacoma, was taken into custody, charged with the murder of Frankie McMahon. It was all there in the morning paper:

PRIEST ARRESTED IN DEATH OF ALTAR BOY
Victim Had Accused Clergyman of Molestation

The cops had rounded up nearly a dozen altar boys who said Father Richardson had molested many of them and, certainly, had molested Frankie McMahon. Some of them had heard Frankie fighting off the priest. Those same boys heard Frankie threatening to tell his parents. Frankie was not to be seen again.

"Have you read the paper?" Gus asked his father.

"Yes," his father replied stiffly.

"I guess you could say I nailed it."

Warren Parker shifted in his chair and said, "Look, Gus, that's enough."

It didn't help Gus's case when, the next day, this headline appeared in the paper:

POLICE SAY PSYCHIC TEEN
SOLVED ALTAR BOY MURDER

And right there alongside the story was a nice photograph, featuring Gus's winning smile.

And lots of quotes that Gus had given the reporter the night before when someone named Pat Jennings called from the *Seattle Post*. Actually, Gus had found the newspaper in the trash that morning; his parents had discarded it that quickly. He would be the next to be discarded. "Your aunt Bettina and uncle Paul have agreed to let you live with them."

"In Ohio?"

"That's right," Meg Parker told her son.

"I don't think so," Gus said.

"You don't have a choice," his father said. "We're doing this for the family's best interests. We can't have the media camping out here every night, waiting for you to come out with your next prediction."

"Or to solve the next crime," his mother added.

"We are guilty by association of your public blasphemy," his father told him.

"Blasphemy?" Gus asked. "Do you have any idea what you're talking about?"

"End of discussion," his mother said.

But it was not the end of the discussion. Gus refused to go anywhere near Ohio. Instead, Bruce Lightener, the Master of the Wedgie Masters, convinced his parents to let Gus stay in their guest room. At least until graduation. In sharp contrast to his own parents, the Lighteners were thrilled to have a psychic among them. "Can we do a séance?" Doris Lightener asked Gus when he arrived with his first boxes.

"I'm sorry, Mrs. Lightener. I'm not sure I'm a medium."

He loved their house (decks everywhere, skylights, a ping-pong table, and, to top it off, a swimming pool), loved Mrs. Lightener's cooking, loved the dogs, and he loved the parrot that said, "Go fuck yourself," whenever someone passed by its cage.

All this, the whole history of Gus Parker's estrangement from his family, came out during that very first meeting with Beatrice Vossenheimer.

"I think we'll be kindred spirits," she said. "But why Phoenix? Was it a vision?"

Gus explained that after graduating from high school he and Bruce moved to LA where they surfed during the day and waited tables at night. About four years later, when Bruce applied to Arizona State University, Gus followed him to Arizona. "So you're in college?" Beatrice asked.

"I was. I left ASU after one semester. It just wasn't for me. I love reading. But I just don't have the head for lectures and research papers. Besides Bruce hooked up with this girl, Naomi, and they took off for New Mexico where they're now teaching yoga."

Beatrice looked at him blankly. Then wistfully.

Gus inferred sympathy. "Please, don't feel bad for me. I don't regret anything I've done so far. I like my life. I like the valley. I don't know many people here, but I'm at peace. And I'm training to be a sonographer, so it's not like I'm flippin' burgers."

She smiled. "No, in fact, I see you building up quite a nice practice here."

Gus's eyes sort of bulged. "You mean like yours?"

"Yes, that's what I mean."

Gus shook his head. "That really wasn't my plan. And that certainly wasn't my intention to come here and solicit help."

Again, she smiled. And her eyes twinkled. "I know that. But that is what I see for you. Your own private practice. And maybe it's selfish of me, but my client list is too big. It's unmanageable. So perhaps I'll send you some referrals."

That was almost twenty years ago.

He sends cards home to Seattle for birthdays and holidays. He has short, awkward calls with his parents. Dead or alive calls, that's about it. The level of curiosity is mutual.

Gus Parker is fine with the detachment.

"Are you tired? Sleepy?" he asks Ivy when he sees her lying in the hallway outside his bedroom. He's just come in for the night after meeting with

Alex Mills. He's not sure he convinced the detective of anything, but the hot tea felt good going down.

The dog picks her head up off the floor.

"You waiting for me to come home?"

She gets up. He bends down to give her a kiss. She growls her growl of love. He has known no greater attachment.

The place is a mess. A total mess. Ransack meets cyclone. He's thought about hiring the lady who cleans the house across the street. Her name is Elsa. Short, round, she's probably forty, and once she told Gus that she was from a very small village in Bolivia. She made a Bolivian fish stew one night for the neighbors and saved a small portion for him. When she brought it over, Gus took the bowl, and as he did he was jolted. Just for a nanosecond he could see it: an image of Elsa on the highway, her car a mangled, crumpled heap. "Don't drive I-10 tomorrow," he told her. "Take the surface roads." She looked at him very seriously, like she, too, was a disciple of mysticism, and said, "Thank you, Gus Parker." The next morning there was a major wreck at the Baseline exit from I-10. An oil tanker had jackknifed. A swath of the highway looked like war-torn Iraq; among billows of smoke were the remains of cars, tossed around like toys, smashed, shattered, crunched. Elsa's was not among them. The next day she came over and kissed him on the cheek, said something in Spanish, and left.

After a quick rinse in the shower, Gus climbs into bed and makes room for Ivy. He holds her tight and begins to slip off to sleep when he feels a subtle vibration in the bed. It tremors softly as if it's in the path of a distant seismic wave. The sensation is familiar to him. He calls it the phantom quake. It has followed him from Seattle to Los Angeles to Phoenix. He thinks once you feel an earthquake it stays with you; once you ride that perfect crest of ocean nothing ever stands still. But now he closes his eyes and sees that woman again. She is closing in on him.

7

Kelly Mills throws the newspaper at her husband. He's still in bed. It's eight o'clock in the morning. "Look at you looking all hand-some and serious."

He rolls over, grabs the paper, and gazes at the headline.

DEAD HIKER FOUND AT SOUTH MOUNTAIN

He looks at the photograph. There he is all serious. Brooding, even. But handsome? Hardly. The lines in his face are hard, his skin calloused by the desert. "I look like a drought," he tells his wife.

"Oh shut up," she calls from another room. "I'm making coffee."

He tosses the paper aside. "I'll have mine with a side of pancakes and eggs," he says. "Bacon if you got any."

His wife doesn't hear him. Or it might be that she's ignoring him. "Get your ass out of bed," is her only reply.

"I'm tired," he whines in three syllables.

"And you think I had an easy week?" she asks, poking her head in the room. "You try cutting a deal for a four-time child molester. You listen to all the backlash. Let's see how you feel, Detective Crybaby."

Kelly Mills is a defense attorney, defending whom she calls, in full deference to Green Day, "American Idiots." Mills loves her like a burst of adrenaline. They've been married, what, almost eighteen years now? And every day he looks at her and his heart becomes some kind of g-force. She just completely astounds him. Still stunning at forty-two, still feisty and fit, still radiant as she was the day, while eating lunch on the courthouse steps, he asked her to marry him. He said,

"Don't ever cut your hair." And she said, "That's an odd thing to say after I've accepted your proposal." And he said, "That's the first of many odd things to come." He still has a love affair with her thick waves and tangles of red hair. Her temptress hair. Her street urchin hair. She is the smartest woman he knows. Sometimes just her voice arouses him.

She's handing him a cup of coffee (no pancakes, no eggs, no bacon) when his cell phone comes to life on the kitchen counter. It rings, buzzes, and Alex Mills reaches for it rolling his eyes.

"Mills."

"Alex. It's me, Gus."

Mills exhales a huge yawn and then says, "Hey, Gus, what's got you up this early on a Saturday?"

"The dog," the psychic replies. "Have you seen the paper?"

"Yep. What about it?"

"Your picture's in it."

"Right. That's not why you're calling, I hope."

"No. I mean, it's your picture with the sergeant and the other officers and that woman."

Mills returns to the bedroom, picks up the newspaper, and studies the picture again. "Oh, right. Bridget. What about her?"

"I'm telling you, Alex, she's in trouble. I can see it even more clearly now. I've been staring at the picture all morning."

"That troubles me, Gus."

Gus says, "No trouble at all."

Alex says, "That's not what I meant."

And Gus says, "I have to meet her."

"Maybe Monday. Okay?"

Gus doesn't answer.

"Is that too late? Is she in imminent danger?"

"No," Gus concedes. "But I'd rather be safe. . . ."

Alex tells him he'll be in touch. "I have to find my victim's family."

"Are you taking me to the scene today?"

Mills stops for a hearty sip of coffee. "Look, I'll call you later."

He throws the phone on the bed.

His wife comes up behind him and wraps her arms around his waist. "Who was that?" she asks.

"The psychic."

"So early?"

"He's insistent about the Bridget thing."

"Wow. I thought you were kidding last night."

"Nope."

"I love the way you smell in the morning," she says with sleepy, flirty eyes.

He turns around and pulls her close. He kisses her neck. She is different every time. Even if they have sex every night, which they rarely do these days, she opens up in a completely different way. He'd like to pull her down on the mattress and go crazy inside her. But he looks at her sheepishly and backs away. He has bad news to deliver this morning.

On his way back to Scottsdale, Alex Mills can really see the city's voracious appetite for development. The Spears live way up there past Bell, where one subdivision after another has backhoed the Sonoran Desert. For Sale signs everywhere. And soldiers of cacti standing guard, it seems, against the next wave of construction. He finds the Spearses' street, parks in front of their house, and hopes for life inside. The sun is bleaching out the sky, so much so that Mills is still shielding his eyes when a man answers the door.

His name is Peter Spears.

Yes, he has a daughter named Elizabeth.

Mills introduces himself and follows Mr. Spears inside. The man is hesitant but shows him to the family room. They sit. Peter Spears calls to his wife, who enters the room carrying a poster. "Peter, I want to frame this," she says and then notices Mills. "Oh, hello. I thought I heard the door."

Mills is steady and calm. Not stoic but cautiously plaintive. He renders the news to Mr. Spears and his wife, Claudia.

She rushes from the room.

Mills can hear a gush of water, then a toilet flush. Claudia Spears is in the bathroom sobbing, heaving. Her husband, Peter, rugged, tan, in his sixties, Mills guesses, is sitting opposite him with a face of stone. The man hasn't blinked in minutes. No one has said a word since Mrs. Spears bolted. A cat scratches across the Saltillo tile, claws ticking like feline Morse code. A refrigerator hums. "Mr. Spears," he says, hunched over, leaning forward, offering more human, less official body language, "I know this is a shock. And there is probably nothing that I can say that will make this any easier. But I'm here not only to notify you. I need to ask you questions."

Peter Spears remains in a trance.

"What kind of questions?"

Mills hears the wife's voice entering the room from behind. She circles around him and sits beside her husband. Her eyes are swollen. Her lips dry. "Are you okay?" Mills asks. "I mean, physically."

"I don't know," she says. "You have to tell me this is a mistake. I want you to bring me my daughter."

And now that, just that statement hangs in the room, hovers all around them, packing a punch, it seems, and sucking the life out of the house.

"We tried to notify you last night," Mills tells them. "We came by here, but no one answered the door."

"We were at the Herberger," the husband says. "A premiere."

Mills clears his throat. "I need you to verify some things."

"Like what?" the woman asks.

She, like her husband, must be in her early sixties. She has almond-shaped eyes; Mills has always liked that shape because it just seems to rest easily on the face. And Claudia Spears's face is an easy one, plain, smooth, a sunspot here and there, but beautiful in a natural way. It seems as if she is the one with questions. And why shouldn't she be? Who the hell killed my daughter? Why would anyone do such a thing? That's what Mills sees in those almond-shaped eyes now; they're hazel and mournful.

"Mrs. Spears," he says, "how long was your daughter renting that house in Ahwatukee?"

"About a year."

"Did she like the area?"

"She loved it. Particularly for the hiking." Her voice starts to break.

"Yes," Mills said. "She was in walking distance to the trails at South Mountain."

"Every so often Peter and I would walk with her into the preserve. Very peaceful. Isn't that right, Peter?" She gently taps her husband's knee.

Peter Spears suddenly shakes his head as if he's waking up from a deep and unplanned nap. "Absolutely," he says. "Very peaceful."

"And did she get along with her roommate okay?" Mills asks.

A smile that can't help itself emerges briefly on Mrs. Spears's face. "They were like sisters."

"Does Elizabeth have any sisters, or brothers?"

"No," Mr. Spears replies.

"How did your daughter and her roommate meet?"

"In college," the woman answers. "They met at University of Arizona, and Liz convinced her to move back here when they graduated."

"Did they work together?"

"No."

"Can you tell me what your daughter did for a living?"

Elizabeth Spears had been working for John Carroll Investments. Mills can't remember if that is the one with the bull or the rock or the helicopter, but he has heard of it, a big finance company with offices everywhere. Elizabeth had been a business major at U of A and had started at John Carroll as an intern. She worked day and night. She ingratiated herself to everyone—from the cleaning crew to the CEO. She got results. She was particularly talented at setting the stage for new clients, making them feel really good about choosing the company. "She was hired in less than a year," Claudia Spears tells Mills. "And promoted a year after that to full advisor status." The mother looks around the room, her head turning in different directions until her eyes rest on a photograph of her daughter. She brings both hands to her mouth as if to hold in a scream.

"Did she have any problems with her coworkers?" Mills asks them.

Claudia Spears shakes her head abruptly. "No. Like I said. Everyone loved her."

"Until she got her latest promotion."

Mills does a double take. "What do you mean by that, Mr. Spears?" he asks.

"I mean, that Elizabeth has toiled now for several years as an advisor with her own stable of clients. Growing stable, I should say. And while she loves the work, she's been feeling stagnant. So she put in for a promotion to management a few months ago. And found out just last week that she got it."

Turns out that the promotion prompted some scathing jealousy in the office with overt resentments pouring out as ugly remarks. And, so of course, Mills wonders about the coworkers, makes a mental note to send Myers over on Monday.

Mills asks about a boyfriend. An ex, the parents say.

"Leland Blankenship. A pompous little asshole, if you ask me," Elizabeth's father adds.

The couple had broken up about a month ago. Leland worked for a pharmaceutical company. He, too, had received a promotion a few months back. His promotion, however, had required him to transfer to San Francisco, and Elizabeth, or Liz, as her parents call her, was adamant about staying in Phoenix.

"She had professional hopes of her own, and knew her own promotion was imminent," Claudia Spears explains. "But Leland wouldn't take no for an answer."

"What does that mean?" Mills asks.

"It means a few knock-down, drag-out fights."

"Was he violent with your daughter?"

"Liz said he never hit her," the mother replies. "But I guess he had a thing for punching in walls and breaking things."

"Where is he now?"

"For all we know he's in San Francisco," Peter Spears says. "I mean, after Liz made their breakup final, we had no further contact with the boy."

"Do you know where in the valley he lived?" Mills asks.

"Oh, yes," the mother replies. "We've been out there quite a bit. He threw some lovely parties. And, well, Liz was out there a lot. Especially on weekends."

"I'll need that address."

Claudia Spears says it out loud twice, and Mills writes it down.

"Will there be anything else?" she asks.

"Not unless you can think of anyone else who might want to harm your daughter?"

Husband and wife look at each other blankly. Both turn back to Mills, shaking their heads. Peter Spears says, "No one would do this to Liz. No one who knew her. Even if someone had an issue with her over something or other, no, she just was the kind of person people appreciated."

"When is the last time you saw your daughter?" Mills asks.

The two of them look at each other and shrug. "Was it last Sunday? Or the Sunday before?" Peter asks his wife.

"The Sunday before," she replies. "She was out here for brunch."

"And the last time either of you spoke to her?"

"I don't think I talked to her since then," Peter says.

"She and I talk, well, we talked almost every day," Claudia answers. "I spoke to her I think on Wednesday."

"Had she seemed upset to you? In any way?"

"No," Claudia says. "Not at all."

"What if you have the wrong girl?" the father asks. "How can you be sure?"

"I wish I were wrong, Mr. Spears, but we found her license on her."

"Someone could have stolen it," he insists.

Mills would probably do the same damn thing. He would debate and negotiate and just fucking deny it was his kid. That's every parent's right. "We don't do this as a procedure anymore, but you're welcome to go to the morgue and identify her for yourself. She's with the Office of the Medical Examiner. I can give you the number."

They both look like they've been shell-shocked. Again. They just stare at him dazed. Peter's eyes are filling. He grips his wife's hands, and Mills sees a tremble in her chin. She wrenches away and rushes back to the bathroom. She is sobbing and heaving again, and Mills wants the man to get up and go to his wife. He wants the man to be a man and bring his wife a remedy for pain. The man should be the remedy. But the man is broken. Mills can tell just by looking at him.

"In the meantime if you have a photo of Liz, or anything that belonged to her, I'd sure appreciate borrowing it."

The father shakes his head, looks quizzically into Mills's eyes. "I've got a photo you can borrow. But most of her stuff is in Ahwatukee."

"I see."

"Unless you want, like, her diploma from high school."

"I don't think so," Mills says as he rises. He turns to the front door.

"Wait there," Peter tells him.

Mills waits and studies the desert capture of the foyer. An aloe plant, several cacti, all stuffed into clay pottery, canvas paintings with colorful renditions of adobe villages. A huge, woven blanket hangs the two stories of the foyer, the phoenix rising from its fibers. Turquoise and brown. Sky and earth. Spears returns.

"Here's the photo," he says, handing it to Mills. "And I found this." He holds up a kachina doll, a miniature, about eight inches tall. "It belonged to her. She bought it in Sedona. It was among the things she left behind in her old room. Don't know why."

Mills takes it. It stands in his hands, an elaborately painted wooden sculpture of a warrior spirit. A blue face with huge, protruding teeth and carved blocks for ears. The doll is feathered and is postured in some kind of tribal dance—at least that's the inference. Mills turns it over. It says, almost predictably, "Warrior Dancer." He looks at the man appreciatively. "Thanks," Mills says. "This is really quite a piece."

"May I ask how that figures into your investigation?"

"It might be of interest to one of the psychics we work with."

"You're kidding, right?"

Mills shakes his head. "Uh, no. If you're uncomfortable with that, I completely understand." He holds the warrior in the air between them.

Peter raises his hand. "Keep it," he says in a deep, resonant voice. "I'm sure my wife would tell you to do the real detective work you need to do to find the killer. You know, none of the psychic nonsense. But as far as I'm concerned you can have Elizabeth's whole damned wardrobe if you think it will help."

Mills hands the man his card. "I wrote the number for the medical examiner on the back. If you think of anything, or remember something, or if you just have a question, please call me."

"Is the medical examiner there on Saturdays?"

"Someone should be available."

The door opens. Mills takes that as his cue. Outside, he's sitting in his car finishing up his notes when he hears the grinding of a garage door opening. From one of the bays emerges a white Volvo. The car backs out of the driveway. Peter Spears is behind the wheel; the passenger seat is empty.

8

Gus Parker's dream veers off course to the southeastern tip of Costa Rica. He's in a lineup just off the shores of Puerto Viejo, the surf roaring as he waits behind the break. The waves are mighty, and he's jonesing for that barrel of solitude, and then suddenly something is banging, banging, banging, like another board smashing into him. He feels himself dart to the left, then to the right, and he feels the sea crashing down and he wakes up. It's 10:06 a.m., and someone is banging on his front door.

"Jesus," he mutters as he tries to collect himself. He had drifted back to sleep after calling the detective.

He pulls on a bathrobe and runs a hand through his sleep-addled chaos of hair. Then he remembers. Damn. A client. At some point yesterday Gary Potter had called and asked for an appointment and Gus had said, "Sure, come over at ten." And then Gus had gotten caught up with a kidney or a gallbladder and forgotten all about Gary Potter's request, had never written it down, and now realizes the banging is the fist of Mr. Potter growing more impatient with every imploring knock at the front door. "Coming," Gus shouts to the hallway. "Coming." He scrambles into a pair of clean underwear, hoists up his sweatpants, and swishes a capful of Listerine around in his mouth.

"I'm so sorry," he tells his client when he finally swings the door open.

"Did I wake you?" Gary Potter asks.

There's nothing worse than a lying psychic with all kinds of hair sprouting out of his head; it's all about credibility, so Gus just smiles and says, "Sorry I was up late working out all sorts of crazy vibes."

Potter just shrugs and follows Gus inside.

Twice Gus has called him Harry by mistake. Gus leads the client to a small office just to the left of the front door. Gary Potter takes a seat on the futon. Gus sits opposite him in a low chair, one of those linen slings made by Scandinavians.

"Let me see," Gus says. "When you were here a few weeks ago you were worried about your mother. I told you she was fine. But you said her voice was breathless over the phone. You thought it was her angina."

"But you were right," Gary says.

"You should have believed her when she said you had called in the midst of an amorous encounter."

Gary Potter laughs. "Who wants to believe their seventy-year-old mother is having an amorous encounter?"

"And what seventy-year-old woman answers the phone during sex?"

"My mother. If she sees my name on caller ID."

Gary Potter is in his midthirties. He is a short, well-built man, with enviable biceps. He hasn't shaved yet this morning, so Gus feels a sort of brotherhood with his client. Gary Potter is wearing khaki shorts, fading and almost threadbare, and a tight T-shirt of the same colorless palette. He is the hue of the desert at midmorning.

"It's obviously another woman on your mind," Gus Parker tells him.

"You think?"

"I know."

Gary Potter is one of about twenty clients on Gus's roster. A few come weekly; most come about once a month. Some of them refer their friends. Gus has never wanted to build a business, has never really acclimated to the cash-for-vibe arrangement. But the income does supplement his modest wage at Valley Imaging. He stares through his client, and the story begins to unfold.

"You are having grave anxiety about your girlfriend," Gus tells the man, and as he does he watches Potter's mouth open to an oval. Gus can see the very first traces of blood recede from Gary Potter's face. Gus has a microscopic view of this that is probably a good minute ahead of the average naked eye. "Do you want to talk about this?"

"You think there's something wrong with Jessica?"

Gus shakes his head. "No. I didn't say that. I said you're worried about her. You think there's something wrong. Don't you?"

The man puts his head in his hands. "I don't know," he says. "I guess I'm waiting for the other shoe to drop. Things are going too well."

"And you assume they will soon go wrong?"

"I do. I guess."

"You've been together for a year."

"Right."

Gus closes his eyes and searches. Something shudders. He hears a woman calling out for help. He can't quite see her. But he sees a woman's hand reaching for him. It's a desperate hand piercing through the earth. "You're afraid some harm will come to her."

"Why wouldn't I be?"

"Why would you be?"

"Like I said, it's too good to be true."

Gus opens his eyes. "She needs your help. I'm not sure why. Your relationship is not in jeopardy."

The guy fidgets nervously. "I don't know what that's supposed to mean. I don't have to worry about my relationship, but she *is* in some kind of trouble?"

Gus can only nod. "I don't even know for sure if it's her. But I do believe there is a woman in your life who may be reaching out to you. It's not your mother. Do you have a sister?"

"No."

Ivy is barking at something outside. It's a root-root-root bark, and it's playful. She likes to sing backup to the birds. Gus smiles.

"Is that it?" the client asks.

Potter is wearing sandals, perhaps optimistic about the weather. Gus studies the tattoos on the man's left ankle. They're symbols of something, he assumes, but he doesn't know what. There's an isosceles triangle, half shaded. Two dark circles, like moons. A star. And a "w."

"Those new?" he asks Potter.

"No. I've had them for a while," Potter replies.

"Oh," Gus says. "Do they mean anything?"

"Not really. Just a pattern."

"I see. The 'w' stands for 'west,' doesn't it?"

The man exhales a one-syllable laugh. "Okay. Something's working here."

"And you want to end up on the West Coast someday?"

"Damn," Potter says. "Yes, I do."

"I think you should go."

Potter gets up to leave.

"No, no, no," Gus says. "Sit down. I think you should go to the West Coast is what I meant."

Potter draws a blank but sits.

"You will never know unless you go," Gus tells him.

"But Jessica has made it clear that she won't come."

"Right," Gus says. "Then I do think this darkness is about her." He closes his eyes again, not waiting for a vision, rather for the message to come whispering. "You will end up in Los Angeles, Gary. But you are afraid to leave her behind. Not afraid that the relationship will falter but that harm will come to her without your protection." He looks at his client.

His client looks back. Their eyes are locked. "You're right," Potter says. "You're absolutely right. So what do you think?"

"What do I think?"

Either the room is spinning, or Gus's visions are getting the psychic equivalent of vertigo. That happens sometimes.

"Is she in danger?"

"I don't think so. I'm not totally sure. But I do know that now is not the time for you to head west. Not yet."

"Wow."

He knows he must stop. "That will be all for today," he tells his client. Gary Potter hands him sixty dollars and leaves.

Two hours later Gus pulls into the Forty-Eighth Street entrance to South Mountain Park. He rolls down the long driveway and finds the parking lot empty, save for two cruisers and an unmarked car. Alex Mills is leaning against the unmarked, talking on his cell phone. There is yellow tape everywhere, like streamers, like a birthday party for the criminally insane. Gus steps out of his car.

Alex walks toward him, shaking his head. Elbow bent, phone to ear. "Shit for brains," says the detective as he stuffs the cell into its holster. "City bureaucrat shit for brains."

"I don't need to go all psychic to figure something ain't right," Gus says.

"The sergeant is getting heat from the mayor about closing down the park. I mean, what do you expect? It's a weekend. We're turning hikers away. And they're all complaining."

"And you're supposed to do what about that?"

The detective shakes his head again, looking at the ground. "Uh, solve the murder, make it go away, open up the park, and serve free punch."

"Like pissed off hikers are more important than a murderer?"

The detective looks up and meets Gus square in the face. "It goes like this, buddy. We turn people away, we remind them of the murder. We remind them of the murder, Phoenix isn't safe. Phoenix isn't safe, then something is wrong with the cops and something is wrong with the mayor. You know how it works, dude. It's like the shark."

"The shark?"

"In Amity. I think his name was Jaws."

"Wow. I see you took a break from the classics to read the Benchley masterpiece."

"Who didn't? It became a classic in itself. And yes, I know I owe you a book."

Then Alex looks decidedly at Gus's feet and shakes his head.

"What?" Gus asks.

"Sandals? Out here on the trails? Are you friggin' kidding me?"

"I've hiked in sandals. No big deal."

"Until you come toe-to-toe with a scorpion. Or toe-to-mouth with a Gila monster."

"I'm fine, man."

"Whatever. We're going off the trail a bit."

Gus follows the detective to the trailhead. A soft wind is stirring. Tumbleweeds, like visitors from an old cartoon, blow across the path and scatter. The sky is a simple blue shield, with no emblem but the sun. But as bold as it may be up there, it's aloof today, keeping the desert mild, temperatures in the midseventies. They walk silently, Gus scanning now every few feet in front of him for critters. Gus has been stung by a scorpion once, and it felt like a fiery cattle prod had been soldered to his foot, only to be followed by an injection of battery acid, but it happened in his bathroom, not on a hike.

Alex leads him off the path toward a cave. Gus kicks a few rocks out of his path. "Someone vomited here," Gus says.

"That's the first vision you're getting?" Alex asks incredulously.

"If by vision you mean I can see the vomit, then yes, Alex." Gus indicates the splatter on the ground outside of the cave.

"Right," the detective says. "That came from the guy who discovered the body. A jogger."

Gus shakes his head. "He's not a suspect."

"So far you're batting a thousand. We checked him out. Looks like he has an alibi through noontime yesterday."

"And I'm guessing the body was here before that."

"Safe to say."

"The jogger was looking for something when he left the trail."

"Is that a question?"

"No," Gus says. "That's what I sense."

"He told us he went off the trail in search of the petroglyph around back." Alex removes a flashlight, shines it into the cave. He brings the sphere of light to the wall. "He found this instead."

The two of them stand there on the fringe of the cave looking at the carving.

"Have you ever seen anything like this?" the detective asks.

No, Gus has never seen anything quite like this. Nor anything like the visions that come at him now at shutter speed. He begins to hum softly to balance himself, to find his center of gravity.

This is the part Alex Mills likes best. He likes the quiet hum that often accompanies Gus's reach into whatever world is out there. It's a serious hum, but a soothing hum, and, while he would never tell a soul, not even his wife, Mills feels a bit more comfortable with mortality every time he hears the hum. He watches as Parker's eyes scan the portrait. His eyes are wide and portentous. Mills came across that word, "portentous," in *Ezekiel's Favorite Garden*, a new literary masterpiece currently on its trajectory up the *New York Times* best-seller list; he's been waiting for an excuse to use the word, but Gus's eyes do it for him. Just look at him, all serious, probing, like a detective but not.

He really shouldn't let Parker enter the cave, but when the psychic drifts inward, Mills holds his breath and slowly follows, placing an arm on the psychic's sleeve to keep him away from the circle of evidence where the body fell.

"You have to put these on," Mills tells him. He pulls a pair of latex gloves from his back pocket and hands it to Gus.

Gus complies. He looks to the ground where Elizabeth Spears had lain, then back at the portrait on the wall of rock. He nods. Then shuts his eyes. He moves forward. Extends one hand and touches the wall. He leans into the wall rigidly, and then after maybe ten seconds his body goes limp. His other hand joins the first. One holds him in place while the other brushes against the carving. He brushes, his eyes still softly closed. He brushes first with the hand, then with individual fingers.

It's like a blind man has come to the crime scene to search for clues in Braille.

He's forgotten how meticulously Gus works. How seriously. He's learned to respect whatever it is that Gus does, but he doesn't fully understand it, so he isn't quite sure he believes what he is supposed to believe about it. Kelly says that there is no way to understand a mind like Gus's. "Stop trying," she tells him. "It's like trying to figure out the beginning of time. Accept the mystery." Mills accepts it. But he's a detective. He's a man of reason. He can't help thinking that somehow, someday, he'll figure out exactly how Gus Parker unearths the truth.

Maybe Gus fell on his head as a baby.

Or stuck a finger in an outlet.

Or witnessed a murder. Maybe Gus saw his father slay his mother.

He knows he's being watched. He can feel Alex's eyes on him like breath on his neck. But that doesn't distract him. The detective's expectations and curiosities are white noise in this realm he explores. He creates white noise himself with a subtle, radio wave hum of concentration. He has retraced the image with his own paintbrush. The portrait is a different dimension than he's accustomed to studying. It's not an article of clothing. It's not a treasured possession, a photo, or a scrapbook. It's the intellectual property of the killer. He feels the killer, not the victim. He feels a rush of anger and pain. Anger and pain that belong to the artist. Two kinds of pain. His fingers go back and forth. He follows the route of the murder, a route that leads him not through the Southwest but through the Northeast. He's suddenly navigating a map of New England and then a map of Massachusetts. And there, near the cold ocean, he knows he's being watched. There are hollow eyes up there in that window in that house on that bluff. And there is rage. A light goes off now; somewhere a candle burns, and Gus sees other bodies. And he sees, to his dismay but not to his surprise, a flash of other etchings.

Now Gus Parker backs off the wall. He turns to face Alex. His hands go to his head as he pushes his hair behind both ears. "Well," he says, "the etching is all about the killer, not about the victim. I don't know what happened to her, but I might know what happened to him."

Alex studies him quietly and then says, "How do you mean?"

"I mean I won't understand this murder until I can really feel something about Elizabeth Spears. But I think this killer is a man. A man with a horrific history."

The detective steps closer. "A history of what?"

"I'm not sure. Something that happened in his life might inform us of what happened here."

"That's pretty textbook, Gus."

"True," he says. "But I think I'm talking about both long-ago history and recent history. I'm pretty sure he's killed before or will kill again."

"How recently?"

"Not sure. But I see more etchings like this in the desert."

"Please don't say that," Alex says, his voice deep and grave.

Gus stuffs his hands in his pockets and shrugs. "I'm just telling you what I see."

Alex kicks the dirt. "I know. I know. I just can't go back and tell the sergeant we got more murders on our hands based on . . . you know, based on . . . these visions." The word "visions" comes out like a theatrical question mark.

Gus just looks at him and sees the discomfort take shape on the detective's face.

"I'm sorry," Alex says. "But we can't go investigate what *might* happen or what *might* have happened. We have to find out what happened here. You know?"

Gus nods. "I do. I'm just suggesting that what happened here is giving me a sense that it's happened elsewhere."

Alex shakes his head. "Okay. I get it. But I have one murder to solve right here. And if I can't solve it, well, I might as well give the case away to Preston or Chase."

"That easily?" Gus asks.

"Yeah. I sound like an ass, right?"

"Hey, I don't know, Alex."

"Preston's old as detectives go. Great guy but feels like he still has something to prove before he checks out. And Chase . . . that guy, smart as anyone I've ever worked with, and he knows it. Always second-guessing me, trying to undermine me, wants to be king of the jungle if you know what I mean."

"I don't know either of them," Gus says.

"Yeah, I think Ken Preston was on the hospital case with us. The psycho nurse, remember that?"

"Of course I do."

"And Chase has only been around for maybe a couple of years. Came since you worked with us last."

"Young ones are always the most ambitious. You'll end up teaching him more than he ever planned on knowing."

Alex laughs. "No, he's not a kid. He came to us from the FBI."

"Isn't that a step down?"

"Thanks, Gus. That's a terrific thing to say."

Gus feels the blood rush to his face. "Sorry. I didn't mean it like that."

"Sure you did," the detective insists. "It's called a lateral hire. Not a step down. Chase was stationed in Virginia. Came here to care for his dying mother. But I guess the FBI was cutting staff in the Phoenix office."

"So you hired him instead?"

Alex laughs. "I didn't hire him. The department did. He's a forensic psychologist. Expert profiler. Huge ego."

"Good. Maybe he'll teach *you* something."

"We've almost come to blows a few times, so I doubt it."

"Come to blows? Over what?"

"I don't remember specifically," the cop says. "I think he's had a harder time getting over his mother's death than he admits, you know, and he compensates for that by being a prick."

"Maybe he just needs a little sympathy," Gus suggests.

Alex responds with a grimace and turns to leave the cave. Gus follows. "So, do you think our killer has a fascination with petro-glyphs?" the detective asks.

"Maybe."

"Maybe? All I'm getting from this little trip is a maybe?"

"Okay, if I had to testify on the witness stand I'd say, yes, the killer has a fascination with petroglyphs."

"Follow me," the detective tells him.

They quickly arrive at a blackish boulder. On the rock's face, front and center and purposeful, as if its bravery out here should be no mistake, is the rendition of an animal of some kind, most likely a mammal, most likely a mammal on the hunt. It is beaten by weather and time, the lines ragged, like a fanciful chalk drawing from the hands of children of an age long ago fossilized. Gus has seen petroglyphs like this before. They're not uncommon, and while they're fascinating, he's never really given them much thought. If he stumbles upon one of them on a hike, he'll stand there for a few moments of abstract and wide-open wonder, really appreciating a certain mysterious history, and he'll move on.

"Well, I don't know," Gus says. "This petroglyph may just be a coincidence."

"But you see more etchings like the one in the cave? Newly drawn?"

"Definitely."

"Can your vision evolve?"

"What do you mean?"

"Like can you go home and then, I don't know, when you're eating dinner suddenly get more details? Is it possible that out of nowhere you'll actually see another murder? Another crime scene? The exact location?"

"Yes, it's possible. You know that. But I don't think I work well under pressure."

Alex Mills has changed, Gus thinks. He's way too nervous, way too amped. Something's not right.

Alex says nothing. Gus looks at him and sees that in only two years or so the detective has aged. Gray is flecking his temples. There is less hair to buzz. He still sees Mills's youthfulness, but from the corners of the detective's eyes there are deeper fault lines brought on by the faults of life: worry, stress, and chagrin. The detective is Gus's age, a fit man, lean; he reminds Gus of a handsome jackal, one that's been around a while, knows the hunt as well as anyone.

"She died around six thirty yesterday morning," Gus says.

"Huh?"

"Your victim here. Elizabeth Spears died around six thirty yesterday morning."

"Seriously?"

"You really don't remember how I work. Do you?"

"I guess not," Mills tells him. "I'll be curious to see if the ME agrees."

They walk back to the trailhead. The only sound is their feet chewing at the ground and the reckless, argumentative chorus of birds overhead.

9

About an hour later Mills is in his office. He had stopped by to check on the staffing at South Mountain and to review photographs taken at the crime scene. He flipped through photo after photo looking for that one thing he had missed. Elizabeth Spears was on her back. She had not fallen. She was placed there. She was lowered to the ground. There were several photos of close-ups: her face, her neck, her hands, and her feet. They didn't tell the whole story. They rarely did. How long had she suffered before she succumbed? How long had she been consciously terrified? The questions, he knew, were morbidly curious and nothing more. Those kinds of questions usually didn't yield helpful answers, most often only answers that satisfied the emotion. Still, he reached for his cell phone, hoping to ring someone in the ME's office. How much she suffered could reveal how expertly the killer killed—or chose to kill. That might be helpful. His phone had been off. That would explain why he had missed his wife's calls.

The voice mail: "Alex, could you please call me? Trevor is acting like a little asshole."

The next voice mail: "Alex, will you please answer your goddamned phone?"

The last voice mail: "Seriously, Alex, you're going to be investigating another murder if you don't get home."

He dials his wife with trepidation. She sometimes scares the hell out of him.

"Well, where the hell have you been?" she snaps.

"You know where I've been, Kelly. What's going on?"

"Just come home. Now."

"Where's Trevor?"

"In his room."

"What did he do?"

"He sold pot to an undercover cop in Mesa this morning."

It's all Alex Mills can do not to throw the phone against the wall.

"This is just un-fucking-believable," he tells his wife and hangs up. He dashes for his car.

Getting in he notices the box he put the kachina doll in. He had meant to give it to Detective Psycho. Fuck. Really, fucking fuck!

He drives off before he even closes the door. His police radio is chirping. He shuts it off with a punch. Then he whips out onto Washington and heads for Seventh Street.

Gus Parker is looking for another crime scene. There's a map of Phoenix on his computer screen. He stares, senses Phoenix staring back, as if the map is watching him think, like a chess master scoring his student's every move, making him earn the taste of triumph. Ivy is sleeping at his feet right now, snoring a bit. He nudges her playfully, and she grunts. While others might look at the map of Phoenix and see a flat square of nothing, Gus sees a valley surrounded by the skyscrapers of nature, those majestic mountains, some with soaring fingers and jagged peaks: Estrella, Piestewa, Camelback, McDowell, Mummy, South Mountain, and more. He closes his eyes and searches. In the darkness he gets a jolt, as if someone has walked into the room and caught him off guard. "Oh, I didn't see you there," he hears himself say. But there is nobody there in the darkness. Just Gus Parker, his eyes closed, and a vision of a million stars. He watches as a blanket of celestial light and vapor fills the valley. Where others might see this vision as stupefying and brilliant, where others might see the promise of life and of God, Gus sees malevolence in clever disguise.

A star is dying.

In its place a black hole. In that black hole a murder. Gus squeezes his eyes shut even tighter, trying to interpret what he sees.

The black hole is a cave. That much is obvious. But he can't see the victim. He can't hear her scream. He's listening, but all he hears are the sonic booms of the cosmos and Ivy barking. Gus opens his eyes. He looks down and sees her head in his lap. But he's disoriented. He looks at the screen and sees the map he started with. It yields nothing. Except the black hole. The black hole of a cave is taunting him, begging him closer, and as he gets closer, as he inches toward it, God help him, the cave morphs into a vagina. He bolts back. Partly he's sympathetic to the metaphor, a tip of the hat to the obvious, but he's also confused as all get out. Which of course is metaphor, itself, for the plight of the modern man. He could sit here, of course, and ponder vagina of all things. But he can't. He just can't. The master stares back at him with hubris and disapproval. Fuck the chess master. Gus logs off.

"You want to go out and sing with the birds?" he asks the dog.

Ivy knows the word "bird." She leaps into the air, jumping and yipping and follows Gus to the door. Gus watches her play for a while; he swears the birds are in on the game, as if they know to fly this way to romp around with their droopy friend. They sing. She barks. They chirp twice. She barks three times. They chirp three times. She barks them one better. Gus feels the smile growing across his face, the elasticity of his cheeks about to snap. There is a warmth rising in his chest much like, he imagines, the love a father has for a child.

"You come out of that room right now."

"No."

"Trevor, I'm not kidding."

"Neither am I."

The shouting begins. "I'll bust this fucking door down," Mills tells the sixteen-year-old. "Don't think I won't."

He won't. That's his own father, Lyle Mills, bluffing, not Alex.

"Whatever, Dad."

"Look, Trev, I'm not taking your shit. I'll let them throw you in jail. Really I will."

He won't. That's Lyle Mills, again. Not Alex.

No response from the kid.

"Trevor, do you hear me?"

Nothing.

Alex Mills feels the blood rising to his temples, the rage clenching in his fists. He doesn't want to hurt the kid, but he wants to destroy something. The door would be fine right about now. He'd fucking bash it to pieces if Kelly were not hovering behind him.

"Where the hell did he get the pot?" he asks her in a whisper. He's noticed that when he speaks quietly he calms himself. It was a hard behavior to learn, still a hard one to summon. But Kelly had taught him how to rein in his anger even when it most threatened to rip him apart.

"You can't be angry at the world for the rest of your life," she had told him.

"I'm not an angry person." And he knew that deeply to be true.

"You internalize it until something happens, and no matter what that something is, you blow up."

He had wanted to ignore her analysis, but faced with no evidence to the contrary, he had to concede her case. She had even helped him understand the source. Of course it was Lyle Mills, no huge surprise there, but it wasn't just because of anger that the guy died; it was darker and more insidious than that. Alex Mills never forgave his father for killing himself. And he never forgave himself for not forgiving his father. There was no justice there. A life so brilliant snuffed out by its own righteousness. What kind of legacy was that to inherit? Alex had seen the danger, hadn't he? But he chose not to speak up. Who was he to thwart the noble path of justice that Lyle Mills seemed, alone, to pave? Truth is he had not had the balls to give the man his due with an earful of brave honesty. So now, instead, he's truly haunted and angry and he carries it around on his back, and Alex sometimes finds himself cussing in the shower or dreaming of the showdown that would have saved his father's life, or wanting to smack Timothy Chase in the head, or something, and thank God for his wife because she had the fucking brilliance to discover this torture and intervene. And at least he's trying. His whisper is his cue to her that he's trying.

But she doesn't know where Trevor got the pot.

"He won't tell me," she says.

"He's going to have to tell us," Alex insists.

Kelly's standing there with her hands on her hips. "He may. He may not."

"Great," he says. "Fucking great."

He backs away from Trevor's door.

"What are you doing?" his wife asks.

"Clearing my head," he replies. "Then I'm going to call the sergeant."

"Seriously, Alex? He was arrested in Mesa, not Phoenix. Don't drag Woods into this."

Mills leads his wife from the hallway. "I'm not dragging Woods into anything," he tells her. "I'm notifying him. And I suggest you notify your boss as well, Kelly. Unless you'd like him to read about it in the paper first."

"Fine," she says.

"You bailed his ass out in a hurry."

"What's that supposed to mean?"

Mills looks away from his wife, stares at a photo of Trevor in his football jersey above the fireplace. The kid's smile is real. Trevor doesn't fake anything. "You should have let him sit in jail," he says to Kelly. "Maybe he would have learned something."

"Easy for you to say. You weren't around to make that decision."

"You're his mother," he seethes.

She's at his shoulder now. "Right. And you're his father. That wasn't a decision I was going to make alone."

His arms are folded tightly across his chest. Again, he's afraid he might explode. His anger is like a storm, bearing down on him, the thunder speaking in four-letter words, the lightning illuminating a hatred that touches the ground. He knows, of course, that like any storm, this will pass. The hatred unsettles him, though. "Fuck him," he mutters.

"You're overreacting," Kelly tells him.

Wrong thing to say. Ever. Those are the kind of words that make him apocalyptic. But he pauses, nods, knows he can't lose control, finds comfort in his wife's voice even if it did utter the ultimate smackdown.

"Maybe," he says.

"In my gut I know this isn't Trevor," his wife insists.

"How much pot was it?"

"You want to read the report?"

"No. I want you to tell me."

She clears her throat. "Under two pounds. With intent to sell."

"Are you fucking kidding me?" he howls. "Where does my kid come up with two pounds of pot to sell?"

"Exactly what the prosecutor will want to know," Kelly says.

He supposes a sixteen-year-old can find pot anywhere. Especially in Phoenix where a "run to the border" is as easy, yet far more dangerous, as a run to the drive-through. But it's not as if Trevor is running his own pipeline. That's preposterous. He has to have connections. He's selling it for someone who's selling it for someone who may be getting it from Los Angeles or San Diego or Denver, for Christ's sake. This could have nothing to do with the border. Trevor is not smart enough to know a cartel when he sees one and not stupid enough to go looking. He's a boy. Not much of a rebel. Up until now.

Mills steadies himself against the kitchen counter. "If only I could put my fist through a wall," he says in the ironic calm of a whisper.

"You're not that type," his wife reminds him.

He waits about twenty minutes and then returns to Trevor's door.

"I hate to threaten you," he says, "but if you don't come out here I'm taking you off the team."

"What?" The voice inside is defiant.

"I said you're off the team if you don't come out here."

"I thought you were going to bust my door down."

"I'm sorry, Trev. I was angry. But I'm serious about football."

The door cracks open. His son stands in the sliver of acquiescence. "What do you want?"

"I want you to come out of that room and talk to me."

"Where's Mom?"

"She's in her office on the computer. This is between you and me, Trevor. She's been through enough with you this morning."

Trevor slips past him, avoiding eye contact, and Mills follows his son to the family room. Trevor reaches for the remote and turns on the television. Mills locks a hand firmly around his son's wrist. "Drop it," he says. "Have some respect."

The boy grunts and surrenders the remote. The television goes black. "Jesus Christ," the kid says.

"Sit down, Trevor. And look at me."

Trevor rolls his eyes, and Mills laughs at the trademark of adolescent petulance. "What's so funny?" the kid asks.

"You. Trying to act like such a tough guy."

"Whatever."

They're sitting diagonally across from each other, a thick wood coffee table between them. "Your mother tells me you were arrested after practice this morning."

Trevor nods.

"How long has this been going on?"

The kid looks away. "This was my first time."

"No it wasn't," Mills says before his son can take another breath or say another word.

"Yes, Dad, it was."

"You're lying to me, Trevor. I listen to liars ev—"

"Every day, 'so I sure as hell know when my own kid is lying.' Heard it all my life, Dad."

"Look, Trevor. All I want is the facts. Don't sit there worrying about punishment. Don't even sit there thinking I'm judging you. I just want the facts."

"Okay. I was selling it for a friend."

"Well, I know you weren't growing it, Trev. I figured you got it somewhere. But 'a friend' is the easy answer."

Like Kelly, his son has marbles of perfect sky for eyes. He has his mother's glare as well. "So?" Trevor says.

"So, you need to tell me who this friend is and how long you've been selling this shit. . . ."

"Dad, look, it won't happen again. I swear. Can we just drop it?"

"Drop it? Are you kidding? We're not dropping anything. His name?"

Trevor shakes his head and shrugs. "I can't."

Mills leans forward, wearing a sly smile. "Again, let me invoke the threat of taking you off the team."

"I didn't tell the cops, and I can't tell you. Which is really the same thing, right?"

"Don't be a smartass, Trevor. I'm not talking to you like a cop. I'm talking to you as a father who's going to ground your ass for the rest of your life if you don't drop the attitude."

Another roll of the eyes. "Sounds like you're interrogating me."

"Of course I'm interrogating you," Mills thunders. "Just like any parent would interrogate any kid who was stupid, fucking stupid enough to sell dope to a cop. How does that sound, Trevor, more fatherly?"

Trevor fidgets on the couch. He's grown a lot physically in the past year. He's almost his dad's height but bulkier. He's been lifting weights, and his muscles, particularly in the upper body, are bulging; he's begun to look like all his friends. Mills never looked like this as a kid. He was lean and fit, perfect for running track where he excelled, but never jockish like his son. Jocks back in his day were dolts. Trevor is no dolt. He's as smart as his mother, wicked and quick. It also explains why he's so haughty and stubborn.

"Dad, I'm not going to narc on one of my friends."

"Is the friendship that important? Or is it the money?"

The kid curls his lip like a bully. "It's not the money."

"How much do you make? What do you do with the money?"

"I'm saving to buy a car. Is that all right with you?"

"Never for one minute will you own a car if you're living under my roof. Unless, of course, you start naming names. No names, buddy, no privileges. Period."

Trevor exhales a sigh of disgust and resignation. "I was just doing a favor, Dad. I'm not in the drug-dealing business."

"Well, that's a relief." Mills's phone rings. He ignores it. "You're ready to take the fall for this 'favor' you were doing?"

"Yup."

"They'll cut you a deal if you name names."

"I don't need a deal, Dad. It's a first offense."

"It's *two pounds*, you jackass. With intent to sell. You're looking at jail time."

"No one's going to put a minor in jail for less than two pounds," Trevor retorts. "Now who's the jackass?"

That's when Alex Mills gets up and lunges at his son.

"What are you doing?" Trevor cries.

"Get up! Get up and call the coach. Tell him you're off the team."

"Dad, let go of me."

Alex Mills has his son by the collar. "You are my son, do you hear that?" He tightens the grip on Trevor's neckline. "You will do as I say. You will not give me or your mother any shit. Pick up the phone."

The two tussle for a moment, and a lamp falls over. It's a heavy lamp of Mexican pottery. It lands with a thud, then breaks open with a small explosion of pieces. They freeze, stunned by the sound of violence. Mills is still gripping his son by the neck. Their eyes meet as if they know what's coming next. The shame and the guilt are that palpable.

Kelly storms into the room. "What the hell is going on in here?"

Trevor breaks free from his father. "He's taking me off the team," he cries.

"Let's all sit down and discuss this," she says in a perfect esquire pitch.

"The sitting down and discussing is over," Mills tells his wife. "If he doesn't name names there's nothing to talk about."

"Trevor, go back to your room," Kelly orders her son. He skulks away. "Sit down, Alex."

He complies. She looks at him with an open face. Mills doesn't understand how, but Kelly seems to maintain a hopeful calm. Like maybe she already worked out a deal for Trevor. Or maybe she knows something that Alex doesn't. "You got a plan?" he asks her.

"He's a good kid. He's never been in trouble."

"It's two pounds of pot for Christ's sake! With intent to sell. That's a lot of fucking trouble."

"I understand."

"Do you, Kelly? Do you understand? I'm a cop. And you're an attorney. We can't let him get away with this. What kind of message would that be?"

"Our occupations are none of his business. That's an unfair playing field for him."

"Unfair playing field? Who are you, Dr. Phil?"

"Alex, I know you're not as angry as you sound," she says. "And I'm pretty sure you're not as mad at Trevor as you are at yourself."

"What is that supposed to mean?"

"You know what it means. I know how your mind works, Alex. You think this means you failed him as a father."

"No I don't."

She just glares at him.

"Well, I don't," he repeats.

"You forget that life is fucking imperfect."

He howls in exasperation. Just one loud, protracted reflex. "I can't even be perfect at being imperfect."

"Stop trying. Go take a walk. Go do something. We're not getting anywhere."

He gets up. "Stop trying to protect him," he says.

"You're acting like he gets into trouble all the time, Alex."

"If we're not firm with him, then this will just be the start of a whole lot of trouble. Don't you see that?"

He walks to the door. He doesn't turn even though he can hear her voice. "I do see that," she says. "I don't disagree with you. But I think there's a better way to deal with this."

He doesn't ask for her to elaborate. She's astonishingly right, as usual, but he really doesn't want to hear anymore. He walks outside and closes the door behind him.

Gus Parker shoots blanks. Real good sperm, healthy sperm, sperm-of-life, could have saved his marriage. He had married Deborah Russ when he was twenty-seven. And they had fucked like crazy. Crazy! It was no effort. They never got tired. They made love with nuclear intensity. They hadn't planned on children for a few years, but once they were ready it was a fuckstorm. And yet the fuckstorms yielded no pregnancies.

"Something is wrong with me," Deborah kept saying.

And he kept reassuring her that there was nothing wrong at all, that it just wasn't the right time.

"When is the right time?" she once asked.

"When the universe is ready."

She laughed. "All you psychics! You all talk like you have fairy dust for brains."

They tried timing her ovulation. Sex became pragmatic (still quite good but pragmatic); they'd scream and yell and really whoop it up, but their sex mania began to sound scripted. The doctor said, "The first thing we do is check Mr. Parker's sperm count."

Gus said, "If I had known I would have counted it myself."

He thought that might have made Deborah laugh, but it didn't. When the results came back, the doctor said, "It's not you, Deborah. It's Gus. He can't get you pregnant."

Turns out Gus had the sperm count of a mermaid, which is to say none. No motility either, he remembers, or something like that. Sorry, sir, your sperm is too small for the ride; it's bad sperm, bad, bad, bad sperm.

"So, we'll adopt," Gus would routinely suggest.

Routinely she dismissed that idea.

"Maybe you should try acupuncture," she told him. "I hear it can increase sperm count."

"Sorry, Deb, that's where I draw the line," he said. "No needles in my balls."

He decided to go inside himself and get Zen about the whole thing. He reached a sort of peace with the limitation, accepted it as part of a bigger plan over which he had no control.

"That is such bullshit," Deb told him. "That is such psychobabble, or psychicbabble, whatever you prefer to call it."

That's how it got.

Again he suggested adoption. Described it as virtuous.

"I want my own baby," she said. "I want a baby with *our* genes, Gus. What don't you understand about that?"

Unlike Deborah, Gus tolerated imperfections, had come to accept them as the loose threads of life. "No," she told him. "This isn't a marriage if we can't have our own children."

"But you love me," he begged.

"Of course I love you."

But she left him. She said she needed to go while her clock still ticked. Now he dates occasionally and unsuccessfully. There's a radiologist who fell in love with him and offered to buy him a Lexus. But he was not in love with her, not in love with cars, not in love with watches and cologne. He dated a massage therapist for a while but broke that off when he walked in on her giving a fast and furious hand job to a client. There have been a few lovely women, funny, smart, beaming. But they didn't like dogs. One of them, Sylvie Moses, acted jealous toward Ivy.

"It's her or it's me," she demanded. "Make a choice!"

Gus did not choose Sylvie Moses.

He didn't choose Jennifer Reilly either. She had completely fooled him. She wasn't a tax attorney, as she had told him. She didn't have an office in Scottsdale. Or a home in Scottsdale. Her name wasn't even Jennifer Reilly. Her name was Donna Dotson, and she and her husband

(husband!) were on the run from authorities in Des Moines where they had duped senior citizens out of their money in a not-so-sophisticated Ponzi scheme. Gus was not a good enough psychic to see through that. He still isn't. He knows that. He can't rely on hunches or vibes when someone is wearing a mask.

And so the love of his life, Ivy, is sleeping now on the couch, exhausted from her recess with the birds. It's about four thirty in the afternoon, and both of them are feeling lazy. Ivy is snoring, and Gus is sitting right beside her, watching a documentary about the great wildebeest migration in Kenya. It's a masterpiece of photography, really, but he's only half watching, because he is so distracted by a vision. There's a woman calling out for help. She's crying and screaming. And Gus almost leaps out of his seat. He looks at Africa, but the migration yields no clues. It yields magnificent perspective on life and the order of nature, on the enormity of the whole and the miniscule speck of everything else. It gives him pause about where he fits in. With his power, and without. He imagines that the African bush at night is a rapturous feast of stars, the sky full of phantasma.

He hears the woman's desperate voice again. It sounds like his mother.

There's a knock at the door.

10

Gus Parker lives in Arcadia, that strange enclave straddling Phoenix and Scottsdale that really can't define itself. Is it retro or metro? Urban or suburban? That kind of thing. With its eclectic mix of mansions, faux mansions, and *Leave it to Beaver* homes from the '50s and '60s, the neighborhood is considered trendy only because someone is always building, fixing, or tearing down something. The people here adore their lawns, that's for sure, as well as the novelty of irrigation in an otherwise brown and rocky desert. Gus's house, a modest ranch, sits on the western edge of Arcadia, known to some as "Arcadia Lite" because you don't have to be a freaking millionaire to live there. Gus bought the home long ago, when supply was considerably larger than demand. He tells Mills he lives there because of the view of Camelback Mountain. "It's like I'm sitting in the camel's lap," Gus once explained, and Mills just shook his head, not really grasping the image. Gus says he feels blessed by the camel, especially at dawn and dusk.

Mills can't begrudge a man his blessings, he reckons.

Gus opens the door. He's wearing drawstring pants and a T-shirt. This guy really likes his pajamas, Mills thinks, imagining Gus going from his hospital attire at work to his pj's at home, with no serious clothes to think of. It's a lifestyle choice, clearly, and Mills self-confesses that he might be a little jealous of the loungey aspect of Parker's life.

"Alex?" the psychic says.

"Hope this isn't a bad time."

"No. You okay?"

"Define okay," Mills says.

He sees the psychic looking through him. The guy's eyes peer into his own and then somehow beyond. It's as if the guy's a human X-ray, which might explain his full-time job.

"There's been an arrest. . . ."

"No," Mills tells him. "No arrest."

"Well don't just stand there," the psychic says. "Come in."

Mills has been here before. Several times. He's always surprised how simple the place looks. He had expected, at first, lots of candles and prisms, and abstract art with mystical references. Parker mostly has photos on the wall. Beach scenes with friends. Surfing photos. Some vistas from the valley's mountains and the red majestic images of Sedona. He still expects the smell of incense, but again he is wrong; instead there is the smell of household cleaner and everyday canine.

"Can I get you some coffee, iced tea, something?" Gus Parker asks him.

"No. I'm fine. Can't stay long. I forgot to give you something earlier today."

"Oh?"

Mills hands him the box containing Elizabeth Spears's kachina doll. "I got it from the victim's parents. I hope it helps."

He follows the psychic to the kitchen where the psychic puts the box on the counter and pours himself a glass of iced tea; Mills is always fascinated with this guy, like is it possible for him, right there as he pours the beverage, to suddenly have a vision? Does he have visions out of the blue, say, when he's scrubbing the toilet or folding the laundry?

"Tell me about the parents," Parker says.

Mills describes the couple and their home, the agitated fear in their eyes that yields mostly to shell shock. "Actually they took it better than most families, which means they are either incredibly spiritual or still incredibly shocked."

"I vote for shocked," Gus says. "Any leads?"

"Possibly. Nothing astounding. A recent breakup, some jealous coworkers."

The psychic looks at him, shakes his head, offers a "hmm" and nothing else.

"What?" Mills asks. "You think I missed something? I'm not done with the parents if that's what you're thinking."

"That's not what I'm thinking." Gus downs almost the entire glass of iced tea. "I just keep seeing an arrest. Like something in my gut tells me there's been an arrest."

"There hasn't. I already told you. I mean, I just hung up from the sergeant. I think he would have said something."

Gus shakes his head. "I don't know."

Mills fidgets. He looks at the floor, avoiding eye contact with the psychic because he can just sense that Gus is sensing something. Mills sees himself in the friendly line of fire. "Well, anyway," he mutters, then points to the box. "Why don't you open the—"

"The sergeant wants an arrest today, doesn't he?"

Mills looks up. "Of course he does," he says. "But he knows that's unrealistic. Said so himself."

"Doesn't matter. He's under pressure, so you're under pressure."

"Brilliant, Gus. A real psychic revelation."

"Dude, I'm just getting a vibe, that's all. You're all uptight. I saw it on your face the minute I opened the door."

Mills nods. "Right. We found the body yesterday. The mayor wants us to find the killer today. That's how it works in city hall."

"My gut tells me you'll have an arrest soon. I keep seeing an arrest. Really I do."

Then Gus looks out the window to the backyard, a yard stuffed with bougainvillea, and he seems lost, adrift, as if he's listening for an elusive frequency. Mills can't imagine the noises going on inside the psychic's brain; it must sound like a pinball machine, or an electric guitar struck by lightning. It must look like a freaking solar flare.

"It's much quieter than that," Gus says. "It's more like an aria right now."

Mills braces himself against the table. The floor seems to swirl. His mouth goes dry. "You read my mind?"

"Not really," the psychic says. "Just an intuition. Sometimes it does sound like a pinball machine, Detective. But that's only when I'm resisting or I'm scared. And it looks more like an electrical storm than a solar flare. But usually it looks like a blue, calm sea."

It's hard to breathe.

"Relax, Detective," the psychic says.

"I'm relaxed," Mills lies.

"Then tell me about the arrest. I know there's been one, but I don't know why you're not telling me."

Mills hesitates, lets out an angry sigh. "All right already. It's my son."

"Your son?"

"Yeah."

"I'm sorry."

"He deserved it."

Mills tells Gus Parker about the charges Trevor is facing.

"Wow. I didn't see that coming," Gus says just as he downs his third glass of iced tea.

"Neither did we."

"I mean psychically. I'm sorry I didn't sense this more accurately. If I knew it was your son, I wouldn't have pushed you about the arrest."

"Don't worry about it," Mills tells him. "Maybe it's an off day."

"So what are you going to do?"

Mills shakes his head. "I have no idea. This isn't Trevor. It's just not him."

"Obviously it's bigger than him," Gus says. "Yeah, that whole team's in trouble."

Mills raises an eyebrow. "You think?"

"I might be having a bad day. So take it with a grain."

Mills asks him to open the box.

"Oh, yeah, let's do that," Gus says. "But let me grab a refill first."

He tells the detective to wait for him out back at the pool.

Gus pulls out the object from the box. He unwraps a small, soft cloth and finds a kachina doll resting in his hands. The first thing Gus intuits is that this little icon has a boisterous personality. There's an energy that bounces. There's clamor. Gus can hear percussion. The doll has something to say. He's happy about this because he knows this is the first step. It's just the way the wooden doll appears to him, like an innocent surprise with significance. Gus lifts the kachina, holds it at arm's length. He inspects it, admires its colors, its posture. He turns it over and reads its name. "Warrior Dancer."

The detective, who's been sitting at poolside dipping his feet, mockingly rolls his eyes. "Not very original."

And then Gus feels a tiny vibration and senses the hum of the doll. "No," he tells Alex, "this *is* an original. This was made by a tribal artist on the Hopi reservation. Made by a woman, an older woman."

"Is the doll telling you that?"

"I think so."

Alex gives a bemused look and says, "Well I'm not so much interested in its history. . . ."

Gus infers the condescension and shakes his head. "I know what you're interested in," he tells the detective.

"Sorry. Of course you do."

"Context?"

"Oh, yeah, sure. It was a doll Elizabeth purchased in Sedona. Something she treasured."

"She had left it with her parents."

Alex shrugs. "Yeah."

"Because she treasured them."

The detective nods. "I guess."

"Why don't you leave this with me until tomorrow?" Gus asks, placing the doll back into the box.

"You'll call if something happens?"

"Immediately, of course."

Alex gets up, rubs his feet against the deck to dry them off. The men shake hands and head around the side of the house toward the front. It's just after six o'clock, and the sky is slowly losing light. But it's still on the white side of dusk, and Gus can feel the warmth on his skin. He closes his eyes for a moment and lets the whiteness seep inward. And then a flash. A pierce of light. And Gus opens his eyes and sees a body falling to the ground. Blood pooling around the head. There's a Medusa splay of hair. A flash. A knife. Another puncture. A dizzying flash. *Chisel. Chisel. Chisel. Metal against rock.* "Wait!" he calls to Alex Mills.

The box falls from Gus's hand.

"Someone is dying right now," he tells the detective.

Alex stops in his tracks. "Come on, Gus. Don't fuck around."

"Huh? I'm not fucking around."

"You're messing with me."

Gus crouches to retrieve the kachina. "Messing with you? About this? Never. I'm seeing this. I'm seeing this now."

Alex grabs him by the shoulder. "Where? Tell me where."

"I don't know," Gus says. "I've been all over the map literally. I was just studying the mountains around Phoenix, and what I'm seeing makes no sense."

The detective shakes his head as if he doesn't understand. His eyes are imploring.

Gus begins to sweat. He feels it trickle down his back. His forehead is moist. He's on to something. His hands are clammy. He sees himself reach for the detective's wrists, doesn't know why, maybe to stabilize himself as he gets to his feet, maybe to affirm a connection, maybe to exchange some kind of power, knowledge, empathy in either direction.

"What are you doing?" Alex asks, recoiling.

Chisel. Chisel. Blood as paint. Blood dripping in rivers.

"A woman is dying right now," Gus says tonelessly.

"Parker, I fucking need something solid. We could catch this guy in the act."

"We could," Gus says. "But we won't. He's almost finished with the artwork. He'd be gone before you got there."

Pooling blood, a soaked floor below her. She sees her death like a photograph. A still picture with borders.

"This is not entertaining, Gus," the detective says. "I gotta go."

Then Gus hears himself say, "Call that woman."

And he hears Alex ask, "What woman?"

"That woman from the press conference. The one I was getting vibes about."

"Bridget?" Alex goes white and wide-eyed. "Jesus. You think it's her." It's not a question. The detective fumbles nervously for his phone.

"I didn't say I thought it was her," Gus says calmly. "But call her. Call her now."

"What the fuck, Gus?"

Gus shakes his head. "Hey, I got a vision about her yesterday. I'm having a vision right now. I don't think there's an overlap. But I don't know."

"Right." The detective dials. Everything about him is frantic.

The wait is fairly excruciating, but Gus tries to go inward and see more, if only to mitigate the protracted silence that sends shivers up his spine. He sees nothing but blood. *Come on, Bridget, answer.*

"She's not answering," Alex says.

Gus sees the stillness of death, of murder consummated. It's over. A lifeless body in the black yawn of a cave.

Gus, having emerged from the vision, is back watching the detective. Every few seconds the man is hitting a button and muttering "fuck." He meets the detective's eyes. The detective peers back. Gus imagines taut elastic between them, about to snap. And then the detective sighs deeply, blowing out exasperated breaths. "Bridget, Bridget," he says rabidly. "I've been trying to track you down."

Gus Parker watches now as Detective Alex Mills tap dances across the stage of apologies. "No," Alex tells the woman. "Didn't mean to scare you. I'm really sorry, but I needed to ask you something about . . ."

He looks up at Gus as if he's reaching for a lifeline.

Gus juggles his empty hands and whispers, "I don't know."

The detective winces and begins to lie. "I wanted to ask you about the story in this morning's paper," he says to the woman. "Have you gotten any follow-up calls from reporters?"

All Gus can hear from the other end of the call is a voice that sounds like sharp fingernails skidding across the surface of a blackboard.

Alex says, "I realize that, Bridget. But I want you to know that you are to make no further statements until you hear from me or Woods. That's right. Decline to comment. You're not the spokesperson for the department."

The detective is shaking his head as he hangs up.

"Well?" Gus asks.

"I guess she's alive," Alex says. "But that was embarrassing. She's finishing up a hike at Squaw Peak. Says her cell service is in and out."

Officially, the mountain is not named Squaw Peak anymore. Officially, it's called Piestewa, the result of a modern name change made about fifteen years ago. But everyone still calls it Squaw, which apparently is offensive to Native American women—or so say white people who think about these things too much. Gus simply calls it the Peak, as do others who prefer neutrality. He also calls it Camelback's angry cousin because it stands there with its jagged omnipotence just to the west of the resting camel, which is higher in elevation actually and far more the mascot of the valley. The Peak is striking, though, with those ancient fingers ripping shreds of blue, its hues grayish and steely. The colors begin to swirl around Gus. He's on a trail, climbing in circles, up a spiral, and the colors are unraveling too fast.

And then it all turns white. A white out. A blank page. A turning page and Gus sees the story. This is the scene of the crime. A man has killed a woman here. He is fleeing now. He has fled into the valley. His footprints are everywhere, but he's nowhere to be found.

He tells Alex.

"Are you sure?" the detective asks.

Gus nods.

"I guess Bridget is lucky it wasn't her," Alex says.

"Can you get a search party to the Peak?"

The detective looks at his watch, then shakes his head. "Not at this hour, man. It's six thirty. By the time I'd get a crew up there, it'll be dark."

"Or you don't want to send a search party based on my visions?"

Alex balks. "It's not that. I'm the fucking case agent. I can do whatever I want."

"Then do it. First thing in the morning, Alex."

"Yeah, well, the Peak is a big place."

"Then the earlier the better."

The detective does a mock salute and a "yes, sir" and turns to leave.

Gus calls after him. "If anyone asks just tell 'em you got a really good tip."

Alex stops defiantly. "I told you, man, I can do whatever I want. I don't need to explain to anyone."

"Right," Gus says. "Tomorrow. First thing. And don't eat the fish."

"Fish?"

"The fish your wife is buying right now at the supermarket. It will make you sick."

The detective raises a hand and waves him off. Then he gets in his car and drives away.

11

Alex Mills sees a crazy-looking car wind through the maze of the parking lot, a flower bobbing from the antenna. He squints but can't make out the driver. The heat is rippling off the pavement. It's way too hot for an October morning at Squaw Peak. He needs to stay hydrated. He needs everybody up here to stay hydrated. But after last night, Mills needs fluids to fight off the food poisoning.

The car comes to a stop, the flower still dancing a jig, and he sees Gus Parker step out of the passenger side. Gus looks like Gus would look on a morning like this. He's wearing a T-shirt and shorts and, again, those ridiculous sandals.

Who the hell is with him?

Mills approaches the car. Gus gives him a hearty handshake, and then they both turn as this little urchin climbs out of the Karmann Ghia. Mills wants to laugh out loud because this person looks like a cartoon character, so petite, so lithe. He vaguely remembers her. Who could forget such a creature?

Gus introduces them.

"Good morning, Ms. Blossomheimer," Mills says.

"Vossenheimer," Beatrice corrects the detective.

"Sorry," Mills tells her. "Must have heard wrong."

"I'd say 'nice to meet you,' Detective, but I do think we met the last time you took Gus on an escapade," the woman says.

"We did."

"Besides, I never forget a handsome man."

The detective laughs. "Quite an automobile you've got there," he tells her.

She gives him a rosy smile. "It's vintage. Like me."

Gus turns to Mills. "I hope it's okay that I've brought Beatrice. I mean, she and I share all that psychic stuff. She's really been my mentor."

"You got some hiking boots, Gus?"

"In the car."

"Put 'em on."

As Gus turns back to the car, Beatrice grabs the detective by the arm and pulls him toward her. Her face is a pinch away when she says, "I don't really do crime. I have a thriving practice."

"How nice for you," Mills whispers to her.

"And I love to see Gus work, if you know what I mean."

Mills doesn't know what she means. He inches away from her slowly and pivots toward Gus. He can't help looking back. Beatrice Vossenheimer is a bit bedazzling. She's wearing lacy gloves (in this heat!) and multilayers that cinch at the waist and seem to form a dress; the layers are gauzy and thin, and she looks like a gypsy.

"I've been calling you all morning," Gus says, all laced up in his boots now. "To ask if I could bring her."

"I was still in the bathroom," the detective tells him.

"The bathroom?"

"All night," he whispers to Gus. "So was Kelly."

Mills stares at the psychic, his eyes urging Gus to connect the dots. But Gus just stands there looking blank.

"The fish," Mills says between gritted teeth. "You were right about the fish."

Then Mills sees the seventy-five watts go off in the man's eyes, and Gus says, "Oh. I'm sorry. You feeling okay now?"

"Well if my ass didn't get enough punishment all night," Mills says, "there was plenty waiting for me this morning. The sergeant chewed my ass out when he saw the newspaper."

"The newspaper?"

"My kid's arrest on the front page."

"Didn't you tell him about it?" Gus asks.

Mills nods. "Right, but the headline didn't say 'Cop's Son Caught with Pot.' It said 'Cop's Son Arrested for Drug Dealing.'"

"I'm sorry," Beatrice says. "I saw the story."

"So, the sergeant calls me and I tell him about the search, and he says, 'Maybe you ought to stay home and take care of your kid.'"

"You argued with him," Beatrice remarks.

"That's a nice way of putting it, Ms. Vossenheimer."

"Please call me Beatrice."

"We don't have a body yet," he tells them.

"I know," Gus says. "And I don't think you'll find one until I really get some vibes here."

"Well, tell your vibes to hurry," Mills warns. "Woods made it clear he has no patience for this."

"What he really means," Beatrice says, "is that he has no patience for you, Detective. He's threatened to take you off the case, hasn't he? Thinks your son's troubles will become a distraction. . . ."

"Not in those words," Mills says, regarding them both. "But something like that."

Gus drifts toward the trailhead. Alex and Beatrice follow. Dust and sand are blowing everywhere and so are the tentacles of Beatrice's dress. "If you're not careful," Gus whispers to her, "we're going to see your underwear."

"Assuming I'm wearing any."

Both men hear her response. Gus recoils. The detective fights back a yelp of laughter, clears his throat, and says, "We have men on every trail."

"No women?" Beatrice asks.

"Actually, there are three women out there," Mills replies. "Sorry for the omission."

Mills says the patrols all met up about eight, didn't get started until nine-ish, and completed a loop of each trail at least once. Now the crews have swapped, he explains, retracing each other's work, getting a fresh set of eyes on every trail.

"What's the cave situation like?" Gus asks him.

"How do you mean?"

"I mean are they reporting back to you the location of caves?"

"Yes. We're mapping them. But even so . . ."

The detective doesn't finish his sentence, and no one, it seems, is paying attention anyway. Gus is staring at the mountain trancelike, and Beatrice is studying the sand around her feet. Mills feels a small cramp in his stomach, and he starts counting backward from one hundred to will the pain away. If he still has the runs from last night, well, there is nowhere to run. He approaches Beatrice. "I don't suppose you people have any kind of healing powers. . . ."

"You people?" she asks.

"You know, psychic people. . . ."

"Right. Well, no not really. We can heal with our answers because sometimes our answers soothe an aggravated mind or an unsettled soul."

Then, instantly, the cramp disappears.

"Are you feeling badly?" Beatrice asks.

"Actually. I'm fine," he tells her, convinced her voice sent a message to his colon.

Then Gus Parker speaks up. "Okay," he says. "I think we need to look on the south side of the French Trail."

Mills points to the map posted on the trailhead sign. "That's number 302. We're close. But the 302 is like one big circle around the peak."

"Right," Gus says. "The body isn't on the peak. It's in a cave off that loop. I can see it as clearly as I can see the tattoo on your ass, Detective."

"I don't have a tattoo on my ass."

"Well someone does," Gus insists. "And there is a cave up there that we need to explore. You can send your chopper up to confirm."

"But how would the murderer get his victim to the cave?" Mills asks. "He'd have to force her off the trail."

"Or coax her," Gus says.

Mills can't argue.

"Maybe," Beatrice says, "the killer acts likes he's just discovered something fascinating in the cave. He gets his victims all excited to see something off the trail. . . ."

"She's right," Gus says. "Our killer has a charade. He's a storyteller."

"That's Ivan talking," Beatrice says.

"Who's Ivan?" Mills asks.

"My dead uncle," Gus replies.

Mills smiles and shakes his head. "I don't even want to know."

"You see," Gus continues, "the killer has a story of his own that he's been subverting for years. I don't know what that story is, but I guarantee you he's rewritten it to appeal to his victims, to capture them, to conquer them."

Beatrice links arms with Gus. "That was brilliant," she tells him.

"Maybe," Mills says, "but you're a psychic, Gus. Are you getting a psychic vibe about all this, or are you trying to give me a profile?"

"Both," Gus says. "My psychic vibe, as you call it, is giving me this sense of the killer's MO. In part it's textbook; in part it's novel and horrifying."

They meet up with Officer Powell at the trailhead. She's a tall, muscular blonde whose arms seem thicker than Gus's legs. She tells them the only cave on the south side of the French trail is about two miles in. "To the east," she says. "The peak will always be on your left. The cave is down about seventy feet from the trail, and it's steep. Very steep."

"Great," Alex says. "We need gear?"

"No," Powell tells him. "No one's rappelling today."

Gus is relieved.

"You'll be good if you go down slow," the officer adds. "Keep your eyes ahead of you."

Alex shakes his head. "I don't know. If I'm going over a cliff I don't know that I should be taking a civilian with me."

Gus's eyes bounce with surprise. "You have to go," he insists. "And I have to go with you."

Alex shakes his head again. "I don't think that's how it's going to work."

Beatrice shuffles over to the detective and puts a hand gently on his lower back. "This is how it has to work, Alex. Gus is no use to you unless he sees the crime scene for himself. Surely you know that. And you are no use to anyone unless you go with Gus. I mean that in the nicest way possible."

Beatrice pauses, shifts her face to the mountain, scanning the muscular rock and the fringes of cacti. She says, "This is not a place that gives up its secrets easily. The fact that Gus was able to penetrate this place and find this cave is rather remarkable. Maybe you'll find something down there; maybe you won't. But, Detective, the fact that you're intelligent enough to trust Gus is fairly remarkable, as well."

The detective nods. "Let me just call the sergeant and let him know what we're up to."

As he drifts away, Beatrice leans into Gus and takes his chin in her hands. "Are you okay? Are you up for this?"

He lifts a hand to meet hers. "Yes," he says. "Of course."

A hawk flies overhead, banking sharply to the left and then curving the opposite way in a graceful arc. Gus can see a chopper hovering way up at the peak of the mountain, and he wonders what the hawk thinks about that, whether it's pleased to have the company, or whether it's feeling somewhat competitive, if not territorial. The hawk calls out loudly with a whoopish song, and Gus senses that the bird is communicating with him, perhaps answering his question.

And then Gus settles on a boulder and shuts his eyes. He sees it all immediately and clearly. The trail, the mountain face, the way his eyes will perceive the infinite rock, and the bottomlessness of the whole endeavor.

He hears Beatrice. "I have no reason to doubt you," she says. "Go over the cliff."

The climb begins with a hike. A roundabout trek as the trail gently ascends around obstacles. He likes to climb. He likes the sound of his own breath because it is proof of life, proof of a heart and lungs. Often on a hike or a climb, he enters a sort of regressive Zen: Who must have walked this terrain before? Who first discovered this very spot? Did the sky look the same as it does today? And if so, is he not sharing the very same sky with people who came millions of years before him; is he not having an experience so similar that he transcends time, and history, in that moment, negates itself?

About twenty minutes later they reach a clearing that looks over the southern side of the mountain. He spots a wide indentation fifty feet or so downward. The cave. Gus loves the height, the sense of stepping off the world; his body shakes for a moment, and he senses that Alex notices the tremor. "Not to worry," he tells the detective. "No fear. That was a psychic shake."

"I'm not worried," Alex says back.

"I mean, I'm having some kind of physiological reaction to my vibe, here. We're going to find a body there. I feel it in my blood and my bones. And I can even hear it in the wind. Or maybe that's just the wind. But I'm getting a confirmation right here. The killer chose this cave for a reason."

Moments later they're scaling the slope downward. Alex's feet hit the rock with precise impact. Gus sort of scatters his feet, creating small avalanches, while the detective never pushes a pebble out of place. Okay, so Alex is más macho. But Gus is not ashamed. He's a great hiker, skier, snowboarder, surfer, whitewater rafter, kayaker, and canoeist. You'd never know it by observing him now, he realizes, but he's a very accomplished outdoorsman. Plus, he's a good bowler when he has to bowl.

"Dude, you okay?" Alex yells to him.

Gus catches his breath and yells back, "Yeah. No problem." He even gives the detective a thumbs-up, which, of course, compromises his balance, but the teeter is barely noticeable.

They settle on a ledge extending from the cave. Gus is grateful to be on a flat surface, any actual surface, and he wants to sit for a moment and reconfigure his breathing, but he knows he can't. He steps immediately into the cave. It's deeper, much deeper than he'd imagined. He sees nothing beyond what the sunlight will yield. Alex brandishes a flashlight and waves him forward.

"How far into the mountain does this go?" he asks the detective.

"I have no fucking clue, Parker. I thought we'd just drop in and find what we were supposed to find."

"What about oxygen?"

With a laugh lodged in his throat Alex says, "We're not going that far in, dude. If we don't see anything in fifty feet or so, we'll know your visions took a detour somewhere."

"They do sometimes," Gus admits.

Their voices are graveyard quiet in here, reverent. Gus looks back at the aperture of the cave; from here it's a small hole with a celestial beam of light. But, save for the flashlight, they're soaked in blackness. There's a damp, coppery smell in here. They step slowly, Alex pivoting the flashlight so it offers a small valley, a half circle, of illumination. They walk a few feet at a time. The smell is stronger, more forbidding, unfamiliar, then putrid.

Something falls.

Both men stop short.

They wait.

Just a rock outside the cave, Gus imagines. And then he touches the wall. "Right here. Shine the light right here."

Alex complies, and the light reveals nothing in the spot that Gus had touched. Gus reaches for the flashlight, and Alex surrenders it. Immediately Gus lifts it to the ceiling of the cave, and up there is a large petroglyph, an ancient depiction of one animal chasing another; Symbols of fire, or what seems like bursts of flames, are etched into the rock above and below the larger portrait. Gus says, "We're here. We're close. That is not a new carving. That's the real thing."

He shines the light at the detective who nods. Alex looks tired. Gus is just waking up. Alex reaches for the flashlight, and Gus places it in his hand. They're about forty feet in. Alex pivots and starts inching deeper when suddenly the flashlight, like a live missile, flies from his hand and hits the wall. Gus hears the detective stumble to the rocky floor.

"Alex?"

"Dude, I tripped on it."

"What?"

"I fell on the body."

"Are you all right?"

"I'm fine. The body broke my fall," Alex says. "Don't come near me."

"What?"

"I said don't come near me," the detective repeats. "I can get myself up. But I'm a mess. I've got body parts all over me."

The words alone bring a heave to Gus's throat. He doesn't puke, but knows it won't be long. He scrambles for the flashlight, which has rolled backward a few feet. He kneels on the ground, grabs it, and illuminates Detective Alex Mills, who is rising from a puddle of slime and human tissue, indeed, clinging to his arms and legs. Gus lowers the flashlight and sees a carcass and bones that have been pulled apart but left in a pile.

Alex is speaking into his radio. "I need recovery. We have a body here. Send the ME. Send the techs. Maybe get me HazMat."

There's no reply.

"Damn it. I probably can't get a fucking frequency in here."

The detective repeats his request. Still nothing. He tries again.

Finally the radio static yields a voice. "We'll pull that together, Mills," he's told.

"We might need a chopper."

"You got it."

"And get Chase out here to take over the scene. My clothes are evidence, so I'll be here when he arrives."

"Ten-four, Mills. As good as done."

Gus aims the flashlight at the detective's face.

"Dude," is all Alex can say.

"I know. This is sick."

"Never," Alex says and then stops.

"I heard you call for HazMat."

"Well, yeah. I'm contaminated."

"Contaminated?"

"This is not the murder you saw yesterday, Gus," Mills says firmly. "This body's badly decomposed. It's been ripped apart by critters, maybe vultures. It's been here for a while."

"But—"

"Trust me on this, Parker. I've seen enough decomposed bodies to know one when I actually trip over one."

Gus aims the flashlight to the body again and sees a hand and an arm, not much of a shoulder. The face lays there crumpled, a shiny parchment of flesh still intact, the jaw, ear, and forehead insanely reminiscent of a Picasso. He moves the light above and around the body, and there, on the walls of the cave, is the killer's rendition of the murder. It's not unlike the carving at South Mountain. A man kneels over a woman and plunges a knife into her body. A wound in the throat. A wound in the chest.

12

The men step out onto the ledge. It's like an escape without an escape. Mills sees revulsion on Gus's face.

"What?" the detective asks.

Gus points, slowly at first, then more urgent, and says, "Those are maggots on your collar, I think."

Mills examines himself and finds the wobbling beans not only on his collar but in his socks, as well. "Shit. Shit. Fuck," he curses. He starts to strip out of his clothes as Gus retches over the side of the ledge into the canyon below.

"I hope no one's down there," the psychic says.

Mills ignores him and brushes madly through his hair to loosen any maggots or bugs that may have landed on his scalp. "I can't fucking believe this," he says. Mills can fucking believe the maggots; what he can't fucking believe is that he's stuck out here in this ugly fucking canyon scraping up the decrepit remains of life, really wading through the sewer of humanity, when he should be at home straightening out his family. He should be talking to his son. He should be saying, "Trevor, you are my priority." You can't imply something like that. Not to a teenager. But, Jesus Christ, this is his job. *This.* This contaminated mess is his job, and it comes as no surprise that this is where he finds himself, covered by maggots, on an otherwise beautiful weekend morning when most men are at home fixing things or frying up bacon or getting the kids ready for a hike. There are probably families hiking all around him now, linen fresh and rosy cheeked.

"Maggots are more likely on a fresh corpse, but I think flies can return and lay more eggs," he says clinically. "Actually, I don't give a shit. Look at me. I'll leave it to the experts."

Gus retches again.

"You okay?" Mills asks.

Gus looks at him confused, as if wondering how you define okay out here. "I guess," he says. "But I'm sorry about my screwup. I must have gotten my wires crossed. I know someone was murdered yesterday. But my visions led me here."

Gus sits. Mills examines for maggots one more time, then does likewise. "Don't apologize, my friend. We needed to find this body."

"You've got a very ambitious killer on your hands, Alex. I mean who would go to all this trouble to murder someone?"

"Something ceremonial, I think," Mills replies. "But what the fuck do I know? I know nothing about these symbols and shit. I really don't get the connection."

"I know one thing," Gus says. "This is a man capable of many murders. You've got a guy on a killing spree."

"Two murders do not make a serial killer."

"Three," Gus corrects him. "The third body will turn up today."

"Hey what if you actually cross your eyes right now?" Mills asks with a smirk. "Wouldn't that actually uncross your visions?"

"I don't think it works that way," Gus tells him. "So, what's next?"

"You stay as far away from me as possible."

The psychic surveys the ledge, acknowledging how little room he has to maneuver.

"How will the ME get down here?"

Mills shrugs. "Not my problem right now," he says. "Maybe they'll bring the body to him. I have no clue."

They wait for help, in whatever form.

Gus, it seems, is fidgety with the wait and can't stand the silence. "Ever uncover anything like this?" he asks Mills.

"Not exactly," the detective tells him. "I've seen a lot of grisly things. I've found body parts in the most unlikely places."

"Like where?"

"Aw, I don't know. The fryolator at Pico Elementary."

"Get out."

"It was during summer break. No kids around."

Gus gestures to the cave. "Well, this is certainly a great story to tell your—"

"Son?"

"Sorry. I'm sure you two have more important things to talk about."

"Do we ever."

Suddenly the rapture of choppers arrives. A war of whirs and the men look to the sky. Mills starts flailing his arms furiously as if waving off the helicopters. "Fuck," he screams. "Fuck the fucking fuckers."

Gus rises, too. "What's wrong?"

"Those aren't my choppers," he says. "Those are news choppers."

"Oh, Jesus. How did they know we were out here?"

"They picked up scanner traffic. Probably been following it since the search started this morning."

The metal vultures are getting closer, lower, their domes almost close enough to see the pilots and reporters inside. The noise is descending, cascading, like a waterfall of scrap metal.

"Stand in front of me," Mills yells.

"Huh?"

"Stand in front of me," Mills repeats. "I'm not going to end up on the news in my underwear."

Gus dashes to Mills's side of the ledge. "I guess that means I'm going to HazMat with you," Gus screams into Mills's ear.

"No, no. You just cover me until I back up into the cave. It'll just take a second. Let's move backward now. Stay a foot or so in front of me."

The men begin the slow retreat.

Mills shrinks behind Gus as the two of them march.

Once in the cave, Mills ducks across the perimeter of darkness. "Shit," he says.

"What?"

"I need my radio."

Gus immediately turns to the entrance of the cave, leans out, and grabs the radio. He puts it on the ground beside Mills. Mills lunges for it. "Get those choppers out of here," Mills shouts into the device. "Tell them they're impeding an investigation."

"They say they have a right to be out here," the voice replies.

"No!" Mills hollers. "Not at all. In fact, we have a right to close off airspace in order to get our own equipment in here. Tell them that."

"Will do, sir."

"Close the airspace," Mills repeats.

"Ten-four, Detective."

Then Mills looks at the psychic. "Do you believe this shit?"

Gus just looks at him and shrugs. "As soon as the news choppers leave, I think I'm going to start my climb back up."

"Huh? You think you're going to climb back up?"

"Yeah. How else am I going to get out of here?"

Mills spits. There's an awful taste in his mouth, worse than death, as if he's gotten human organs on his lips. "Dude, I can put you in one of our choppers," he tells Gus. "You know, an airlift."

"I'd rather just climb back up, if that's not a problem."

"It's not a problem for *me*," the detective tells him. "But based on your skills coming down, it may be a problem for *you*."

Gus rolls his eyes and then leans forward. "I'm not a big fan of helicopters," he says.

"Scared."

"Yep. Totally scared."

"I appreciate your candor, Mr. Parker. When we get the media out of here, you're free to climb."

The climb up is a whole lot easier than the hike down. Perhaps it's because Gus is fleeing the scene. That's what he thinks as he muscles up the mountain. He's escaping a monstrous scene, a hideous corpse, a vortex of evil. And he attacks that mountain, grinding away with his hands, with his feet, and it all reminds him of the rope climb in high school gym. He was always the first to the top. Never liked the way down. Now atop the ridge he catches his breath, walks in circles with his hands above his head, at once reaching for the sky, for purifying air, for salvation. And then he wipes the sweat from his face and shrugs off the idea of salvation. "You ready to head back down the trail?" someone asks him.

Gus hadn't noticed the patrolman coming toward him. He recognizes the kid with the wide and eager face. The name is Hall. The badge confirms it. "Yeah," he tells the kid. "Let's go."

They descend the trail in silence for about ten minutes before Hall turns to him and asks, "What was down there?"

"A corpse."

"Well, I know they found a dead body, Mr. Parker, but was there, like, anything unusual?"

Gus stifles a laugh. "A dead body down there would be considered unusual," he tells the rookie.

"I hear Mills tripped over the body."

"It was very dark in there. We're lucky we found the remains."

The kid has a swagger, but it's refined and not discourteous. "Yeah, well, that makes three bodies and three caves."

That kind of math would account for Gus's visions, but he doesn't share his psychic arithmetic with the officer. "Two bodies so far," Gus says instead. "Unless you've been reading my mind."

"No. It's three bodies, three caves," the officer repeats with intrigue in his eyes. "I sense a pattern here."

Gus dispatches a clear signal of confusion from his face.

Hall moves closer. "Oh. You probably didn't hear."

"Hear what?"

"While you were climbing up from the cave, a call came in from Camelback. Somebody found another body up there."

Gus feels his eyes rip open. "Where? When?"

"About half an hour ago, maybe. On the south side of Camelback."

They're walking swiftly now. "Really? I didn't think the south side was all that popular with hikers," Gus says.

"I don't know."

"Has anyone told Alex?"

"He'll be told as soon as someone from his squad gets here," the officer replies.

They descend the rest of the trail in silence, but Gus is full of commotion in the regions of his mind where he goes to clarify visions. The Camelback body is the murder he saw yesterday. Has to be. On *his* Camelback. You live in its shadows long enough and you begin to think of it as your shelter, as your hunkering guardian. There is something about that big, red mountain that Gus trusts instinctively even if the huge beast occasionally strands a hiker, injures a cocky climber, and requires rescue choppers to dip between its humps.

Down at the trailhead Beatrice is gone.

No sign of the Karmann Ghia. He pulls out his cell and dials.

"I had a client," she explains. "You were gone forever. But I left with every intention to come back and get you," she coos. "Don't feel abandoned."

He tells her about the grisly remains in the cave and the body at Camelback.

"Oh, my dear God," she says, and Gus imagines her holding a fluttering hand to her heart. "Let me see if I can work on this for a few minutes."

"Beatrice, you don't do murder," Gus reminds her. "Besides, I know the body at Camelback is the death I saw yesterday. Because the victim here is obviously not fresh." And then he walks toward Hall's cruiser, the cell phone still in his hand. "Beatrice, hold on," he says. He sticks his head into the officer's car.

"Hall, can you give me a ride to Camelback? I'm stranded out here."

"Those are my instructions," Hall says.

"From who?"

"Mills. Just heard from him. Apparently he got the news."

Gus flies to the passenger side and hops in. "Beatrice. I'll call you later."

This place is so familiar. It's Gus's backyard, this street that starts out flat in Arcadia and starts its climb up to the base of the mountain. It curves and bends, and Camelback towers overhead; he has studied this big rock for years, and he is still so awestruck. The closer he gets, the bigger it grows until he is just a tiny factor of dust.

"You know this area?" Hall asks.

"Uh, yeah."

"This isn't exactly a hiking spot."

"I know."

"But there's a ledge up around here where people climb to take pictures. Nice views."

"Yeah, and it's all being sold off to developers. It's immoral."

They make a sharp turn, and the road heads steeply downward before twisting, again, up and around another bend. That's where they find about six cruisers parked end to end. A crime scene van is blocking the road. They get out and walk to the van where they're greeted by Detective Morton Myers.

"Looks like you don't need me here," Hall says.

Gus senses the void in Hall, the enough-for-one-day disintegration of the soul. Hall is so young and already jaded enough to retreat from the big case of the day. Doesn't need to be here. Perfectly happy to go home and eat pasta and walk the dog.

Myers nods. "Go back to the Peak," he tells Hall. "They need your help working the perimeter and closing the trails."

Gus is not looking at either of them. Instead he is studying the ledge above the road and watching the scramble of feet up there. He closes his eyes. This is where the body lies, the one he saw slain yesterday. The vibe rattles deep within him, a kettledrum of affirmation. He opens his eyes, shielding them with one hand from the sun. "There's a cave up there?" he asks Myers.

Myers flashes a bubba grin and says, "Oh damn right there is. Party cave. All the kids come up here to drink and smoke. Neighbors are always complaining."

"And nobody saw anything last night?"

"Not that we know of," Myers says.

"A hiker found the body, right?"

Again that grin of the Wild West, where body counts make a cop like Morton Myers salivate, as though without the bodies, without menace of criminals, how would he justify the uniform? "Hysterical neighbor is more like it," Myers says. "This ain't no hiking trail."

"I'm out of here," Hall says. He extends a hand, and he and Gus shake.

Gus turns back to Myers. "Show me the way up."

Myers looks to the ledge, then back to Gus. "Uh, not so fast, buddy. I don't have the authority to let you up there."

"Where's Mills?"

Myers twists his mouth as if he's savoring his favorite pastry. "He's probably at headquarters taking the hottest shower of his life. That's if they let him leave the scene; I hear his clothes are evidence. Heh-heh."

"They are."

"Well, that just sucks. Doesn't it? I'd make 'em give me a Silkwood shower. If you know what I mean."

"I do," Gus says. "So, I guess I'll call for a ride home."

Myers puts a hand at the back of Gus's neck, gently turns him away from the crime scene, and says, "I don't know about that, Mr. Parker. Sergeant Woods is on his way right now. Maybe you should talk to him."

Gus shakes his head. "I don't think so. I'm sure Woods has more important things to do here than talk to me."

Myers laughs, then adjusts his weight. "We have two orders from the sergeant," he says. "Block the road from the media and keep you here if you show up. Woods is the boss. Mills's boss. Best you comply."

"I'm flattered. I think."

About twenty minutes later a tank-size SUV rounds the bend. It's a box of armor and rubber. Colored lights pop up everywhere like menacing eyeballs. The car comes to a thunk at the side of the road. Sergeant Jacob Woods emerges from the heavily tinted interior. Another man exits the SUV. Gus doesn't recognize him.

The two men cross the road without seeing Gus and confer with Myers and a few others. Jacob Woods looks up at the ledge, while one of his men points to a walkway that will lead him there. Someone says something to make the sergeant laugh. Woods gives the comedian a slap on the back. Then he narrows his eyes and looks Gus's way.

Gus stares back.

It's narrow eyes versus narrow eyes.

The men climb the walkway and disappear above the ledge. They're up there for a few minutes when Gus is summoned. It's Myers's voice from above. "The sergeant would like you to join him up here," the cop says.

A sound cracks through the air as Gus reaches the walkway. A sound Gus, by now, is familiar with. It's the wobbly cutting of chopper blades through the sky. He can read the logos on the closest two. The news channels have arrived. "I guess we have company," he says to Myers who has come down to escort him.

"Too bad we can't shoot 'em down," Myers says. "They'd make for great target practice."

"I guess the whole first amendment thing rubs you the wrong way."

"I love my guns."

Gus sighs. "That's the second amendment."

"Who's counting?" Myers retorts. "Let's just say I'm no fan of the media. If they even start to interfere we'll get them out of here."

In less than a minute they're at the top and Gus sees a semicircle of crime scene techs hovering around what he assumes is the cave. As he approaches he sees the sergeant break from the group and come his way.

"It's Parker, right?" Woods asks, extending a hand.

Gus nods. They shake firmly.

"Good to see you again," the sergeant says. "It's been a while."

"Yeah. Can I help you with anything here?"

The sergeant sizes him up anew. "Help with anything? Two bodies in one day, buddy. And Mills tells me you called it."

"In reverse order, if that makes a difference."

"As long as we can put it all together, I don't care what order you see the bodies."

"You think there are more. . . ." Not a question.

"Yes," the sergeant says. A more definitive answer than Gus expected.

"Me too."

"Can you come over to the cave and take a look?" They start to walk, and then the sergeant stops abruptly. "It's not your typical desert cave, you know. Lots of beer cans. Kids, that sort of thing."

"Right," Gus says. "I'm guessing no petroglyphs either."

"No ancient ones. But we have a brand-new drawing in there."

They reach the periphery of the cave. "Come on, everybody, give us room," the sergeant demands. The small army disperses. And then Woods leans into Gus and says, "Look, you can't touch the body. You know the drill?"

"Of course."

"Don't even approach the body. Stay as close to the walls as possible. You hear?"

Gus nods. He enters the shallow cave to find a woman on the floor, facedown, her head turned to one side. The side of her neck that is visible is slashed from her ear to her throat. Orbs of blood soak her clothes at other puncture points: her left shoulder, her right rib cage; a dried-up pool has seeped from her stomach.

"Her name is Lindsey Drake," the sergeant says. "She's from Wisconsin. We found her rental car parked along the road."

Gus nods. He studies the depiction of the murder chiseled into the side of the cave. It has every characteristic of the killer. Again, a self-portrait of crime. The killer and his victim. A knife. Gushing stab wounds. The artwork is unrefined, a classic message from a child. There's hesitation, mania. There's anger, joy, and Gus sees that fire again. And he sees that New England town again, a house by the water. He bows his head.

"We don't know what brought her up here," the sergeant says. "Her boyfriend just said she was missing around Camelback last night."

"Boyfriend?"

"Yeah. Some guy who called 911 when she didn't show up back at the hotel."

"And what happened? Did anyone go looking for her?"

"It was after dark when he called. It had only been a few hours since she went missing," Woods explains. "An officer went over to the hotel, took a report. We had a few patrols come up to the neighborhood. But it was too dark for anyone to go up the mountain."

"Did anyone follow up with the boyfriend this morning?" Gus asks.

"After Mills cleans up he's going to the hotel to question the guy."

"Okay," Gus says, looking squarely at the sergeant. "But what I don't understand is why the killer would have been lurking here. This is not a trail. There are no petroglyphs. Hikers are interested in the mountain, not this little ledge."

"So you see no connection?"

"Oh, no, I see a connection. I get the same vibe here as I did at the other two crime scenes. I'm just curious about this spot."

"It doesn't fit the profile?"

"I'm not a profiler, Sergeant."

Woods smirks. "Yeah," he says. "I know that, Parker. We got a guy for that."

"Right."

Outside at the clearing, the sergeant introduces him to Timothy Chase, the other man who Gus saw getting out of the SUV. Chase examines Gus, nods, and shakes his hand. "Pleasure," the detective says. He's wearing a linen blazer, blue jeans, and one of those Wheaties smiles. Timothy Chase is a large outline of a man, long arms, legs, and wide chest.

"So, you're the profiler?" Gus asks.

The man, who towers over Gus, laughs and shakes his head. "Forensic psychologist," he says.

"Right. Of course. I thought the terms were interchangeable."

"They're not."

"My fault," the sergeant says. "At least I don't call him Mr. Hollywood anymore."

Gus laughs, then acknowledges that Detective Timothy Chase does, indeed, possess that Hollywood look, those impossibly chiseled features and gleaming eyes. Gus sees the emergence of self-help guru Tony Robbins in the face of the detective, those huge teeth, those happily catatonic eyes. The similarity to Robbins is actually quite striking. Gus had almost dismissed the man as a jarhead; now studying him closer he feels a bit emasculated. Ain't nothing wrong with this guy's sperm count, Gus observes resentfully. He's probably impregnated half the women in the valley just by brushing by them on the street.

"He's my scene investigator. Supervising until Mills gets back," the sergeant explains.

"Former FBI?" Gus asks the towering detective.

Chase nods. "I see my reputation precedes me. Or is that your psychic thing?"

"I think Mills mentioned it to me," Gus says. "But didn't he call you out to the Peak? To take over the scene there?"

Chase bristles. "Well, turns out I was needed here, Mr. Parker. We sent the very capable detective Ken Preston out to the Peak. So I think we got it covered. Do I need to clear it with anyone else?"

Distinctly put in his place, Gus apologizes. "I hope it didn't sound like I was second-guessing."

"No apology needed, Mr. Parker," Chase says. "It was good to meet you. I've worked with psychics before on FBI cases. I'd welcome any of your hunches. Now if you'll excuse me. . . ."

Gus nods. "Look, if I can have some time in the cave alone, that would be very helpful."

"Uh, no. I can't let you in there alone, Mr. Parker," Chase tells him. "Totally against protocol. With all the evidence, and everything . . . Can't have you disturbing the scene, you know."

"I'd like to go back in," Gus insists. "You could have someone escort me. Just give me some space."

A few moments later Gus is back at the hole in the mountain, latex gloves on his hands, surgical shoe covers on his feet, and Detective Morton Myers at his side. They circumnavigate the body, giving it a wide radius on all sides. They steer clear of the bloodstains and the splatter. Then he sits by a distant wall of the cave, across from the drawing. Gus might as well have the chamber to himself now, the way he is able to shirk the presence of Morton Myers and the techs working nearby, the way he tunes out the exterior chatter and the other noises of the day. He closes his eyes. Yes, there's New England again. And the ocean. And there is a man grunting and a child screaming. And the man is in flames. And now it's the child grunting as he pulls fish from the water and cuts their heads off. He picks up clams and crushes them with his hands. He is bloody and older now. He is throwing furniture at a cowering woman. She's beautiful but terrified, her makeup running. And he's grunting as he curses her. *Fucking cunt, fucking cunt, fucking cunt!* This madman kicks the woman in the face. He kicks her repeatedly. Gus can't see his face, but he sees thick veins in his neck. He sees the man's feet; what he believes at first to be blood is actually ink. His ankles are tattooed. He can't decipher the tattoos, but they look like a signature, like an artist had signed the man's feet. He hears a drumbeat, a crash of cymbals, and applause. He opens his eyes. The light comes in. It's like he's just been watching theater.

Someone is shouting his name.

13

Detective Alex Mills takes a good whiff of himself and smirks. He smells like a baby fresh from a bath. He reeks of soap, completely sterile, completely disinfected. They had given him a hazmat suit to wear just so he wouldn't have to ride back to headquarters in his underwear. He had stripped off the suit and stepped into the shower where the water was set at a furious temperature and velocity. And he just stood there, slack, surrendering to the torrent, grateful for the cleansing, yearning to touch his wife's skin, to go home to her and curl up in bed, under the cover of their big fleece blanket, and sleep. A deep, dark, center-of-the-earth kind of sleep. But such an expedition would have to wait because Mills has been sent to the downtown Hyatt to seek out Neil Carmody, the boyfriend of the Camelback victim.

The man opens the door on the second knock. He's unshaven and disheveled, his eyes sunken and surrounded by circles of ashy gray. "Mr. Carmody?"

"Yes?"

"I'm Detective Alex Mills from the Phoenix Police Department."

The man's face sort of collapses right there in the doorway. "This can't be good."

"I believe we found your girlfriend's body on Camelback Mountain. We're investigating this as a murder."

Then the man goes weak in the knees and grasps the doorjamb. He just stands there and says nothing. His chest is heaving.

"May I come in?" Mills asks.

The man lets him pass.

Mills looks around the hotel room. There are two suitcases, a garment bag, and some kind of carry-on. One bed is unmade. The room smells of human sweat and sickness. Gone is the institutional fragrance of Generic Hotel, replaced by the odor of a man who has been up all night in desperation. He's in a black T-shirt and gray sweatpants.

"What happened to her?" the man asks, wide-eyed, a minor tremble in his voice.

"What happened to *you*?" Mills studies him from head to toe. So there's no mistake about his question, he stares hard at Carmody's fat lip, the dried-up blood, the laceration above the eyebrow, and, of course, the crudely bandaged right hand.

"Oh, God," Carmody says. "I must look like I've been in a brawl," he adds somewhat absently.

"You do."

"I fell."

"You fell?"

"On a hike yesterday morning," the man says. "Lindsey and I were hiking Camelback."

"And you fell?"

"Hard."

"Did you go to the hospital? Did you need a rescue?"

Carmody laughs. "No. We were on our way down. I tripped and got banged up, but I made it to the car and Lindsey drove us back."

"Did the two of you have a fight of any kind?"

"Huh?" And then, "No, no. We never fought."

"What do you think she was doing up at Camelback alone?"

"I know what she was doing. She was going up there to take some more pictures. I had just handed her the camera when I tripped, so she never got the shots she wanted."

"But you were already on your way down when you fell," Mills says. "I would think the only shot worth getting was the view from the top."

"No, Detective, Lindsey wanted to document the climb from ascent to descent."

"Oh. I see. So you let her go off alone to finish taking pictures?"

"Let her? What do you mean? It didn't seem particularly dangerous. I mean, it was daylight. I figured there would be lots of hikers around. And I sure as hell wasn't in any condition to go climbing again."

"I understand," Mills says. "Now I need you to come with me, Mr. Carmody. Do you need a few moments to get yourself together?"

"To see her body?" the man asks with a shiver.

"The body is still at Camelback. I need you to come with me to the police station."

"To the morgue?"

"Like I said, the body is still at Camelback, but it will eventually be taken to the ME's office, and, yes, if you wish you may view the body."

And then Carmody sits at the side of the unmade bed and sobs. "I don't think I slept at all last night," he says in between gasps for air. "Every hour that went by took more and more convincing that she was all right. You know what I mean?"

"I do."

There's always a mix of sympathy and healthy suspicion. The sobbing is not uncommon, nor is the drama. But Mills senses a melo-drama, here, and melodrama is often an overcompensation. Hard to know at first.

Still crying the man says, "I mean, it's like with every hour you feel the hope slipping away and you have to fight that much harder to believe otherwise. I don't think I can do this."

"I'm sorry, Mr. Carmody," Mills tells him. "But I don't think we have an option. We ID'd your girlfriend through her driver's license, but we still need a full statement from you."

Carmody then goes facedown on the bed and wails.

Mills waits and says nothing. He stares out the window at the view of the northwest valley, sees nothing remarkable except the late-day sky.

Carmody groans, then rolls over. "I don't believe this," he says, getting up. "This can't be happening."

"Where you from?"

"Boston."

"Interesting," Mills says. "I'm told her license was issued in Wisconsin."

"It is," Carmody tells him. "She moved to Massachusetts to be with me. Just a month ago. She hasn't switched things out yet."

"Go wash your face."

Now the two men are heading toward the police headquarters, driving big squares of the central Phoenix grid around the station because Mills is hoping to give Carmody time to process. Time to talk.

"What brought you to Phoenix?" Mills asks.

"Business conference," Carmody says.

"I figured."

"You did?"

"Yeah. Most tourists don't stay downtown. They stay at the resorts."

"My company used to put me up at the Phoenician. No more. Too expensive."

"What kind of work do you do?"

"I work for a consulting firm. Human Resources."

"How long have you been in Phoenix?"

"Three days. The conference ends today."

"So you came in Friday night?"

"No," the man replies. "Thursday afternoon."

"You have your travel documents?"

The man fidgets. He lifts his hands as if to exaggerate their emptiness. "Not with me. At the hotel."

"I'll want to see them."

Neil Carmody is staring vacantly at the road ahead.

"Are the two of you experienced climbers?" the detective asks.

"What do you mean?"

"Camelback is not for beginners exactly. Certainly not for beginners who don't climb in the desert. You're a long way from home."

"We're not beginners," Carmody says. "There are mountains in New England, you know."

The man speaks evenly, almost eagerly now, the lack of guile suggesting to Alex Mills that Neil Carmody doesn't know he's being questioned when he's being questioned. Mills slows to stop for a red light at Twenty-Fourth Street, and that's when he pivots his torso and says to Carmody, "I've got to tell you, the sergeant takes one look at you and you become a person of interest."

Carmody's expression doesn't change. "With all these bruises, I wouldn't blame him."

"Well, you cleaned up okay enough."

"Yeah, but the bruises are still bruises. And the scratches on my face don't look like I was playing with a cat."

"No, they don't," Mills says. "But, hell, if you were the killer I imagine you would have hightailed it out of town by now. You'd be long gone, man."

Carmody doesn't say anything, and this bothers Mills.

"You know," the detective says, "even if you weren't all banged up, you'd still be considered a suspect. Everyone's a suspect. Especially boyfriends and husbands."

And then, finally, "Do I, like, need a lawyer?"

"If what you've told me so far is true, then no, sir, I wouldn't think so."

The man's shoulders sink. "Okay. That's a relief."

That would have been Carmody's cue to say, "I'm innocent" or "I didn't do it." But he didn't. He said, *"That's a relief."* And now he's clamming up again. On one hand Mills would expect the guy to speculate wildly, either as a deflection or, just as credibly, an honest reaction. On the other hand, Mills fully understands if Carmody is shifting into denial and burrowing away from the truth.

Mills thinks Carmody's silence is fascinating even if he doesn't exactly consider him a serious suspect for now. After all, there are three bodies, not one. If the murders are connected, Neil Carmody was a busy man during his business trip to Phoenix.

Five minutes later they're at the PD without either of them saying another word. But as Mills escorts Carmody into the station he can see fear return to the man's eyes. The building has that effect even on the most innocent of visitors. Mills introduces a slightly jittery Carmody to Detective Morton Myers who has just returned from Camelback. Mills will leave Lindsey Drake's boyfriend here so Myers can casually question him. That was the plan. To make sure the guy's story is consistent.

"You have a picture of Lindsey on your phone?" Mills asks the man.

"Yeah. Several."

"Myers will have you text one to me," Mills says, suddenly transactional, all business. "I'm heading to Camelback."

The mountain is already casting its mammoth shadow over its lower neighbors as Mills approaches the cave. This is as typical a Phoenix afternoon, of life and death, as any other. He has dug bodies out of Dumpsters under the valley's glorious sunlight; he has fished bodies out of canals beneath a cerulean sky; he has stumbled upon humanity's inner darkness on the calmest, breeziest, easiest desert mornings and afternoons. There was always darkness, even in the Valley of the Sun, a contradiction that had started to turn off some kind of light within him, as well.

"The boyfriend is now with Myers, as you requested," he tells his sergeant who's standing at the mouth of the cave. "He just sent me a picture of our likely victim."

"What happened when you questioned him?"

Mills describes in copious detail his conversations with Carmody at the hotel and in the car.

"A business trip. . . . A hiking accident," the sergeant recites as if he's scribbling mental notes. "Have you checked out his story?"

"Not entirely."

"Make it entirely," the sergeant orders. "Proof of his every move here in Phoenix."

"Like I said, he's with Myers," Mills explains, the umbrage in his voice not entirely subtle. And then he tells his boss, with just enough hubris to level the playing field, that they have to rethink the Elizabeth Spears case.

"So soon?"

"I had Myers running background on her ex, her coworkers, her roommate, but I think it's a waste of time. Unless we can establish a personal connection between the three victims, their personal relationships with others don't matter." Mills pauses. Sergeant Jacob Woods says nothing. "We have one killer," Mills continues, "and three random bodies."

The sergeant completes the logic. "We're ruling out a copycat," he says, "because the scene at South Mountain has been sealed."

"Exactly," Mills says. "There would be nothing to copy. I want to keep Preston on the Squaw Peak case. That's a Jane Doe someone forgot about."

His boss gives him a sober nod of affirmation.

"Now if I can get in the cave and compare the picture to our corpse, that would make my day."

"Just so you know, Mills, this is an asshole-free crime scene."

"You sure about that?"

"Don't test me. Not in the mood," his boss warns him. "The cave is yours, but you might want to get your psychic friend out of there."

Mills peers into the hole in the mountain, then back at Woods. "You let him in there?"

"With supervision, of course. Myers went in with him first. Now a tech is keeping a watchful eye over your psychic."

"Gus doesn't disturb crime scenes. He penetrates them."

Woods ignores him, bends a few degrees, and cups his hands around his mouth. "Parker," he shouts. "Come outta there."

Gus emerges at that moment, dust and dirt coating his arms and legs, frosting his hair. "You don't need to shout, Sergeant. The cave's not very deep."

Mills laughs quietly, admiring how unflappable Gus can be.

"Hey, Alex," Gus says with a wave. "You okay?"

"Okay?"

"Disinfected?"

"Fully."

"Recovered?"

"Not sure what you mean."

"I sensed you were traumatized at the Peak."

"It takes a lot to traumatize me, Gus. More than a few maggots."

"But there were more than a few maggots," Gus says.

The sergeant leans in close. "If you boys are done socializing, I'd like to keep the investigation moving."

"Don't mean to impede, Sergeant Woods," Mills assures him, then to Gus, "You get any solid vibes in there? Pick up on anything?"

"Confusing images. A man beating a woman. Blood. And tattoos."

"Nothing specific about the victim?"

"No. But I keep seeing a house in flames. In New England."

"New England?" the sergeant asks.

"Yeah. I don't know why."

"Carmody's from Massachusetts," Mills says.

"You do know we're looking for something really specific here?" the sergeant asks. "You know, like a lead. Like a place where the killer might be hiding? Or maybe what he's wearing, or what kind of car he's driving?"

Gus nods. Then he squints and asks, "Has anyone searched the victim's car?"

Only now Mills notices the cave dust caked in Gus's eyelashes.

"Of course. Chase is on it now," Woods says. "He's doing a preliminary with a couple of techs before they stick it on a flatbed and send it to the lab."

Mills has to bite his tongue. Seriously, he has to grind his teeth into his tongue and tighten his jaw lest he release a slew of obscenities (fuck, damn, fucking fuck, Jesus, fuck)—not directed at the sergeant, and not necessarily at Timothy Chase either, but at the circumstances, the circumstances that sort of apply the writing to the wall. *My fucking job, my fucking life, I thought I had it all figured out.* But no one has it figured out. Mills has burned a tremendous quantity of mental calories trying to avoid the inevitable. He had checked into a successful life; he'd been a strong husband and a strong father, and he'd been a local hero. But nothing stays the same. Inevitably things change. Inevitably you lose your grasp on power or success, or both. Usurpers line up. Shit happens, and you get evicted from your successful life. Trevor is the latest author of Alex's inevitability, but he had a hunch when Chase joined the force. "Chase," he says casually. "When did he get here?"

"He came with me," the sergeant replies.

Mills nods. Then he rolls his head and cracks his neck, if for no other reason than to feign indifference.

Gus asks, "Did he find a coffee cup?"

The sergeant looks at the psychic confused and says, "What's that?"

"A coffee cup. Did Chase find one in the car?"

"I don't know," Woods replies. "He wasn't looking for a coffee cup. The techs are looking for signs of a struggle, hair, blood, broken glass, that sort of thing."

"Of course, but isn't everything in the car considered evidence?" Gus asks.

"Yes," Woods replies. "And everything in the car that is not obviously or overtly suspicious will be inventoried, as well."

"Good," Gus tells him. "I sensed the victim stopping at some kind of convenience store for coffee. She might have even filled up with gas on the way here."

"We'll check it out, Mr. Parker," the sergeant assures him. "But let's wait to hear from Myers. I'd be interested to know if all Mr. Carmody's statements are consistent."

The men descend from the ledge and meet up with Chase who's watching a tech bag evidence from the car.

"Wow," Gus says.

"Wow, what?" Woods asks.

"The car. It radiates a certain sadness."

"Come on, Parker, the car . . . radiating sadness?"

Mills jumps in before Gus has to. "Sergeant, Gus takes his cues from everything."

Woods shrugs. "Whatever."

"Look at it just sitting there," Gus continues as if he had not considered a word the sergeant has said, "implicated in a crime unwittingly, regretfully, and now it understands that it had no power to save Lindsey Drake."

Woods says, "Really? You've got to be kidding me, man."

"I'm not," Gus insists. "Just let me sit in the car for a few minutes. I bet I can all but solve the crime. I feel . . . actually, I know the answers are in there."

The sergeant bows his head. "I'm sorry, Mr. Parker, but we can't let you do that. You might compromise or destroy evidence. We have a good idea what happened in the cave. We have no idea what, if anything, happened in that rental."

"But, Sergeant . . ."

"No," Woods insists. "Maybe when we're done going through the car."

"All I'm saying," Gus argues, "is that I know I can tell you more from inside it."

"Look," Chase says to the group, "once the car is completely processed, if and when it ends up in the impound lot, it does no harm to give Gus access. There's no risk of evidence tampering if we sign off."

"Right," the sergeant concedes. "But that might take a while. I'd sure like to catch this fucking psycho sooner than later."

"You know there are two sets of tire prints," Chase tells them, a remarkable happiness in his eyes.

"Two sets?" Mills asks.

"Yeah, one set right in front of the rental's. Both equally fresh."

"What about a coffee cup?" asks the sergeant. "Or a recent receipt?"

"Bagged them both," Chase says. "I got a cup from Circle K. And a gas receipt."

Gus offers one of his signature all-knowing smiles. *A prophet among us*, Mills thinks.

"Good work, Tim," the sergeant says. "It's getting dark. Get the car out of here and finish tomorrow."

"We need to finish with the tire prints. You know, in case it rains tonight," Chase tells him.

"Rain in the desert?" Mills mutters.

Chase just glares.

"I think we're going to have to make a statement," the sergeant tells them. "We found two bodies today. The place is buzzing with the media. We blocked them off down the road."

"Gus, would you mind excusing us for a moment?" Chase asks.

Gus looks immediately to Mills.

Mills does a quick assessment of the politics. There's no ground to stand. Not yet. He nods at Gus, and the psychic steps away.

"So, what is it, Timothy?" Mills asks his colleague.

"It's obvious," he says with mild condescension. "I think we hold the boyfriend."

Mills does a mental double take. "Are you serious? What's his motive for all three murders? This guy, for all we know, has no connection to South Mountain or the Peak."

"For all we know," Chase tosses back.

Mills plants his feet firmly in the ground. "I think the body at the Peak was there long before Mr. Carmody showed up in Phoenix."

"For all we know," Chase repeats, taunting passively.

"But something about the guy's story concerns me," the sergeant interjects. "He said his girlfriend came back to Camelback to finish taking pictures after their hike was cut short by his accident. So what is she doing here?" He gestures upward to the cave, now unseen, above them.

Both detectives look at each other and then at the sergeant.

"Well?" the sergeant continues. "She would have gone back to the north side where they were hiking. How would she have even known to come out to this ledge? Out-of-towners don't just stumble upon the view here. No one hikes over here."

"She followed someone up here," Chase says.

"Two sets of tire tracks would indicate that," Mills affirms. "So if

Carmody is our guy as you suspect, then why do you think he'd lead his girlfriend up here in separate cars?"

Timothy Chase narrows his eyes.

As counterproductive as it might be to the investigation, Mills can't help but find pleasure poking holes in this guy's theory. The thrill comes on so fast he doesn't have a chance to chastise himself for acting like a child. When you poke holes in Chase's theory, you poke holes in his ego, and Mills can justify that because the guy is just a fucking blowhard half the time. Bill O'Reilly with a badge.

"Maybe he didn't lead her up here," Chase concedes. "But maybe he has an accomplice. Maybe that accomplice has a connection to South Mountain and the Peak."

"So Neil Carmody and his buddy come to Phoenix to go on a killing spree?" Mills asks.

"Stranger things have happened," Chase muses in a stage whisper.

"I'm sure they have," the sergeant says. "But that's not what happened here. And I think you know that, Tim. Look, you go figure out the personality of this killer. And let Alex go find him."

"You can't let Carmody leave," Chase insists.

"We can't make him stay," the sergeant says.

"He's a person of interest," Chase argues.

"Agreed. And we can question him until the cows come home or he calls a lawyer. Whichever comes first. But we can't make him stay," the sergeant says.

Then Mills says, "Of course he's going to stay. You think he's going to up and leave his girlfriend's body here?"

And the sergeant says, "Alex is right."

Chase shakes his head and turns back to the victim's car.

The sergeant makes a silent, calming gesture, as if he's smoothing out ruffles with his hands, as if he's a kindergarten referee. But then he pivots sharply, perhaps sensing Gus's presence behind him. "I thought I asked you to excuse us."

Gus, his face a mix of Zen and crazy awe, says, "Yes, you did. But I sensed you were talking about the boyfriend."

"Sensed? Or eavesdropped?" the sergeant asks.

"Sensed. I'm sorry to interrupt, but the boyfriend was never here, on this side of the mountain."

"And you know this how?" Woods asks, his tone betraying his impatience.

"All I'm saying is that the victim was in that cave with a stranger. No one else," Gus explains. "I don't know about the boyfriend. I think maybe he took a fall. But not here."

The sergeant takes a step back as if yielding, physically, to the swath of Gus's power. "You knew about the hiking accident?" Woods asks wide-eyed.

Mills tries to conceal the smile of vindication rising on his face.

"Uh, not specifically," the psychic says. "But I sensed the man was hurt somehow and that he wasn't here with her."

"That might be true," Woods says, then shifts to Mills. "But we're keeping Carmody until Myers—or you, Mills—checks out his story."

It's not a suggestion. It's a signal to Mills to yield to the swath of the sergeant's power.

"I'm going back to the cave to ID her with the photo," he tells his boss.

"Be my guest," Woods says. "But, Mr. Parker, you stay here."

14

Gus wants to leave before the press conference begins. He finds the vapidity of reporters alarming and distracting. They could never know what he knows. Few people could ever know what he knows. But he particularly cringes when watching reporters trying to figure things out as if they're amateur sleuths from Sherlock University. The TV people are actors and actresses. The newspaper people take themselves too seriously. He supposes they're in the same game, though: truth.

He sees Detective Timothy Chase coming down the road.

"You heading out?" he asks Chase.

"Just for a bit. Gotta check on our guy at the Peak."

"I don't suppose you mind dropping me off. I need a lift."

"You don't want to wait for your buddy Mills?"

"No. He's busy. I've been gone all day. I got to feed the dog, let her out."

"Let's go," Chase says. "Anything for a man with a dog."

"You have a dog?"

"I did."

They're quiet for most of the drive. Gus gives the detective street directions and watches Chase watch the road. Chase must know that Gus is studying his profile, the way the detective flexes his face, the way he emphasizes his jaw; it betrays a self-consciousness, as if Gus has invaded his privacy. Gus makes a stab at modesty. "Well, I think I really fucked up," he says.

Chase doesn't turn, doesn't take his eyes off the road. "How do you mean?"

"I saw a murder last night, and I assumed it was the murder at Squaw Peak. But that body's been there for a while."

"So?"

"So the murder I saw last night had to be the one at Camelback. But I had no clue."

"The way I see it," Chase says, "is that there was a murder last night. And something else led you to the Peak. Both hunches were true. And like I told you before, I welcome any hunches."

"Is this your case now?"

Chase turns to him abruptly. "Of course not," he says. "I'm not the case agent."

"No, but I'm betting from this point on the case is all about psychology."

"That's probably a good bet, Mr. Parker."

And that's about it. Gus mutters directions. Chase confirms with a grunt. The ride takes maybe ten minutes.

As soon as Gus steps in the shower he realizes that Alex Mills will not solve these murders. The second the blast of water hits his face he knows it will be Timothy Chase. Timothy Chase will find the killer. He stands there soaking it in. He stands there inundated with certainty. He lathers up and wonders, frets really, if or when he should tell Mills the truth. He doesn't know if it will make a difference. Mills won't want to hear it. Mills will just try harder to change destiny when destiny can't be changed. Gus saw it in the profile of Timothy Chase as the detective drove him home; he saw a man with a homing device fixing in on the killer. Rinsing off, he's troubled. Mills is going to lose the case. Should Gus warn him?

He feeds Ivy, who solicitously wags her tail, and he feeds himself. Beatrice calls.

"I just want to say I'm sorry again for leaving you up there all by yourself."

He tells her not to worry.

"I saw choppers coming in as I was heading out."

"Yeah, the news," he tells her.

"What happened up there?" she asks, the scales of her voice rising.

"It'll be on the ten o'clock news. Watch."

"Are you okay?"

"Yes," he tells her.

"What's wrong? I can tell something's wrong, Gus."

"I can't put it into words." And he can't. He has a scramble of stimuli coming at him, and yet he regards it the way most people regard a pile of laundry or a sink full of dishes, a sort of default to ambivalence. "I'll make you dinner tomorrow night. Come over."

At ten o'clock Gus turns on the news. Tonight it's an anchorman named Doug Duggard with the breathless details of the Squaw Peak and Camelback murders. "Is there a serial killer in the valley?" he asks an audience who can't answer. His eyes jolt and chin dips. "Let's go to Mary Raney who joins us live from Camelback. Mary?"

Mary Raney grips her microphone and gestures with her free hand to the dark mountain behind her. "This is not the side of Camelback popular to tourists. And yet this is where the body of a tourist was found today by authorities. That, after another gruesome discovery at Piestewa Peak, more commonly known to Valley residents as Squaw Peak. Just hours ago Sergeant Jacob Woods of the Phoenix Police Department held a press conference where he would not rule out a connection between the murders. Let's listen in."

The press conference appears on-screen, washed in twilight and rinsed with caution. "I'm not going to speculate," the sergeant tells the media. "But some evidence does suggest the crimes are connected."

"What kind of evidence?" a reporter shouts out. "Did the victims know each other? Was it a HazMat situation at Squaw Peak? Hazmat suits were spotted by the chopper."

"I can't comment on evidence," the sergeant replies. "To our knowledge the victims did not know one another, but that is not conclusive at this point. There was a possibility of contamination at the Squaw Peak investigation."

"Is Mills leading this investigation?" another reporter asks. "We heard scanner chatter that it's Mills who was contaminated. What's his condition?"

"Detective Alex Mills is currently leading the investigation," Woods tells them. (Gus notes the word "currently"). "He was removed from the scene due to possible contamination with the remains at the crime scene. His condition is fine. He's standing behind me now."

Gus smiles. Indeed, Alex Mills is standing back there alongside a few officers, offering that official frame of law enforcement around the sergeant.

Suddenly there are rapid-fire questions from several reporters, all of them jockeying for attention as if it's some kind of competition, which it is, Gus realizes. But for what? Who can ask the most probing question? Or who can yell the loudest? The sergeant raises his hands and says, "Look, people, I'll take your questions. Just one at a time."

And then he calls on the next reporter.

"Do we have a serial killer on our hands, Sergeant? Any leads? Are you tying this to the murder of Elizabeth Spears at South Mountain, as well?"

"These murders may be the work of one killer," Woods says. "But we have not defined these yet as 'serial crimes.' I'm not going to discuss leads right now. We are gathering evidence. But we won't be commenting on the evidence at this time. Next?"

"How are the murders similar? Same murder weapon? Same MO?"

"We believe the same type of murder weapon was used, a knife. All the victims seemed to have died from stab wounds," the sergeant, blatantly fatigued, explains. "That is, of course, pending autopsy reports. If we knew for sure it was the same knife involved we would assume this to be the work of one killer. I'm not going to speak to motive. It's too early in the investigation."

"Will you be reopening South Mountain Park and the Peak?"

"I'll be meeting with the leaders of Phoenix and Maricopa County tomorrow to discuss the possibility of reopening those areas," Woods replies. His voice is getting edgier. "Though, the crime scenes will remain sealed."

"Will Detective Mills be taking questions tonight?" inquires still another reporter.

"No."

Then the same reporter dives in before anyone else can spit out a word and asks, "Will Detective Mills be making a statement about the arrest of his son?"

Woods, even edgier, says, "That's unrelated to this case."

"Unless it distracts the detective from this case," the reporter persists.

"Was that a question?" Woods asks the group, the anger in his voice now unabashed. "I didn't hear a question, so if there are no more questions . . ."

"What did the bodies look like?"

"Thank you all for coming. That will be all for tonight."

Mary Raney reappears on camera. (Gus had forgotten all about her!) Her hair is wispy in the light desert wind. Her lips are juicy and seductive. "And so, more questions than answers tonight in a series of killings that have stunned the residents of the valley. We'll be following this case every step of the way, and we'll update you as warranted."

"That is kind of your job, Mary," Gus says to the TV.

But he is interrupted by Doug Duggard who asks Mary, "Do residents of the valley have any reason to fear, Mary?"

She sucks in her cheeks and gazes into the lens like a soap opera ingénue into the eyes of her lover. "There's a killer on the loose, Doug. I'm sure people won't be resting easy until the killer is caught."

"Mary Raney reporting live tonight from Camelback Mountain. Thank you, Mary."

Thank you? Gus wonders. *For doing her job?*

"And in other news," Duggard chants, "a ninety-two-year-old woman is in stable condition after driving her car into a Chick-Fil-A."

Gus Parker lifts the remote and extinguishes the evening news.

One of Kelly's partners, Michael Susso, a youngish attorney with long legs and a short torso, will represent Trevor Mills. Susso is wearing an impeccable suit and a smile that just won't quit for a Monday morning. They're sitting in a conference room on the second floor of the courthouse. "Thanks for taking the morning off," he says to Mills.

Mills bristles. "Well, of course I did. You'd think I wouldn't be here?"

"Oh, no, Alex," Susso says. "It's just I assume you're up to your eyes with the cave murders."

"Even still . . ."

"I mean it's all over the news," the attorney says.

Mills had seen the morning paper.

POLICE FIND TWO MORE BODIES IN MOUNTAIN CAVES

That was the headline. There were two other related stories, one below the fold and another taunting one on page three:

THREE DAYS, THREE MURDERS, NO LEADS

Mills rolls his eyes. "Whatever," he says. "I'm here. Aren't I? Family is more important right now."

Trevor releases a snarky laugh.

Mills glares at his son.

They'll enter a plea of not guilty, but Mills would like to sentence his kid right now to ten years of hard labor.

"The DA is offering a deal," Susso tells them. "It's a first offense, so he has a lot of latitude."

"We'll take the deal," Mills says.

"Well, wait, Alex," Susso tells him. "Let me explain. He'll wipe out some of the charges altogether if Trevor names names."

Mills looks to his son who is seated across from him. Trevor doesn't move. His face is frozen; his eyes are fixed on the opposite wall.

"Trevor has already told us that he won't name names," Kelly says.

Mills leans forward. "Yeah, that's what my son says. But that's not what we decided."

"Well, he's looking at two and a half years in juvenile corrections," Susso tells them. "Possession with intent to sell. I mean, it was almost two pounds of pot."

Mills bolts out of his chair. "We know."

"Plus an extra year for selling in a drug-free school zone," the attorney adds.

"You sold pot to a cop in a school zone?" Mills asks his son. Then he puts his head against the wall and knocks his head gently. "I don't believe this," he whispers.

"Honey, sit down," his wife begs.

Mills will not be mollified. He circles the room. Prowling.

"The state suspects that your son was selling the drugs for someone else. Someone higher up," Susso explains, still with that irritating smile.

"Obviously," Mills says aloud, then to his son, "Do you realize the complete fuckup shitpile of trouble you're in?"

"Honestly, Dad, I do."

Surprised, Mills backs off. That was the first lucid statement from Trevor in two days.

"You'll be in a whole lot less trouble," Kelly says to the child, "if you tell us who gave you the pot. Who were you selling the drugs for?"

Trevor lowers his head. "Mom, I could get killed for saying anything."

"Killed?" Kelly begs, panic in her voice. "You never said anything about that."

"Now you know," the boy says.

"Did someone threaten you?" Mills asks. "You absolutely have to tell us."

"It's just something I heard after practice, that's all."

"Wait a minute, Trevor. You went to practice yesterday?" Mills asks his son. "I told you no more practice. You're off the team." And then, "Kelly?"

"I thought he was going to tell the coach," she says. "You could have gone with him if it were so important."

"Look, folks," Susso interjects.

"No, wait a minute," Mills insists. "Let me make it clear. Trevor is off the team, and, yeah, I'll go to school with him, tell the coach myself if I have to. 'Cause it's that important."

Trevor looks up. "Either way. On the team or off the team, I'm not saying anything. I swear they'll kill me. And even you," he says to his parents.

Mills scoffs at his son. "Seriously? Your dad's a cop; your mom's an attorney. No one's going to touch you, boy. You think you're working for the mob, or something?"

"Something," his son mutters.

"We can work out some kind of protection for Trevor if he gives us the full scope," the attorney tells them.

Trevor pounds a fist on the table. "No," he rages. "No. I'm not going to sign anyone's death warrant."

Mills sidles to his son. Leans his face close to Trevor's. "Knock off the melodrama, Trevor. You're not signing anyone's death warrant. Michael's going to enter a plea of not guilty for you this morning. Then we'll have a discussion with the DA. That's how it's going to be. If anyone is going to lock you up for twenty years it's going to be me, not that fat-ass fuck Maricopa County sheriff. You get that, son? Your mother and I are going to help you get your life back because otherwise your life is never going to be the same again. Never. You can kiss all you ever wanted good-bye."

Trevor's face reddens and twists. He is a boy, an infant, a baby, and everything out there in the world frightens him. He is ashamed, and yet he is too young to modify his behavior. He is too young. And Alex Mills sees in his son's watery eyes an innocence he had all but forgotten, an innocence that betrays Trevor's affectations. Trevor is nodding repeatedly. His heavy foot beats on the floor.

"I got the drugs from a few guys on the team," he says.

"Thank you, honey," his mother says.

"Can you tell us who those guys are?" Susso asks.

"Yes. I can," Trevor replies. "But that's really it. I don't really know who we were selling the stuff for."

Alex sits and sighs. "That's a start," he tells the others in the room. "But I have a feeling that we're not hearing the complete truth."

"What, Dad?"

"How do you not know who you're selling this stuff for?"

"Because I'm smart enough not to ask," the kid says. "These players get it, distribute. And we sell."

There's a knock at the door. It's a clerk. Trevor's case is up next.

"The arraignment will take five minutes," Kelly tells her son.

"I'm calling the department," Mills says. "I think the narcs will want to pay a visit to the high school."

"Leave it to the DA," his wife says. "She may want her guys on this."

How fucking embarrassing. Not just for him, or for Kelly, but for the legacy of Lyle Mills. For the first time ever he hears himself say, "I'm glad my dad is not alive."

"Talk to the DA," Kelly insists.

He nods.

It was a routine day of mammograms.

The women were pleasant. Except for Candy Harperfin who insisted that a woman administer the procedure. "How could I let a man handle my breasts?" she screamed at the receptionist after bolting from the exam room clad only in a crispy blue johnny. Even after Candy Harperfin was pacified and a female tech was freed from another pair of breasts to take over for Gus, the patient continued to rant and rave about the sanctity of a woman's breast. "A woman! I'm a woman! I have control over my own body! This is not a man's domain!"

Gus just shook his head and smiled cordially. Then he went to finish the mammogram that his colleague had been forced to abandon.

Mrs. Campbell was very understanding. In the midst of the exam, Gus did observe strange objects floating in Mrs. Campbell's breasts. He studied the images closer. What were those things? Footballs? It's not like he could ask.

Gus finished the exam, and now three unprotested mammograms later he's home and cooking dinner for Beatrice. She arrives around seven o'clock and offers to take Ivy for a walk while Gus grills the salmon.

"Yeah, sure," he tells her. "She loves you."

Which is obvious. Ivy greets Beatrice Vossenheimer ecstatically, leaping, barking, and drooling. The dog buries her face into Beatrice's chest. The two leave for a neighborhood walk. Gus is food prepping for about ten minutes when the phone rings. It's Gary Potter.

"Do you have any time available tomorrow or Wednesday?"

"I think so," Gus tells his client. "Is everything okay?"

"Oh, yeah. Just great. But I'd like to ask some questions about something new."

"Sure," Gus says. "Tomorrow night. Eight o'clock."

"Thanks, man," Potter says.

The salmon sizzles, and Beatrice returns. Gus delivers the meal to the table. They sit quietly for a few seconds. Beatrice smiles at him relentlessly. She won't turn away. She just holds him there in her loving gaze.

"I know something's troubling you," she says finally. "I could tell last night."

Gus shrinks into his chair, acquiescing. "I owe you an apology," he says.

"For what?"

"For making you witness my huge embarrassment," he says.

"What embarrassment?" She slips out of her shoes. She always slips out of her shoes.

"White or red?" he asks.

"Red," she replies. "Merlot if you have it."

"I do," he tells her. "The embarrassment of watching a total psychic screw up."

He pours the wine. "I don't follow," Beatrice says.

"Beatrice, really, I fucked up. We were all operating on the assumption that the murder I saw in real time was the murder at Squaw Peak. But that body's been there for days, maybe longer than a week. The murder I saw was actually the one at Camelback. I'm sure of it."

Beatrice offers a sympathetic smile. "Oh, my dear, this is really bothering you."

"Well, yeah, I've been beating myself up about it all day. I'm surprised all this worry didn't interfere with my work."

"Because it's insignificant."

"Not to me. I actually got two murders mixed up."

"No," she says, reaching out to him. "You got two murders misplaced. But then you found them."

She takes his hand and squeezes.

"And what's all this nonsense with 'real time'?" she asks. "Your generation is so hung up on live feeds and streaming video and getting all your information in real time that you have distorted the very essence of time altogether."

"What in the world are you talking about?"

"Have you ever heard of such a thing as fake time?"

Gus laughs. "Well, of course not."

"Because there is no such thing as real time or fake time. There is only time. And if you try to base your senses on real time, or if you try to place your visions in real time, you're only going to throw yourself off. It's unnatural," she proclaims. "Now let's say we put on some good music, eat dinner, and talk afterward. Let's just eat to the music. Let the music be the conversation."

Gus smiles at her fascinating eyes, at her mystery. The kitchen is open to the entertainment room, so all he has to do is step to the couch and grab the remote. "Classical okay?"

"Perfect," she says. "The instruments actually talk to each other."

He playfully rolls his eyes. Beatrice chuckles, and Gus shakes his head.

"What?" she asks.

"You're too much," he tells her, returning to the table.

The music really does provide conversation. The winds talks to the horns, and the reeds play a losing game to the percussion. And there is no spoken word. Just wallows and crescendos and the occasional munch of a crouton. And yet Gus suddenly hears an unfolding of events. He is very sure that the gas receipt from Lindsey Drake's car will show that she stopped at Circle K on the way to Camelback. He is also convinced that she asked somebody at the gas station for directions. Maybe the clerk inside the store, maybe someone filling up nearby her. He isn't sure, but he really feels that somehow those directions got Lindsey Drake in trouble. A manic flutist. So much for GPS. So much for the kindness of strangers. A bang of the drums. He feels a rush in his heart for the woman who never saw what was coming. And then he sees the crude artwork in the caves, and he knows it will happen again. He doesn't say anything. He doesn't have to. He learned a long time ago that this ability to sense things doesn't mean he can control things. All he can do, when the full picture comes together, is report it. The violins sound like they're weeping. He feels a lump in his throat and brings the wineglass to his mouth and sips.

When they're finished eating, and he's clearing the dishes, he tells Beatrice about the events he's intuited. "Maybe nothing," he says.

"Or something. Probably something. You must stay tuned in, Gus."

Beatrice is beaming, a radiance that goes deep beneath the skin. She is glowing, really. Gus cannot sense why. Then he can.

"Beatrice, did you meet a man today?"

She hoots with laughter. "Indeed, I did. Very good, my boy. You are wide open and listening. Don't you be chiding yourself for misplacing your murders when you can still pick up on the other vibes out there. I'm impressed."

"What's his name?"

"Max."

"Well, good for you," he says. "And where did you meet him?"

"At the deli at Safeway."

"I've never seen you eat lunch meat," Gus says. "You're just not the type."

"I ordered cheese."

"You're lactose intolerant."

She waves her hand. "Oh, whatever, Gus. A girl's gotta do what a girl's gotta do. I was actually in produce, thank you very much, and I felt a very strong force pulling me to the deli. And there he was."

"I wish that would happen to me."

She grabs his chin. "It will."

"Does this Max have a last name?"

"I assume so," she says with a laugh. "But I don't know it. I gave him my number. Hopefully he'll call."

"He will," Gus says emphatically.

"So you really do sense something?"

"I do," Gus replies. "I'm not feeling his last name, though. I'm thinking maybe Irish. Or Jewish."

Judaism was going to be Gus's next stop after he left the Catholic Church. But he got stuck somewhere on the road between atheism and Buddhism—a place where you create your own Zen if God doesn't show up.

"Mind if we drift over to the couches?" Beatrice asks. "This chair is beginning to hurt my ass."

Gus grabs the bottle of wine and meets her at the couches. He stretches out on the long part of the "L"; she sits on the short end with her feet resting on the coffee table. The windows are open, and the night is breezy and fragrant. Gus lowers the music and thinks he hears the low howling of coyotes in the distance, which isn't typical, but they do come, the coyotes, displaced from their habitats, wandering from one shrinking swath of desert to another.

"I need your help again," Beatrice tells him.

Gus adjusts a pillow behind his back. "Anything. . . ."

"Friday night. Charla McGregor. Tucson."

"Charla 'Channeling with Charla' McGregor?"

"Yes. Do you mind taking the drive?"

"I'd love to."

Later that night, Gus is in bed and he thinks he's dreaming, but he's not. Not entirely. He's in the overture to sleep, the orchestra swaying him like a hammock, and he sees his client Gary Potter standing over a body. Potter growls, then screeches, then laughs insanely. Gus hears the cries of a woman. She tries mightily to crawl away from her death. But Gary Potter pulls her by the ankles. And then everything goes dark. Gus bolts up in bed. He can't see. He lunges for the light. Seventy-five watts of confusion. And he remembers Potter's tattoos, the symbols on his legs. He understands, suddenly, that Potter is coming to confess.

Gus tosses and turns. His night is a twisted wreckage of sheets and blankets, so fitful that even Ivy moans to register her complaints. In the morning he stumbles through the fog to fetch the paper from the front door. The headline:

COP'S SON PLEADS NOT GUILTY IN DRUG CASE; PROSECUTOR DROPS MOST CHARGES

He shrugs. He doesn't really know what this means for Trevor Mills, but he thinks the headline still spells bad news for the boy's father.

15

Gus Parker spent most of the morning working the ultrasound and watching happy couples say hello to their blobs of life. He tried hard to detach, to not think about his useless sperm, to not think about the futility of his fertility, or the woman, whomever she is, who is supposed to be in his life forgiving him his backfires, loving him anyway, loving him wholly, to not think about the beautiful children he might have adopted and their beautiful smiles and their perfect teeth and their gleaming eyes and the way they'd love him, too. He tries to avoid the ultrasound altogether, but when he can't he tries to detach.

"Is that his you-know-what?" the patient asked, a big smile birthing on her face.

"I think it is," her husband replied with manly affirmation.

Gus was happy to move into MRI for the last two hours before lunch.

That's where he meets Clark Smith. Ankle injury.

Clark's a big guy, not fat, but boxy and muscular, about thirty, with boyish features.

"How did you hurt yourself?"

"Soccer. Ever play?"

"Uh, no. I was a beach bum."

"Cool."

That's where he also meets Rosemary Nichols, a pleasant fifty-year-old with shoulder issues. It begins with her voice. When Gus greets her she speaks musically. "Well, hellooooooo," she sings, her words climbing the scales.

"You're in a lot of pain?" Gus asks.

She says, "Terrible," as if she speaks in italics. "But people are getting really sick of hearing me complain, and I can't say I blame them," she adds.

"Ms. Nichols, people don't generally understand the depth of anybody's pain but their own," Gus tells her. "That's human nature."

She smiles. "Thank you for saying that. I bet you hear a lot of moaning and groaning in this job."

Rosemary Nichols is heavy-breasted and heavy-bottomed; everything in between is rather compact. "If people can't express their pain here, where else can they express it?" Gus says.

"You are such a kind man," she tells him.

He shows her to the dressing room and then, once she's wrapped up in her robe, to the table. It is only now, when she's in a generic robe like everyone else who files past him on any given day, that he sees her beauty. It emerges like the quiet salutation of namaste. Despite the voluptuous, curvy shape of her body, Gus sees her stretching long, wide, gracefully, bringing hands to heart. "You do yoga, don't you?"

"Oh my gosh! How could you tell?"

"I'm just getting a vibe. That's all."

"Crazy," she says with a throaty laugh. "I love my yoga classes."

She lays back and rests her head on the pillow.

"Where does it hurt the most?" he asks her. "The left or the right?"

"On both sides. And my neck. It's awful in my neck."

Gus taps her arm. "Well, I'll be looking at the whole area, Ms. Nichols. Now you lay still for me, okay?"

"Of course."

The procedure takes about twenty-five minutes. Gus is in and out checking on his patient, reminding her to lie still, and then he's telling Rosemary Nichols that she can get dressed. She leans on him as she shimmies off the table. Gus smiles as the patient turns away and disappears into the dressing room. It's a disk issue in the cervical region; the disk is pinching a nerve. That's not something he can actually see on the study himself, but it's something he is sure of. What he can see on the study are the ghostly bones of the human body.

He clicks through the pictures, making sure they're accurately labeled, and something catches his attention. As he is scanning from one screen to the next, he notices an anomaly in the image. He zooms in, then zooms out halfway. A shadow obscures the left shoulder. He eyes it suspiciously. Although Gus Parker is not a doctor, he knows the shadow is not a tumor. Perhaps she moved during the procedure. He inspects another image. Again, it is stained by a shadow, like a blob of ink, this time over the cervical region. How could he have been so careless? He continues clicking through all the shots hastily, nervous that he botched the entire procedure. Some of them are intact, but most of the cervical shots are obscured. And suddenly, he knows why. There, on the last screen in the series, is not a shadow, not a blob of ink, but a distinct image of a rope around Rosemary Nichol's neck.

He feels a bubble of panic in his chest. His breath escapes him, and he can feel his eyes bulging. He looks at the rope and studies its coils, its knots and its fibers. It fits noose-like around the victim's neck, and yet Gus does not sense that Rosemary Nichols is a victim. He gets no image of her, precisely. He didn't get that kind of vibe in her presence. But he wonders. He wonders if she'll be next. Gus knows this is a sign, but the harder he concentrates on the meaning the more abstract the image becomes. He shuffles madly through the screens again, almost mangling the keyboard in his hands.

"Easy there," says another tech who passes by in the hallway.

"Wait," Gus tells him. "I need you for a second."

"What's up?" It's the tech, the randy guy in the lab coat, who loves to date patients, the policies be damned.

Gus points to the images on the monitor.

"You screw up, Parker?"

"No," Gus says. "Well I don't know. You tell me. What do you see here?"

The tech narrows his eyes and cups his chin in one hand. He smells like an overdose of Armani. "I see two shoulders and a neck. That's what I see. The contrast ain't the greatest. But it's okay."

"That's it?"

"Well, dude, we don't do the diagnosing, you know. . . ."

"No, I mean do you see any obstructions on the images? Anything that looks unusual?"

"Nope. Just disks," he says. "Why don't you get out to the court-yard for a minute? The light in here must be messing with your eyes."

"Yeah. That's it," he tells the tech, and the serial dater wanders off.

But that's not it.

The images are fine, and Gus is relieved. But there was a rope around that neck, and in his own bones, as though he is imaging himself, Gus Parker knows that the killer is not scared of the cops, of the media attention, of anything. Gus knows that the killer is stalking his next victim. So, when Alex Mills calls and asks to meet for lunch, Gus doesn't hesitate.

The morning hadn't started well for Alex Mills. He had been summoned to the sergeant's office. Timothy Chase was sitting opposite the sergeant when Mills walked in. Mills studied the room soberly, then smiled knowingly.

"Glad to see the news about your son," the sergeant told him. "Bet you're relieved to get that off your plate."

"Thrilled."

"What do you think it'll take to get the other charges dropped?" the sergeant asked him.

"I don't know," Mills replied absently.

"I bet you do," his boss sneered.

"I suspect that we're not really here to talk about my son."

"Have a seat, Alex," the sergeant said.

Mills isn't psychic, but he knew what was coming next. He sat beside Chase.

"Morning, Alex," the other detective said with a boomingly cheerful voice.

"So the FBI has offered to step in," the sergeant told them.

"Offered?" Mills asked.

Woods smiled. "Suggested, recommended . . ."

"And you told them what?"

"Well, that's what I called in Chase for. After all, he's an FBI dropout."

Chase cleared his throat.

The sergeant laughed. "Actually, I'm able to use Chase to keep the bureau out of our hair for now. They may want in if bodies start to turn up outside the city."

"They don't want us as the lead agency?" Mills asked.

"They didn't. Until I played the Chase card. They were very friendly about it, as usual. They seemed satisfied when I told them Chase was on the case."

"And taking over as case agent?" Mills asked. It was almost as if, from the day Chase landed at the Phoenix PD, there was a certain deference that was expected from Mills—unspoken but implied—and it stoked a burn in him that he couldn't quite douse.

"What? Absolutely not," the sergeant barked.

"Then what are we doing here?" Mills demanded to know.

"I've called you both in here to tell you we're fucked. The commander is all over my ass; the chief is all over his ass; the mayor is all over everybody's ass. If we don't solve this crime like yesterday we are totally fucked. Right now we're the lead agency. But we're on a short leash, guys. A very short leash, getting tugged in all directions. I need a killer. Or we'll likely let the feds take over. You got that?"

Mills drew a deep breath. "Yeah, I think so," he said. "I'm inferring we're fucked if we don't make an arrest."

"All right, wiseass," Woods grunted. "Get out of my office and take the psychologist with you."

Mills spends the rest of the morning in his office with Timothy Chase. They hash and rehash. Every trail they imagine turns cold, even as Mills feels like the two of them are finally warming to each other.

"There's something I don't get," Mills says. "Chiseling into rock makes noise."

"I suppose you're right. And?"

"I don't think our artist is working during the day."

"Artist?"

"The killer," Mills says. "Think about it. All that chiseling noise would call attention to itself. Other people on the trails would hear it. The killer would be asking to be caught in the act."

"Yeah, but, look at Squaw Peak," Chase tells him. "No one would have any idea what was going on down in that cave."

"Maybe. But think about South Mountain. And think about Camelback. Both more open, obviously, to hikers, to neighbors. I don't think the killer is doing this during the day."

Chase twists his mouth and says, "He has to be. He's grabbing these women during the day."

"Because?"

Chase laughs. "Because no one is out on these trails at night, Sherlock."

Mills shakes his head. So much for warming to each other. The guy can't help being a condescending fuck. "The opportunity is during the day," Mills argues for the sake of arguing. "But the means are at night."

"Right," Chase says. "So, you think the guy is grabbing these women when he has the opportunity, like they're out hiking, and he sneaks up on them when no one is around; he abducts them and then brings them back to the caves at night to finish the job?"

"Maybe not. I don't know. I don't even know if it's a guy. I need a profile of the killer. That's your department."

Chase nods. He gets up and pours himself some coffee. "We're looking at a guy, Alex. Or a very strong woman. The killer is confronting his victims and dragging them to the caves."

"Maybe not. Maybe he just hikes along the trail and approaches these women like, 'Hey did you see the ancient petroglyphs in the cave back there,' and they follow him into the cave willingly where he stabs them. A male or female assailant could do that."

"That scenario is plausible," Chase says. "But the brutality of the crime matches a male pattern."

"And yet, there's no sexual element."

"Doesn't have to be," Chase argues. "But I don't see female-on-female aggression here. Of course we don't know yet about Jane Doe at Squaw Peak, but the other victims are all in their late twenties. That's a prime target for a man in his midthirties to forties. A single guy or a guy who can't form real relationships with women. He's in good shape. He fits in well with the hikers. He needs strength to maneuver the victims. He needs agility to handle the murder weapon, the chisel, the body, all at the same time."

"Unless he stashes the knife and the chisel in the cave beforehand," Mills says. "That is, of course, if the murders are actually happening in the cave."

"Where else would they be happening?"

"Well, if the guy is abducting his victims, he could be killing them somewhere else, like at his house, and bringing them back to the caves for a proper burial."

Chase shakes his head emphatically. "No, that's too much trouble. And there's no evidence that the body was moved in or out of the caves. And how do you think he'd transport his victims back and forth?"

Mills shrugs. "No, no. You're right. Forensics pretty much confirm the murders are happening in the caves."

"That and all the blood splatter," Chase reminds him with a patronizing, penetrating stare. The guy is making Mills's fingertips burn.

Instead of slugging the forensic psychologist in the eye, Mills stares out the window. The valley is surrounded by mountains. Walls of rock. Jagged peaks. Caves everywhere. Bodies anywhere. "What do think the significance of the carvings is? Is the killer sending us a message?"

"Maybe," Chase says. "The way I see it, he's taking ownership of his work. Like each murder is an accomplishment. I don't know if he's sending *us* a message. But I think he's sending someone a message."

"Who?"

"I'm not there yet. I'm going to call over to Arizona State. A friend of a friend is a professor. Teaches Native American Studies."

"And?"

"Maybe the message is tied into the whole folklore."

"You think our killer is Native American?"

Chase laughs. And, again, Mills wants to throw a punch. Smack that superior grin off his face. "No. I don't think he's Native American," the fucking genius says. "But obviously the murders, the carvings, the petroglyphs are no coincidence. Our killer may be trying to adopt some kind of ancient symbolism."

They both turn to the doorway at the sound of clicking heels. Bridget Mulroney poses in the doorframe, her makeup vibrant and cartoonish. She looks like Raggedy Ann put on an inky black wig and a business suit. And Mills is guessing Raggedy Ann Mulroney has had breast implants. She stands there with a gleam in her eyes and a wicked smile across her face.

"Hello, Bridget," Mills says.

"May I come in?"

"Of course," Mills tells her. "Grab a chair."

As she does she says, "People don't like what they're seeing on the news. The mayor's office is freaking out. Calls, e-mails, everything. Is there any way we can fix this?"

"Fix it?" Mills asks.

She tilts her head. "You know what I mean. Don't make it so sensational. Keep it simple. Don't overdramatize. It's all over social media. Hashtag 'Deadly Phoenix.'"

"What the hell are you talking about?" Mills says to her. "It's a fucking murder case. Three bodies. We can't help it if the media makes it all dramatic."

"I guess what I'm saying is that maybe there's a way to restrict the media," Bridget tells them.

Chase laughs.

Mills rolls his eyes. "Really? The city is asking us to restrict the media? It's a lose-lose proposition. If we don't restrict the media, they take the case and *they* sensationalize it. If we do restrict the media and they find out we're withholding information, we're in deep shit with the public."

"*Deep* shit," Chase says.

"You should know that, Bridget," Mills adds. "Weren't you a TV reporter?"

"Don't hold that against me," she replies. "TV news people are crazy."

"And yet you speak about them in the third person," Mills says.

She ignores the remark. "Is there anything you guys can tell me? Anything I can take back to the city?" she begs.

Chase says, "We're putting together a profile of the killer. We're examining and comparing forensics from all the crime scenes. And we intend to work with any agency or jurisdiction in the valley."

"Is that on the record?" she asks.

Chase looks to Mills. Mills nods.

"Fabulous," she says. "Now tell me something I don't know."

"Like what?" Chase asks.

"Like, do you have leads? What should the women in the valley do to protect themselves? Are we closing off hiking trails? What evidence is interesting?"

"No comment. Hike in groups. No. No comment," Mills recites.

Chase gives him a smart look of approval. As if he needs one.

"You guys are being so cagey," she whines.

This goes on for about ten minutes, during which Mills zones out and thinks about Trevor and really disappears into the notion that his son's drug dealing is not simply a juvenile transgression. There is something more here. He tried reaching one of the guys in Narcotics yesterday and hasn't heard back, but Mills's gut tells him that the volume and value of the weed is way beyond a typical high school bust. Everyone knows the drug trade from Mexico has spilled over the border and has become very much a Phoenix problem. It's an intractable problem that persists despite the smoke and mirrors of Sheriff Clayman Tarpo's very public crackdowns on illegals. America is the inhaler of Mexican drugs. The drug gangs are lethal not because they're Mexican. They're lethal because they're gangs. He worries it might be too late to extricate Trevor. Sure, most of the charges were dropped, but he worries his son is too entrenched somehow. At the courthouse there was real fear in Trevor's eyes, not fear of punishment, fear of a graver danger. Alex can't help but think that, even if all the charges are dropped, this will not have a good ending. He languishes there with this bleakness, with this sense of resignation, when a fist pounds the surface of the desk. Everything rattles.

"Are you even listening to me, Alex?"

His eyes meet the fist of Bridget Mulroney, then her eyes.

"Don't you ever do that again, Bridget," he tells her. "Ever." And then he looks away, wondering if that warning was really for his son, if it's Trevor clenched in his jaw, not Bridget Mulroney; the spastic woman just happened to pound the wrong desk at the wrong time.

"Well, pay attention, Detective. I'm not here for my health," she says.

Mills doesn't even know why she's here. And he tells her that. "We don't do department relations or public information. We don't deal with the media. You should be talking to Sergeant Woods or one of our PIOs."

"I did," she insists. "They sent me to you guys."

Chase shakes his head. "Of course they did."

Mills recognizes the deflation of Bridget Mulroney. She just sits there sinking into herself. Ten minutes ago she was full of fire, and now she's wilting, curling in, going fetal. Could she really be a victim? The question has been needling him but hard to entertain, what, with all her histrionics, but it's been there, poking at him, like maybe he has some responsibility for this woman, the one sitting here, her layers peeled back. His jaw is still an aching vise. He tries to imagine what Gus Parker has seen, the actual vision of her in danger. What the fuck does that look like? He shakes his head, it begins to throb, and he doesn't know what to tell her, or whether to tell her anything at all.

"What do you say we do lunch?" he asks her.

Her brows go up. The rest of her face is cartoonish surprise. "Alex, I don't fuck my colleagues."

"And I don't fuck . . . whatever it is you are."

"Then why ask me out to lunch?"

"Maybe he's hungry," Chase says.

"Gus Parker wants to talk to you," Mills says to her.

She twists in her chair, does a half spin. "Who's Gus Parker?"

"The psychic," Mills replies.

"Oh, come on," she says with a hearty tavern laugh. "Is he seeing my future?"

"He just wants to ask you a few questions," Mills says, rising from his desk.

"I get it. He wants to hook up. What are you, Alex, my pimp?"

Chase laughs. Mills does not. "No, but why does everything out of your mouth seem to involve fucking?"

"Everything in my mouth, too, Alex," she says with a cackle.

Chase roars. Mills seethes at him. Then he turns to Bridget and says, "Keep it up and HR will want to have a chat with you."

"Oh," she purrs, "am I offending you? Little me making the macho cop nervous? What kind of healthy male isn't turned on by a little flirtation?"

"What kind of healthy woman behaves like this?" Mills asks her.

"Who says I'm healthy?" She looks to Chase. He smiles but averts her gaze.

Mills grabs a few files from his desk and makes for the door.

"Are we still on for lunch?" Bridget asks.

He shakes his head and scoffs. "I don't think I have a choice. Gus Parker for some reason wants to help you."

"Help me? With what?"

And then, fuck it. "He thinks you might be in danger."

"In danger of what?" she asks, then stands to face Mills. Again, there's a real person there, not a bold temptress, not an actress, not a frost queen. She's shaking. Her neck is turning red.

"Meet me in the lobby at one o'clock," he says.

Chase and Bridget look at each other, then at him.

"We're done for now," Mills tells them.

Two hours later Bridget shows up in the lobby, hands on hips. "Look, Mills, this is a complete waste of my time. I've got lots of work to do. Yours is not the only project on my plate."

He just stares at her blankly and says, "I cannot tell you how glad I am to hear that."

They meet Gus at Café Nana in Tempe. Gus is already in a booth by the window when they arrive. Mills offers a fist bump, which Gus returns awkwardly. Bridget extends her delicate hand. "Pleasure," she says. "I think."

"You think?" Gus asks.

She smiles saucily. "I'm prepared to be intrigued."

"Didn't know intrigue required preparation," Gus tosses back.

Mills studies the volley across the table. Clearly Bridget is sizing up Gus Parker, but the calculation in her eyes is hard to follow. Mills knows she's on the prowl, but he also knows that her lively masquerade must be covering for something too hot to touch. There's that constant affectation, as if she's still on camera, craving attention, coyly playing to the audience for its validation and for its love. He's no shrink, but Mills knows damage when he sees it. Right now he sees the woman trying to unlock the possibilities of Gus Parker, studying him like maybe he could save her life.

"Detective Mills, here, says you're psychic."

"There's probably some truth to that," Gus tells her.

"So aloof," she says.

A waiter with a British accent brings them water and menus. His name is Kent.

"He's faking it," Gus tells them when the waiter drifts off.

"He's not Kent?" Bridget asks.

"He's not British," Gus says. "He's a theater major at ASU, and he's doing an act."

"You know him?" Bridget asks.

"No," Gus tells her. "I just know."

She rolls her eyes.

Mills turns to Gus and says, "Bridget hasn't been with the city long."

"Just under a year," she says. "And no one ever told me that we had our own special Psychic Friend."

"You're not familiar with my work," Gus tells her.

She laughs again. "Uh, no, Mr. Parker. I'm not."

Mills shifts toward her. "Gus has led us to several suspects over the years. He's helped us wrap up some really difficult murder cases."

"I don't know whether that says something about Mr. Parker or something about this department," she says.

"Enough with the attitude, Bridget," Mills warns her. "Gus thinks you're in danger."

She leans forward. "In danger of what? Boredom?"

"Knock it off, Bridget," Mills snaps. "Just listen to what the guy has to say. If you want to ignore it, ignore it."

"I'm sorry," she says, "but surely you can understand how all this talk of danger might make a girl like me nervous."

"We don't want to make you nervous," Gus assures her.

The waiter returns to take their order.

"So where in England are you from?" Bridget asks him with a juicy grin.

He hesitates. "London," he says as if he's drawing a number from a hat. "Now what can I get you?"

They order lunch. Bridget takes a big gulp of water, swallows and says, "Seriously, guys, should I be scared?"

Gus ignores her question and asks, "I want you to think carefully and tell me if you've noticed anything unusual in your daily routine."

"Like what?"

"Really focus on the last few days."

"But I don't know what you mean by unusual."

"A car that reappears in your midst. A face that doesn't belong," Gus explains.

She laughs nervously. "You have to be kidding me."

"I'm not kidding."

"Please," she scoffs.

"Please what?" Gus asks. "Do you pay attention?"

"To what?"

"Your surroundings."

"I don't know." Impatience is growing in her voice.

Gus clears his throat. "I saw you on TV at the first press conference last week," he begins. "I don't know if the killer was there camouflaging himself among the media, or whether he was watching from home, but I really got the sense that he was watching you."

"Me? I was way off in the background. I watched a clip from the press conference too, and you could barely see me."

"I saw you," Gus says dryly.

"Did you notice anyone unusual in the crowd?" Mills asks her.

She shakes her head. "No," she replies. "I know all the reporters here. I don't remember seeing a strange face."

"I think he was watching you on TV," Gus says. "That's all I'm saying. The killer connected with you for some reason. I get this vibe, a strong vibe, that he might want to stalk you."

Bridget Mulroney stares at him. She moves her lips around as if sampling the taste of something, considering the palate of it. "I appreciate the warning. But why did you wait four days to tell me?"

"I'm sorry," Gus says. "Our paths should have crossed sooner."

"At first I didn't want to alarm you," Mills adds. "But then all of a sudden I try to call you and you're hiking Squaw Peak and the next day we find a dead body there. You know, things added up."

She folds her arms across her chest, tilts her head, and nods as if she finally gets it, but she doesn't get it or doesn't want to get it. It's all mockery. "Assuming I buy into all of your psychic mumbo jumbo, what do I do with this information?" she asks them.

"Be totally aware of your surroundings," Mills says gravely. "Notice everything."

"And assuming I don't buy into any of this?"

"Totally ignore your surroundings," Gus retorts. "Notice nothing."

Mills lets out a good laugh. Gives Gus a high five.

"Well, aren't you boys just the coolest and the smartest," she says. "You come to me with these, uh, serious assertions, and then offer the most laughable advice. 'Be totally aware of your surroundings.' How about you give me something more to work with? What does the guy look like? What does he drive?"

"We don't know," Gus says. "I'm working on it."

"And you call yourself a psychic?" she asks.

"Actually, that's what other people call me. It just kind of stuck. I actually work as an imaging tech. You know, MRIs, ultrasounds, that sort of thing."

"Right," she says. "But I'm curious. Is Mr. Parker's role in this case public information?"

"No," Mills replies. "Not yet. Gus isn't looking for any kind of attention. Ain't that right, Gus?"

The psychic nods.

Bridget engages Gus in a tempting bout of staring. He counters without a blink.

Lunch arrives. They eat, mostly in silence. Bridget comments on the salad dressing. "Savory," she calls it. "Very savory."

Mills looks at her hard, studies her through the lens of unsavory crime, sees her in abstract places running from shadows, down a dark alleyway, her office after hours, a deserted parking deck; he doesn't have the same gift as Gus Parker, but now at least he sees the possibility. She's sitting right next to him, and she could disappear tonight. The thought just lands in his lap, thud, and it's not a thought he can easily dismiss.

"Would you mind checking in with me a few times tonight?" he asks her.

She turns to him. "Seriously?"

"Seriously."

"If I happen to remember."

Kent returns to ask if everything is to their liking.

They assure him it is.

Bridget asks Gus if he ever dates his patients.

"No," he tells her.

"Do you ever fantasize about them?" she persists.

"All the time," he says. "The problem is my fantasies are not like your fantasies. My fantasies tend to be visions of what will come to them."

"No sex," she says.

"No sex, unless of course that's what's coming to them, and then, of course, not explicitly."

"Wow," she says, clearly ignoring what he really means. "You never fantasize. That's so sad."

Mills shakes his head and crunches a french fry. Under his breath he mutters, "Thank you, Sybil," which no one hears.

Kent, the non-Brit, returns to clear their dishes.

"I know this all seems kind of strange to you," Gus says to Bridget. "I appreciate that. But I'd hate to be right about this and you be wrong about heeding the warning."

"Damn, you're good," Bridget tells him. "Just the right amount of Disney, and just the right amount of Stephen King. I don't suppose you talk to dead people."

"Only my uncle," Gus says. "I'm not that kind of psychic."

"Because if you were," Bridget continues, "you could just ask Elizabeth Spears and Lindsey Drake who killed them."

"That is, of course, if they knew their assailant."

"Of course. But wouldn't it be great to at least get a good description from them?" the woman muses.

"It would be," Gus concurs. "Great."

Bridget offers her business card to Gus, says she has to pee, and tells the men to wait for her outside.

The men say nothing until they reach the sidewalk.

With traffic blowing by, Gus turns to Mills and says, "What the hell is her deal?"

"Her deal . . ." Mills successfully pauses for dramatic effect. "Her deal . . . Where do I begin? It's a long story, Gus, but the short version is this: Mulroney comes from an influential family. Mulroney Construction is her father's company."

"I don't know the name," Gus says.

"I'm sure you've seen their signs everywhere," Mills tells him. "They're huge. They build schools, libraries, banks . . . that kind of stuff. The Mulroneys are loaded, Gus, and the word is whatever Bridget wants, Daddy makes sure she gets."

"Hence her job with the city."

"Yeah, hence that." Mills scratches his chin. The stubble sounds like sandpaper. He feels pale. Even now under a brilliant sun and its reddening rays. "But before she henced her way into the city," Mills continues, "she was a TV reporter. She got a job at one of the local stations as soon as she got out of college. Again, Daddy doing the bidding."

"I don't recognize her from TV."

"Well, she didn't last long. I mean, she had no experience. She was in over her head. And then, of course, she fucked the vice president and general manager."

Mills races through the Cliff Notes of "Mulroney Fucks a Mormon" to the gaping face of the psychic.

"So she leaves Channel Six and ends up with the city," Mills says, wrapping up the tale. "On her feet. No consequences, no remorse."

Those words—no consequences, no remorse—are hanging in the air with a peculiar palpability as Bridget emerges from the restaurant.

"Alex, you gotta get me back to work," she tells Mills. "I've got projects up the spiral staircase of my ass."

He glares at her, then shakes his head apologetically at Gus who is stifling a laugh. "Hey, Parker let's talk later. Okay?"

"Actually, there's something I need to tell you now."

"Okay. . . ."

"Privately."

Bridget exhales a hyperbolic breath of disgust. "Seriously?" she groans. "I don't have all day."

Mills tosses her a set of keys. "Go wait for me in the car."

She turns and storms off.

"She rattles easily," Gus observes.

"That's her reputation," Mills says. "So, what's so urgent?"

"I thought you should know about what happened with a patient of mine this morning."

Mills lifts his eyebrows, offers a probing look.

Gus tells him about the rope around his patient's neck.

"Well, geez, that's creepy," Mills tells him. "You think she's our next victim?"

"No, actually I don't," Gus says. "But I think another victim is imminent. Maybe that's the real message here."

"Yes," is all Mills says.

"Something wrong?" Gus asks.

"No. Nothing. But I think we better give this lady some surveillance, just in case."

"Okay, but I think you're probably wasting your time. I don't see her as a victim. I just see the rope as a sign."

"Do you have an address for this lady?"

"It's in the system, but technically . . ."

"You can't give it to me."

"Right."

"Technically I'd have to get a subpoena."

"Right. HIPPA and all that."

"But getting a subpoena would be impossible based on, what, a psychic at Valley Imaging?" Mills asks.

"Exactly."

"Then what do you suppose I do?"

"Watch for an e-mail."

"An e-mail?"

"With an attachment."

"Okay."

"I may accidently take a picture of her record with my phone."

"And accidently e-mail it to me?"

"I might."

"That would be very careless of you, Gus Parker. It could get you fired."

"That's why any observation of Ms. Nichols must be very stealth. She must never catch on that she's under surveillance."

"Stealth," Mills repeats with benign irony. "You have my word."

Then Gus leans in as if he has a secret to tell and says, "I saw the paper this morning. I guess that's good news for Trevor," which isn't a secret, but Mills appreciates the discretion.

"Good news is relative these days, Mr. Parker," he says.

"You don't sound hopeful."

"We don't need the publicity," Mills tells him. "That much should be obvious."

"By 'we' you mean the department or your family?"

"I mean both. Equally."

Gus says something, but Mills can't hear him over the sudden approach of a blasting horn. The eruption, blaring and insistent, displaces all the other noise of the street, stops people in their tracks, and hurdles forward. Both men turn.

"What the fuck is she doing?" Mills roars.

The car collides with the curb. Bridget is at the wheel, her hand leaning on the horn. Gus blocks his ears. Mills bangs on the window.

Slowly, the passenger window lowers. And the horn abruptly dies.

"Get the fuck out of my car," Mills tells the woman. "I could get you fired for this little stunt."

"But you won't," she says.

"You're a freak," Mills tells her.

"And I'm late for a meeting, Alex," she says as she crosses to the passenger side and winks at Gus. Before her door is closed, the car peels out with an angry shriek.

16

Gary Potter shows up promptly at eight o'clock. Gus had only been home from work about an hour (two extra patients were squeezed into his schedule) and had dashed out to walk Ivy, rushed a shower, and shoved a slice of spinach pie in his mouth. Still chewing, he swings the door open and ushers his client inside. "Welcome back," he says.

"You were right," Potter says as they sit opposite each other.

"About?"

"You told me I would end up in Los Angeles."

"Yes, I did," Gus says. "But I also said it wouldn't happen immediately."

Potter's smile is almost audible. "I auditioned for the Out-of-Workers and got accepted."

"The Out-of-Workers?"

"Never heard of them?" he asks incredulously. "They're the number one improv group in LA. All their members go on to sitcoms and movies."

Gus nods and smiles. "Congratulations. This is good news."

"My show closes at the Herberger in two weeks, and then I'm good as gone."

"And your girlfriend? We talked about her last time. You were worried."

Potter leans forward. "And this is the best part. Totally knocked me for a loop. She wants to come to LA."

"No kidding. This is all working out."

"Yeah. I got to get the hell out of the desert," Potter says.

Before his client even finished that sentence, the visions were back. Roaring visions of murder.

Potter is standing in a cone of bluish light, his hands holding a knife above his head.

And plunge. And plunge.

And a woman below, wailing like a siren.

Knife ripping through cloth, ripping through skin.

She cries in scales from high piercing to low moaning, from the breaking of glass, to the sweeping up of the dust.

Potter has no eyes.

Gus grips his chair, wills the visions to scatter. He closes his eyes and fetches a blank page in his mind. He says nothing until the sheet is in place, and then he lowers his head and says, "Gary, I see you violently upset about something."

"You do?"

It's not like Gus can just open his eyes and say, "Dude, I saw you kill someone." Instead, he says, "Yeah. I think there's something here in the valley that is making your departure even more urgent."

"Really?" the man says, and Gus immediately hears a change in the man's inflection. He hears a bubble of suspicion, then a bubble of surprise.

"Maybe it's nothing," Gus stalls, "but I feel like your move to Los Angeles is not only an opportunity but also an escape."

"What would I be escaping from?"

Gus opens his eyes. Gary Potter's face is fractured by a frozen crack of a smile. The man looks a bit like a happy corpse. "Is there anything you did here, Gary, that went wrong?"

Potter shakes his head. "I can't imagine what you're talking about."

"Well, I just wonder if there aren't other reasons you want to leave the valley."

"This place bores me to death, if you must know."

"That's a pretty strong word."

"What is?"

"Death."

Potter laughs. "Excuse the exaggeration."

"I'm not sure it's exaggeration. I'm seeing something about death, Gary. I must tell you that."

The man sits back. "Now you're freaking me out."

"Am I? I'm sorry."

The guy throws his arms in the air. "Man, I came here with good news, and now you're just messing with my head."

Gus smiles thinly. "I'm sorry. Didn't mean to. But why are you here? What do you want from me?"

Potter collapses in the chair. "I want you to look into my future and tell me the move to LA will work out, for Christ's sake. What do you think I'm here for?"

Gus nods. "Would you like some spinach pie? I just picked it up from Whole Foods on the way home."

"Uh. No thanks."

"Okay," Gus says. "I can tell you that your move to Los Angeles will work out well. I don't see any problems in California for you. Your girl-friend will be happy too. I see her singing in a café. She's really going to discover herself. Is she the only woman you've dated here in Phoenix?"

"No. There's been a few others."

Suddenly, again, a puncture, a scream, a puncture.

"Maybe that's what I'm getting to," Gus says. "Maybe you need to make peace with them before you go."

"Make peace?"

"Did any of those relationships end badly?"

Potter laughs deeply. A resonant stage laugh, from the belly. "They all ended badly. I'm a bit of an asshole."

"What I'm seeing is you in Los Angeles, suddenly feeling bad for what happened here in Phoenix. It's going to get in your way."

The client shakes his head, lowers it to his hands. "Whoa, man, this is deep. I've pissed off a few chicks, but I'm sure they're over it."

"Why are you so sure?"

"Because it's been a few years since I dated anyone but Jessica."

"People don't forget their hurt."

"Yeah, well, two of them never stopped calling me."

"Oh?"

"They acted like I ruined their lives."

Gus sees an image of Gary Potter lunging in the dark, rivers of blood at his feet. "So there you go," he says, feigning ambivalence. "Apparently, they're not over it." Gus's hands are clammy, and he can tell his face is a sheen of sweat. "I need a cold drink. Can I get you something?"

The client says no.

Gus rises steadily, overcompensating for the tremors in his legs. He walks from the room and grasps a wall. Takes a deep breath. Aims for the kitchen sink. He splashes cold water on his face. Then he reaches into the refrigerator and swigs some pomegranate juice straight from the bottle. *Okay, everything's fine,* he tells himself. *I may have a killer in my house. But I'm a professional. And I'm hydrated.*

"I think I'll take you up on that beverage."

The shudder is obvious. Gus actually feels his feet leave the ground.

"I'm sorry. Didn't mean to startle you," Potter says. "But actually I'm really parched. Another reason to get out of the desert."

Gus laughs nervously. "Water? Juice?"

"Water's fine," Potter says. "You know, I'm thinking about what you said. You may be right. I don't want to be haunted by any ghosts once I get to Los Angeles."

"Of course you don't."

"So what do I do?"

"Make amends in the way that fits for you." Gus hands him a glass.

"What does that mean?"

"Well . . ." Gus draws his own pause. He scrambles for words; his hesitation is palpable. "Maybe this is the bad breakup equivalent of going to confession."

Potter takes a gulp from the glass. "I'm not a good Catholic, but maybe I should just call them and tell them I screwed up. Ask for their blessing and all that."

"That sounds about right," Gus says, swallowing hard.

The two men stare at each other for a protracted moment. Ivy is snoring in the next room. There is no other sound. Eyes lock on eyes. Gus looks deeply into the man. The man is a cave. A dark hole in the universe.

"Wow, you're good," the man says. "Really, really good."

"Am I?"

"Yeah. I was embarrassed to admit it, but it's true. I did something awful to those women. I cheated on all of them. Probably ruined their lives. Jessica is the first woman I've ever been faithful to. For Jessica and me to work out, I have to make amends to the others."

Gus's breath is shallow. "Is that how you see it?"

"Thanks to you, man."

"Okay. Well, our time is up," Gus tells his client. "Let me know if you need another appointment before you leave Phoenix."

Potter reaches into his pocket and pulls out an envelope, hands it to Gus. "I don't know if you'd call this a tip, but I brought these for you."

Gus peers into the envelope.

"Two tickets to see my show at the Herberger. Saturday night. Can you make it?"

Gus examines the tickets. "Yeah, sure. That's really kind of you. Nice surprise."

"Can you get a date?"

"I'm sure I can find someone."

"Jessica has a sister if you're looking, dude."

Gus laughs. "Not really, but thanks. I have a few people in mind."

"I bet most chicks are scared to date a psychic."

Gus shrugs. "I don't know."

Potter digs out cash from his wallet and hands it to Gus. "Here's your fee for tonight."

Gus follows Potter out the front door. "Hey, I don't suppose you have any rope in your car," he asks his client.

"Rope?"

"Yeah. I need to rig something in my garage," Gus fibs.

"Uh, no. I don't think so. I have some tools. But no rope."

"Okay. Just thought I'd ask."

Potter drives off. The taillights are bloody red eyes, and they're watching Gus as they retreat into the socket of the night. Gus is still standing in his front yard. He's swaying there, considering all kinds of implications.

The next morning Gus wakes up groggy. Kind of a psychic hangover. He decides right there, still squashed in his pillow, not to think about last night. But somehow he's going to have to tell Detective Alex Mills about his visions of Gary Potter. But not now. Now he needs a cup of coffee that's an 8.0 on the Richter scale. And a really long and really hot shower. He has forty-five minutes to get to work. He flips on the TV, then listens to CNN as he roams around the house.

North Korea still crazy.

Afghanistan still bloody.

White House spokesperson Hallie O'Halloran still dumb as a brick.

A fire kills seven in New York City.

A bank robbery gone bad in Chicago.

And a serial killer on the loose in Phoenix. The anchor people are talking about the desert murders. Now it's a national story.

17

Bridget Mulroney, leaning at the doorway to Alex Mills's office, tells Mills and Chase that the networks are poking around. "The television networks," she emphasizes.

"And you would just love to get in front of the network cameras and make a statement for the city," Mills says. "Isn't that right?"

"That's not it," she insists.

"Then what is it?" Chases asks.

"They want to know why the FBI isn't involved."

Chase gives her a look.

"What?" she begs.

"I'm why the FBI is not involved," he tells her.

"For God's sake, Bridget, refer them to the sergeant," Mills says with some chagrin. "He put out a press release. It clearly states we have a former agent on the case."

"Well they're not buying it," she tells them.

Mills gets up and gestures to the door. "Then you're not selling it hard enough. We're busy, Bridget. Could you take this up with Woods if you're really that anxious?"

She puts her hands on her hips. Her business suit is tight in all the wrong places. "Don't you fucking discount me, Alex."

"Really, Bridge," Chase says.

She pivots, stops, grunts, and leaves.

"I guess I should applaud," Mills says. "That was one performance."

Chase turns to him. "I think you should really cut her some slack. She comes in here on the defense because she knows you can't stand her."

"Did you just call her Bridge?"

Chase shrugs. "I don't know."

"You did," Mills says. "You called her Bridge. That's sweet."

The phone rings. Chase leans forward as though he's about to pick it up. Mills gives him a look, a territorial look, like what the fuck, dude; he points a finger to the phone then to himself. "Mills."

"Hey, Alex, it's Brett in the lab."

"Hey, man. What do you got?"

"Nothing conclusive, but I wanted you to know we're sure these victims were gagged before they died."

"Right. We figured from the facial injuries. Something tight to silence them from screaming."

"Yeah. We definitely got trace fibers in the teeth. Probably rope and other fabric."

"Thanks. I'll send Myers down to see the samples. What about my Jane Doe from the Peak?"

Brett laughs. "That body's a hot mess. But we're trying. I'll keep you posted."

"Cool. Thanks, man."

Mills hangs up and tells Chase what he just learned. The former FBI agent smiles and nods. He picks up a small stack of papers from the chair beside him and drops it in front of Mills.

The report on Carmody's rental car is incomplete.

The tire tracks on the other vehicle are a likely match for a pickup or an SUV. They are no fresher, no older than the tracks from Carmody's rental. Both vehicles likely arrived at the scene at the same time—or within minutes of each other.

The Circle K receipt is linked to a location on Camelback Road, 2.1 miles from the murder scene. Time-stamped at 3:01 p.m.

Hotel video surveillance shows a woman leaving the parking garage in a vehicle consistent with the rental Lindsey Drake was driving. Her departure time is consistent with the statement given by her boyfriend. Video surveillance of all entrances/exits shows no evidence that Neil Carmody ever left the hotel after returning from the original hike.

"Maybe Carmody's not our man," Chase says.

"Yeah, well, I never really suspected him."

Mills looks at the board on the opposite wall. He sees how many officers are on patrol at area hiking trails. A lot. In shifts. Sheriff Tarpo is lending a few deputies to the effort. The crime scenes are still secured. But the trails are open. The last patrol shift will end about an hour after dusk. Mills closes his eyes and tries to imagine the killer. He always does this. And the same image always comes to mind. It's a bald white guy in his late thirties. He has smooth skin, save for a soft shadow of a beard at the edge of his jawline. His eyes are gentle and deceiving, his lips soft and boyishly supple. He's wearing a nylon jacket with a striped collar and cuffs. He doesn't know who this man is. Generic Killer, maybe, but it's always the same man, with those same features, who lingers in his imagination. The face is not familiar; it's not similar to any particular perp he's apprehended. The face does not remind him of a high school nemesis or a neighborhood troublemaker. He doesn't know why he sees this image whenever he's looking for a killer, and he's mildly envious of Gus Parker who not only gets images but visions, as well.

In walks Detective Morton Myers who interrupts Mills's reconnaissance. He hands Mills a thumb drive. "Do you guys have time to watch?" Myers asks.

The videotape from the Circle K is fuzzy and frustrating to watch. It had successfully been subpoenaed from the convenience store's corporate headquarters. Despite the graininess of the video, the detectives do see a woman emerging from a vehicle that matches Lindsey Drake's rental. They see her walk into the convenience store. And then they see nothing. Myers inserts another thumb drive into the computer, and they watch as another camera picks up a woman approaching the cashier inside.

"That's her," Mills says. "That's our victim at the counter."

"Right," Myers says. "But so far no sign of her making contact with anyone else."

Mills calls up the other video source. "You can see her leaving the store, walking back to her car. . . . And now she stops before she even gets to the pump. I can't make out what I'm watching here. Is she responding to someone? Or is she calling to someone?"

The tape is jumpy, and though it's in color, the lighting is weak like a smudge of fluorescence, not really light.

"I don't know," Myers says.

But she stands there, Lindsey Drake does, mulling something over and motioning with her hands.

"She's talking to someone at another pump," Chases says. "Isn't there another camera out there with a different angle?"

Myers grunts a no.

"Damn."

They watch as she disappears out of frame; the next thing they see is her car pulling away from the pump. For a split second they see a vehicle fall in behind her, and then, it seems, the vehicle, a white van or SUV, inches up beside her. Then both cars are gone.

"Play it back in slo-mo," Chase says.

Mills plays it back several times, but there's just no making out the details of that white vehicle. He can't even tell if it is, indeed, an SUV; it's just not on-screen long enough. It's gone in a flash. It's white. That's all.

"Well, it's better than nothing," Myers says.

"You think?" Chase asks.

"I can take it down to our A/V guys and see if they can enhance it."

"Wait," Mills says. "Let's take another look at the indoor camera. Just because we don't see anyone in the store when she reaches the cashier doesn't mean there wasn't someone in there earlier who might have been lurking."

They examine the indoor video again. They go back thirty minutes before Lindsey Drake's image appears at the counter. A few people buy cigarettes. A construction dude buys Gatorade. Three high school kids, all hyper and spastic, buy Slurpees and try stealthily to camouflage a few beers in their purchase. It's funny. Myers and Chase both laugh at the same moment when the cashier simply slides the beers away from them. And then it's dead, except for a guy who comes in and buys a lottery ticket, and he's hard to see through the sunglasses and the low-lying cap.

"Our guy?" Myers asks.

"Let's see the outdoor shot again," Mills says. "See if it picks him up coming out."

It does. The detectives watch and replay, watch again.

"He's going in the direction of the white truck," Myers says.

"Hard to determine," Chase responds. "We can't see the car in the shot. We can only guess he's walking toward it."

"Okay, fine," Mills says. "Then match up the time codes. I bet if we look at the scene where the girl seems to be talking to someone we can match the clock to the time he would have reached his car at the pump."

"Assuming she was talking to him," Chase snaps.

"Confirming she was talking to him," Myers insists.

The men are interrupted by heavy footsteps, someone entering the room. Mills looks up from the screen, but his eyes take a split second to adjust. Then he sees Sergeant Jacob Woods standing there. He says, "Hey, Sarge, what's up?"

"We have a body. Call went to Glendale first. About thirty minutes ago. They're out there. Confirmed a body."

"Glendale?" Mills asks as he tries to reconcile the utterly suburban image of Glendale to the topography of the other murders. He can't.

"Woman," the sergeant says. "About thirty. I guess there's something at the scene Glendale wants us to look at. Lieutenant Cole just texted you the address."

"We're talking about a house?" Mills asks the sergeant.

"Yeah. Crystal Ledge subdivision."

Mills drives mostly in silence toward Glendale, Myers riding shotgun. Chase follows in his own car. Myers stares vacantly at the road in front of them, shaking his head incessantly. Occasionally, he'll rest against the window beside him, and Mills can tell that a string of murders is not what Myers signed up for. A murder every six months, fine, but Morton Myers just doesn't have the head for anything more sinister. And Mills supposes that's a good thing, that there's something about the man's simple-minded, hometown boy approach to life that makes him a good all-around scout.

Crystal Ledge boasts the same charm as most of the newly built subdivisions in the Phoenix sprawl. That is to say none. Three styles of homes, a left-oriented one-story, a right-oriented one-story, and a two-story, alternate on streets of zero lot line plots; there are no trees, save for the saplings of palms and transplanted saguaros. You can see too much air and not enough green. The homes are colorless, too. The homeowners association has clearly written two shades of beige into its covenant. Crystal Ledge is one big circle with short streets branching off and lonely coves tucked into the middle. The big circle, itself, is called Crystal Ledge Circle, not leaving anything to the imagination, and Mills considers that as a metaphor for the whole subdivision. They drive about two-thirds of the way around the circle and take a left on Crystal Ledge Cove. They stop at 5668.

Glendale Police has a few cars here. The sheriff's office has a few as well. The mingling of officers and deputies outside the house comes to a hush and a freeze when Mills, Chase, and Myers approach.

Mills recognizes a detective from Glendale. "Hey, Scotty. What do we got here?"

Detective Scott Bradshaw looks at him emptily and says, "Either a copycat or your killer is getting more domestic. Take a look and tell me if you want in. I mean, do whatever you need to do, but my sergeant wants some answers."

"No problem," Mills assures him.

Neighbors have drifted to their lawns, mostly stay-at-home moms, some with babies in strollers, most of them cliquing off into small circles of curiosity and fear. The fear is lodged in their eyes, probably climbing up their spines, as they take surreptitious glances at 5668.

Myers stays on the lawn as Mills and Chase enter the home.

A sheriff's deputy leads the detectives to a back bedroom.

"The victim is Andrea Willis, thirty-eight," he tells them. "We found her DL."

Mills enters first. The wall opposite him, the one above the bed, is torn up, pieces of drywall hanging like flesh. This is where the killer has carved his rendition of the murder. The carving depicts a body dangling from a noose.

"Fucking weird," Chase says. He kneels to get a better look at the body. The victim is sprawled on the floor, her arms and legs akimbo.

"The bedroom door is off the hinges," Mills tells him from behind. Chase turns around. Mills lifts the door a few inches.

"You want a look at her?" Chase asks.

Mills comes forward and kneels to examine the woman's face. It must have been beautiful before her death. He can tell from the high cheekbones, the well-defined jawline; her lips, though gray, look sculpted by hand.

"Who ID'd the victim?" Mills asks.

The deputy says, "The homeowner did. We removed her from the house. She's out back with Glendale giving a statement."

"They can stand down," Mills tells the deputy, his gaze never leaving the body. "I'll resume the interview."

The deputy nods and leaves the room.

Myers approaches and says, "Looks like we have a copycat."

Mills studies the victim's neck. It's purple, deep purple, almost black. She had obviously been strangled. He sees the imprint of some kind of cord. Gus Parker saw rope. He saw rope around a neck. "A copycat?" he asks. "Why do you say that?"

Myers clears his throat. "Uh, Alex, because we're in a house, not a cave. Same idea, maybe. But different method. Inconsistent."

Mills rises to his feet. "C'mon, Myers. You know better. This is just as easily the same killer throwing us a curve."

"Ya think?"

"Dude, we still haven't released the details of the crime scenes. They're airtight for chrissakes," he says, noting his exasperation.

"But the trails are reopened," Myers insists.

"The crime scenes are still secured. At least during the day," Mills reminds him. "No one's described the cave drawings to the press. And none of the witnesses are talking."

"How do you know?" Chase asks.

"Because the press would be all over it," Mills tells him. "There's been nothing in the paper about the cave drawings, nothing on TV. Nobody knows enough of the details to effectively copy those murders."

"Hey, Mills, I'm just considering all possibilities," Myers says.

Mills pats him on the arm. "I know you are."

"What about the broken mirror?" Chase asks.

Mills turns. "Where?"

"Right there toward the floor."

A mirror-paneled closet door is open, halfway off its hinge, and, indeed, there are cracks all across the bottom third. "She was most likely alive when she hit the floor," Mills says. "When they struggled he either slammed her head into the mirror or she bumped it herself."

Chase kneels by the victim's head, studies it, looks closely, but doesn't touch the scalp through the woman's hair. "There are some lacerations here," he says. "A few punctures, it seems."

Mills backs toward the bedroom door. "All right, Tim. You bring in the techs and take over in here if Glendale truly wants to yield. I'm heading out back to talk to the homeowner."

On the way back down the hall with Myers on his heels, Mills notices a few photos askew, doesn't know if that's the result of too many responders crowded into a narrow hallway, or more evidence of the struggle that preceded death. Mills enters the great room and gets a better sense of the house. A typical open floor plan that draws your attention, ultimately, three places: a fireplace, a flat-screen TV, and the sparkling pool out back. Through a mangled French door, he sees a cluster of uniforms surrounding a woman. She's shaking her head. Mills is careful not to touch the busted handle of the door; he opens its partner instead. The partner door has all its panes intact. The other door is a chessboard of shattered glass.

"Hello, I'm Detective Alex Mills from the Phoenix Police Department." He extends a hand. The woman shakes it. "This is Detective Myers."

Her name is Marcy Stone. She's sitting at a small wrought-iron table. Her hair is streaked blond, and it falls to her shoulders. She's wearing a tight blouse unbuttoned halfway down her cleavage, revealing a chest that is ruddy from sunburn. Her skin is finely freckled. She looks about forty.

"Guys," Mills says to the others lingering at the pool, "can I have some privacy for a minute?"

The men look at each other, faces full of professional umbrage, but they all disperse.

"Ms. Stone—" Myers begins.

"I gave a statement already," she says, her voice as vacant as her eyes. "Two actually."

"We realize that," Mills tells her, taking a seat across the table. "But we're not asking for a statement. We just want to talk."

She asks if she can smoke. Mills nods. She lights up.

"Ms. Willis was staying with you?" Mills asks.

"Temporarily."

"When did you find her?"

"I've answered that question several times this morning."

"I know, I know," Mills tells her. "And I apologize for putting you through this again. But for us it's better that we ask a few times to make sure we get it right. For you, not so pleasant. Again, I'm sorry."

"I found her around six thirty when I came home."

"Came home? From where?"

"I stayed at my boyfriend's last night."

"I see. Did you provide us with his name?"

"I did."

"His address?"

"Yes. He lives up in Moon Valley. I sleep there a few times a week. We take turns."

"Where is he now?" Myers asks.

"He flew out this morning. On business."

"Does he travel a lot?" Myers asks while jotting down notes.

"About twice a month. He sells eyewear."

Mills looks at the woman as she looks away. She pushes a strand of hair back behind one of her ears and gazes off into nowhere. It's quiet here, save for the fountain that trickles into the pool.

"How long have you known Andrea Willis?" Mills asks her.

The woman takes a long drag of her cigarette and exhales it slowly, almost luxuriously; she seems to admire the smoke as it drifts away. "About eight years."

"How did you meet?"

"At the gym. She was in my Pilates class. That lasted about three months. But she loved hiking. So we hiked together."

"Have you heard about the murders on the hiking trails?" Myers asks.

"Of course," the woman says. "But we haven't been out there in weeks. My fault. I met Matt a few months ago, and, well, you know."

Mills offers her a smile. "Where did you usually hike?"

"Dreamy Draw."

"My wife and I go there sometimes," Mills tells her. "It's nice and quiet. We like it. So, you came home, saw that someone had busted in . . ."

"Yeah. And I immediately went to her room to make sure . . . but, you know, I saw her. . . ."

Mills inches his chair closer. "I'm really sorry about your friend, Ms. Stone."

"Marcy."

"Yes, Marcy, I know how upset you must be."

She looks at him fiercely. "You know what," she says. "I'm all cried out. Don't think I don't care or anything. I do. I just lost my best friend. In my house! But I've cried all morning."

"Actually, you look kind of numb to me. Maybe in shock. Can I get a paramedic to look at you?"

"No. That won't be necessary. A monster was in my house last night. How do you expect me to look?"

"I understand," Mills assures her. "Now, I need you to tell me the circumstances around Ms. Willis staying here in your house."

"Again, I've already been through this. You know, Detective, I'm cried out and talked out. You smoke?"

"No."

"You?" she asks Myers.

He shakes his head.

"Well, don't mind if I have another."

"I don't, if you will give us a few more minutes of your time," Mills tells her.

"I will," she says, exhaling the first wind of smoke. "Look, Andrea was thinking of leaving her husband. I told her not to make, you know, any hasty decision, to come here and think it through."

"How long ago was that?" Myers asks, still writing.

"About three or four weeks ago."

"Did her husband know where she was?" Myers continues without looking up.

"No."

"But he knew you were best friends, so did he call here, or stop by? Did he call her? You?"

"He did call her several times, but she didn't answer. That was not my advice. That was her decision." The woman narrows her eyes and takes a long drag. Mills knows one thing doesn't make sense: a woman who does Pilates, who hikes the desert, filling her lungs with poison. And Mills can tell she's been smoking for a very long time. It's betrayed in the roughness of her skin, a slight sandpaper quality to her voice, and, of course, the pursed wrinkles around her lips. "He never came by that I know about," she tells the detectives.

"What's his name?" Myers asks.

"Bobby."

"Willis?"

"Yes," she replies, stretching the syllable with annoyance.

"I'm sure she confided in you," Myers says. "What were the problems in the marriage?"

"She complained about his laziness, for one thing. He never helped out around the house. Really unmotivated. He lost his job a year ago and kind of started dragging her down with him."

"I suppose a job loss could do that to someone," Mills tells her. "Make them feel helpless or worthless."

She shrugs. "I don't know. I only know what she told me."

"Did she ever mention violence in the marriage?" Mills asks.

Marcy Stone peels with laughter. "You're like the tenth person who's asked me that this morning. Everyone suspects violence," she says with a mock shudder.

Mills decides he's not fond of Marcy Stone. He looks at her squarely. "Under the circumstance, I'd think you'd understand why."

She raises her eyebrows impetuously. "Yeah, I suppose, but that would make it so easy, right? He beats her, she walks out, and he kills her. I don't think this is one of your Lifetime movies, if you know what I mean. He never hurt her . . . as far as I know. I think she would have told me. Bobby is actually kind of meek."

Mills nods pensively. "Do you have any cords or rope in the house?"

"I suppose," Marcy Stone replies. "I mean, I've got extension cords, for sure. Maybe some rope in the garage."

"Okay, Ms. Stone. Thanks for your time," Mills says. "Make sure if we call you for any follow-up, you get back to us promptly."

She nods. "No problem."

"And your house is a crime scene. My guys aren't leaving anytime soon," he tells her. "You better make arrangements to stay elsewhere."

She coughs and says, "So I've been told."

"We can get you assistance if you need it."

She doesn't say anything, nor does she move when Mills gets to his feet. She limply shakes his hand and stares into some kind of endless void.

Out front, Myers wanders off, takes notes about the house, while Mills gets with a few of the crime scene technicians. They tell him that they've picked up fibers from the bedroom floor but most are too fine to analyze with just a visual. "Here," one of the investigators says, handing a plastic bag to Mills, "this is the best sample we have, the closest we've seen to rope."

Mills examines it through the plastic. He toys with it in his hands. "Yeah, looks like rope to me. Has Chase seen it?"

"Yep."

"The marks on her neck seem more consistent with a cord," he tells the tech, giving him the bag.

"I would agree, but we'll get back to you on that."

Mills nods and steps over to a Glendale detective who's leaning against a cruiser. "Hey, Marco, what's doing?"

"Mills. You slumming today?"

"When I saw you I knew I was scraping at the bottom, man."

They shake.

"Look," Mills says, "I want to go talk to the victim's husband. Have any of your guys gone to notify?"

"No," the detective says. "We were told to wait. Looks like you guys are taking jurisdiction."

"Don't make it sound like we're stealing your dessert."

"You can have it, Mills. I'll release my guys now. Not sure you're going to shake the sheriff as easily."

"Sheriff?"

The Glendale cop points.

Mills turns and sees the sheriff's car parked down the street at the opening of the cul-de-sac, almost out of sight. "What the fuck?" he says.

"He's been here for at least a half hour."

"Doing what?"

The guy shrugs. "I don't know. Some reporters showed up, and he answered some questions."

Mills feels his face turn red. "Are you fucking kidding me?"

"No, dude, relax. That's why he's parked down there. He's stopping the media so they can't get into the neighborhood. You think that's a bad thing?"

Alex Mills has the sheriff in his crosshairs. He doesn't turn back to the Glendale cop. He says, "Thanks. I'm sure once we get all the paperwork in order you guys can scatter."

"It's all in order, Alex," the cop says. "The fat one's been out here taking in all the work we did for you guys."

"Myers?"

"Yeah, him. The roly-poly one."

He takes one look back at the cop. "Be nice, Marco. And trust me, man, my department is doing its share here." Then he slips away in the direction of the waiting sheriff.

It's the same old Clayman Tarpo from the fiery press conferences, the defiant interviews, the front-page photos (above the fold), the bulbous swagger, the central casting, red-meat-and-potato-chomping-salads-are-for-sissies sheriff of Maricopa County. His arteries are clogged, but his conscience is clear. Tarpo is the silhouette of a motel sign somewhere on the road between here and Yuma.

"Sheriff, thanks for the help," Mills says. "But I got everyone in place. So you can take off if you'd like."

"Someone's got to talk to the press," Tarpo says with a puff of disgust. Clayman Tarpo is as blustery as an August monsoon. He snickers and snarls and looks down at Mills even though Mills is a good inch taller. Tarpo accomplishes the condescension by addressing the detective at chest level.

"Well, I'll let my sergeant determine that."

Tarpo folds his hands across his chest. "Will you now?"

"Yes," Mills says, his eyes meeting the sheriff's, lingering there until the sheriff blinks. "This is not your case. Not your jurisdiction. Now, why don't you tell me now what you told those reporters?"

Tarpo laughs. "Ah, no harm done, my friend. The same disinformation they come to expect from me."

"And bravado, no doubt."

"That too," the sheriff says. "I gave no details. No names. No theories. Though I did say the crime scene reminded me of the murders in the caves."

"You did say that?"

"Was that wrong?"

Mills wipes his brow. "Of course it was wrong. I thought you offered no theories."

The sheriff puts a hand on Mills's shoulder. "My boy, there's a difference between a theory and a description. You do understand that, don't you? And the description was very, very vague. A comparison, that's all. Of course the reporters wanted to know what the crime scenes had in common, but I just said, heck no, that information ain't coming from me."

Tarpo smiles as if he just came all over his pillow.

"No more talking to the press. That decision will come from my department," Mills tells him.

"Hey! Why all the attitude? Haven't I been generous lending my deputies to your trail patrols?"

"Yeah, generous. Thanks," Mills says before turning back to the house.

"Hey, Detective," the sheriff calls after him. "How's your kid?"

Mills keeps marching forward. "Trevor is fine."

"Sure hope you get him out of this mess. There's a program called DARE, you know."

Mills doesn't flinch. "Go stick a cactus up your fat ass," he mutters under his breath.

He meets up with Chase and Myers in front of the house. Myers's shirt is stained with sweat. Beads of it are running down his face. "Morty, you need to get in shape, man," Mills tells him. "You've got water?"

"Yeah."

"I'm going with Chase to go look for the husband. You stay here 'til things are wrapped up." Then he tosses Myers his keys. "Take my car back when you're done."

18

They find Bobby Willis's townhouse in a well-groomed subdivision just adjacent to the Biltmore. The neighborhood is a curvy one, with lush desert vegetation protecting most of the homes from passing eyes. "What makes you think a man will be home in the middle of the workday?" Chase asks the detective.

"Unemployed," Mills answers.

"Potentially explains the rage."

"Potentially," Mills says.

Small boulders, in hues of rust and gold, line a path that leads to the front door.

Mills knocks. He hears footsteps. Someone is on the other side of the door. Mills can feel a presence there, a person spying through the peephole. He hears the person breathing. "Hello, Mr. Willis," he calls.

"Who is it?" a man calls back.

"Phoenix Police," Mills replies.

The door opens slowly. "Police?" says a man in drawstring pants, looking up, assessing his visitors.

"Mr. Bobby Willis?" Mills asks.

"Yes."

"I'm Detective Alex Mills. This is Detective Chase. May we come in?"

"What's this about?" Willis is unshaven, short, and stocky. He's wearing a clean T-shirt.

"Your wife."

Willis's eyes pop wide. "Andy? Is she okay?"

"I'm afraid not, sir," Mills tells him. "We believe your wife was found murdered this morning in Glendale."

As the color drains quickly from his face, Bobby Willis begins to tip toward the wall. Mills steps forward to steady the man. "Please let us come in and talk, sir."

"Whatever you want," Willis says.

The man leads the detectives into the house, to a room that overlooks a golf course through a wall of glass. A small, lagoon-like pool is carved into a portion of the patio. The ceiling soars above them. Two couches face each other—a huge marble slab between them. Willis sinks into one couch; Mills and Chase sit opposite him.

"We have a positive ID on your wife, Mr. Willis," Mills tells him. "Her body was found at the home of Marcy Stone."

"Marcy?" Willis begs. "Is she . . . you know, involved?"

"We don't think so," Mills replies. "It seems she has an alibi."

The man's face is contorted and suddenly red on fire, as if he's about to howl. Mills has seen this kind of agony before, on the guilty and the innocent; the agony is never a true indicator of either.

"How was she . . . uh, how was she murdered?" the husband asks.

"We think she was strangled," Chase says.

"Strangled," the man repeats. He looks at them, his face vacant, his eyes wide and blank; he sees everything but downloads nothing. Then, a few moments later, a light goes on, a switch, a Control-Alt-Delete reboot, and he says, "You think I killed her. Don't you?"

"Why would we think that, Mr. Willis?" Mills asks dryly.

Willis shifts uneasily. "'Cause, you know, we were separated."

"Legally?" Mills asks.

"No, not really. She bolted on me."

"Bolted? I bet you were angry," Chase says.

The man stares evenly at Timothy Chase. "Yeah, angry. But I didn't kill her."

"We're not asking you that," Mills tells him. "Nor are we accusing you of that, sir. But we do need some information. Do you know anyone who would want to hurt her?"

"No."

"When is the last time you talked to her?"

"About three weeks ago when she left. I mean, I've been trying to reach her, but she doesn't answer."

"When she didn't answer, you didn't worry?" Chase asks the man.

"About what?"

"There's a serial killer on the loose," Chase says.

The husband says nothing. He sits there with his head in his hands. Mills wishes he could have left Chase in the car.

But Chase will not be stifled. "You've heard about the murders, haven't you?" Chase persists.

"Of course," Willis says. "It's been in the newspapers and on TV, like, every day. But I never gave it much of a thought. I didn't think Andy was missing. She was mad, but not missing. Are you saying she could be one of those victims?"

Mills leans forward and shakes his head. "We're not saying anything, Mr. Willis. We're just trying to put the pieces together. Your wife worked?"

"She did hair. But she had taken the last two weeks off from the salon because we were supposed to go to Hawaii."

"Really?" Chase asks. "You must have been pretty mad that she would walk out on you right before that trip."

"I was upset. But I had no idea where she went. I had no way to find her."

The bong of a grandfather clock echoes through the house. It's two o'clock.

"Does your wife have family here in Phoenix?" Mills asks.

"No," he says. "We're both originally from DC."

"I worked in DC for years," Chase tells him. "FBI."

"No shit," the man says. "What are you doing back here?"

"Family stuff."

"We visited her family a lot," Willis says. "She really missed DC. Phoenix doesn't even come close."

Chase nods emphatically.

Mills indulges their small talk, ignores them for a few minutes, gets up, walks to the window, and studies the fountain that spills lazy waves of water into the pool. The lapping is hypnotic. He turns around and wanders as the two men discuss the Redskins, the Orioles, whatever. Apparently, Bobby and Andrea met in college. Mills isn't listening fully enough to decipher which college. It's just two men colliding with deep-voiced familiarity. Their exact words, in fact, disappear into the generalized manliness of a frat house. A frat house of grief and sympathy, doubt, fear, and distraction. There must be something in it for Chase, psychologically speaking. Mills is back in the foyer. He ducks into a room on the other side, a den of sorts, with a love seat, a desk, a computer, and the source of the bong. Mills admires the handsome grandfather clock, the dark mahogany, the gilded edges, and the etched glass. He sees a small fissure at the top of the glass face and traces it slowly downward as it opens to a gash and then to a distinct hole at the bottom; the hole looks as random as a piece from a jigsaw puzzle. It's 2:10.

There's a bookcase opposite the clock. Mills looks for something he recognizes. But he can tell from the spines of the books that someone in the house is a big fan of frothy romance. He can see it in the feminine fonts, in the titles, too. *Her Secret Man. Rescued By a Stranger. She Takes a Dare.* Perfect reading for the salon, he guesses. Not a trace of the classics anywhere.

"I see your wife liked to read," he says to Bobby Willis when he returns to the living room.

Both men look up.

"And I see that your beautiful clock has been banged up a bit," Mills adds.

Bobby Willis stands. "Well, hey, don't you need a warrant to be snooping around my house?" He annexes his question with a laugh, bouncy and insincere, as if he's joking.

"Sorry," Mills says. "Just admiring the place. But do you mind telling me how the glass on the clock broke like that?"

Willis shrugs. "The clock used to be in here. We decided it would look better in the study. You know, more . . . studious or something. But I lost my balance, and it went into the wall when I moved it."

"That's too bad," Mills tells him. "It's a beautiful piece."

"Thanks. Will that be all?" Willis asks, his voice breaking, and then he sobs.

"Can you tell us about your activities between five p.m. last night and five a.m. this morning?" Mills asks.

"There's not much to tell," Willis says, choking back the tears. "I was here the whole time. You know, I was laid off a while ago."

"You had nowhere you had to be?" Mills probes.

"I went to the Home Depot yesterday around noon. And then to Safeway about two o'clock, grabbed stuff for dinner, and came home."

Mills asks, "And you stayed home?"

Willis says, "Yes. All night."

Mills asks, "Can anyone verify that?"

Willis shrugs. "I don't think so. I was alone." He wipes his face, sniffling.

"So, no one can actually place you here in the time frame we're talking about?" Mills asks.

"I didn't kill my wife," Willis tells him. "I think the only verification you could find would be on the cameras as you enter and exit the neighborhood. The association elected cameras, instead of gates. I'm not a fan of people knowing when I come and go, but there you have it, boys. Get the video, and you'll see that my car never entered or exited during your time frame."

They're in the foyer now.

"That doesn't mean you didn't leave," Mills says. "You know that presents us with a problem. I'm not accusing you, sir. I'm actually trying to eliminate you."

Willis nods. "I'm sure you are." His eyes fill again, tears brimming. "Now, really, I need some time, gentlemen...."

"Fine," Mills says. "Thank you for meeting with us." He hands Willis his card. "If you think of anything, call me right away."

"I will."

"And, one more thing, Mr. Willis. Do you have an article of clothing or something that belonged to your wife that you don't mind parting with?"

Willis narrows his eyes, cocks his head. "For what?"

"It'll just help us with the investigation," Mills tells him. "You know, something important to her. Might give us some clues to who she was and who she knew."

Chase clears his throat.

Mills doesn't give a shit.

Willis wipes a tear from his cheek. "Sure," he says. "Wait here."

The man disappears down a hallway off the living room. Mills can sense Chase eyeing him uneasily. Before Chase has a chance to speak, Willis is back holding a necklace. Hanging from the chain is a solid gold lightning bolt. "This meant a lot to her," Willis says. "She's a big fan of some rock singer who wears one just like it. I forget . . . what's her name? I don't know, but Andy was always wearing it and dancing around the house."

He puts the necklace in a small cardboard box and hands it to Mills.

"Thanks, man," Mills says. "If you need anything let me know."

"Do I go to the morgue?" the husband asks, and then he backs into a wall, sobbing.

"Not necessary," Mills replies. "When the body is ready, someone will call you."

In the car the men decide to head back to Glendale. Mills isn't too concerned about Bobby Willis. "If he was near the murder scene, we'll get a ding off the cell tower," he tells Chase.

"*We* know that," Chase says. "Doubt *he* does. Crime of passion. Better to let him speak. 'Til he unravels."

"Suppose so."

"You ever met a murderer who left his cell phone at home?" Chase asks.

"Not yet."

"'Course not. Most of them are fucking sending out tweets with one hand while they're killing with the other."

Mills laughs. And then he doesn't. He has a sense of doom.

19

Gus Parker gets home about 4:30 in the afternoon. The days still feel like summer, so he's not surprised when he takes Ivy for her walk that she's panting before they reach the third corner.

"We'll make it a short one, girl," he tells her. The air smells of creosote. The image of Gary Potter killing a woman has been haunting him for days. He's been so distracted he mistook a kidney for a gallbladder. Only momentarily. But still. It's times like this when he misses surfing the most. There's nothing quite like having that much energy and that much solitude. A neighbor approaches with her baby in a stroller. The woman says hello. Gus smiles. The baby squints at the sky. Gus has an urge to reach down and pull the child toward him, not in a malicious way but to somehow make up for what he never had. Gus doesn't know this woman, but he knows that he's jealous of her husband.

A bird swoops down, and Ivy barks.

"C'mon, girl, let's go home," he tells the dog. At home he turns on the TV and mixes a heap of salad for dinner. Vanna White is turning a letter. "Not in my house," Gus says to the television as he surfs to another station. He lands on another local station and a rerun of *Seinfeld*. It's the one about Elaine's nipple. He's seen this one about a half a dozen times, and he still laughs. He thinks Julia Louis-Dreyfus is sublime. The five o'clock news comes on as he's carving up some chicken.

"Murder in Glendale," the anchorman belches. "A neighborhood on alert."

Gus barely listens until he hears the bellowing voice of Sheriff Clayman Tarpo and the comment that the crime could be linked to the desert murders.

"So, Tony," says the anchorman to a reporter on the scene, "did the sheriff explain why there might be a connection?"

"He offered little in specifics, but he did say that something about the crime scene was consistent with what investigators found in the desert."

"Intriguing," the anchorman muses for the camera. "Thanks, Tony. Good work out there."

Gus drops the carving knife and reaches for his cell phone.

Alex Mills doesn't answer.

He tries again. He leaves a voice mail.

He takes the chicken salad and forks at it while he walks into his den and turns on the computer. He goes to the *Arizona Republic*'s website. The victim's name is Andrea Willis. She's thirty-eight years old. A hairstylist, separated from her husband. The *Republic* has the same vague, offhanded quote from the sheriff. It's unclear to Gus why the sheriff would be involved now. As he's finishing the article his phone chimes. A text message from Alex: "Interesting vision. Victim was strangled by rope or cord. Busy. Let's talk in AM."

He thinks about the rope and the MRI. Interesting vision, maybe. But it doesn't explain the connection between a suburban crime scene and a series of cave murders. Still, affirmation goes thud in his chest. The rope around Rosemary Nichols's neck was a sign, not for her but for Gus, and, sadly, for Andrea Willis. The rope, Gus knows, is how the killer ropes them in. That's it. He changed the murder weapon, but there has to be something else about the crime scenes that are connected. He knows this.

"Same killer?" he texts back to Alex.

"Affirmed, not confirmed," Alex replies.

Gus shaves before bed. He had been sporting two days of stubble. He gives his face a final splash of water and looks up to the mirror. For an instant he sees the faint image of his mother. She's there in front of him but far away in the mirror, reduced to a horizon dweller. He thinks she's calling to him. Her mouth isn't moving, but he can hear her voice. It sounds as if she is trapped in a fog, the way her voice carries with strange echoes. He suddenly understands that she is not talking to him. She's saying, "How long do I have? What are my options?" And she's saying it to someone else.

He feels a chill.

It's been a while, maybe two years, since he has talked to Meg Parker. He doesn't remember the occasion of that conversation, but he remembers the tone: short, cordial, and detached. Gus listens to himself juggle his options. The more he hears himself the more he realizes that he doesn't have any.

He calls her in the morning.

"Hi, Mom."

"Who's calling, please?"

"Who's calling? It's me, Mom."

"Oh, Gus. As if I didn't know. But out of sight, out of mind, as they say."

He shakes his head. She's hopeless. "How are you?"

"I'm fine," she says. Her tone is chipper and manufactured. "What can I do for you?"

"Just checking in," he says.

"For what? Money?"

He sighs deeply. "Really? When have I ever called you for money?"

"It's inevitable, Gus. We know you can't really sustain a life as a palm reader."

He laughs bitterly. "I'm not a palm reader. And you know that. You also know that I have a full-time job in healthcare."

She laughs.

The c-word is on the tip of his tongue, but he stuffs it down his throat. "Speaking of healthcare, Mother, when's the last time you saw a doctor?"

"Not lately."

"I think you should."

She clears her throat. "You do? Let me guess, you got a sign that I'm ill."

"Maybe I did."

"Look, Gus, your father is walking in for breakfast. You do remember we're an hour earlier than you."

"Only half the year," he says.

That hour, or that half a year, is a metaphor for everything.

Gus shuts his eyes now and concentrates. From his world, the curtain closes. He stares at the square of black. He can feel his eyes squeezing in his head, exerting the mental muscle to open the curtain to their world. Slowly it slides aside, and the first thing Gus sees is an image of Jesus in a painting on the kitchen wall. It's right next to the sign that says, "Bless This Mess," and a corkboard sprouting coupons at the height of harvest. And his father.

"Tell Dad I really like the tie. Red is such a power color."

"Good guess," she says.

"When did he grow the moustache?"

"I see you've been talking to your sister."

"It's been nearly a year since I've spoken to Nicole," he tells her. "Go to the doctor."

She says nothing.

"Oh, and Mom, is that toast burning? Before the timer? You're usually more accurate than that. But I hear the timer going off in four, three, two, one . . ."

Ding.

"And Dad's toast is charcoal black," he adds.

She slams the phone down.

Gus reads about the Andrea Willis murder in the morning paper. The report is nearly as void of detail as the stories he saw last night. The article does include a quote from Sergeant Jacob Woods of the Phoenix Police Department who says, "We are looking into any and all connections to other currently open cases. Certainly if anyone has any information related to these crimes, they're urged to contact us as soon as possible. Let it be clear that we, not the sheriff's office, are the lead agency on this case."

He's getting ready for work when the phone rings. It's Alex Mills, who fills him in on the murder scene in Glendale.

"Carved into the wall?" Gus asks.

"Yeah."

"The message is obvious."

"We know. He's everywhere. He's emboldened."

"But this is different," Gus says. "All along he's used the desert petroglyphs as some sort of compass of his crimes. Now he's committed a crime in a completely arbitrary place."

"There was no petroglyph near the Camelback cave," Alex reminds him. "Besides, Chase says not to get too hung up on them as some kind of symbols. We were all set to map out the petroglyphs within a ten-mile radius of Phoenix, no easy feat, and then send out surveillance teams looking for bodies, but then Chase talks to this professor friend of his at ASU who tells him the symbols mean nothing."

"Nothing? I doubt that."

"According to this professor, the petroglyphs, themselves, are arbitrary. They basically serve no other purpose than art."

"Of course they're art," Gus says. "But I always assumed they carried some kind of spiritual significance."

"Not according to Chase."

"So the murderer is putting together a portfolio of his own artwork?"

"He's leaving proof that outlives the crime," Mills replies.

"Good point."

"Chase feels the killer is documenting his work with pride."

"I wonder who the killer's trying to impress."

"Why do you say that?"

"Because I see more into this than proving a point, or marking an accomplishment," Gus says. "He's trying to impress someone, or maybe even seek approval."

"Maybe you should talk to Chase," Mills tells him. "You sound like you'd be more helpful to him than me."

"I take it you two aren't getting along."

Mills laughs. "We're getting along fine. But in this kind of case the profile is everything. And that's what Chase does. He's the expert."

Gus feels himself lunge for the next remark. "But maybe I can lead you to the killer before Chase even finishes his profile," he says, thinking of Gary Potter.

"Go on, my psychic friend. . . ."

Gus bristles. "You know, I haven't figured out how to tell you this. But I may have a lead."

"The case isn't getting any warmer."

"I can't tell you who it is, but I can put you right in front of him."

"Don't be coy, Gus Parker."

"I'm not. I just have to be careful what to say. He's a client of mine. And I have a plan."

"Meet for lunch?"

"Can't. I'm working through lunch so I can leave early for Tucson."

"What's in Tucson?"

Gus tells him about Beatrice's investigation. About Charla McGregor's appearance in Tucson. "Wanna come?"

"Tonight?"

"Yeah."

"I don't think so, Gus. It's such short notice. I mean, I'm intrigued and all, but I don't want to spring it on Kelly."

Then Gus knows exactly what to say. "Bring her to the theater tomorrow night."

"The theater?"

Gus offers to give Mills the tickets to Gary Potter's play. "That client I'm telling you about. He's the lead character."

"Why do you think this guy's linked to the murders?"

"Why do I think anything? Why do I get a hunch or a vision?"

"Fair enough."

"I wish I could give you more details, but I can't. He's a client."

"I get it, Gus."

"Look, it might be nothing," Gus tells him. "But treat your wife to a nice night of dinner and the theater and get all the stress of work off your mind. If nothing else, that should make it worth it. I know you're under a lot of pressure."

"Speaking of, we don't leave Trevor alone these days."

"I can understand that."

"So, I think it's thanks but no thanks on the play."

The words come out before Gus fully assembles the logic. "Leave him with me. I'll keep him out of trouble."

"You want to babysit a teenager?"

"No," Gus replies. "I want to hang out with him."

"Yeah, I don't know how well he'll take to that. I'll talk about it with Kelly and let you know."

Gus says that's no problem. What Gus really wants is for someone to shadow Gary Potter. But he knows it doesn't work that way.

And then Alex says, "Hey, Gus, I have something for you."

"What?"

"Personal effect from Andrea Willis."

"Intrigued. How about you trade it in for those theater tickets?"

"Like I said, I'll let you know, man."

Gus laughs. "Deal," he says. Then he's off to work where he's met by four pairs of breasts in a row.

Followed by a gallbladder, two livers, and a kidney.

During a break he stuffs a burrito in his mouth, then returns to his work and a cranky old fellow named Mr. Harvey. "Let's just get this done with," the man says. "I don't have time for this nonsense. You know what, young man? I'm seventy-eight years old, and I still run a company. How about that? Huh? Most people my age are playing golf! Bored to death and probably going broke. Not me. No way."

"Good for you, Mr. Harvey," Gus tells him. "Keep active. Stay active."

"I was running five miles a day before my knee started cramping up. So, what am I supposed to do now? Go to some idiotic senior center and play chess? I don't think so. Not Ted Harvey. Not me. No way."

Gus smiles. "I don't see that happening to you, sir. Just give me a few minutes and we'll get you out of here."

During the procedure, Gus scans the pictures, as he usually does, to inspect the images for quality. One image comes up, not as the lateral meniscus but as a face. A *face*. He closes out of the window and calls it up again. And there in the box on the screen, smiling as if she just won the Joan Crawford Mother of the Year Award, is the defiantly beautiful face of Meg Parker.

20

Beatrice and Hannah show up at four o'clock.

"You don't look well," Beatrice tells Gus. "Are you sick?"

Gus ushers them in. "Not really. Just tired, I guess."

"Don't let your mother get to you," Beatrice tells him.

He looks at her and bursts into a smile. "Damn, you're good," he says.

She does a coquettish half spin and says, "Of course I am. I see what you see."

"You ladies ready to hit the road?" he asks.

They are, and they pile into Gus's car and head out of Phoenix. They're halfway to Tucson, well past Casa Grande, when Beatrice tells Gus that his house is being cased.

"For a robbery?" he asks, looking away from the road.

"I don't think so," Beatrice says.

"What did the car look like?" he asks, observing the jitters in his own voice.

"I don't know," she tells him. "Keep your eyes on the highway, dear."

He talks to the windshield in disbelief. "How did you not see what the car looked like?"

"Because I didn't see a car."

"She had some kind of vibe when we entered your neighborhood," Hannah explains.

"Oh," Gus says. And then he wonders who. *Who would be casing my house?* Officially, no one outside the police department knows that Gus is working on the desert murders. Certainly not the media. "Do you have any idea who it might be or why?" he asks Beatrice.

She utters a chain of tsks. "We can't worry about that now, Gus. All I'm saying is that your house has been watched."

"That's all you're saying," he says mockingly.

"I don't sense any harm," she tells him. "Besides Ivy is a fine watchdog."

They're mostly quiet for the rest of the journey. They pass the exit for Mission San Xavier del Bac. It's a place that Gus, not a religious person, would normally pull off for a brief visit. Called the White Dove of the Desert, it's a silent place, wholly spiritual and serene. On a trip south, Gus never misses the chance to visit. There he would stare at the soaring white arches against the crisp, impossibly blue sky and just dream. His connection would require no work. The place just is.

But he moves on down the highway. The desert rushes by like a conveyor of burlap. Beatrice removes a CD from her pocketbook and slips it into the player. "I want you to hear some new music."

A woman sings delicately to the strumming of a guitar. Her voice builds to a flourish, and then the percussion drives her into a thrashing chorus about ghosts—*"Ghosts don't need a place to hide . . . they never do, they never do . . . ghosts are with us, with you . . . always inside."*

"Who is this?" he asks Beatrice.

"Billie Welch."

"You're kidding." Billie Welch was a rock and roll chanteuse who came to fame in the late 1970s when women in rock were rare and all of them owed a debt of gratitude to Janis Joplin. Billie Welch was every adolescent boy's dream. Beautiful, doe-eyed, sultry. Her songs were seductive, never sexual, but fetching and mysterious. Her career had endured, though as the years passed she seemed to drop out of sight, releasing less music, following, it seemed, in the elusive footsteps of Greta Garbo. "She's still making music?" Gus asks.

"Apparently," Beatrice says.

"I think I had a crush on her when I was seventeen or so," he confesses.

"Well, now you can probably meet her," Hannah says. "She just moved in two houses down from Beatrice."

"I brought her a pie. She gave me a CD," Beatrice adds. "She said she was tired of the LA life and was looking for a retreat."

"Wow," Gus says. "That is so cool. How old is she now?"

"Probably a few years older than you," Beatrice guesses.

Gus listens to the music as if it's translating the white noise of the highway.

"I think this is our exit," Hannah tells him a few minutes into the interlude.

Turns out Charla McGregor is the real deal.

Never once did she exploit Hannah's feigning story of a lover lost at sea, told, following protocol, with shivering drama and high volume prior to McGregor's introduction. And if there had been any tendency to exploit, the lover lost at sea would have been perfect bait. The attendance was not even half that of Eric Young's appearance in Phoenix. The people who showed up were uniformly tepid, if not sheepish. There was no sense of arousal in the crowd, not even a buzz of anticipation. But there would be recognition and tears, and apparently truth, as Charla worked very hard to connect with the individuals seated in a semicircle around her. She was tall and thin, with a bowl of black hair, intermittently spliced with gray. She had perfect posture. And powder sand complexion. She spoke softly. She made no ringing pronouncements, preferring to speak to her guests as though they had come for a cup of tea, not a show. It did seem like a sort of exquisite tea party, the intimacy she created in that space.

No need for Beatrice to burst out from the bookshelves to rescue anyone from malfeasance.

"Charla might have caught wind of my investigations," Beatrice told Hannah and Gus after the event. "Maybe word is out, and she recognized Hannah as one of my plants."

No that's not what happened. They all knew that. They all witnessed the same thing when Charla McGregor wrapped up her session for the night.

The crowd ran out of questions. There was nobody left hoping for a meaningful prediction or a soul-stirring connection with the dead. Charla smiled beneficently. "You have been a great, great audience tonight," she said. "Let me just ask you for a few minutes of silence, if you'll indulge me. Throughout our session here I have been getting a palpable sense of unfinished business. It's one of those things that will keep me up at night if I don't figure it out. That's what psychics lose sleep over."

Her audience laughed sweetly.

And they gave her their silence.

In the meanwhile, Gus started to fidget and gave Beatrice a look. *Can we go now?*

She shook her head.

Then Gus's ears tingled, burned.

"I know someone in this room is searching for a man who has done something wrong," announced Charla McGregor. "This man is not dead. He's very much alive and dangerous."

Her audience responded with a muffled gasp and horrified looks.

"Any takers?" Charla asked.

People turned their heads anxiously. Gus's ears were pulsating. Beatrice elbowed him in the ribs.

"I'm stuck on the letters 'I' and 'L,'" Charla told the gathering. "Does this mean anything to anybody?"

Suddenly, Gus stood, pulled by some external force, and said, "It might mean something to me."

"Are you a detective?" Charla asked him.

"No."

"Hmm. I'm seeing a detective," she said.

Gus shrugged and said, "I've been spending time with a detective."

There was a nod of recognition. Something passed between Charla and Gus that only they could sense, like a seismic wave or the sonar of dolphins who often gathered around Gus while he surfed the ocean. Those dolphins communicated with him. They sensed his sixth sense; at least that's what he told himself. And now, there was that same glassy but sentient look in Charla McGregor's eyes and a distinct signal that she was talking to only him. The room hushed. The two psychics gazed at each other.

"You don't need my help," Charla said. "You will find this man. Your search may feel more like research. And I encourage that. Start digging. Read what you need to read." Then, pointing to Beatrice, she added, "I'm sure that lovely lady to your side would be happy to help."

Beatrice purred.

Not an eye blinked in that audience.

"I'm assuming the letters 'I' and 'L' are initials," Charla said.

"I don't know," Gus told her.

"Keep them in mind," she suggested. "Do not forget them."

"Is this man still in the area?"

"He's in Phoenix if that's what you're asking me," she said. The crowd, for some reason, applauded. Even Charla seemed confused. Then she said, "He's involved in something this weekend. Keep your detective close. There is something happening this weekend."

"What do you see?"

"It's vague. But a woman is crying. She's desperately afraid."

Gus sensed some fear among the audience, as well. "Maybe we should continue this privately."

Charla shook her head. "No. I have nothing more. I'm sorry. Just remember. 'I.' 'L.' And, okay, two more letters. 'M,' 'D.' ILMD. Four letters. Perhaps not initials."

"Perhaps not," Gus agreed, entering the letters into a note page on his phone.

"Or," she added with a gush, "he's a doctor. Initials 'I,' 'L,' medical doctor."

Again, the group applauded.

"A doctor?" Gus heard himself ask.

"Thank you all for coming. I'm so honored to be with you tonight," Charla McGregor told her audience. "I'll be happy to sign some books before I leave."

The crowd scrambled toward her. "You should get her phone number," Beatrice says to Gus now.

"No. I'm good. She said it herself. She has nothing more. You know how that is."

Beatrice nods.

"But I think the research begins now. 'Read what you need to read,' she said. Before we leave I want to look and see if there are any books here on Native American art or folklore, or something like that."

"Go ahead," Beatrice says. "I have to pee."

Hannah giggles. "Me, too."

Gus moves trancelike to an information desk. He silently chants the letters "ILMD" like a mantra. He recognizes the pretentious aroma of coffee done seriously wafting from the café.

He approaches a clerk. "I'm looking for something on desert petroglyphs," he says.

The clerk, a young, waifish woman with big eyes and dandruff, assesses him oddly. "Geography?"

"No, no," he says. "Those Native American symbols in the desert."

She smiles widely. "Oh, yes, of course. So sorry. Let's look it up."

He follows her to a kiosk and watches as her spindly fingers punch information onto a keyboard. She hums softly as she waits for results. Gus assumes she's a student at U of A. Majors in music. "Well, here we go. I'm not getting a direct match with anything in stock. Something comes up in art. But that's a special order. And there's this . . . *Hiding in the Desert: A Memoir from the Reservation*."

"No," Gus tells her. "I don't think so."

"Then there are all these travel guides to Arizona," she says. "They all seem to mention artifacts. Mostly in museums, though."

Gus shakes his head.

"Here's another art book," she says. "And we do have it in stock. It's a photo book of desert artifacts."

"Now, that sounds like a good start. Can you write down the name?"

She smiles. "I can do better than that. I can take you to the book myself."

Gus knows the women will be waiting but also knows he's getting a flirtatious vibe from this musky-smelling coed. "Oh, that's fine," he says. "I'm heading back to Phoenix. If you could just write it down, I'll look for it at one of your stores up there, or maybe online."

The woman shrugs. "The only other thing that comes up is this: *A History of Symbols*. But it doesn't say Native American symbols, and it's been out of print since 1980. Looks like it was self-published."

"Doesn't matter," Gus says. "I'll take that info too."

The woman scribbles a few lines on a scrap of paper and hands it to Gus. "The name of the photo book we have in stock," she recites, "and the details about the symbol book. Anything else?"

"No, thanks. That was a great help."

She twirls a finger into her hair. "My pleasure," she says as an unfortunate sprinkle of dust falls from her head. "I'm here until closing if you need any more help."

Gus nods politely and smiles.

Beatrice slept the whole way up I-10, snoring softly, wistfully, delightfully, as though a baby hummingbird had landed right below her nostrils. Hannah, however, chatted into Gus's ear for the length of the ride, telling him her own stories of psychic revelations, like the time she and her first husband, Mitch, were in Los Cabos and it rained for three days straight. "I had a feeling it would," she told Gus. "I know that doesn't make me officially psychic, but it made me listen more to my intuition. If you know what I mean." Gus wasn't sure what she meant.

Back at Gus's house now, Hannah wakes Beatrice and guides her to the car. The women offer him butterfly kisses, a squeezy hug, and depart. Once inside, Gus pours himself a glass of wine, takes two sips, turns on CNN, takes two gulps, and promptly falls asleep on the couch.

He's probably down for half an hour before a throaty growl from Ivy wakes him up. He opens his eyes, but she's not there. "Where are you, girl?" he calls. "You need your walk. . . ."

The dog offers a distant yelp from the hallway, maybe the bedroom. "Ivy?"

He looks at the clock. Midnight. In his stupor, the time makes no sense. He drags himself to the bedroom, his eyes half-closed. "Baby, you in here?"

He feels for the bed in the dark and hears a voice. "Gus Parker, Gus Parker, I hope you don't mind the company."

21

That yanks him from his stupor. Suddenly, he's wide awake. He spins around for the light switch, but in the dark he's disoriented and he has spun too far. "What the fuck? Beatrice?"

"No. It's me."

"Who?"

And then the room is flooded with light. The glare splinters his eyes for a moment, but he clearly sees Bridget Mulroney in his bed, her hand on the switch of the night table lamp. "Hi," she says.

"Bridget?"

"I didn't want to disturb you," she tells him.

He scratches his head and looks at her uneasily. The room smells perfumed. "And this is your definition of not disturbing me?"

"You were asleep on the couch. I didn't want to wake you up. So I figured I'd sleep in here."

"How did you get in?"

"Your slider to the pool was open."

"Oh."

"Why don't you come to bed?" she asks.

He shakes his head vigorously. "Come to bed? I don't even know what you're doing here."

She taps the mattresses. "Come sit," she says.

"Bridget, I think you should go."

She throws the covers off. She's in a bra and panties and in magnificent shape, like a gymnast but longer, like a dancer, a trapeze artist. "I said sit, Gus," she orders.

Gus tries to stare her down, but her eyes are annihilating, like two grenades coming his way. Her lips are moist. He can't look at her, but he stands his ground. "I'm not sitting anywhere," he says, "until you tell me why you're in my house."

She groans. "Because someone is following me, Mr. Parker. Are you happy?"

"What are you talking about?"

"You were right. I should have listened to your warning. All night I was distinctly aware of being followed."

"All night?"

"Yes. Wherever I went I felt like I was being trailed."

"On the road? By a car?"

"Yes!" she gushes.

"Do you have a description of the vehicle?"

She lifts a leg and stretches. "It looked like an SUV or a pickup."

"Color?"

She reaches for her ankle, clasps it in her hand. "I don't know. It was dark, and he was well enough behind me."

"But the car had to be close enough for you to sense you were being followed."

"I guess you're right," she says. "But all I can really remember were those headlights. I was just focused on the headlights. Every time I rounded a corner, those headlights would follow. It was kind of like a monster."

"But Bridget Mulroney doesn't scare easily. At least that's not the impression you give."

She releases her leg and dips it slowly to the mattress, her toes pointed. "Did I say I was scared?"

Gus gestures to the bed.

"Well, I didn't want to go *home*," she explains. "I didn't want this freak to know where I live."

"So, you came here, and now this freak knows where I live."

"I parked two blocks away so he wouldn't, Gus. I risked my life and ditched my car, and I shook him loose!"

Gus remembers: Beatrice had a vibe about his house. Someone

might be casing, watching; someone might be stalking. Was the vibe about Bridget breaking in? he wonders. Or was it even darker? Had Beatrice felt the presence of a killer coming for his prey?

"Did he follow you?" Gus asks.

"No. I hid behind a cactus until he left. I think I woke a neighbor."

Gus shifts on his feet, puts his hands on his hips. "Did you call Mills?"

"Not yet."

"Why not?"

"I thought you'd do your psychic thing first."

"What psychic thing?"

"I don't know . . . go out and touch my car . . . confirm for sure it was the killer who was following me."

He sits on the bed. "It doesn't work that way, Bridget."

"And you call yourself a psychic?" she says. In her voice there is a very subtle tango of umbrage and flirtation.

"I already told you the killer was watching you," Gus reminds her. "You chose not to believe me."

She brushes her hair back. "It wasn't that I didn't believe you, Gus. I just honestly didn't trust you. I'm not a huge believer in psychics. I don't expect you'll change my mind. I just thought you came to me with a sort of made-up warning because what you really wanted was to fuck me."

Gus coughs instinctively, a decoy reaction. "Excuse me?"

"It could have been a creative come-on. You know, scare me into fucking you."

Her fingers skitter across the mattress in his direction.

He fidgets. "Furthest thing from my mind," he tells her emphatically, though he does, indeed, sense the faintest stirring in his groin (faint, very faint, could be anything).

"So you don't want to fuck me?"

"I wanted to warn you. I wanted to bring you into the fold."

"Well, okay then. Consider me warned. And I'll come into the fold if only to find out who was following me tonight. But I can't believe you don't want to fuck me."

"That's not what I'm saying, Bridget."

"Then you do want to fuck me?"

"What I'm saying, Bridget, is that you were wrong to think that sex was my motive. It wasn't and isn't."

She pouts her full, moist lips. Here she is, an insanely fuckable woman in his bed. Or perhaps she is fuckably insane. He suspects the latter, but even so, there's that stirring, that very faint stirring. He hates that his dick has a mind of its own. *It's probably the wine*, Gus tells himself. The wine and the smell of perfume. Perfume can kill him. Maybe some other time, some other place, at some other age, but if nothing else, age has taught Gus Parker that a few minutes of pleasure is not worth the crazy. Beatrice thinks he's asexual, a spiritual guru who knows all pleasure through the Zen of the universe, not the flesh of a woman, but if that were true, which it is not, why would his healthy dick be coming out of hiding?

"Well, I just can't go home right now," she says.

"You can sleep on the couch, Bridget."

She gathers her clothes. As she walks from the room, she turns to him and smiles. "I'll make a deal with you, Gus Parker. You prove to me you're really a psychic and solve this crime. And I'll prove to you that you really do want to fuck me."

"Can't you think of a nicer way to put it?"

"Resolve this case? Give us closure? Apprehend the suspect? What do you want, Gus Parker?"

He shakes his head. "A good night's sleep," he says and shuts off the light.

In the morning Gus rolls over and swings his arm over a soft mass lying beside him. Then he feels a tongue brush against his cheek, leaving behind moist heat and bad breath. He scrambles for the covers and sees a face staring him down.

"Thank God it's you," he tells Ivy. "Where the hell have you been?"
She whimpers.

"I know. I know. I've been a bad dad. A very bad dad."

She paws him softly. He kisses her head. He stretches, rises, and wobbles to the living room to check for remnants of Bridget. The couch has been slept in but abandoned. It says so in the subtle imprint of a body, the pillows askew. His next stop is the bathroom where he pisses out his bladder. The relief is unusually satisfying.

The relief across town is satisfying, as well. Nothing like some morning fornication to put a smile on the face of Alex Mills. They love Saturday morning sloppy sex, he and his wife. No expectations, just bed hair, cotton mouth, musky smells, and the overnight sheen. Kelly has bitten his ear, and it's a sting he's learned to love. "If I had a maid who could bring me coffee I'd never leave this bed," she tells him.

"You really want some hot chick joining us?"

"Who said she was going to join us? And who said she'd be hot?"

He squeezes her waist, and she writhes with laughter.

"Stop it," she pleads. "I hate being tickled."

"No, you don't."

She rolls over on top of him and pins him by the wrists. "I wish for one day we could lock the world out completely. Your job, my job, our son."

"I love you, Kelly."

"I love you, too," she says.

He looks at her in disbelief. Not that he's surprised that she loves him, but he has just seen another layer of beauty unfold across her face, unravel around her body. She constantly regenerates her sexiness, her clarity of self; it's that clarity that surprises him—it resides in her eyes, as if she has just discovered a precious jewel.

He grinds beneath her. Not to start anything; it's just a lusty affirmation.

"Oh, Alex," she says.

"I couldn't live without you," he says.

She releases his wrists. "I'll deny I ever said this, but fuck Trevor. He's staying with Gus Parker tonight while we go to the theater."

"Really?"

"Yep."

"That's great. Really great."

Later that morning he calls Gus to let him know.

Gus sounds tired, ambivalent about the plan. His sentences are short, his voice awkward.

"Everything okay with you?" Mills asks.

"I guess."

"I'm not the psychic here, but something's up."

"That's why you're such a good detective." Gus describes a surprise visit from Bridget Mulroney. "She was gone when I got up."

"I admire your self-control," Mills tells him.

"Well, she is a bit crazy, isn't she?"

"She might be," Mills replies. "But I've fucked crazy before."

"Before Kelly. . . ."

"Yes," Mills says emphatically. Then he says, "I'm not going to tell you to stay away from her. I'll just say proceed with caution."

"I'm not proceeding."

"Maybe you should focus on whoever was following her," Mills says. "I think we need to look at that closely."

"Yeah," says Gus. "I'll do that."

Mills tells him he'll drop Trevor off at six.

That gives Gus pretty much the whole day to hunt down those books. First, he takes Ivy for a long, hearty walk. Then he's off to Turning Pages. It's a total clusterfuck of a bookstore in Tempe that has everything ever written by anybody about anything, new and used. That's an overstatement, of course, but that's what it feels like every time Gus walks in and smells the assorted breeds of paperbacks and hard covers that are piled from floor to ceiling. He likes getting lost in the musty coves and dungeons of the place. There is no real first floor, no real second floor, just ramps that take you from one nook to another. And there's a basement. He likes the basement a lot. The isolation of it gives him silence from the world. He often has visions in here for the utter lack of distraction. And he often finds really good biographies, too. About real people— not just celebrities and hacks—who did historic things, like Dr. David Livingstone, the Scottish explorer who named the great falls in Zambia after the queen. Gus isn't a big fan of the British explorations in Africa, but that book was so damned well written, like a great novel.

He lets himself get lost for a while, loses track of where he is, what he's looking for; he stares at a book called *Sew, A Needle Pulling Thread: Life of a Hollywood Costume Designer*. He has absolutely no interest, but figures if Turning Pages has this obscure book, they should have what he's looking for.

He stops by the café and orders an exotically named coffee. Good buzz on the first sip. Then he goes to the customer service desk and asks about the book on desert artifacts. "It's a photo book," he tells the clerk. He sees her name on the tag attached to her blouse. *Joy*. Such an optimistic name. With a heavy burden. How can *Joy* ever be sad? And get away with it? Her smile is a knockout, he has to admit, not dopey and gaping but really smart and radiant. She's pretty, in a Whole Foods sort of way. Joy's skin is pale. Joy doesn't really have any breasts, which doesn't surprise Gus considering her tiny frame. She reminds him of a hatchling.

"Name?"

"Gus."

"I mean the book."

An instant heat rises to his face, and he musters a dopey smile of his own. "Right, of course." He pulls the notepaper from his pocket. "*Lens of Time: Artifacts from the Southwest*," he tells her.

She takes him to the photography section. They meander through two rows of stacks until Joy finds the book and removes it from the shelf. "Just one copy," she says. "Anything else?"

"There's another book that's out of print," Gus says. "I figure if I can get it anywhere, I can get it here. It's called *A History of Symbols.*" He gives her the scrap of paper.

She looks at Gus coyly. "I'll check for you," she tells him. Her eyes are green.

Gus feels a shiver. "Uh, I'll be over at the café going through this," he says, holding up the photo book.

"I'll find you there," she says.

He orders another cup of Lion Thunder African Hill, or something like that, and starts perusing. The images don't tell him much, and the text is limited, identifying only the artifact, the tribe, place of origin, and date. There is some explanation about how some pieces were used, like the carved wooden stick (a pipe for smoking), bowls of pottery (preparation of meals; no surprise there), and a small wooden tube and a stone dish (extracting dyes from berries and other desert growth). Gus flips to the index to see if there's an entry for *symbolism.* There isn't. He wonders if there actually exists some kind of very magical, very spiritual, very sacred symbolism that the tribes have simply chosen to keep to themselves. After all, from what Timothy Chase has learned from the professor at ASU, there doesn't seem to be some universal glossary of petroglyphs.

"*A History of Symbols* by Theodore Smith." It's Joy, standing over him.

"Oh," he says, looking up. "Thanks."

"We don't have it. We don't have a record of ever having it," she says grimly. "I'm sorry." She hands him the rumpled notepaper.

"No, no," he tells her. "Thanks for checking. Really, I appreciate it."

"You do know it was self-published."

"Yes."

"Which probably means it had very limited distribution. And it was a long time ago."

"Right."

"But I bet if you look it up on Amazon you can probably find someone trying to sell a used copy. These days Amazon has everything we don't."

She looks defeated, and all at once Gus Parker understands that she's a lover of books who stands witness to the digitalization of expression, the foreign code of binary numbers taking the breath out of imagery and storytelling. Those are her words, not his. He's sort of reading her mind.

"I can check Amazon if you'd like," she tells him.

That's the last thing she really wants to do, he knows. "That's very kind of you, but I can do that later myself," he says. And then he hears himself add, "Can I get you a cup of coffee?"

Her face turns red. She smiles and says, "I really don't get a break for a while. I have to get back to work."

"Okay," Gus tells her. "Maybe some other time."

"Maybe," she says and drifts away smoothly, gracefully, like a joyful muse looking for a suffering artist.

He scans through more pages of the photo book but gets an overwhelming sense that, while interesting and quite beautifully compiled, the collection of photos is not revealing anything of importance to him—nor is it provoking anything psychically. One curious thing does, however, catch his attention: a photo credit to Theodore Smith. He checks the notepaper again. Same name as the self-published author. He examines the photo. It's a photograph not of an artifact but rather of a painting of artifacts. Smith used the hues of clay as his canvas, and upon that canvas placed his crude rendition of artifacts (pottery, tools, weapons) and framed it all with symbols that evoked the petroglyphs of the desert. Gus can feel a huge smile emerge on his face, a tingling in his cheeks as if he just bit into something tart and tangy.

The caption reads, "*Desert Remains*, a painting by Theodore Smith. Photographed by Theodore Smith, 1956, Phoenix, AZ. Smith was a graduate student in fine arts at Arizona State University and donated this painting to the university collection upon receiving his master's."

Gus asks one of the café workers for a pen and makes some notes on the scrap paper, jotting down "1956. *Desert Remains*. Smith. ASU." And then he returns the book to the shelf and leaves.

22

"It's been a long time," Kelly Mills says, standing behind Alex and Trevor. "Thanks for doing this," she says with an earnest smile. "We'll have you over for dinner some night soon. Okay?"

"No problem," Gus tells her. "It's good to see you." He extends a hand to Trevor. "Hey, Trevor. What's happening?"

Trevor Mills ignores the hand and enters the house.

"Get back here," Alex snaps. "And shake the man's hand."

"That's okay," Gus whispers.

"It's not okay. Trevor?"

Trevor returns and shakes Gus's hand. "I don't need a babysitter," he says.

The kid has really grown up. It's been a few years since Gus has seen Alex's kid, and he looks like the years have been healthy. Trevor is muscle-bound and handsome, the prom king, the big man on campus, but the sneer on his face looks indelibly adolescent.

"I didn't offer to babysit," Gus tells him. "But I'm not going to bullshit you. If I were your mom and dad, I wouldn't be leaving you alone at home either . . . all things considered."

Trevor almost smiles but self-corrects by squaring his jaw and rolling his head until his neck pops and cracks. It's a pregame locker room gesture. Stoic for the sake of being stoic.

"He has tons of homework," Alex says. "He won't be a bother to you."

Gus looks at Alex and Kelly. "It's okay if he is. I don't mind the company."

"If he gets his work done you guys can toss a ball around," Alex suggests. "You got your football, kid?" he asks his son.

"It's in my backpack," Trevor replies. Then he turns around and struts into the living room.

His father calls to him. "In your backpack? With all your homework?"

"That's right, Detective," the kid yells back.

"Hey, you two enjoy your night," Gus tells the couple. "I'll make sure he gets dinner. Pizza okay?"

Kelly nods. "Really, Gus, you're doing us a huge favor. He'll eat whatever you put in front of him."

Gus walks them to their car. Alex ducks in, reaches for the compartment between the two front seats, and grabs a small cardboard box, then hands it to Gus.

"What's this?"

"Open it."

Gus lifts the top off and finds a gold pendant resting in a cloud of cotton. He pulls it up by the chain. "A lightning bolt?"

"From our last victim," Alex says in a stage whisper. "Go crazy."

Holding the lightning bolt in his hands, Gus watches as Alex and his wife drive off. Ivy barks a hefty good-bye.

"Let's go say hello to our guest," he tells the dog, stuffing the small box in his pocket.

They find Trevor sitting perfectly in the middle of the couch staring at the television. He has a book in his lap. Notebooks are scattered to his right; his football is tucked under his left arm. Two things are clear: no one is welcome to join him on the couch, and ESPN trumps homework.

"Whatcha reading?" Gus asks.

Trevor holds up the book and says nothing.

"*Great Expectations*? I love that book," Gus says. "You know, I think that is my book."

"Huh?" the kid mutters, his eyes unable to migrate from the television.

"Did you get that book from your father?"

Finally, Trevor turns, curls his lip, and says, "I guess. It's been on the bookshelf at home forever."

"Oh. I lent that to your dad a long time ago."

Trevor shrugs. "I'm reading it for English. Is it okay if I keep it for a while?"

Gus sits on the arm of the couch. "Yeah, sure. Of course."

"Thanks, man." Trevor turns back to the broadcast.

Gus says, "You're welcome." And then he asks, "Can you concentrate okay with the TV on?"

"I'm fine," he says.

He tells Trevor he'll be out back with Ivy if he needs anything. The kid nods as if he's hypnotized.

I don't know what the fuck I'd do if he were my kid, Gus tells himself as he ushers Ivy out to the pool. All these years Gus has longed to be a dad, thought he'd make a really great father, but now with this case study parked on his couch, he's not so sure. He probably wouldn't have the patience for it. Probably would be deeply wounded to watch a kid grow out of love with him. You know, one day they can't get enough of being thrown up in the air, and the next day you're threatening to throw them out of the house. Dogs on the other hand . . .

"Jump in if you want to jump in," he tells a tentative Ivy who wobbles at the edge of the swimming pool. She looks at him expectantly. "No. I'm not coming in tonight," he adds.

He pulls the small box out of his pocket and removes the gold chain and dangling pendant.

A strike of lightning.

He hears the crackle of electricity and the crash of a storm.

He imagines the gold shard against a black sky. He hears drumming, but maybe it's thunder. He hears music, but there is no music. Gus lowers himself to a lounger. He twirls the bolt, and then he lets it float like a pendulum. A list. A list! A list!! So many things come at him, a burst of visions in rapid-fire flashes.

A raging fire.

Rage in the eyes of the killer.

Green eyes.

A child screams, "Daddy!"

A woman goes down, her hands hitting stone, her head oozing blood.

Love, raging love.

Gus clenches his fists, but the bolt drops to the ground. He's breathing heavy. His heart is pounding, and his body is awash in sweat, cold sweat. What the fuck?

He stares at the pendant and tries to stare it down. Rarely does the psychic energy scare him. It scares him now. He feels a bubble of panic. Like a killer is close, watching him maybe, like if he doesn't act fast there will be blood and horror everywhere. A child screams, "Daddy! Daddy! Daddy!"

"Hey, Mr. Parker?"

Like whiplash to his brain, Gus snaps to attention. He turns and sees Trevor Mills standing in the frame of the slider. He rises. "What's up, Trevor?"

"I was just wondering if you have anything cold to drink."

"Of course."

Gus gives Trevor a choice from the refrigerator. The kid actually makes a play for a Heineken, but Gus simply says, "Seriously?" and Trevor removes a bottle of Aquafina instead.

"How are you coming along with your work?" he asks Trevor.

"All right."

"Let me know when you want dinner."

Trevor nods and returns to the couch. Gus calls Beatrice, tells her about the lightning bolt, and listens to the silence as she conjures up an answer. He hears the drumming again, but this time it's coming from her end of the call. He also hears the jangling of wind chimes. "Something is going on this weekend," she finally says. "From last night in Tucson to your lightning bolt tonight, I do think there's another murder happening in our desert."

"Yeah. So do I."

"The killer may be on to you," she says tonelessly.

Gus squints, as if the sun is in his eyes. "I don't see why or how."

"I don't know, Gus. You're in deep, as they say. It's all around you."

"That's reassuring," he says flippantly.

"Of course it is. It means you're close."

"Somehow I'm not sure. I went to the bookstore today. I think maybe I stumbled upon something. Probably an odd coincidence."

"We'll do some research together, Gus," she says. "You come over for dinner tomorrow night."

It's an instruction, not an invitation.

Later Gus finds Trevor asleep on the couch. He clears his throat, hoping to wake the kid. That doesn't work, so he snaps his fingers and directs Ivy to hop, which she does with a happy pounce upon the kid.

"What? What the f—" Trevor yelps. "What happened?"

"You fell asleep."

"Bored to death more like it."

"Hey, why don't you take a break? Let me order dinner, and while we're waiting we can toss the ball around."

The kid shrugs. "Whatever."

Gus dials Giovanni's and orders a pie with as much garbage as it will support. He leads the teenager out front.

Trevor is about to throw, his arm drawn back, his hand caressing the football, but he stops and says, "I didn't figure you for football."

"Oh. What exactly did you figure me for?"

Trevor laughs. "I don't know. Yoga."

Gus snickers. "Pass me the ball. You must be rusty."

"Why?"

"I heard you've been taken off the team."

Trevor whips the ball at him. Gus leaps and catches it, but he's stunned for a moment and so are his hands. *Damn, there is such rage.* Gus solidly and smoothly tosses the ball back. His hands are still tingling. Trevor catches it expertly. And starts to dash. "You gonna take me down?" the kid hollers.

"Uh, no. I don't tackle minors. If that's okay. . . ."

"C'mon, dude, my dad and I do it all the time."

"Right. And if he breaks your elbow no one's going to sue."

Trevor is running serpentine and doesn't stop. Instead he aims for Gus and brushes him. "Take the handoff," Trevor says.

Gus scoops the ball and cradles it tight against his abdomen. Trevor dashes on.

"What if I tackle you?" Trevor yells across the yard.

"I don't think so, Trevor. Let's just toss it around, okay?"

"Don't be a pussy, Gus."

Gus feels every muscle stiffen. "A what?"

"You heard me."

"I'm done." The ball spirals to Trevor.

"Aw, come on, man, I didn't mean it like that," Trevor calls, his pitch elevated.

Gus looks at his hands. Something isn't right.

The ball comes soaring back.

"I said we're done, Trevor."

He leaps anyway and catches the football high, tries to tug it to his waist, but loses his balance and falls to the grass. Clutching the ball, now, he sees everything.

"You okay?" Trevor calls.

He sees a locker room. The blackness behind the basement windows suggests to him it's night. There are voices of young men like Trevor. Only one of the hanging lights is lit, casting a yellow murky hue over two parallel benches where the boys sit opposite an older man. The man is wearing a cap. He's got small hands but a tight, strong grip on a wad of cash. The boys follow him outside.

Gus squeezes the ball tighter.

"Get up," Trevor shouts.

A trunk opens. A bale of pot is loaded. Then another. As if the boys are tossing luggage into the belly of an airplane. Their cargo is wrapped in blankets. Weighted with football helmets. The older man smiles. Pats one of the boys on the shoulder. The kid shrugs.

It's very late. Almost midnight.

The coach hands Trevor a beer.

The trunk slams shut. Tires peel out. The older man turns back to the gymnasium door.

Gus shakes his head vigorously, and the vision ceases. He rises from the ground.

He seals this knowledge. He protects even the nuance. He wants to ask, but he can't. He goes inside. Trevor follows. The food arrives, and they eat in abundant silence. Then Trevor returns to the couch.

Around 10:45 p.m. Gus hears the thud of a car door, then another. Two drum beats of relief.

"He's sleeping," Gus tells Alex and Kelly as they cross the threshold.

"Did he get any work done?" Kelly asks.

Gus bobbles his head and says, "I guess so. But he's been sleeping mostly since we ate."

"I'll wake him in a minute," Alex says. "But first I think you should know you were right about your client. He's a murderer."

Gus reaches for the wall to steady himself. "Are you kidding? Why didn't you call?"

"Because we didn't want to miss anything," Alex says. "We couldn't take our eyes off your client for a second."

Kelly laughs. So does Alex.

"What the hell?" Gus asks.

"I think we should talk," Alex tells him.

Gus leads them to his office. They sit on the futon opposite him. "Did you make an arrest?"

First Alex buries his face in his hands, takes a breath, and then looking squarely at Gus, he says, "Your client . . . is a murderer . . . on the stage!"

"What do you mean?"

"He means your client is playing a murderer," Kelly tells him. "That's his role in the play."

"Oh shit," Gus says, biting his lip, the heat of shame rising to his face.

"Oh yeah," Alex begins, "there's a very graphic scene where he kills his mother, then his girlfriend. He goes totally fucking insane, and he murders them both. You had a good vibe about Gary Potter. That is to say his character. The one he's playing."

Then Alex laughs again.

"Well, you know," Gus says, searching the room, his gaze sweeping as if he's looking for salient clues, "it's possible that he's taking his murder cues from the play. Maybe the part he's playing is the perfect fit." Gus knows he sounds as if he's amateurishly building a case, but he keeps climbing, keeps digging his way out. "I mean, maybe he got so immersed in his character that it made him a killer."

"You're not serious, are you?" Alex asks. "This is no slight to you, man. You really did see him kill people. But you really saw him do it as an actor. In a play."

"So that's it?" Gus asks.

"Well, he left the theater pretty quick after the show was over. I got his license plate. We'll run it. Give him a basic check. Just to rule it out. And to satisfy your psychic hunches."

Kelly play punches her husband. "Don't be an asshole, Alex." Then to Gus, "We really, really enjoyed the night out. We needed it. We owe you."

Gus says nothing. Just stares at them.

"Let me go wake Trev," she says.

"No." Gus stops her. "No wait."

Alex raises an eyebrow.

"I need to tell you something," Gus says. "Tonight was very portentous."

Alex smiles. "Big word."

"I had a ton of visions. A ton. There's going to be another murder real soon. Maybe tonight. Maybe tomorrow. But it's imminent. I think I should meet with you and Chase in the morning. If we put our heads together I'm almost sure we can catch the guy in the act."

Kelly sighs.

"Well maybe not in the act," Gus concedes. "But close to the scene."

"With all due respect, Gus. I really need Alex to spend some time with Trevor tomorrow," Kelly tells him. "I want Sundays to be their time."

Gus hesitates. There is not a sound, save for the low murmur of the manly men of ESPN in the other room. They're debating an NBA trade with all the gravity of a UN Security Council resolution. Gus shakes his head and notices that Alex notices the awkward silence between them. Kelly interjects with a smile, and, just as she's about to say something, Gus says, "Yes, and then there's Trevor."

Both of them look chilled.

"We tossed a football around earlier," he tells them.

"He's good," Kelly says.

Gus speaks with no inflection. "The marijuana is coming from the school."

Alex opens his hands and says, "We kind of figured that considering what Trevor has admitted so far."

"I mean it's coming from somebody at the school. Not another student," Gus explains. "I think Trevor may be getting it from his coach."

Kelly gulps. The sound is a cross between a laugh and that first heave of vomit.

"Gus, really," Alex says. "That's a bit of a leap."

Gus describes his vision. He describes the image of the coach.

They listen intently, their eyes like bulbs of surprise.

Trevor shuffles into the room. "Mom? Dad? When did you get back?"

"Just a few minutes ago, honey," Kelly tells her son. "You go wait for us in the other room. We'll be ready in a minute. Get your stuff together."

He yawns, shrugs, and retreats to the living room.

"I don't know what to say," Alex says. "I want to take you seriously, dude. But you did just mix up an actor and a murderer. Not very psychic."

Gus winces and says, "Thanks a lot."

"I'm sorry," Alex says. "That came out wrong."

Gus doesn't respond.

"But thanks for sharing that," Alex tells him. "Of course, it's worth investigating. Of course it is." He then turns to his wife. "It's not out of the realm."

"No," she says. "It's not."

"But I can't be the one to investigate. Nor would I be," Alex says. "Drennon in Narcotics has always been a close friend. I'll go to him."

Gus watches as Alex rises, extends his hand to his wife, and leads her from the room. He doesn't move. He listens as they gather their son, the sound of a family configuring itself. He hears them approach the front door. Alex ducks his head in the office door and says, "Thanks, Gus."

The night is so quiet after the family departs, just still and muted. He sits there for a moment pondering the silence, then pondering himself, which breaks the silence with loathing and doubt. How had he been so wrong about Gary Potter? How had he so monumentally fucked up? His embarrassment onstage for all the world to see. *That's right, Gus, go for your own jugular, your own catastrophe. Pile it on. You do this so well.* He curls up on the futon and lets himself be eaten alive, cannibalized by failure. Overinflated as it might be, the failure consumes him, digit by digit, first his fingers, then his toes, then his ears, then his chin. Then it smacks him in the face. But that's it. He'll just stop. He'll turn it off and turn away. He'll never do this again. He'll ignore the intuition. He'll take drugs to make the visions go away. He'll do whatever it takes to see only what he sees and nothing beyond what he sees. That can't be too much to ask. Then he hears a woman singing, somewhere in the distance. Outside, in the night? In his house? In his dreams? She's singing out there about her own angst as if to say, *I get you, Gus,* but he's done searching for the unexplained. Is she real? Is she a vision? He doesn't give a shit. He drags himself off the futon and stumbles to his bedroom.

23

He doesn't hear from Alex Mills at all on Sunday. Just like that. Alex has gone dark. Gus wonders if he is recanting their partnership, what with the Gary Potter screwup; he's not sure, doesn't want to speculate, but he's anxious because he suspects something is going down today and he's being shut out. He's slept off his self-indulgent madness, as he always does, though he's aware that this time the wipeout was more profound than usual.

He takes Ivy for a very long walk. "Thanks for the exercise," he tells his dog. As usual after a psychic meltdown, he's reconciled himself to himself. Maybe it was that woman singing, maybe it was sleep, maybe it was the kale and pineapple yogurt smoothie he made this morning and gulped down like a champion, but it's just a different freaking day, and that's enough for now. As if to reaffirm and reconnect, he's carrying with him the lightning bolt. He has the leash clutched in one hand, the pendant in the other. If anything, he feels a vibration from the dog, not the bolt. This animal is a smart animal, and this animal is connected to the inner Gus, to that extra realm that sees things no one else can see. It's like Ivy is saying, *Don't worry, buddy, I get it, you're not alone.* Gus smiles and laughs to himself. *This is what it has come to. My easiest communication is with my dog.*

Then he hears, "Daddy, daddy, daddy!" And it's not the Golden Retriever.

He listens intently. But he hears nothing more. He smells smoke.

He surveys the neighborhood, scanning for signs of life. A dad, maybe, working a grill with his son, steaming hot dogs or grilling burgers. He spies into backyards. Nothing. No father. No child.

Across town a father is tossing a football with his son.

"That arm of yours is getting too strong, if that's possible."

Trevor doesn't respond. He just smirks.

"I'm almost worn out, Trev."

"C'mon, Dad, we've only been out here for twenty minutes."

Mills wipes his brow and squints into the sun. "Damn. I'm really out of shape."

He runs and leaps for the ball. Snags it. *Dear Lord, my kid is going to kill me.*

"Hey, throw it real long, Dad."

Mills pulls back the ball, feels the shoulder and elbow flex, and flings the ball past his son. Trevor runs. Trevor leaps. Mills is on him as the ball snaps against the kid's chest. They tussle. They throw their weight. They both tumble to the ground.

"That would've been a foul, Dad," his son says, catching his breath.

"Tell it to the coach," Mills replies.

"Get off me."

"All right, already."

"Jesus, Dad. This is a friendly game."

Mills rolls over on his back, looks up to the sky, and takes in the expanse of Arizona blue. Screaming, perfect daylight. As if to taunt him, it's a perfect day for everything that isn't. Sure, he's come out to play, but the two of them, father and son, are tossing back frustration and anger, resentment and rancor, and nothing seems to be mitigating that, no joy of game, no zesty endorphins as they reach, toss, rush, as they crash to the ground. There's no relief.

Trevor begins to rise.

"Wait," Mills tells his son. "If this is a friendly game, let me talk to you as a friend."

The kid snorts.

"I'm serious, Trevor. I want you to know that whatever is going on with those drugs, the truth will come out. I'd rather hear it from you, but if we have to wait for investigators to uncover the truth, that's fine because this whole dirty business is going down. You understand me?"

"Doesn't sound like a friend to me," Trevor hisses.

"That's because it's hard for a dad to shut off the dad speech. But objectively speaking, Trevor, you're just the tip of the iceberg. You're not some hotshot football player living a double life. That's something you see on HBO. You're in this at the bottom. There's no cartel here. No glory. And it doesn't make you more interesting."

Mills is still looking at the sky, worshipping something about infinity and scale.

"So now you're a psychologist?" his son says with a smirk.

Mills rolls to his side and pulls Trevor by the collar of his T-shirt. Now their faces are inches apart. "Let me tell you something, Trevor, the truth is going to come out before this case makes it to trial. We will never let this thing go to trial. So if you're planning some kind of reality TV moment, forget about it. You're forgetting what I do for a living."

"I know what you do for a living."

Mills gets up. "I know, I know, Trevor. You're rebelling because your life has been so fucking hard having a cop for a father. Look at you, the poor kid who can never fuck up. Can't act like the others, has to live to a higher standard. Trust me, I know what it's like. But I respected my father for everything he did."

A teenage sigh. "Why do you still have a problem with me, Dad? They dropped most of the charges."

"I still have a problem with you because most isn't enough. If you tell the whole story, Trevor, they'll take it in exchange for immunity."

"Maybe I don't know the *whole story*," he says, his tone mimicking.

They're still inches apart, and now Mills grabs his kid by the chin. "You're smart, you're talented, you could go to any college on a scholarship," he tells his son. "Probably a football scholarship. Why would you throw all that away? No one will touch you, Trevor. No one will ever take a chance on you if this thing goes to trial."

"I think you're more worried about your reputation than mine."

"Really? Is that the kind of man you think I am? The kind of father who raised you?"

"I don't know."

"You don't know?"

Trevor says nothing.

"Jesus Christ, Trevor. I will only ever want the best for you even if you have no idea what the best for you means."

Trevor looks away and says, "Just so you know, I do respect you, Dad."

Then, with a hesitant nod, Mills turns and walks into the house.

After a nap, Gus heads over to Paradise Valley to have dinner with Beatrice. She opens the door, and he can immediately envision a hearty dinner; the house is steaming with flavor.

"What are you cooking?"

"Vegetarian lasagna. Nothing special."

"It smells very special."

She smiles. "I'm trying out some new spices. I'm also making my own dressing for the salad. You like cactus?"

"Surprise me."

Over dinner he tells her more about the gold lightning bolt.

"That vision of fire has been consistent," she says.

"And the kid screaming. . . ."

She piles more lasagna on his plate. "Delicious," he whispers.

"Do you have the pendant with you?" she asks.

Gus nods.

After dinner, while Gus cleans up and stacks the dishes, Beatrice leans against the counter with the bolt in her hand and closes her eyes.

"You slept with that guy from Safeway. Didn't you?" he asks.

"Yes. I did. Now shush. I'm concentrating."

"And I think there's a murder this weekend."

"Silence!"

Gus goes quiet. He suds up the silverware and listens to it squeak between his fingers. Off in the distance a hawk calls out to the valley. It's a lone call of authority, like a father or a coach.

"I don't hear a child," she says, her voice cooing like a songbird.

Gus watches her intently.

"But I do see smoke."

"Where there's smoke . . ." he says.

She shakes her head. He shuts up.

Then she opens her eyes. "You're losing confidence, Gus," she tells him.

"Huh?"

"I guess the biggest sign I get from this lightning bolt is about you."

"Oh?"

"Gus Parker, you really need to believe."

He laughs bitterly. "Believe? In what? I'm not feeling very task oriented."

She gives him a look, like a teacher on the receiving end of bullshit. "What does that mean?"

"It means I don't feel close to a suspect in these murders. It's been days and days, Beatrice, and all I'm getting are vague nuances. I don't think I'm misfiring. I just don't think I'm firing enough."

"We all get into slumps."

"I'm not in a slump."

"What does the suspect look like?"

"That's the thing. I don't know. I don't have a face. I should have a face by now. I should have the kind of face that I would identify lingering around a crime scene. I think this guy is watching. I know he's watching."

"You think he's coming to the crime scenes and observing police work?"

Gus stuffs his hands in his pockets. "Yeah, I do. But that's not psychic. That's just basic criminology."

"Not necessarily," she says. "Come sit."

He follows her to the big living room, the cube of glass that looks to the neck of Camelback. She drops to a sleek leather chaise and tucks her feet beneath her. Gus pulls an ottoman close and sits.

"You're just not really listening to yourself," she tells him. "If you feel this guy is at the murder scenes, you need to focus there. But you're not. You are looking too far afield. You're looking for his history, but his history doesn't mean anything unless you indulge that physical vibe about him. You have to concentrate on his presence. Let the detectives tell you about his history."

He nods and says, "I guess that means you're not interested in the history of the petroglyphs or the research we were going to do tonight."

She sits up. "Oh, no. That's not what I said."

Now they're sitting at her computer. Gus is Googling *A History of Symbols* and Theodore Smith.

With speed that defies logic but defines the Google generation, 283,000 results appear in .26 seconds.

There are, apparently, quite a few Theodore Smiths in the world.

But only one who has written *A History of Symbols*.

Beatrice scans the page of blue links. They read like headlines. For the most part they're articles about Smith's book.

"Self-published," Beatrice reads. "In 1973."

"He got a lot of press for someone who couldn't find a publisher."

"He was a known artist," she says. "Apparently."

They click on several articles. The actual headlines are not kind.

"Look at this," Beatrice says. "'Local Artist Writes Fantasy as Facts,' 'Author Invents His Way through Symbolism,' 'His Story of Symbolism Symbolizes Nothing.'"

Gus is scrolling down and reading with her. "'Theodore Smith Fakes Archeology Credentials,' 'Symbolism of a Raving Lunatic.' That must have hurt," Gus says. "Reviewers then were meaner than they are today."

"These aren't just reviews," Beatrice tells him. "I think they're articles about the book. Like there was some kind of investigation to expose him as a fraud."

"Right up your alley."

She nods, then continues to read. "I sure wish I could get my hands on a copy."

"Unlikely," Gus tells her. "It's out of print. No surprise there."

After another click, Gus lunges his head forward, as if he needs a closer look. "Jesus," he whispers.

"What?"

"Jesus Christy Christ!"

Beatrice pulls him softly back.

"What is it?" she asks.

"Maybe another reason his book is out of print."

Beatrice reads.

LOCAL MAN KILLED IN BEACH HOUSE TRAGEDY

Theodore Smith, 40, perished in a house fire late last night at his summer home in Cape Cod, Massachusetts, authorities said. Smith, a 1955 graduate of Arizona State University, was a lifelong resident of Phoenix.

The Massachusetts State Police told the *Arizona Republic* that there are few details of Smith's death at this time. Smith's wife, Priscilla, survived the blaze. The couple's seven-year-old son, Theodore Jr., has not been accounted for.

Smith was the author of the recently self-published and controversial book, *A History of Symbolism*, which claims to interpret cultural symbols through the ages. Of particular interest to those here in Arizona are his statements about desert artifacts and petroglyphs, which are widely regarded as erroneous if not outright falsehoods. His work was disputed by archeologists, historians, members of the Native American community, and even journalists here at the *Republic*. Smith had no known occupation at the time of his death, but sources say he was mainly an artist and his work had sold well at area art festivals.

"I knew it!"

"The fire?"

"Not just the fire, Beatrice! The house, Cape Cod, the seashore. All things I saw at the first crime scene."

Her hands are on his shoulders. She squeezes. "And you had the audacity to doubt yourself."

He allows himself a laugh, but he is braced with intensity. "I've been seeing the fire ever since. It's a persistent image. A relentless vision. Whether I'm at a crime scene or just holding that necklace, it's all around me."

"A seven-year-old boy," Beatrice recites. "Your screaming child?"

"I know. I know. I know. I don't know," Gus sputters. He shakes his head. "I don't know. Too many convulsions."

"Convulsions?"

"I'm describing my brain."

"Are you conjuring anything?"

"Nothing."

"Okay, then," she says, "let's just study this. The article was written in 1973. That means Smith died the year his book was published."

"Humiliated to death?"

"Not funny," Beatrice says.

"But it could be a suicide."

"Could be," she concedes.

"There must be some other reports about his death. I'm sure the *Arizona Republic* followed this very closely. And obviously the press in Massachusetts, too."

"Unless it was something benign like a kitchen fire."

"A missing kid, Beatrice. A missing kid is not a kitchen fire."

"Right," she says. "Let's Google 'Theodore Smith' and 'death,'" she tells Gus.

There are 330,000 results in .22 seconds.

"Shit," Gus says. "It was a kitchen fire, all right. Mr. Smith was toasted like a sesame seed bagel."

"By his wife, apparently," Beatrice utters softly.

SMITH DEATH WAS LIKELY MURDER, POLICE REPORT
Massachusetts Authorities Say Fatal Fire May Be the Result of Spousal Issues

Priscilla Smith, 27, is being questioned about the death of her husband Theodore, 40, after their summer home was engulfed in flames four days ago, according to investigators. The couple and their seven-year-old son were on their yearly break from Arizona's desert heat when tragedy struck in the small Cape Cod town of Chatham. Their son is believed to have perished in the blaze along with Theodore Sr., according to State Fire Marshal Patrick O'Leary. "Right now this looks like a case of arson," O'Leary told reporters. "We, of course, are looking for a suspect."

"There's no way she did it," said Margaret Shanley, a Chatham neighbor. "She was the nicest person in the world. She was so quiet, so unassuming."

John Lafferty, another neighbor, disagreed. "I always heard lots of fighting coming from that house. Like clockwork. Every summer. You see, we're year-round people. Summer officially starts when the Smiths start screaming."

Authorities said they were following leads about spousal problems. "We have some leads and mounting evidence that this was not a happy marriage," said Lieutenant Detective Paul Kalowich of the Massachusetts State Police. "If the fire marshal tells us he's thinking arson, we start talking to the wife. Perfectly routine," he added.

No one in official capacity would speak to the *Republic* about the whereabouts of the son.

Gus and Beatrice keep searching and reading and scrolling and searching.

Beatrice excuses herself to pee, and when she returns Gus gets a whiff of something spicy and rich. "Did you light up incense on your way back?"

"Nag Champa."

"Oh."

"Gus, you haven't had sex lately."

He says nothing.

"Gus?"

"What?"

"Sex. What's up with you?"

"Nothing."

"Not interested?"

"Look, Beatrice, I'm over forty. My libido has matured."

"I know you don't think the way most straight guys think, but you do need to get laid."

"Are you having a vision?"

"You're still haunted by your marriage, but there's a woman out there who wants you."

He smiles. "Anyone specific?"

"Not yet," she says. "I'll keep you posted. But you should know that plenty of women want you, Gus. You just have to be at the right place at the right time."

"Sounds like I'm looking for a job."

"No," she says. "You're doing a wonderful job right now. Look there," she tells him, pointing to the computer screen, "the wife was arrested."

PRISCILLA SMITH CHARGED
IN HUSBAND'S DEATH
Prosecutors Say Wife of Eccentric Artist
Started Fire That Killed Him

Authorities in Massachusetts have arrested and charged Priscilla Smith, 27, with the murder of her 40-year-old husband, Theodore. The arrest comes two weeks after the Smiths' summer home in Chatham was destroyed by fire. Mrs. Smith has also been charged with arson in the case.

"Traces of an accelerant were found on Mrs. Smith's fingernails and dress," explained Lieutenant Detective Paul Kalowich of the Massachusetts State Police. Kalowich said the wife had waited for her husband to go to sleep for the night before she torched the home. No motive is known at this time.

The Smiths were parents to seven-year-old Theodore Jr. His body has not been recovered from the scene, and his whereabouts are unknown. "We believe his body may have been burned beyond recognition," Kalowich said. "This house was incinerated. We were able to identify Mr. Smith because when the fire woke him up, he apparently tried to escape through an upper-story window and fell to his death on the lawn below."

Lawyers assigned to defend Mrs. Smith had no comment.

Theodore Smith and his family lived mostly in Phoenix, Arizona, where he was known as a local artist and author of the recently self-published book, *A History of Symbols*.

"You'd think they'd have some forensic evidence from the little boy," Gus says.

"You would think," Beatrice concurs, "but you'd be assuming that investigators had the same kind of forensic technology that they do today."

"Even so, there should still be some trace of him," Gus says. "I just don't get this."

"I know," Beatrice whispers, as though they're working a top secret case. "Why would a woman let her child die in a house fire?"

"That too."

"What else?"

"I can't figure out the connection to the serial killings," he replies. "And who's to say if there even is one?"

"You need to look deeper."

"I don't know," he says.

"Well, let's see," she says, and Gus senses a patronizing inflection in her voice. "You saw a fire. We found a fire. A fire that killed the author of *A History of Symbols*. The family lived in Phoenix. Theodore Smith had an interest in petroglyphs, for whatever reason. Of course, there's a connection. It may not be connected specifically to the killer. But it may be connected to more evidence, a true lead. Remember, as I always say—"

"No coincidences."

"I bet this case is legend in Massachusetts," Beatrice says. "I think you should ask Detective Mills to investigate further. In the meantime Google 'Priscilla Smith trial.'"

Gus complies.

"Yikes," he says.

There are 299,000 results in .18 seconds.

He clicks on an article from the *Boston Globe*. It's dated June 27, 1974.

PRISCILLA SMITH TRIAL BEGINS
Smith Says She Murdered Husband in Self-Defense

Priscilla Smith, 28, went on trial yesterday for the murder of her husband, Theodore. In opening statements, Smith's attorney, Kelvin Kennedy, told the jury that his client was a battered wife who was desperate to do something to stop the abuse. "Theodore Smith had physically and emotionally abused Mrs. Smith since she was a bride at the age of seventeen," Kennedy told the jury. "With a full heart, she tried everything she could to save the marriage."

According to Kennedy, Theodore Smith had also been abusing the couple's only child, Theodore Jr. "Theodore was a vicious man, hiding behind his affinity for art. But that affinity was really part of his pathology as we will show in this case. You will see graphic, horrific examples of the wounds sustained by his wife."

Prosecutors, however, called Smith a cold-blooded killer, who was embarrassed by her husband's eccentricity and public humiliations. "She wanted to be rid of him. She wanted to deny any association. She did not believe in divorce. But she believed in murder," District Attorney Stephen Pastorelli told the jury of six men and six women.

Pastorelli hammered on about the humiliation the family suffered after the publication of Theodore Smith's controversial book,

A History of Symbols. "Priscilla Smith couldn't handle it. She was shunned by neighbors, by family. Even her little boy tried to run away. She thought murder was the solution to their problem."

For a moment yesterday afternoon, the courtroom was rocked by the bombshell statement that Priscilla Smith would be on trial for double homicide if only the body of her son had been recovered. Kennedy leapt to his feet with objection. Judge Marcus St. George quickly sustained the objection.

The first witness, likely State Fire Marshal Patrick O'Leary, will be called to the stand today.

"This certainly adds a whole new spin to the case," Gus says.

"It does. I've sensed domestic abuse all along," Beatrice says softly. "But, you know what? None of these search results says anything about a verdict. Keep scrolling, honey. Looks like we have several more pages to go through."

Gus sighs a huge, canyon-sized sigh, stretches his arms over his head, and says, "I'd love to, but I'm exhausted. It's getting late. I need to get home."

Then Beatrice whips her face into his and says, "How could you not want to know how this thing turns out?"

"I can wait," he assures her. "I like a good cliffhanger."

"I don't," she says. "We're probably only one click away from finding out."

"But I'm stumped," he retorts. "Frankly, I don't want to go any deeper with this until I get a sense of context. Where it all fits."

"I know what context means, Gus."

Admonished, he shrugs and scrolls. He goes to the next page. Scrolls there, too.

"This is better than searching through microfiche," Beatrice says. "Remember that?"

"No."

She tugs his ear. "Of course you do. I'm not that old."

"Yes you are," he tells her. "I'm just amazed all this stuff has been digitized."

He clicks on a *Boston Globe* article dated July 18, 1974. He reads the headline aloud: "'Smith Found Guilty in Husband's Death, Life in Jail.'"

He and Beatrice soak in the article.

"Wow," Beatrice says. "First-degree murder with malice aforethought. Automatic life sentence without possibility of parole."

"So, I guess we know where to find Priscilla Smith."

"If she's still alive. I don't see how anyone could survive that long behind bars. She has to be in her sixties or seventies."

Gus Googles "Priscilla Smith jail."

"Now you're just humoring me," Beatrice says.

"It's working," he retorts.

The results are fast but inaccurate. They see stories about jails in Smith County, Arkansas. Stories about jails in Smithfield, Virginia. And a clip from a bondage movie called *Priscilla's Jail*.

"Well of all things," Beatrice says. "There's a movie for everyone."

"I think I know what the problem is," Gus tells her. "She was probably sentenced to state prison, not jail. There is a difference."

"Oh, please," she begs. "Do you think Google would really know the difference?"

"I do. And it does."

He types in "Priscilla Smith prison."

There are 249,000 results in .20 seconds.

They stare. Scan the screen. Gus swallows hard.

He points to a headline. "This was written just a month ago!"

"I see it. I see it, Gus."

PRISCILLA SMITH GRANTED CLEMENCY, LEAVES PRISON

(Framingham)—Priscilla Smith, 67, convicted of first-degree murder in the death of her husband nearly 40 years ago, left MCI-Framingham last night to rousing applause of supporters outside.

Smith's release follows in the footsteps of the famous "Framingham Eight" case of the early 1990s when the state first recognized battered woman syndrome as a murder defense and commuted the sentences of seven of the women who had argued that they should have been allowed to present evidence of battered woman syndrome during their trials. Smith originally petitioned for clemency in 1991 and was denied. She had brought her case before the board several times since. "We applaud the State and welcome the release of Priscilla Smith with open arms," said Lila Jackson of the Battered Women's Clemency Project.

Smith was found guilty in 1974 in the arson-related death of her husband, Theodore Smith, after she burned down their Cape Cod summer home. Mr. Smith died trying to escape. Their son vanished at the time of the crime and was first thought to have perished in the fire. Due to a lack of evidence, however, the State declined to prosecute Smith in connection with her son's disappearance. His whereabouts remain a mystery today. Smith did not have much to say to the media outside the prison last night. "I cannot and will not discuss my son. Let me just state that I am grateful to be free, grateful to all the women who supported me. My freedom is overdue."

"No current member of the parole board was a member back in 1991," said attorney Martha Higgins. "So I can't say that we know why her original petition was denied. We do know subsequent petitions were denied because there was no evidence that Mrs. Smith actually acted in self-defense at the time the fire was started. Various members of the board had a hard time connecting the dots over the years. Had it not been for the advocacy of several women's rights groups, the board might not have truly understood the motivation and impetus of Mrs. Smith's crimes. The State has become, over the years, duly enlightened to the plight of battered women."

The District Attorney's Office was not available for comment.

Smith told reporters that her immediate plans were not clear. "I would like to work on behalf of battered women. But I'm headed back to Arizona. That is my true home."

Gus sits back and studies the screen. He sees Beatrice scanning the article again. His intuition is all over the place. He feels its pulse quickening. He clicks back to the search results, and there it is: a one-paragraph story in the *Daily Courier*, reporting that Priscilla Smith, paroled murderer and arsonist, had been spotted in Prescott. A few townspeople quoted in the article said she's come back to Arizona to be with her sister who lives in Yavapai County.

Beatrice waves her hands in front of the computer. She's deep in ritual.

"I don't know. I don't know," she says. "I feel a connection. I really do."

Gus nods.

"And you?" she asks.

"Yes. I think so."

"Do you *see* it though? Do you *see* the connection?"

"No," Gus replies. "I don't see it. But I don't think it's that complicated. In purely detective terms, if the story of Theodore Smith is linked somehow to these murders, then the timing is no accident. You don't need to be a psychic to figure that out."

"Her release from jail practically coincides with a string of murders that are begging for symbolism."

"Something like that," Gus says.

He hits Print, and all the articles start surfing out of the machine.

"You do have to share this with the detectives."

Gus gets up. He backs into the kitchen, grabs his cell phone from the counter, and dials Alex Mills.

Voice mail. He leaves a message. "You have to hear about this. Call me."

Beatrice is still staring at one of the articles.

"I'm waiting for it to speak to me," she says. "It has to. It must."

Gus understands exactly what she means. "It's like my intuition is ready to dive off a cliff," he tells her.

"Take me with you."

He tells her he will.

24

The light is on in the hallway bathroom. Gus doesn't remember leaving it on, nor turning it off. He doesn't care. All he wants is sleep. He has to work in the morning. His shift starts at 7:00 a.m. He has to be in at six thirty. His yawn is a quiet howl. He inventories the workday to come. MRIs. There will be back pain, lots of back pain; there will be explorations of the spine, from disk to disk. There will be headaches and surveys for tumors. And shoulder pain. And neck pain. And there will be cancer patients. They will come to see how their disease has progressed. Maybe he'll intuit something in a mass of tissue and spidery fibers. Maybe he'll see another rope. Or maybe he'll just watch and see nothing. He knows he won't be able to take his mind off Theodore Smith.

A candle flickers in the living room. He knows he didn't leave a candle lit. He scans the kitchen, then the living room; there's no sign of anything being disturbed. Ivy is sleeping in the corner singing a few melodious snores. His home is utterly quiet. Beautiful, but mysterious. Who lit the candle? Someone has been here. Or someone is here.

It's not a psychic hunch. It's just a hunch. He bounds for the bedroom, flips the switch, the overhead light goes on, and he's speechless. He can't utter a word. Not even a groan. There she is splayed across the bed. There she is completely naked. There she is with flaming orange hair, pubic hair to match. With chopsticks twirled into her fiery tresses high up on her head. Heavy eye makeup, smudgy, her body limp.

"Welcome home," says Bridget Mulroney. "Did you have a good day?"

He stands there trying to interpret the hair color. Why so drastic?

And yet as he tries to fathom the fiery hair, he knows he is not trying to grasp anything in particular; rather he is doing what he can to avoid the obvious monster in the room: the vagina of a clown, the vagina of a crazy woman.

Gus Parker is sweating.

"You don't look happy to see me," Bridget says. "And that makes me sad."

"Bridget, get out of my house."

The woman has not broken her pose. Her porcelain breasts have not shifted, or jiggled, or bounced. "You don't mean that," she whimpers.

"Seriously? Do you know how much shit you're in now that you've broken into my house twice?"

He backs himself away, shuffling toward the door.

"I didn't break in," she tells him.

"Of course you did."

"No," she insists. "The other day when I was here I grabbed one of your keys and made a copy. So technically I did not break in tonight. I hope that clears things up so you can take off those clothes of yours and stuff your manhood deep inside me."

Gus sputters.

"Don't be so shy," the intruder says.

"Bridget, I think you need help. I don't really know what you want. But I think you need help."

She sits up but spreads her legs even wider. The chopsticks wobble on her head. "I'll tell you what I want, Gus Parker. I want you to come over here and fuck me like I'm your precious geisha slut."

He shakes his head. "What did you just say?"

"You heard me, Gus Parker. Get in bed and fuck me like I'm your precious geisha slut. It's my fantasy."

"It's . . . disgusting. It's . . . so . . . I don't know . . . insane."

"You will come to love my fantasies."

"I don't think that's possible."

She clutches one of the chopsticks from her head and flings it at him. "Fuck your geisha and fuck her now. Damn you!"

"Look at you," Gus says. "You're not only insane, but you sound like a freakin' racist. And I don't find that attractive."

"I love the Far East."

"This has nothing to do with the Far East."

"It's a Far Eastern tradition."

This kind of reasoning is going nowhere. "Bridget, if you leave now, and you leave quietly, I promise to keep this between us," he says.

But she doesn't leave. And she isn't quiet. "Who is she?" she howls. "You have a girlfriend, don't you?"

Gus says nothing. He considers sex as a tactic. What if he just fucks her and sends her home? Will that be the end of it? He spies her nakedness. There's nothing stopping him. After all, Beatrice was just having visions of him getting laid. And here is Bridget Mulroney, her legs spread wide, her entry like a canyon, every detail of it in his face—like porn in IMAX. But he is just too repulsed to be aroused. Not even the slightest stirring in his groin.

"Who is she?" Bridget screams again. "Do I know her? Where does she live? Where do you fuck her? I need to know, Gus Parker."

"Lord, Jesus, have mercy on me," Gus cries, feeling nothing religious in particular, just a larger-than-life desperation.

And then she pulls the bedside lamp down to her lap, aims the halo of light on her female parts. "Look at it," she demands. "Look at it!"

"Bridget, really . . ."

Gus is drawn to her naked crotch again; as much as he'd like to, he can't break away, for in a flash, he sees something there: he sees one man and another, and another, and another. He sees Bridget stifling tears, her eyes closed, her legs spread. A man is slamming at her. A man with tons of flesh.

"You fucked Clayman Tarpo? You fucked the sheriff? What the hell is that about?"

Suddenly modest, she puts her hands to her chest and lunges for the blankets. She slams up against the headboard. "What did you say?" she cries.

"I'm having a vision of you getting fucked by Sheriff Tarpo."

"Oh my God. No. You can't know that."

"Then it's true?"

She swipes the lamp, and it crashes to the floor. The bulb blinks off, then on again. The woman gasps for air. She seems on the verge of hyperventilating when Gus steps forward, extending a hand.

"No. No!" she fires at him. "Who told you Tarpo fucked me? Who told you?"

Gus lowers his head and stares at the floor. "No one told me, Bridget. I just know."

"Right," she says bitterly. "Because you're a fucking psychic. One look at my twat and you know my life story. Fine, then. Yeah, the sheriff fucked me. And so did the superintendent and so did the head of the school committee. And so did the president of American Bank, and the head of the airport authority, the CEO of Valley Computers, the pastor of Valley Church United . . . and the list goes on, Gus Parker!"

"Really, Bridget—"

"How do you think my father won all those construction bids? Huh? How do you think he made his millions?"

Gus is horrified, his mouth agape. A chill rushes down his spine. He is thinking a thousand thoughts, a raceway of questions, but he can't say anything. He doesn't doubt her; there is no doubt. With great certainty he sees her life as the torture she has described; he sees the men. He sees the money, the machinery, the cranes, the ribbon cuttings, the suits, the ties, the champagne bursting; the images are flashing at him like a life coming to an end.

"My cunt built schools, jails, office towers, banks, terminals, churches! You name it, my cunt built it. There should be a monument to my cunt in the middle of Phoenix."

She's not crying. She's laughing hysterically.

Gus approaches to lift the lamp.

Bridget gets up and charges him. Bridget Mulroney is very strong. She flattens him against the wall. He pushes back. "Look, Parker, are you forgetting that you are the one who came forward to save me?"

"Say what?"

"I thought so! First you want to meet me with the pretense that I'm in danger. And now you want to cast me aside like some kind of geisha slut. After everything you know now?"

Spit lands on his face.

He takes a deep breath. "All I did was warn you that the killer might be stalking you," he says slowly, carefully. "I had no idea about the rest of this. But now it makes sense."

"What does?"

"That this is the only way you know how to operate. What happened to you defined you."

"You're a genius."

"I think I sensed this all along, Bridget," he says tentatively. "You weren't flirting with me when we met. You weren't coming on to me. You were begging me to see your life. You do need someone to rescue you. You've known it all along. And now I know it, too."

He's out of breath.

Bridget leans an elbow into his chest. "Well, now I have a vision for you, Gus Parker. I envision you going down. And I don't mean on me where you might have enjoyed it." She laughs. "Where you *would* have enjoyed it. No, I see you going down. I see you falling from grace. And I don't see you ever getting back up again."

"Is there any way I can help you? That's all I want to know," he says. The sympathy is warming his chest, flooding him.

"Rescue me, you mean? Your words, not mine."

"I don't know how to do that," he admits. "But I can help you put the past where it belongs."

She laughs. Her eyes are on fire. "You can't do a damn thing for me. I hope the sedative wears off soon."

"Sedative?"

She smiles wickedly. "Oh, I'm sorry. Didn't you notice how deeply your mutt was sleeping on the couch?"

It takes a moment. And then he says, "Ivy? You gave her a sedative?"

"I didn't want our fucking to be interrupted," she tells him. "You understand. Don't you?"

"Are you really that nuts?"

"Yes."

He grabs her wrists and flings her away. "Get out of my house," he shouts, pushing her from the bedroom. "Get the fuck out of my house."

He listens as she escapes into the living room. He hears her throwing on clothes. And then the front door slamming. Gus can hear the woman sprinting down the street. She has playground feet, and her playground noise finally recedes around a corner; in the distance a car engine comes to life.

Then he rushes to Ivy. He shakes her, but she won't wake up.

25

Alex Mills wakes up to Led Zeppelin.

There's steam coming from the bathroom where Kelly is showering. He looks at the clock.

It's 6:00 a.m.

He shakes his head. "Jesus fucking Christ," he shouts.

The bathroom door opens, and out pops Kelly's face. "What is it?"

"Who told him he could play music at six o'clock in the morning?"

She shakes her head. "You want to have another confrontation with him?"

Mills rolls over. "Damn it, Kelly. I'm not the reason he's having problems. Would you get that through your head?"

"You know what? Go fuck yourself," she tells him, then retreats to the bathroom and shuts the door. He hears the shower surging again.

He juggles his options, to kill his son or not? To shove a fist in his mouth? Or put him through a wall? To explode or implode? He's aiming for eight o'clock. He's got a meeting with the squad at 8:30. He gets out of bed and brews the coffee.

"Turn the music off," is all he says to Trevor when he sees his son rummaging through the refrigerator.

The kid nods and disappears into his bedroom.

Mills sips coffee and waits for his wife to join him. They languish over breakfast in silence. When he gets out of the shower, she's gone. But there's a note on the kitchen counter.

Took Trevor to school. This morning never happened.
Sorry. I love you, K.

On his way to work Mills notices that he missed two calls from Gus Parker last night. He listens to the messages. First, Gus says he has new information but doesn't elaborate. The second call came hours later; it's breathless, and it's about Bridget breaking in again, something about chopsticks and drugging his dog.

"Jesus Christ," he groans.

He dials Gus. But the phone tag continues.

At 8:30 he joins Chase, Preston, and a breakfast-chomping Myers in the sergeant's office.

"We've got the best crime lab in the whole state," Woods begins. "But it's no use to us if we have no evidence to analyze."

The detectives look at each other, but no one replies.

"Where's the damn evidence?" Woods demands. "The chief is breathing down my neck 'cause the mayor is breathing down his. The FBI wants in. The state prosecutor wants his investigators in. Let me put it this way, gentlemen, we're on a short leash. A very short leash."

Mills clears his throat and says, "We've collected plenty of evidence from the crime scenes."

"You've collected bodies," Woods hisses. "There's no trail to the killer. There's nothing that leads us to him. No trace of a weapon, no traceability at all on anything."

"It's been a week," Mills reminds him. "Does the city actually expect us to wrap this thing up in a week?"

"Yes," Woods replies. Then he turns his eyes to Timothy Chase and says, "And you? Anything?"

Chase stiffens. "Like Mills said, Jake, it's barely been a week, but—"

"A week with four murders," Woods snaps.

"I was working on a report all weekend, and I'll share what I have so far."

Mills eyes Woods, who sits there and makes a gesture with his hands, a sweeping one that says, *Well come on, let me have it.*

Chase exhales deeply, squares his muscular shoulders, and says, "Here's what I surmise. The killer doesn't know all of his victims. He may know one of them. But not all. He's raging at women because his wife walked out on him, which I think makes Mr. Willis the strongest suspect. He's the only one we know linked to the crime who has a motive."

Woods nods. Chase's profile, so far, is consistent with what the detectives have discussed and completely plausible, Mills thinks. Still, it sounds like ass-covering.

"We have nothing actually linking Willis to the crime," Woods says. "And his motive is really singular. A crime of passion against his estranged wife. He would have no motive to kill the other women."

"Unless, the rage unleashed something uncontrollable in him," Mills suggests. "Something psychotic."

"But the sequence bothers me," Woods says. "Why kill the other victims before killing his wife?"

"Because he couldn't find her. She was hiding from him," Chase replies. "Besides, if his wife turns up dead first, then the finger points to him immediately. But if she shows up dead in the camouflage of the cave murders, she's the victim of a serial madman."

"And he breaks into the Glendale house to kill her?"

"We think so," Chase says. "Sign of forced entry."

"Unless Andrea Willis brings a guy home for the night and the guy kills her and he makes it look like a break-in," Woods argues. "You've considered that, right?"

"We've considered it," Mills tells his boss because he has to say something even if it means making shit up as he goes along. Then, another spontaneous declaration. "But we're focusing on Willis."

"And that's it?" Woods asks, cupping his hands to the ceiling.

Chase shakes his head. "Not exactly," he answers. "Let's go back to the night his wife was murdered. The Crystal Ledge subdivision has cameras at the gates. Five white trucks were seen at the gates in the twelve hours prior to the woman's estimated time of death. Five in, three out. The three out match the five that went in. We know the makes and the models."

"No license plates?" Woods asks.

"No," Chase replies. "These cameras are cheap, low quality. We've tried brightening the picture adding filters, but no plates."

"What's the point of having cameras that don't snatch license plates?" Woods asks the room.

"Deterrent," Mills says. "It's a subdivision, not a military base."

"Thank you, Alex," Woods snaps.

"But, I'm planning to go up to Glendale today and go door-to-door looking for white pickups, getting plate numbers," Mills tells his boss.

Chase turns back to Woods. "On the videotape you can see that one of the trucks entered Crystal Ledge with its lights off. At ten thirty at night. Figures into the time of death."

"Does Willis own a white truck?" Woods asks.

"No," Mills tells him.

Woods pounds the desk. "Goddamnit, would you guys get your stories straight!"

Mills leans forward. "Look, we have a possible link between a white truck and the death of Lindsey Drake at Camelback."

"And even if Willis doesn't own a white truck he could have borrowed one or rented one," Myers adds, suddenly waking up from his Pop-Tart stupor. "I've been reaching out to Budget, Hertz, and all the others. Avis and Alamo already told me I'll need a subpoena."

"Then get one," Woods says, his jaw clenched. "For every damn rental car company in the valley."

"It's in the works," Myers assures.

"Meanwhile, I am pretty sure I've figured out how this guy's handling the victims," Chase says. "He doesn't kidnap them and bring their bodies into the desert. The evidence we do have doesn't support that. The blood and other matter at the crime scenes suggest it's been there as long as the victims have been expired. There's no trail of fluids entering the caves, or leaving. The killer grabs his victims from a trail, drags them or carries them into these caves. They put up whatever struggle they can, which is to say not much considering we don't see evidence of the attacker's skin or hair under their fingernails or foreign objects in their hair, or evidence of any blood other than their own. And he stabs them to death. It's not that complicated."

"And no one witnesses this?" Woods asks. "The victim doesn't kick or scream?"

"He waits for a lone hiker, obviously," Chase replies.

Mills understands the need to muscle in. "Plus, fibers found in the victims' mouths suggest they were gagged to prevent screaming," he explains. "Also the lab says their facial skin shows obvious signs of stretching and abrasion around the mouth."

Preston clears his throat. "Or the guy simply approaches the women in a friendly way and tells them they ought to follow him to see the petroglyphs," he explains. "You know, he coaxes them."

Woods flinches. "Jesus Christ, you guys have next to nothing! And goddamnit, Chase, you're supposed to come up with a profile and find a fucking suspect, not the other way around." He lets out a deep, exasperated breath. "God!"

Silence rattles through the room in an unnerving way.

Mills senses a warmth rising from his chest, creeping up his neck.

Everyone tries to avoid eye contact with Woods, but no one is successful. He's just sitting there daring them all to say something, anything, to have the balls to prove him wrong. The protracted misery just hangs there, the sergeant shaking his head.

Then Woods stands up and starts to circle them, a coach furious with the team. "And what about the cave drawings?" he growls. "Explain why this Willis guy has such a fascination with those fucking petroglyphs."

"Look," Chase says, "I think we have to understand how this guy is thinking."

"No shit," Woods mutters.

"It's clear our killer is enjoying himself," Chase tells him.

"Enjoying," Woods says. Not a question. Just a statement.

And Mills wonders where the hell this is leading.

"Yes," Chase continues. "The rage makes him do it. But once it's done, he enjoys the accomplishment. Like he hasn't accomplished much lately, and finally he can take credit for something."

"Also consistent with a man like Willis who's been unemployed for a while," Mills interjects, as though the teamwork had been planned. Which, clearly, it hadn't.

"Are you telling me unemployment leads to serial killing?" Woods asks.

"Of course not," Mills replies. "You know exactly what I'm saying. If Chase's theory about accomplishment is true, then it very well could apply in the Willis situation."

"Hmm," from Woods.

"Look," Chase continues, "the profile I'm going with suggests the killer is enjoying all the attention. They usually do. This guy enjoys being in the news. That's pretty standard, too. But I'm also getting the impression that he's enjoying leading us on a wild goose chase. He doesn't actually enjoy the act of murder as much as he does the game that he's engineering."

"I'm not sure I follow," Woods says.

Neither am I, motherfucker, Mills wants to add.

Chase leans forward and squares his chin. "He doesn't really like stabbing these girls. He doesn't really like the blood and guts. But this hide-and-seek sort of thing is a game to him. It reminds him of being a little boy. He's getting off on that."

"But what about the artwork?" Woods asks.

"We know it doesn't mean anything symbolically," Chase replies.

"Says who?" Woods persists.

"Says a professor friend of mine at ASU, something I already discussed with Mills," Chase replies curtly. "But I also talked at length to the people at Deer Valley."

Surprised, Mills turns to his partner. "The Rock Art Center?"

"Yeah, Alex, the Rock Art Center. On Saturday. Spent a couple of hours there. They schooled me."

Schooled you? Are you fucking kidding me? Mills shrugs him off but can't shrug off the doomlike encroachment of the man's shadow. This is not a guy who shares territory, Mills knows. "Well, what did you learn, Tim?"

Chase smiles. "Without giving too much away to them, I found out that the meaning of all these petroglyphs is either steeped in mystery, or completely meaningless. They might just be artwork. Or the result of boredom. You know, ancient civilization doodling, like Myers is doing right now in his notebook."

Myers looks up red-faced. Chase laughs. Preston rolls his eyes.

"So the killer is an artist?" Woods asks. "You don't find any messages in the drawings?"

"I don't think so," Chase replies. "They may mean something to the killer, himself. But they don't mean anything in Indian lore, so to speak."

Mills bristles. It's time to take a whack at this fucker. "I don't disagree with Chase, but I think he's missing the point. If the guy is enjoying this, if he's feeling a sense of accomplishment, you know, the need to take credit for something, then of course the artwork means something. It's his signature. The guy sees the petroglyphs as signatures of an ancient civilization, proof of life, proof of accomplishment. He's trying to make his own mark. It's pretty fucking easy to understand."

"What's pretty fucking easy to understand," Woods snaps, "is that you boys aren't working together. There's no alignment here. And I won't stand for it." He returns to his chair and sits. "That's it. I have a meeting with the commander in an hour, and I need to prepare. Get out of here."

Mills asks Chase to follow him back to his office. He closes the door. Chase is about to sit, but Mills remains standing. "I don't like hearing your profile for the first time in front of the sergeant," Mills says. "Why didn't you call me this weekend? Or did you purposely go rogue?"

"I figured you were busy with your son, and all." And then a patronizing grin. "I know how hard it must be."

"You don't have kids," Mills says. "You don't know shit."

"Hey, buddy, what's with all the anger?"

Mills stuffs his hands in his pockets. "You're a fucking opportunist. But you probably already know that. That's my profile of you. *Buddy.*"

Chase waves his hands in the air. "Come on, now, Mills. I know you're under a lot of stress. I'm gonna just pretend I didn't hear that." Then the former FBI agent turns around and walks out.

The reference to Trevor reminds Mills to seek out his friend in Narcotics. Mills is on the third floor, walking down the linoleum hallway to the office of Jeremiah Drennon, when his phone rings. It rings loudly because the hallway is like a tunnel, and people passing by pause long enough to issue their chagrin because rings are frowned upon around here; there's even a sign that says SILENCE YOUR CELLPHONES.

It's Gus Parker.

"I have so much to tell you," Gus says, "but I'm between patients so I can only give you the CliffsNotes."

Mills listens as Gus describes his visions of fire and an anguished child.

"You've been seeing a lot of fire lately," he says to Gus.

"Yeah. But this is no ordinary fire."

Gus races through a story about a real fire in New England and the death of an artist named Theodore Smith. There's something about a woman convicted of murder. The signal in the tunnel-like hallway of the third floor of the Phoenix PD is crappy at best, so Mills has to keep asking, "What? What's that?"

"Can you hear me now?" Gus asks.

"Yeah."

"Now I can't hear *you*. Can you hear *me* now?"

"Jesus," Mills snaps. "Meet me after work."

"Wait, wait, wait," Gus insists. "I had another visit from Bridget. You got my message?"

Mills backs up to a window at the far end of the hallway. "Yeah. I called you back. Is your dog okay?"

"Barely," Parker whispers. "I have to get back to work. Ivy woke up this morning stumbling all over herself. I dropped her off at the vet on my way in. They say she'll be fine."

"Good. And Bridget? You want a restraining order or something?"

Gus says, "Ask her about the networking she's been doing for her dad."

"What?"

"She's his whore to success. I gotta go."

Mills is standing there, the dead phone in his hand, a churn in his stomach, bile in his throat. *Man, they do not pay me enough.* Seconds later he's in Drennon's office, exchanging a firm handshake and small talk. Drennon's wife, Martina, is doing fine. So are the twins. They're both studying abroad next semester. Anthropology for one, economics for the other.

"A huge hole in the wallet for me," Drennon says with an exaggerated groan. He's a bald guy with a goatee. And a huge smile that compensates for something.

"Oh, come on, Jerry, I can see it on your face. You've never been prouder."

"And you holding up okay with your boy?"

"That's sort of what I'm here to talk about," Mills says. "I got a good tip." He tells Drennon that it might be worth his while to visit with Trevor's coach.

"Hadley? Dick Hadley?" The narc is incredulous.

"Yeah."

"Wow. He's a legend." He pauses and then asks, "Who told you this?"

"I said it was a tip."

Drennon shakes his head. "C'mon, Mills, you know better."

"Look, when an athlete gets arrested for selling drugs, why is it so unusual for you to go out and talk to his coach?"

Drennon doesn't answer.

"I'm telling you, Jerry. This comes from a good source."

"Does it? Or does this come from your kid? Naming names without having to do it in court?"

Mills takes a deep swallow, understands the narc's concern, and realizes how this must look. "No, that's not it. I just promised my source I wouldn't mention his name. I'm not asking you to go raid the school. I'm just sayin' go talk to Hadley. You don't have to railroad the guy. Go talk to the principal, some of the teachers, as well. Make it look informational, that's all."

Drennon checks his watch. "I gotta run to a meeting, Alex. But thanks for the tip. I'll let you know."

Climbing the stairwell back to his office, Mills has a firm understanding that Jeremiah Drennon didn't have to run, or walk, or go anywhere. But he has no fucking clue if the guy will actually go to the high school and ask anyone anything.

26

"You wanted to see me?"

Bridget Mulroney stands at the threshold to his office.

"Yeah. Come in. Shut the door."

She sits and crosses her legs. The upper foot dangles a white stiletto.

A plane heaving out of Sky Harbor rumbles overhead. Bridget is wearing a purple blouse, modestly buttoned, with just a dash of cleavage revealed. Her hair is swept up in a crazy bouffant, shockingly red. She's been generous, if not theatrical with the eyeliner.

"You broke into his house twice," Mills says. "And you thought it wouldn't get back to me?"

She leans forward. "I can explain. Really I can."

He leans to meet her halfway. "Don't bother, Bridget. Gus told me everything."

Her face freezes. "Everything?"

"Enough to get you arrested."

She shrinks back and sobs. Her top button pops open; underneath she's wearing a lavender camisole. Her shoulders are shuddering.

"Not here, Bridget. Please. Keep it together."

"I'm going to get fired."

He reaches across the desk and grabs her hand. She's startled and stops sobbing. "You should get fired. But I didn't say anything about that."

"You're not going to report me?"

"I didn't say that either. But it's not like you need this job."

She's gulping back tears again. "No, no, you don't get it," she begs. "Why do you think I'm working? Why do you think I'm working a crappy job like this? Not because I want to, that's for sure."

"Then why not stay at home or work for Daddy?"

Suddenly, she's in his face. "I thought Gus Parker told you every-thing," she growls.

That's right, Mills thinks. Gus said something about Bridget whoring for her father. "Almost everything."

And then Bridget describes how, since the age of sixteen, she has helped her father grow his construction empire by spicing bids with sex. Mills is stunned, just stunned.

"I don't know if I can believe you," he says. "That's just disgusting."

She's choking back more tears. "Please. Please believe me."

Another plane. This one rattles the window. "Why don't you do something about it?"

"Like what? Call the sheriff? I fucked the sheriff!"

"Oh God." Mills wants to retch.

"I know. I know. Hard to believe. But it's true. I swear," she pleads. "Ask your friend Gus." She points to her crotch. "He took one look at me down there and saw everything. I confessed everything when he used his psychic powers on me."

Mills sits there shaking his head. "I think you're fucking nuts, Bridget. But I want to help you."

Suddenly, her head snaps around. She's looking behind her, left to right, probably wondering who's witnessing her meltdown through the glass fishbowl of Mills's office. Everyone is. But the people out there are decent enough to turn back to their computers with mock indifference as soon as she catches them rubbernecking. "I can't get fired. I need this crappy job so I can support myself. Don't you understand that? If I don't have an income I have to rely on my father."

Mills puts his hands in the air as if he's stopping traffic. "No you don't. You can get real work and stick with real work like the rest of us."

"That's what I'm trying to do here," she cries. "I don't want to be depen-dent on him. But once he croaks, I inherit the business and I'll be set."

"But he abused you. Your father abused you. That's a crime."

"I know."

"And he rigged the bidding process. And you helped. And that's a crime, too."

"I know."

"And all these assholes who slept with you, they're all guilty of crimes, as well."

"Again, Alex, you're not telling me something I don't already know."

"I think the attorney general would be very interested."

Immediately she bolts from the chair and grips the desk. She's leaning almost horizontally across it and pulls Mills by the shirt. "You can't do that."

"Get your hands off me, Bridget, and sit the fuck down."

She complies and begins to sob again.

"Why shouldn't I go to the AG with this?"

"Because," she wails, "they'll kill me."

"Who? Who will kill you?"

She says nothing.

"You think your father will kill you?"

"No. He'll hire someone."

There's a knock on the door. It's Chase. He waves him off. Chase doesn't move.

"No way," Mills says fiercely to Bridget, his jaw clenched. "A father doesn't do that. This is bullshit. You're making this shit up."

"Ask your friend Gus Parker. I told you, Alex. He knows everything."

He rises from his chair. "Look, if this is true, we're doing something about it. For now go back to work."

Then he opens the door as wide as it will open and ushers Bridget Mulroney from his office. He exhales deeply, really fucking wiped out. "What is it?" he asks Chase, who's looming.

"We got a body," Chase says. "At White Tanks."

White Tanks sits on the western edge of Maricopa County. The mountains are bold and mostly bald, its ridges serrated against the sky; there's a certain quiet drama between man and nature here: the urge to conquer is marginally quelled by the instinct to worship. Hikers hike devoutly. Families gather like pilgrims. The gardens of saguaro and patches of white granite suggest a rugged place of worship. Grace resonates.

This is the place where Alex Mills would bring Trevor as a child and make up a story about exploring an uninhabited world. And when they'd spot a petroglyph, which are as ubiquitous here as they are anywhere, he'd tell his boy the drawings were messages from other planets. Directions to outer space! Invitations to visit! Clues to different languages! Then he and Trevor would make up gibberish speech and talk like that for maybe half an hour, sort of understanding everything as they canvassed one of the easier trails. He'd forgotten all about those trips, the way his son would take in the scene with greedy curiosity, with relentless wonder. White Tanks is such a haul; who has time anymore?

Apparently the media does.

They're already here.

"How they'd get here before us?" Mills asks when they see the vans lined up at the visitors' lot.

"Probably a tip. Hot story," Chase says.

"It was a rhetorical question, dude."

"Rhetorical or not, if people saw a body here, they probably started posting pictures to Facebook."

"Let's hope not."

Myers is in a separate car with Preston. He rolls up beside them and opens his window. "We got officers from Buckeye and Goodyear scrambling to clear the trails of hikers."

"They better not remove my witnesses," Chase thunders.

"Our witnesses," Mills reminds him. On and off throughout the day he's also wanted to say, *Okay, dude, take the damn case; I don't give a shit*, but then he'll think, *No, someone needs to prove to this jarhead that there's a hierarchy here, and it might as well be me*. Mostly he's been ambivalent, wishing for moments here and there that he'd been a zoologist.

Chase gets out of the car, and the other detectives follow, Mills last so he can gather his cool.

"The sheriff's office is closing the park down. And the reporters are being kept in the parking lot," Preston says. "A deputy's waiting for us on the Waterfall Trail."

Exactly the trail Mills would explore with his son. Waterfall is a short hike. Only about half a mile to Petroglyph Plaza, and then maybe another half mile to the waterfall, which is generally a misnomer. It only flows after an exceptionally heavy rain.

"About forty feet or so beyond the petroglyphs," Preston tells them as they pass the trailhead.

"Of course," Mills says.

It's 3:20 p.m. The sun is high and hot and blinding. A dry desert wind blows in blustery circles.

Myers is trudging behind them.

"You okay?" Mills calls back.

Myers clears his throat and says, "Yeah, sure. Don't worry."

Chase puts a smirk on his face that Mills would like to defy with a swift right hook.

They reach the so-called Petroglyph Plaza, and Mills looks at the ancient artwork with a different understanding. The way Chase had described the rock drawings that morning to the sergeant makes the petroglyphs sound like stone-aged graffiti, but Mills can see that these rock drawings took hard work, hours of dedication, maybe longer; they had to mean something. To him, the drawings are like primitive newspapers, recording life events or observations; they're the documentation of plants, animals, strangers, and storms that passed through. The killer must see the murders as news events in *his* life. Mills senses something coming together, something vague, but something prompted by the old news stories Gus Parker rattled off this morning.

A few minutes later they round a bend and find two deputies standing with a small circle of hikers. Witnesses.

"Howdy, guys," Chase says. "What do we have here?"

A tall, reedy-looking deputy turns and comes forward. "Hey, Detectives. Mitch Jefferson." Mills doesn't recognize him. "We just briefed your techs. They're with the body."

"Thanks," Chase says. "Call came in as a female hiker or jogger. Was she alone?"

"Yeah."

"Who are the witnesses?"

"We got the spotter. He went behind those boulders to take a leak and found the victim," the man says, outstretching a thin branch of an arm to indicate the massive boulders at the side of the trail. "The two others were hiking together, and they saw him come running back onto the trail all crazy and blathering. He does have a rather odd story to tell."

The detectives look beyond Jefferson, squinting into the sunlight at the tableau of witnesses assembled with the other deputy. Mills's jaw recoils.

"Do you see what I see?" Chase asks.

"Willis," Mills says tonelessly.

"You guys know him?" the deputy asks.

"You might say so," Chase replies.

They approach the witnesses: a tall redhead probably in her late twenties, clad in Spandex, and her hiking partner, a shorter woman, kitten-like, also in Spandex. Then they turn to Bobby Willis.

"I don't think the cops believe me," the red-eyed man says. A big teardrop stain of sweat covers his T-shirt. He's breathless.

"Believe you?" Chase asks.

"I told them I was meeting Detective Myers out here."

"What?" Myers asks. "What did you say?"

Willis shuffles his feet in the dirt and says, "That I got your call and I came rushing out here to meet you."

Mills asks the deputy to guide the women away for a moment.

"What exactly are you pulling, Willis?" Chase asks when they have the man cornered.

"Pulling? I'm not pulling anything. Myers here called me and told me you all found big evidence about Andrea's murder."

Myers emits a short squeak of surprise and says, "No, no, no. I never called this guy. Never."

"Yeah you did, about an hour and a half ago. You told me to meet you up here to see the evidence."

Chase and Mills turn to Morton Myers who is just standing there shaking his head. Then Chase and Mills look at each other. Mills's brain is working overtime, the inner eye darting back and forth at possibilities, none of which add up.

"You have a cell phone with you?" Chase asks the man.

"Yeah."

"Give it over."

Mills watches Willis nervously wrestle the phone from his pocket and, his hand in little human earthquakes, turn it over to Chase, no thought in the world of a search warrant or a lawyer.

"You have two calls from blocked numbers," Chase says.

"Right. Myers called back to make sure I was here, and I said I was but I had to piss really badly so he told me he always pisses behind the boulders here when he's hiking. So I did. And then I saw the body back there."

Myers steps between Willis and Chase. "I never hike out here. I never hike. Look at me," he says, pointing to his ample waist.

"Then who called me?" Willis asks.

"Well, certain calls from the PD would read as blocked numbers," Preston concedes. "But thousands of people block their numbers. Does Detective Myers sound like the caller on the phone?"

Willis scrunches up his face into a beaten ball of confusion and says, "I don't know. I don't think so. It sounded like he was on speakerphone or in a bathroom. But he knew about me and Andrea."

"Or," Chase says, crossing his arms over his chest, "you have an accomplice who you arranged to place those calls as some kind of alibi. Amateurs never think things through."

Willis is shaking now from head to toe. "No. Stop! This is ridiculous. I was lured out here. Why would I kill someone and then point out the body to strangers? Please," he begs. "Think about it."

"Trust me," Chase says. "We're thinking about it. All the angles. That's exactly what we get paid to do, Mr. Willis."

"Then what goddamnit is the connection to Andrea?" the man wails.

"You are," Chase says. "Don't you understand that?"

The sun has drifted overhead farther to the west. There are shadows crisscrossing the trail.

Willis lowers his head and buries it in his hands.

"You wait right here," Mills tells Willis. Then he nudges the other detectives aside. "Preston, I'd like you with the body. Go check in on the techs. Chase will be there in a minute," he says. "And, Myers, go get a statement from the hikers."

"The deputies got one already," the portly detective says.

"Go over it with them," Mills tells him. "Then you can let them go."

Myers shrugs and retreats down the trail, following Preston.

Mills turns his eyes to Chase. "Look, we're walking a fine line here, Tim. We got nothing on this guy but a bizarre coincidence."

Chase spits. "Nothing? Are you kidding me?"

"We haven't even seen the body. For all we know it's been here for a week. Why would Willis be out here now?"

"He wants to get caught," Chase announces.

Mills shakes his head. "Where's the weapon? If he wants to get caught why not give up all the evidence?"

"The weapon's buried somewhere in the desert," Chase says.

"Where's the blood?"

"The blood?"

"Yeah, the blood," Mills insists. "Not a drop of blood on the guy. What was he wearing during the crime?"

Chase studies Mills from head to toe. And then he tonelessly chants, "He was wearing clothes during the crime, then swapped them out. They're buried with the weapon. I'll bring in the K-9s, and they'll find exactly what we need."

"Until then?"

"We hold him. Take him down to the station. Get a confession."

Mills shakes his head. "Good luck with that."

"You got a better plan? You think Myers actually called Willis out here?"

Mills plants himself firmly. "No, I don't. But there's something else here that we're both missing."

"Like what?"

"Like the facts, Detective," Mills says sharply. "It's inconvenient, but we need some facts. And nothing here adds up. I can't point my finger on it, but this is a mind fuck. The killer is still out there, and he's laughing at us. It's a psychological game, Chase. And we're losing."

"Maybe we are. Let's leave Willis with Myers while we go check out the body."

They both look down the trail to Myers who is standing, happily it seems, with the two young hikers. Then Chase and Mills turn to each other. Their eyes do a pregnant volley in the silence. Mills looks to the ground and exhales a recalcitrant sigh. No, he thinks, there's no way. There's too much paunch, too many years, and too many blissfully idiotic smiles. There have been no signals. Certainly no red flags. Myers is a good ole boy. He likes his meat and potatoes with a side of bacon. He plays bingo, goes to church, bowls, and does the toy run for Christmas. He is so above average at being average that average people are afraid of him.

Maybe that's what Chase has been getting at all along.

"You think we should talk to him?" Chase asks.

"Protocol says yes, but personally I say no."

"We have to."

"I know. But not here. We'll catch up with him back at headquarters."

Myers is finishing up with the witnesses. As the women drift away, Mills escorts Bobby Willis down the trail, leaves him with Myers, and the two men immediately begin to argue about the phone call. Mills turns away, shaking his head. He rejoins Chase, and they both duck behind the boulders where they find the crime scene technicians hovering over a body.

"Victim's name, according to the DL, is Monica Banfield. Age thirty," Preston tells them. "Sheriff's office says they got a call about a missing person yesterday matching the description of the victim. Five-seven, 130 pounds, brown eyes. Tramp stamp, I mean tattoo on the very lower back."

Monica Banfield has short-cropped hair, dusty with trail dirt. Her legs are long and lean. She's wearing purple sneakers. There's dried-up blackish blood everywhere. Bruises tug at the corners of her mouth.

"How many knife wounds?" Mills asks.

"Six," a tech says.

Another tech is busy scraping through the dirt. She looks up and asks, "Hey, boys, did you see this?"

She leads Mills and Chase to a lone boulder just north of the big ones, an isolated chunk of stone in the middle of a wash, with a freshly carved depiction of death on its face: the agony of Monica Banfield is the killer's newest installation in the desert.

"Un-fucking-believable," Mills whispers.

"Where are the photogs?" Chase asks.

"They're here," she replies. "They got shots of it."

Chase taps Mills on the shoulder. "You want a closer look?"

"No."

They return to the body. The male tech, Matt, is holding tweezers above the victim's head, ready to sample tissue or something else of interest. "I don't think the crime happened today."

Chase nods. "No, it doesn't look like it did."

The body has been picked at.

"Probably sometime over the weekend," Matt tells them.

"Probably," Chase says.

Some of Monica Banfield's facial flesh is missing.

One eye is open.

"The OME is ten minutes out," Preston tells them.

There's no weapon. Footprints of the victim and the killer, if there were any, were disturbed by onlookers, compromised by traffic back and forth to the scene; it couldn't be helped. Besides footprints weren't all that reliable in the desert anyway, with all the predators that scramble around at night disturbing the tracks of humans. The air is finally cooling.

"We'll be back later," Mills tells Preston.

Onlookers and other hikers are long gone when Mills and Chase return to Petroglyph Plaza. Chase tells a crumbling and bewildered Bobby Willis that he can come back to the station and answer some questions, or face arrest right there at White Tanks.

"Do I have a choice?" Willis asks.

"I just gave you a choice," Chase says.

"Do I need a lawyer?"

"That's your call," Chase says. "But I bet you'll be out of there in ten minutes if you don't."

Mills says nothing.

Then Willis removes his hands from his pockets and uses them to indicate, palms open, not a surrender but a willingness. "Whatever you need to catch Andrea's killer," he says. "But I guarantee you I have nothing to do with this."

Mills tells Myers to get the victim's details from Preston and check out her background. Then, Chase on one side, Mills on the other, the detectives surround Bobby Willis as they descend the path to the trailhead.

At the station Bobby Willis decides to lawyer up. Timothy Chase is about to release a Patriot missile from his head; you can just tell by the combustion in his eyes. This is not the way he had planned it. This is not the way he wanted to control it. And Alex Mills is amused watching Chase teeter as if his nerves are working their way up the Richter scale.

Attorney Samuel Vargas arrives. He's compact, neatly tailored, and olive-skinned. He has tiny hands.

Before they greet him, Chase asks, "You want in on this?"

Mills tilts his head, puts his hands on his hips, and says, "What do you think?"

Ultimately the meeting with Vargas and Willis yields nothing. Vargas had consulted with his client in private first. Then, in the interrogation room, the lawyer went on and on about a lack of evidence, a conspiracy, a setup, and insisted there were no reasonable grounds to detain his client, and Willis said nothing. Smart man, Mills observed. Chase's fuming was audible and visible under the malignant haze of the fluorescent lights. He tried ranting, then raving, then a passive-aggressive cast of the line verbally reminiscent of fly-fishing; he waded and waited, his questions dangling, smart, even, and casual, but no one spilled the truth. There was no catharsis. No theme song. At 4:30 p.m. Bobby Willis walked out of the Phoenix Police Department a free man.

"For now," Chase quipped as he and Mills watched the man and his meticulous lawyer exit into the plaza below.

They head back to White Tanks in separate cars. All Mills really wants is to see his wife and son right about now, but there's still light in the sky, a body in the desert, and more vultures ready to swoop in and further desecrate the crime scene. His phone rings. He assumes it's Kelly wondering where the fuck he's been, but it's Gus Parker wondering where the fuck he's been.

"I thought we were supposed to meet after work."

"Shit."

"I called you a few times but didn't bother to leave a message."

"Sorry, man. Long day. We found another body."

"Wow," Gus says with a gust of energy. "I knew it."

"Yeah. You did. It happened sometime over the weekend."

"Where?" Gus asks.

"You tell me."

Gus offers a curtailed laugh. "Let me guess. In the desert. Off a hiking trail."

"White Tanks."

"Oh? I love White Tanks."

"Yep. So do I. Same pattern, Gus. You won't learn much by watching the news. But watch anyway. I'm heading back out there now."

"Can we meet tomorrow? I've got those news clippings. I think you'll learn a lot by reading them," Gus suggests, an affectation of intrigue in his voice, maybe self-deprecating, maybe not.

Mills brakes at a red light. "Right, of course," he says, and then, "Just so you know, there's going to be a ton of follow-up tomorrow. But I'll try to break free for coffee or something."

"Okay, just call me," Gus tells him. "And you're fine to go right on red."

"You heard my brakes squeal."

"No, I didn't. Now make that turn."

"Yeah," Mills says and hangs up. He just wants to get the fucking day over with.

27

Gus is off the phone from Alex Mills for maybe two seconds when it rings.

Ivy is sniffing at his heels. "Yes, girl, yes, we're going for a walk!"

The dog yelps at the word "walk."

"Just let me get out of these clothes."

His phone is still ringing. It's a Seattle area code. He answers.

"Gus?"

"Yes."

"It's your father."

He had called his father last year to wish him a happy birthday but never heard back. He tries now to think, how old is the man anyway? He tries to picture Warren Parker the same but older.

"Gus?"

"Yes, it's me. What's up?"

His father takes a deep breath. "It's your mother. She's sick. Just wanted to let you know."

Gus drifts into his bedroom and sits at the edge of the bed. He pulls a sock off. "What's wrong? Can you give me some details?"

"She hasn't been feeling well for about a month or two. She's been very tired. And she's been complaining of nausea. Violent nausea."

Gus nods, registering his understanding as if the man is in the room with him.

"I couldn't get her to the doctor. But finally she just gave in."

"Did she tell you I called her?"

Silence. Then, "No. I don't think so. When did you call?"

"Doesn't matter."

His father takes another breath. "Well, Gus, your mother has cancer," he says. "We found out this morning."

And Gus is surprised by his own reaction. He had never stopped loving his mother; he had stopped liking her a lot. He had left home, and what is left now is the rice paper of memories, fragile etchings, tiny deaths and their inscriptions. Those memories have always been cold and wet and misty like Seattle, like portraits of regret, or something like that. And so here he is dumbfounded, floored in a physical way, as if someone pulled the rug and down he went with a thud. Sure, he had had his vision, and, yes, his heart had been a simple, bare hyphen between before and after, but here he is facing the force of nature, nascence, specifically, and a tug that, if nothing else, is a cliché of womb to child. He's not sad, but he's deeply saddened; there are no tears, but there is a hollow call from somewhere like his inner cave.

"Should I come to Seattle? Would she like to see me?"

His father murmurs. The sound is soft and distant and thoughtful. "It's in the pancreas. Supposedly it was caught early. But she's probably got less than two years."

"I can make it before then," Gus says.

"Of course you can," his father replies. "She could be in the hospital another day, or another week. We really don't know."

"Has anyone told Nikki?"

"I called her this morning."

Ivy comes back to Gus's heels. She moans, then nuzzles into his leg.

"Okay," Gus says. "I'll be in touch."

And that's it. Gus shakes his head as he hears the line go dead. He considers the sound of nothing that replaced the sound of something. He studies the sound of detachment and understands it as the separation of life and death, and he doesn't want to think in black and white right now, but that's what he sees when he surveys the room. He nudges Ivy. "C'mon," he says, "let's go chase ghosts."

Later, after a hearty walk into the dusky night, after a layer of the sky became a glowing pink mattress, each pocket a swirl of cloud in perfect formation, after Ivy yelped at the wind and the birds, Gus came home to a quiet, wordless house that stayed that way through dinner, through half a bottle of wine, through four chapters of *Moby Dick*, until the phone jarred him from his stupor.

"Honey, are you watching the news?" It's the curly, shrilly voice of Beatrice Vossenheimer.

"Oh, shit, right," he says, scrambling from his office, racing to the TV, lunging for the remote.

"There's a murder," Beatrice says. "They say it's coming up on the news."

Gus looks at the clock on the cable box: 9:59.

"Thank you, Beatrice. I lost track of the time."

"Is this your murder?"

"My murder?"

She laughs. "You know what I mean."

"Yes, it's the one that kept haunting me all weekend."

Then he tells her about his mother.

"I'm so sorry, my dear. I know how complicated this is for you," she says. "But I also know how strong you are. You'll do whatever you think you have to. Call me after the news if you want."

Trevor is in his bedroom absorbed in a video game. He had actually smiled a few times during dinner, and, for Mills, that was progress. Progress around the Mills dinner table did not mean, *Hey, now you get to play video games because you smiled*; it meant, *Hey, we might be communicating better so I'm not going to come in your bedroom and hassle you tonight. Even if you are breaking the rules we issued when we grounded you. You fucking punk.* Mills realizes, here in this moment, that you can only truly hate your son if you truly love him.

Kelly is curled up to him on the couch. They're watching the ten o'clock news. The anchorman introduces a reporter who is standing in a parking lot surrounded by thick darkness.

"Earlier this evening the medical examiner removed the body from the scene," the reporter chants. "Police aren't naming the victim, but the scene is eerily familiar to the string of murders that have recently turned the valley into a killing ground for a monster."

Mills rolls his eyes. His wife offers a disgusted laugh.

"The victim is described as a thirty-year-old female. She was stabbed six times."

The reporter is no longer on-screen. Instead he's talking over video from earlier in the day when cruisers were coming and going, and lights were flashing, and crisp uniforms were supposed to comfort viewers with the sense that somebody was in control.

"The Phoenix Police Department is the lead agency investigating the serial murders, and while Sergeant Jacob Woods would not confirm that this crime is linked to the others, he did leave that door open."

Woods appears behind a small orchestra of microphones.

"We see some similarity in the appearance of the crime scene to the others we've discovered over the past week," Woods says. "We're not releasing any other details of the scene itself, and we have made no other connection at this point to the other murders."

Then the reporter is back.

"We do know a woman was reported missing to the sheriff's office over the weekend, but we don't know if that woman is the victim found today. Again, authorities are not releasing the identity, pending the notification of next of kin. I'm Juan Carlos de Castillo, on the Nightbeat."

The anchorman thanks Juan Carlos de Castillo and then turns to the anchorwoman sitting beside him.

"This is the fifth body found in the valley in little over a week," she tells the viewers. "And investigators have made no arrests. They're being pretty tight-lipped except to say they've been following up on multiple leads. But that's not enough for one Scottsdale family. Elizabeth Spears was the first victim identified by police in this recent rash of killings. The twenty-seven-year-old's body was found a week ago Friday. Tonight her parents held a last-minute news conference to say, 'Enough is enough.' Let's go live to Scottsdale where Bhagyavi Gupta is standing by with the story. . . ."

Mills feels a coil of rope tighten around every muscle. He sits up, and Kelly whispers, "Oh, shit."

Bhagyavi Gupta stares into the camera like a deer that has noticed the headlights just a fateful second too late. The microphone shakes in her hand. There is no escape, and so she opens her mouth and speaks.

"The aching, grieving Spears family has finally come forward to speak about the death of their daughter, Elizabeth. Her body was the first one found linked to the current string of murders in the valley."

Gus Parker is transfixed. He has no real psychic vision of what the parents will say, just plain, easy intuition. And he knows it does not bode well for the Phoenix Police Department, particularly for Case Agent Alex Mills. Gus imagines the kachina doll from the Spears' Scottsdale home, and he sees faces streamed with tears; he sees a bedroom door that has remained closed for just about a week and a ghost that comes and goes, unable to connect, unable to let go; it is there, and then the ghost is gone.

"Our daughter's body was found almost two weeks ago," Peter Spears tells the group of reporters gathered at the sidewalk. "My wife and I called this press conference to call for action. We've seen no progress in the police investigation. They were out here to talk to us once, then nothing. Except more bodies. How many women have to die before they catch this killer? Where's the urgency?" The man steps aside and lightly guides his wife, a bereft woman, her arms wrapped around the cocoon of herself, to the microphones.

"Naturally, we're frustrated," she says, her words sedated, her eyes heavy. She scans the members of the press slowly. "Every time we hear of another murder, we relive the murder of our beautiful, beautiful, little girl. How come there's been no arrest?" She chokes up, takes a deep breath. "We're losing faith in the ability of the Phoenix Police Department to do the job, here. It's hard for everybody. We know. But where's the FBI? Why is the police department going it alone? Why is a man who can't even control his own kid in charge of the investigation?"

"Claudia," her husband says tentatively.

The camera zooms in closer. This is one of those moments television news cannot resist. Real human misery and drama, as if viewers need the aperture of agony fully opened, the grief fully exposed to understand it, as if members of the TV audience can't figure out for themselves that the mother of a murdered woman might be, well, sad. It's a slow and steady zoom. Gus shakes his head.

"No, this needs to be said," Claudia Spears tells the reporters. "The lead detective of this investigation has too much on his hands. Read the newspaper. His son is on trial for drug trafficking. Drug trafficking! Talk about a distraction. If he cared as much about finding justice for our daughter as he must for his son, he should step aside and let someone else take over."

"That'll be all," Peter Spears announces as he steps forward.

Reporters dispatch questions, but the couple turn their backs and head inside.

Bhagyavi Gupta reappears on the screen. "We've reached out to the Phoenix Police Department for a response to Mrs. Spears's comments. But we haven't heard back at this time," she reports. "We did check, however, and while it's true that the son of Detective Alex Mills has been arrested on drug charges, the boy is not accused of trafficking and is not currently on trial. Back to you in the studio."

The anchorman offers a somber nod and says, "Chilling either way. Truly chilling."

Yeah, Gus Parker thinks, very chilling for Alex Mills. Very fucked up and very chilling.

Mills says nothing. Neither does his wife. She takes him by the hand and leads him to the bedroom where they lay together staring at the ceiling. She strokes his arm, then his shoulder.

He doesn't even try to sleep.

The next morning the White Tanks murder is on the news again. It's in the paper. He hears a replay of the Spears press conference and turns on the coffee grinder to drown out the resounding inevitability of his fate. The couple's picture appears below the fold in the *Republic*.

VICTIM'S PARENTS DEMAND ACTION

Kelly swipes the paper from him, shaking her head.

Trevor pokes his head out of his bedroom. "Dad, I saw the news."

Mills ignores the boy. Kelly turns to Trevor and says, "Your father doesn't want to talk about it. Now get a move on. You're not making me late again."

"No, really, Dad, I saw the news. I got bored gaming and turned on the news last night and—"

"Trevor," his mother warns.

The boy shuts the door.

About an hour later Mills is at his desk, his eyes heavy. He senses the eyes of everyone else focused on him, and he's not wrong. People pass by, pause, and stare. Others look up, watching. The silence seals around him; suddenly he's a crime scene. So many bystanders, but nobody wants to get involved.

Except Bridget Mulroney. She's all tragedy mask this morning, standing there in his doorway, pouting, chin to the floor, hands folded. "I'm so sorry, Alex. I don't know what to say," she tells him.

She's wearing a lime green headband that matches her lime green heels.

Her eye shadow is a frostier green.

"Can I help you?" Mills asks.

Bridget advances. "No. But can I help you?"

"With?"

She stands there halfway between his desk and the door. She and her staged compassion. Nothing is real to this woman; her life is too fucked up even for a reality show. "With anything, Alex. I know you're going through a hard time."

"Do you?"

She stiffens. She blanches. "Oh. I guess you . . . I guess they . . . I mean . . ."

"You mean you've already been asked to draft a press release about my reassignment."

Again, the sad face. "Look, Alex, forget I ever came in here. I just thought . . . Well, I didn't think. So we can talk later. Okay?"

She's backing out of the office, her heels clicking in reverse.

He sits for about ten minutes after her withdrawal and then strides the gauntlet to the sergeant's office, scrutinized by everyone, as if he's taking a perp walk.

The sergeant looks up from his desk. "You're early," Woods says.

"Early?"

"I asked Chase to call you at ten thirty."

Mills looks at his watch. It's 10:17 a.m. "I guess I'm psychic."

"Sit down, Alex."

Mills complies, and Woods launches into a speech of admiration that cuts a swath as wide as Mills's career has been long. Integrity. Respect. Trust. Rinse. Repeat. The verbal anesthesia offers no comfort to Mills, for when the appendage is cut, he feels it. He feels the slice through his skin, the teeth of the blade eating through his flesh, grinding through his bone, and the rest peeling away as the appendage begins its descent to the floor.

"Surely, you understand, Detective," Woods says. "It's a PR move. That's it."

Mills will be reassigned. Chase will be named case agent. Effective immediately. There are lots of very important cases piling up, critical, high-profile cases, yours to pick from, blah, blah, blah, integrity, respect, trust, blah, blah, blah.

"I think you're making the wrong decision. But I understand," Mills tells his boss.

"Look, Alex, maybe it's not a permanent reassignment," Woods says. "Maybe things will die down, and, if time allows, we'll get you back on the case. But, to be honest, we better find a suspect before that."

"Is this your decision alone?" Mills asks.

"Of course it is."

Of course it isn't. Mills knows the short leash between Woods and the chief, between the chief and the mayor. It's not difficult to triangulate the points of his reassignment.

"Unless you have any questions," the sergeant says, "that'll be all."

Mills leans forward. "Why wasn't I the first to know?"

Woods leans back. "What do you mean?" Not a denial.

"I mean Mulroney."

"Oh, that," Woods says, waving a hand like a lazy conductor. "Just a matter of efficiency. The city wants this released before the TV stations broadcast at noon."

"Yes, sir," Mills says. And then, sarcastically, because he really can't help it, "I imagine the whole valley is tuning in waiting for this announcement. Because it will make everything that much better."

"I'm sorry," Woods says. "Really I am."

It doesn't matter to Alex Mills how sorry Jacob Woods is. He doesn't blame Woods. If anything, the sergeant has always been Mills's cheerleader. Still, there's something (Mills can't quite get it on the radar) perverse about what has just happened on the gurney of his career.

Not as perverse as what awaits him in his office when he returns.

The morning edition of the *Republic* is spread open across his desk, its wingspan almost as wide as the desk itself.

Timothy Chase is standing by the window, blocking a chunk of sunlight with his silhouette. "Did you make it past the first page this morning?" Chase asks.

Mills tosses the guy a deadly look and says nothing. He aims for the desk, reaches for the newspaper, but stops when he sees the photograph of Petroglyph Plaza in a box that nearly covers two inner pages. No, he hadn't made it this far into the paper before Kelly intervened. He reads now through the articles stacked around the photo. One suggests the murders have become like a ritual; the reporter, Matt Segal, points out the pattern of desert locations:

> Some of the trails in these areas are known for the presence of petro-glyphs. A spokesperson for the Phoenix Police Department would not comment on any link between the murders and the Native American art. However, the *Republic* has confirmed that the police are looking into that link. "I was contacted by a detective," said Pro-fessor Romero Lincoln of the ASU Department of Native American Studies. "We haven't had a chance to speak, but the message indi-cated an interest in the history of petroglyphs." Lincoln declined to say whether the Native American renderings suggest anything about the murders.

Chase steps out of the light. "It's about time someone in the media made the connection. I mean, it's not exactly brain surgery."

Mills thinks hard for a moment and then says, "You told us you spoke to the professor."

"I did."

"Not according to his quote right here in the paper."

"I told him it was off the record."

"So he lied to the paper?"

"I don't know," Chase says with a dopey grin.

Mills nods. "Yeah, I see how it's done in the FBI." Then he stares Chase down, a face-off that has all the percolating anger of a hockey brawl. "I'm not on the case, Tim," he says. "You can take your fucking newspaper."

"You talk to Woods?"

"I said I'm not on the case."

"Tough press conference last night."

Mills folds his arms across his chest. "Whatever," he says sharply. "It's your case. Congratulations." He sits, logs on to his computer, and tries to tune into white noise.

"We're going to get Willis one way or another," Chase tells him.

Mills could not feel any more ambivalent. He just stares.

"The more I think about it, Mills, the more I'm convinced," Chase continues. "The guy is classic. He's so full of rage at his wife, and he just falls in hate with any random woman."

Mills looks up. "Falls in hate?"

Chase sits on the edge of the desk, peering down at Mills with stormy eyes. "Yeah. It's a behavioral thing with these guys. They take their rage with them wherever they go. Any woman is vulnerable. They're on a random search to project their hate, to find a body who will define it, take responsibility for it."

"Right," is all Mills says.

"Damn right," Chase tells him. "Like the guy is just living his raging life, and if there's a woman in front of him at the checkout line who's taking too much time, he hates her. He turns her instantly into the enemy. And he wants to kill her. Or maybe it's a woman who is talking too loudly on her cell phone in the post office. He falls in hate swiftly and wants to kill her. He assigns her his rage and feels justified in killing her."

"Well, I've felt that way before," Mills says with a laugh.

Chase doesn't acknowledge the humor. "Sometimes it's just a chick he thinks is ugly. Her ugliness offends him in some primal way, and she's as good as done."

"Wow," Mills says. "You really know your shit."

"Right," Chase says. "I'm all over Mr. Willis."

"Then tie him to a fire."

"A fire?"

"Yeah," Mills says. "Our psychic friend keeps seeing fire at the crime scenes. Remember?"

Chase smirks. "Our psychic friend," he repeats. "Of course. I remember. I'll get right on that. A fire." He sniffs the air and laughs.

"Maybe the fire will give you the evidence you need to really bring him in," Mills says, turning back to the screen, his voice passive, his thoughts aggressive.

"Fire or not, Willis fits the profile."

Then go arrest him, you fucking jarhead, Mills thinks. "Get out of my office, Chase," he says instead. "And don't come back unless you're asked."

Chase offers a strangely timed thumbs-up and leaves the room.

Between patients, Gus gets a call from Beatrice. She says she's quite upset by the press conference last night, how it stirred her in such a worrisome way. "It's way too dramatic for my taste," she says. "Especially at this point in time."

"What point in time?"

"I think they'll have their killer by the end of the week."

"Why am I not seeing that, Beatrice?"

"I don't know."

"I'm really not seeing anything."

"Well, I am. I got the sense of it when I read the paper this morning. I took one look at the photo a few pages in, and I just knew. I feel this in my bones," she insists. "I see an arrest."

"Let me know if you get anything else. I'm running on empty."

"Exactly why you need a new client," Beatrice tells him.

"A new client? I'm not taking on new clients," Gus says. "If anything, I'll drop the few I have."

"Don't be ridiculous," she argues. "You need a fresh start. I want to refer someone to you."

"Don't risk your reputation," he says with a snort.

"Can you come by my house tonight?"

"Who is it?"

"You'll meet her tonight."

Gus shakes his head. "I don't know, Beatrice. Can we make it maybe another night once my head is clear?"

"Let me know," she says, and she's gone.

Gus stares at the phone and considers calling his sister, Nikki. What would he say to her? Would they laugh? Commiserate? Talk each other into feeling remorse of some kind? They don't really know each other. Instead he pulls up his calendar, checks his appointments, and calls his clients to cancel. "A short vacation," he says mostly to their voice mail. The only client he reaches is Gary Potter who says, "No problem, but I might not be here when you get back. Headed to LA."

"So, you made the decision."

"I did. The play wraps up in three weeks. Then I'm gone."

"Good for you," Gus says.

"Yeah. I'm stoked. An agent from LA was in the audience last weekend. Saw my acting. Told me he'd work with me if I came to Los Angeles."

"Wow. I didn't know agents scouted Phoenix theater."

"Said he was on vacation. Called me a convincing killer."

Gus imagines Alex Mills at the theater that evening and wonders how to break the news to poor Gary Potter. "My sixth sense says he was a tall, fit, and thin man, wearing a tweed jacket, with a lovely lady hanging on his arm," he tells his client.

Gary Potter laughs. "Oh, no. Definitely not tweed. The guy was very LA. Leather jacket. Diamond ring. And gay. No lovely lady. A big, bald, Italian-looking dude with the same freakin' diamond ring. Actually, they made a nice couple."

Gus swallows hard. Not a psychic. Not a sleuth. "Well, good luck to you, Gary."

"Thank you. Thanks for everything."

"Everything?"

"Form of speech."

A few minutes later Gus is staring at a gall bladder thinking this is his destiny when his uncle Ivan whispers in his ear, "Don't be such an asshole, asshole."

28

Mills is not surprised when he gets a call from Kelly. "You all right?" she asks.

"Yeah. It's done."

"I know. I saw it online."

"Sorry, Kelly."

She pauses. "Why are you apologizing to me?"

"I guess this must be embarrassing for you."

"Are you kidding me?" she begs. "You know what I think about other people's opinions."

Of course he does. Kelly does not live her life according to the opinions of others, not friends, not family, not colleagues, and certainly not strangers. How does he tell her that that's what he loves about her, when he loves so many other things, too? Like her voice, for example. Like the healing clarity of her voice, right now, which kind of sucks all the malevolence out of the room.

"Kill them with your resilience, Alex."

"One at a time I will," he tells her.

"Love you," she says.

He says he loves her too and hangs up.

Bridget Mulroney is standing in his doorway.

"What now?" he asks.

She looks at the floor. "I'm sorry to bother you. It's just that as far as the city is concerned, I have to inform you that you're not at liberty to comment on your reassignment."

"I had no plan on asking the city's permission," he hisses. "But I also had no intention of commenting to anyone."

She looks up and smiles. "Whew," she says, feigning relief. "I didn't think so, but I had to be all official about it anyway. I mean, your phone will probably be ringing for the next day or so."

"I'll refer all calls to Woods."

She looks around the room, as if she's searching for broken pieces of him. She shakes her head. There are tears in her eyes.

"Bridget? You okay?"

"I just hate seeing good people get knocked down."

He gets up. "I'm not knocked down. I'm fine."

"Really?"

He reaches for the football sitting on the windowsill, the football autographed by former NFL quarterback Jake Plummer, and tosses it at Bridget. She goes all spastic but catches it.

"Nice," he says. "This job . . . life, actually . . . is a game of football. Sometimes you're up. Sometimes you're down. Sometimes you make that special play. Sometimes you fuck it up and there are people like pigs piling all over you and you get dragged through the mud and you just get your ass up because tomorrow's another game."

Bridget studies the football in her hands. "Jesus, Alex, this is signed by Jake Plummer."

"Yes, it is."

"In his heyday I came very close to f—"

"Please don't say it, Bridget. It's not flattering."

She recoils. "I'm sorry."

"Please tell me you weren't responsible for the stadium."

She rolls her eyes. "Of course not." And then she adds, "Well, maybe."

He walks to the door and closes it, returns to the desk, and gestures for his visitor to sit. She does, and as Mills sinks to his chair he says, "This is hard for me to tell you, Bridget, but I have to notify the state attorney about your father and his business dealings."

Mills watches as the woman crumbles. Her head does a wide roll and collapses forward. He hears the shuffle of her shoes coming off her feet. She begins to sob.

"I'm sorry, Bridget."

"No. You can't do this," she begs. "I told you my life might be in danger."

"If you cooperate, there will be protection for you."

"Easy for you to say."

"Bridget, look at me," he says. He waits for her eyes to meet his, and he says, "I will insist on that."

"Why are you doing this to me?"

"First of all, to free you. And then, of course, it's my duty. As a law enforcement official I'm obliged to report this. Particularly because it involves the abuse of a child."

Her arms go flailing. "Who's the child, Alex? Who's the freakin' child? I'm an adult, goddamnit."

"You were a child when the abuse took place."

"It was consensual," she says with a spit.

"It was rape," he tells her. "You know that. I know you know that."

She says nothing. She breathes heavily.

"Besides, your father bribed officials. They subverted the bidding process on who knows how many projects. . . ."

"Lots."

"They're all criminals. And they'll all go down, Bridget."

She covers her face. "No, no, no, Alex. I can't go through this."

"I'm not promising it'll be easy."

She pulls herself to her feet. She grabs a tissue from his desk and blots her eyes, dabbing her makeup, leaving behind smudges that look black and blue.

"I want to help you," Mills tells her.

She coughs, then clears her throat. "Yeah, right."

"No. I do. You need to talk to someone. We can get you a name of a good doctor."

"We?"

"My wife and me."

She says nothing.

"I promise you, Bridget, I won't report this until you've seen a doctor. I won't say a word until I know you're getting help."

She turns away from him. "What if I leave town? What if I disappear?"

"I'll find you."

She opens the door and walks out. The phone on his desk rings. Off the case? Why should he answer? But his diligence forces him otherwise. It's Cal Dixon, from the medical examiner's office. "Just thought you'd like to know," Cal begins, his voice crisp and official, "the remains at Squaw Peak were probably there a month. So—"

Mills interrupts him. "But I had fresh maggots on me."

"You did, and you didn't. That body had been decomposing for a while, and the insects likely appeared in waves, with new generations appearing in cycles," Dixon explains. "The environment was conducive. The first adults that hatched after two weeks probably laid eggs, themselves. The corpse was a family affair, my friend. We see evidence of fly eggs, maggots, pupae, and adults. I'd say three to four weeks. I'll send you the report."

"Don't bother," Mills tells him. "I'm off the case. Send it to Chase."

Gus learns about the reassignment of Alex Mills while watching the six o'clock news over a sloppy dinner of beans and rice and some Cajun shrimp he had left over from lunch.

"As we first reported at noon today, the Phoenix Police Department, under mounting pressure from community leaders and at least one victim's family, has reassigned the detective who was leading the ongoing serial murder investigation across the valley."

Just as Gus had expected. Just as he had sensed. More intuitively, he reasons now, than psychically. Ivy's head is in his lap. He strokes the dog gently, turns off the TV, and looks at the empty bowl in front of him. A wave of laziness washes over him; he just doesn't want to move, clean up, put away, or, God forbid, mop and vacuum. He can't ever see himself picking up a vacuum again. And, once again, he thinks about hiring Elsa, the cleaning lady, stealing her from the neighbors, eating Bolivian fish stew, and never ever scrubbing a toilet again. But there's more to Elsa. He can see it. She has a secret layer of soul, like a haunted messenger. Ivy lifts her head and sniffs.

"What is it, girl?"

She lets out a bark, and then the doorbell rings.

"Even my dog is more psychic than me," he says to himself as he rises from the couch.

He half expects to find Elsa when he opens the door. At least that would affirm his ability to predict. There's a woman standing there, but she's not Elsa; he recognizes her, but he's not sure who she is. She stares at him doe-eyed and smiles softly.

"Hi," she says. "I'm Billie Welch."

Of course she is. Gus Parker is staring at a rock n' roll icon, a face he would probably know under any other circumstance, but not here, on his front porch, without a guitar strapped around her neck, a microphone to her mouth, stage lights, some kind of context.

He takes a deep breath. "Hi," he says. "Can I help you?"

"I'm here for my appointment," she says, her voice dusty like the air.

"Appointment?"

She smiles demurely. "Oh, no. Maybe I have the wrong address."

He looks to his driveway and sees a black SUV parked there.

"This is so strange," he says, still mesmerized. "My friend was just playing your CD."

"Beatrice?"

"Ah, that's right. Turns out you know Beatrice Vossenheimer," he says. "Just turned down an invitation to have dinner with her tonight."

"Still have to work on that last name," the woman says with an easy laugh. "But, yes, she's the one who set up the appointment. Are you Gus Parker?"

He shakes his head, as if he doesn't understand, but then quickly nods. "Yes, yes. I'm Gus Parker."

She looks down and grabs the tails to her shawl and swoops them around her shoulders. "Okay," she says, "this is strange. I'm here for a consultation. Beatrice referred me. Did I come on the wrong night?"

He lies. "Oh, no, I was expecting you. I'm sorry. But Beatrice just said she was sending someone over named Billy. I was expecting a guy."

"I get that a lot."

"No you don't. You're famous," he says. "Please come in."

He is going to kill Beatrice Vossenheimer.

Gus ushers Billie Welch to his office, tells her he needs a minute to finish up something in the kitchen, and then heads to the bathroom where he looks in the mirror and sees a train wreck staring back at him. There he is in a fraying T-shirt and sweatpants. His face is whiskery, and his hair is a skirmish. "Fuck," he says. He brushes his teeth, runs a comb through his hair, and dashes into the bedroom and into a new set of clothes.

"You didn't have to change for me," Billie tells him when he enters the office.

"First impressions, and all . . ."

She stares at him. Gus tries to do the math. Billie Welch spilled onto the national stage when he was still living in Seattle, when he was in high school and living with his friends. He figures that must make her about six or seven years older than him, but he looks into her face and sees no age, not a wrinkle, not a crease; she is frozen in time, a chanteuse, a surfer girl from the old school.

"Beatrice didn't tell you I was coming," the woman says.

"Is it obvious?"

She smiles. "I really have never consulted with someone like you before," she tells him. "And I don't have any particular questions. I just wanted to see what it would be like."

"Why not let Beatrice show you?"

"I asked, but she deferred to you. I think she wants to keep our friendship neighborly."

"Of course," Gus says, remembering. "You're neighbors."

"We are."

And then a silence. A long protracted silence. He hears Ivy flopping around nearby. A neighbor starts a car. Billie wears a Zen-like smile on her face. And a chain around her neck. And a lightning bolt on the chain. The lightning bolt! The Andrea Willis lightning bolt! The charm that almost knocked him off his feet with its heavy implications. He has it right there in his top drawer. He shivers. He can't say anything. He just can't. He closes his eyes, and for some reason he sees himself at the side of the stage waiting for Billie as she leaves her fans in awe; some of them are crying, and there are tears in Billie's eyes as well as she flows off the stage in her diaphanous gown. She takes his hand. And then he sees them on a narrow street in London, and they're talking to Dickens, and Billie is taking notes, and the night is foggy; you can't see people's eyes.

He opens his and finally says, "I liked the CD. A lot."

"Thank you, Gus. I'm touring with it now."

"Where should we begin? Can I call you Billie?"

She leans forward and touches his hand. "Of course."

The light in the room has an orange glow, like a distant flame, like a burnt sunset, and the muskiness of her perfume suggests a burning, too. She has been everywhere, this star that occupies his office, this woman who makes his skin all goosey and hot.

"I don't really have any questions," she reminds him. "I just want to see if anything comes to you."

All of a sudden, something does. "Your family," he says. "They're very important to you."

"They are."

"Your parents are still living, and they adore you."

"They do. They still treat me like I'm their little girl."

"They're worried about you."

"I thought so."

Gus sees them now. Two older people with the same expectant eyes as Billie's, the same gratified smiles on their faces, the same soft energy and glowing intensity. "They want you to go back to Los Angeles."

"I keep a place there," she says. "But right now I want the solitude of the desert."

"Speaking of solitude, I think they're worried that you'll end up alone."

"True. My mother, especially."

"They'd like to see you settle down."

"They know better."

"Still, they worry that when you retire from music you'll turn around and have nobody."

She tilts her head and gazes up at Gus. "First of all, I'm never retiring. I'll still be singing when I'm old and gray. Second of all, I have the greatest friends in the world, all over the world."

Gus nods. "Of course. But the only thing I sense about you right now, Billie, is a missing piece," he says. "I wish I had something more to tell you, but right now that is the strongest message I'm getting."

"Maybe next time," she tells him. "I'm intrigued."

He nods and smiles. He can't believe he's been allowed to gaze into the life of a legend. He offers to walk her to her car. Before they get to the door, he stops and turns to her. "That was rude of me. I should have offered you something. I opened a bottle of wine with dinner. Can you stay for a glass?"

She reaches out and grabs his arm. "You offer a girl a glass of wine before she gets behind the wheel? I had you figured for more responsible."

He feels himself blush. He knocks his fist against his head. "Of course. My bad. Some decaf?"

"Next time," she says and continues toward the door.

"So you are coming back?"

"Absolutely, Gus," she replies.

He watches her drive away.

Damn, he thinks to himself. *What the hell was that?*

29

Gus calls Beatrice Vossenheimer on the way to work the next morning. Billie Welch music had been drumming in his head all night. "What were you thinking?" he asks Beatrice.

"It had nothing to do with thinking," she replies.

"Which means you weren't thinking."

"I was sensing."

"Sensing what?" he asks, frustration with her edging into his voice. "That I was completely unprepared for a new client to land at my door? Especially someone like Billie Welch who, if you don't mind me saying, is completely out of my league. Why would you set me up like that?"

"Now you're getting it," she says, her voice clinking like a champagne toast.

"Getting what?"

"Oh, Gus Parker, must I write it out for you phonetically? I was setting you up."

"Huh?"

"I. Was. Setting. You. Up."

She chuckles as if she's high.

"With Billie Welch? Are you crazy?"

"No," Beatrice replies. "She was over here the other day, and we were talking, and I suddenly got this vision of the two of you together. I just saw you walk into her life."

"Does she know that?"

"Not really."

"I'm not completely amused, Beatrice."

"Oh, please. How are you going to meet someone, Gus? You never get out of the house except to come see me. This asexual mystique of yours is a total fraud!"

"Asexual?"

Beatrice scoffs. "It's a disguise, Gus Parker. And I've exposed it!"

"You make me laugh. You really do," he says, welcoming the smile that's beaming across his face. "I may not have a black book full of hookups. But I get mine when I have to."

"Not the same thing, my dear. You are oblivious on purpose. No romance in your life," she argues cheerfully. "You've fallen in love with that dog of yours. And while I love her, too, her companionship has limits."

He merges onto the highway and scans the morning sky. "Interesting," he says. "The subject of companionship came up last night. There was a very strong signal."

"Of course there was," she says.

"I gotta go, Beatrice. I need a few moments before I face the day at work."

She ignores him. "Have you heard from the detective?"

"Mills? No," he replies.

"Just wondering," she says. "Now that he's off the case he probably has some free time to go over our research."

Gus rolls his head and hears a crack. "Yeah, but like you said, he's off the case."

"So what?" she barks.

She rarely barks, but she's right. "I know," Gus tells her. "If I can sit him down and show him what we found, he'll find a way."

"Exactly. I see him going rogue."

Gus laughs. "You're whacked, Beatrice. I'll call him now."

She disconnects, and he dials. He gets a recording and leaves a message. Just hearing the detective's voice, even though it's the same voice on the same recording as always, Gus gets the sense, a very potent sense, that the man is not going rogue; he's going dark.

Alex Mills walks the hallways of the Phoenix Police Department as if nothing has changed. He smiles, nods, and carries himself at an altitude uncharacteristically high for someone who has been reassigned. He's killing them with his resilience, and the body count is mounting. *Oh, yeah, look at me brewing a new pot of coffee in front of everyone. Look at me reading the paper. Look at me staring in deep thought at my computer screen* (he's actually searching Amazon for Henry James). The thing is, Mills has made the not-so-stunning realization that Woods's talk of very important cases piling up, critical, high-profile cases, yours to pick from, was the sergeant's very best attempt at mollification.

Myers drifts into his office and shuts the door. "It's still bugging me," he says.

"What is, Morty?"

"Why would anyone call Willis and pretend to be me?"

Mills looks up. "I have no idea."

"You believe me, don't you?"

Mills tries his best not to sound ambivalent, but he does. "Sure," he says.

Myers leans against the wall. "You don't give a shit."

"I'm off the case."

"Right," Myers says. He's quiet for a moment. His eyes are probing. His lips move a few seconds before he speaks. "Do you have any advice for me? Huh, Mills?"

"Turn in your phone. That'll clear you."

"They already took it."

Mills shrugs. "Good. I honestly don't think Chase suspects you of anything. Stay under the radar."

The portly cop nods and walks out, brushing by Preston who walks in.

Mills just looks at him and says, "Jeez, I didn't realize they installed a turnstile at my office."

"Sorry to bother you," the older man says. His face is creased, tired, and unshaven. "I'm having trouble with Jane Doe."

"Squaw Peak?"

"Yeah."

"So why are you talking to me? Doesn't anyone understand that I'm off the damn case?"

Preston stuffs his hands in his pockets. "Because I respect you. How's that for an answer?"

Mills smiles his first smile of the day. "It's a good answer," he tells his colleague. "Nothing comes up on NamUs?"

"Nothing."

"What about FBI or Interpol?"

The guy rubs his eyes. "I haven't heard back."

"You will," Mills tells him. "I'm sure Chase has faith in you. I know I do, buddy."

Preston nods and smiles.

"And you're welcome at my turnstile anytime," Mills says.

Gus Parker pulls into his driveway, starving because an unusually high mammary volume usurped his lunch hour, and he hears Ivy barking rambunctiously inside the house. That never happens. She'll leap all over him when he walks in the door, but the sound of his car rarely excites her. Maybe it's the birds.

When he enters the house the dog is still howling like a wolf but not running to him, not bounding at him to welcome him home with a frenzied tail and a sloppy tongue. He follows her bark and finds her in the office, standing on the futon, her paws on the windowsill. She's yelping like a siren.

"What is it, girl?"

She turns to him and barks.

"Ivy?"

Her nose is at the window again.

"C'mon, let's go for a walk."

Responding to the magic words, the dog strikes an immediate silence, leaps off the futon, and into his arms.

Outside the air is crispy as if maybe the desert is finally cooling into fall.
Gus looks to the sky and sees a few gleaming stars even though the sky is still
blue; it's one of those afternoons. "I don't know what's bothering you," he says
to Ivy, "but whatever it is, I'm home now, and it's nothing I can't take care of."

She's ignoring him, now, her face to the trees, searching for birds.
She pads along beside him, and they walk quietly. About twenty minutes
later, Gus's head is clear and Ivy is panting. They head home. Halfway
up the driveway, someone calls Gus's name. It's Elsa, the cleaning lady,
emerging from the neighbor's house. She's wearing her standard uniform:
a combo, seemingly, of men's pajamas and surgical scrubs.

"Hey, Elsa," he says with a wave.

"Gus Parker. Wait there for a second. I have to ask you something."

The woman, a canvas grocery bag in each hand, approaches, and he
meets her at the street. "What is it?" he asks.

"You know anybody with a white pickup truck?"

The hair on his arms begins to rise. "No," he says. "I don't."

She looks at him. Her lips form a thin, grim line.

"What happened?" he asks.

She shakes her head. "I'm not sure. I've been here all day working
for Mr. and Mrs. Russo, and I see this white pickup truck sitting at the
end of the street. For a very long time."

"How long?"

She shrugs. "I don't know. I lost track of time. But whenever I
check back I see it there."

"When did you first notice it?"

"About noon."

"Was it still there at, say, two?"

"I don't know. I think it came back a few times," she replies.
"Whoever was inside had no idea I'm watching from the front window."

Gus rests his chin on his fist. "Okay," he says, trying to intuit something, anything. "Did anyone get out of the car?"

"Not that I saw, Gus Parker."

He smiles briefly at her formality. "Did the car ever come into the
cul-de-sac?"

"I see it drive around twice. But the windows, they are so dark and tinted. I think maybe he roll down the window just a bit and take a picture of your house."

"My house?" His thoughts go immediately to Beatrice's vibe about someone lurking, casing his house. The presence of a stranger would certainly explain Ivy's unusual frenzy when he got home from work.

Elsa puts a bag down, reaches into the pocket of her drawstring pants, and removes a slip of paper. She hands it to him. "It's the license plate number. I write it down."

Gus says, "Thank you, Elsa. You'd make a great neighborhood watch lady."

"What? What's that?"

"Oh, just someone who protects the neighborhood."

She smiles. "No, remember, Mr. Gus Parker, you protect me. You saved my life."

He looks at her puzzled, but then she reminds him.

"The crash on the highway, *mi amor*. I live today because of you."

She brushes his cheek with her hand.

"Have a good night, Elsa."

He watches as she grabs her bag and heads for her Corolla parked in front of the Russos'.

"C'mon, Ivy, let's go get you some water," he tells the dog. On his way in, Gus unfolds the piece of paper.

ILMD 73.

Gus is sitting in front of CNN in a sort of news stupor. He watches and listens, zombielike, but doesn't really see or hear what's going on in the world. It's all white noise and a low-grade angst. There's so much going on, he thinks; the valley is hot. That's his gut feeling. The valley is hot. A fire burns not in the valley but under the valley. It's a remnant of a tragedy, and it stews there in the belly. There's a monster feeding off the stew, stalking the desert and maybe stalking him. He sees the letters, ILMD, like stencils now, cut from the air in front of him, across the screen of cable news, crawling at the bottom, now, a redundant ticker, I-L-M-D, I-L-M-D, I-L-M-D. . . .

Then he remembers.

Of course he remembers. Last week, Tucson. Charla McGregor and the initials. He checks his phone for the notes he took that night.

ILMD.

He shudders. A real involuntary shudder of his body. Those letters. Right there in front of him. A small, electrical charge buzzes through him, as if the pieces fit like a plug into a socket.

Charla McGregor guessed a doctor. She might be right. Maybe it's a doctor with a vanity plate. For the second time that day, he calls Alex Mills. The least the detective can do is run the plate. But for the second time that day, Gus gets the guy's recording.

30

The third time Mills thinks, *Jesus F. Christ*, and answers. "I'm off the case, Gus," he says.

"Hello to you, too," Gus retorts.

"Sorry, it's just you're going to have to go through Chase now."

"I'm sorry to hear about what happened, Alex. You should still be on the case."

Mills laughs. "Yeah, well . . ."

"Yeah, well, I have lots of stuff to tell you. I've been trying to reach you, and leaving you messages, and—"

"I know, Gus, I know. But the truth is, considering the circumstances, there's not much I can do with your information. Let me give you Chase's extension."

"No," Gus insists. "You need to see what I have."

"Like?"

"Like those news articles I've been telling you about. That old murder in New England and the guy obsessed with symbols," Gus reminds him. "The woman who killed him might be living in Prescott. I think she's somehow connected to the cave murders, too."

"You think?"

"You'll think so, too," Gus tells him. "And I have a license plate. I was hoping you could run it for me."

"What license plate?" Mills asks.

Gus says, "Remember that psychic I went to see in Tucson?"

Mills says, "Yeah?"

"Well, she came up with these initials, said they were linked to our killer."

"And you were waiting to tell me this when?"

"Dude, why do you think I've been trying to hunt you down?"

"What are the initials?"

"I-L-M-D," Gus chants, perhaps a bit too dramatically for Mills to believe.

"I'll run it, see if there's anything to it. I got plenty of time on my hands."

"There is something to it," Gus insists. He tells Mills about a white pickup truck stalking his neighborhood. About license plate ILMD 73. Mills taps his fingers on his desk like an impatient father; on one hand he's trying to humor Parker, on the other he's trying to detach himself from the case completely. But what the fuck? He's intrigued by the plate, if nothing else.

"Like I said, I'll run it," he tells Gus. "But I'll have to pass the information on to Chase."

They make a plan to meet tomorrow for lunch.

Gus Parker is staring at a pancreas, and he's thinking about his mother.

"Oh, that gel is so cold," the patient says.

"Sorry."

His mother's pancreas is coming apart. What a horrible disease, he thinks as he glides around the patient's belly. It's out of her control, and Gus knows that must be the hardest thing for Meg Parker to accept. Life to her is an alphabetized spice rack. And Chivas. He wonders how Nikki is taking the news, if she's making a pilgrimage to Seattle. In that instant he gets a whiff of jet fuel and sees himself on a plane, sitting over the wing. He thinks about weight and balance, and then the patient says, "Are we almost done?"

Gus punches a few notes into the computer and says, "Yes. You're all set."

At 12:25 Alex calls and says he's waiting for Gus at a diner down the street. Gus changes into his street clothes and is out the door.

"How long do you have?" he asks Alex as he sits opposite him in the booth.

"I'm fine," Alex says. "Nobody's looking for me."

A waitress stops by and asks if they're ready. Alex orders a burger. Gus hasn't opened the menu but tells the woman he'd like a club sandwich. When the server is gone, Gus reaches down to the bench and retrieves a file folder. He pushes it across the table.

Alex looks but doesn't touch the file. "Your news clippings?"

"Yeah," Gus says.

Alex takes an index card from his chest pocket and, with a bit of melodrama, drops it on the table and slides it with one finger to Gus. "An exchange of information," he says. "The license plate."

Gus turns the card over and reads. He instantly gulps.

Smith, Theodore.
3589 N. Angel Gem Rd.
Phoenix, AZ

He can't find his voice, but he finally whispers, "Read the file. Read it."

Alex opens the folder and begins to scan the pages. Gus follows the man's pupils as they meander from line to line. He watches the crease begin to crawl across the detective's forehead, and he sees the man, subtly but visibly, grip the pages tighter. Alex finishes one page then quickly jumps to the other, and then the next, and then he goes back, and his face seems to be calculating an equation of evil and disbelief. He keeps reading like that, one page to another, then back, as if he's taking an open book exam. And then Alex puts the papers down neatly in front of him, raises his face to Gus, and they sit there staring for a few moments across the island of the table, isolated, the two of them, in a warp of affirmation. The truth penetrates. Gus begins to smile. Alex says, "Holy shit, Parker."

"Yeah," Gus says. "There's a Theodore Smith who isn't dead."

"The son. . . ."

"Right."

"Apparently he survived the fire."

"And he drives a white pickup."

Mills twists his face and races through the pages again. "And, it looks like Priscilla Smith was released a month ago. As far as we know, that would coincide with the first murder."

"What?" Gus begs.

"The ME thinks the remains at Squaw Peak have been there about a month."

"So there's your connection!"

"That's not a connection, Gus. That's a coincidence."

"You know how I feel about coincidences."

Alex shakes his head. "No, this is actually a coincidence, a good coincidence. But who are we trying to tie to the murders, her or her son?"

"Whoever has a motive. . . ."

"That's just the thing," Alex says. "I can't go before a judge and get a warrant to search the guy's house based on a few old news articles and a coincidence. There's no connection. This isn't sufficient evidence."

"What about the truck that could be connected to the Camelback victim?"

"It's not solid, Gus."

Gus leans forward. "Exactly why you have to search the house. You have the address. You'll find evidence there. I'm sure of it."

Alex shakes his head. "C'mon, Parker, this isn't your first go-around with this. I can't secure a warrant based on your visions or your hunches or even your research. With all due respect."

"What if I prove there's a connection?"

"How you planning to do that?"

"Maybe a trip to Prescott to talk to Mrs. Smith."

Alex puts his hands up as if he's directing traffic to stop. "Hold on there, captain, I can't have you doing that. Totally against protocol. I'm already 'reassigned.' You want to get me fired?"

"So I never told you."

"No. You can't go to Prescott."

"Then you go talk to her."

Now he's waving his hands, dismissing the whole stretch of ideas. "No," he says. "I have to get Chase in the loop."

"You do," Gus tells him. "Or you don't."

"Huh?"

"You want this case back, don't you?"

Mills fidgets. "That's not how it's done."

"I realize that," Gus says. "I'm not saying you should do it on company time."

"Then what are you saying?"

"I'm saying go freelance with this. If you can wrap this thing up, you're a hero. If not, nobody has to know."

Mills shakes his head. "I don't think so."

The waitress returns with the food. "Anything else, guys? Are you fine with the water?"

Both men nod, and she retreats.

"Meet me after work and let's go to the address," Gus says, holding up the index card.

"We can't just show up at the guy's house," Mills tells him.

"We can at least drive by."

"Maybe," Mills says. "But not today, Gus. Let me think about it. I need a chance to make heads or tails out of this new dump of information."

Gus doesn't exactly know what that means, but he doesn't bother to ask.

Later, after lunch, they're standing in the parking lot and Alex asks if he can keep the file.

"Oh, yeah. That's for you. I made copies," Gus tells him.

Alex reaches out for a handshake and says, "I'll be in touch."

31

Mills is maybe twenty feet from his office the following morning when Timothy Chase stops him in the hallway. Twenty feet! Had he not stopped at Starbucks on the way in for the stupid fucking latte, he would have been safely ensconced in his office with the door closed by now, enough to remind the hulking Chase to keep his distance. But, no, here Chase is, his elbow resting on the wall, bracing his neck in his hand, looking down a good three inches at Mills. "Interesting development," Chase says. "Looks like our killer is smart enough not to carry a cell phone."

"I'm off the case," Mills reminds him.

"Yeah, well, just thought you'd want to know that we've got all the cell tower data. No matches from crime scene to crime scene."

Mills starts to walk off. "Then I guess that blows your theory about Bobby Willis."

"How do you mean?"

"If your killer doesn't travel with a cell phone, how does that explain Bobby Willis at White Tanks? He had his phone with him."

"We're looking at that now. I'm thinking it's an anomaly."

Mills is almost at his door. He turns back and laughs. "An anomaly? Seriously? Sounds to me like you're starting from scratch. Good luck with that. Maybe you ought to call Gus Parker."

"The psychic?"

"Yeah. Someone's stalking him. He's got the license plate."

"Who'd want to stalk him?"

Mills looks down, then up, his hands juggling theories for show. "Maybe the killer knows Gus is on the case. Maybe the killer's afraid that Gus will reveal him to us. That's kind of how it works."

Chase chews his lip and nods. "Like I've said, I got nothing against working with a psychic."

"Ask him about the fire. It'll be worth your while."

Then Mills steps into his sanctuary and closes the door behind him.

Gus is working a half day today and has spent most of the morning hunting for Priscilla Smith's address in Prescott even despite his own hunch that she has no address in Prescott because those townspeople told the newspaper that she was staying with her sister. He tries to conjure up an image of a house, the sister's house, but all he can come up with is a generic box with a picture window. He thinks there's an old Ford sedan sitting in the driveway. Gus knows if he heads to Prescott he'll find her.

He calls Alex to tell him.

The man's voice is flat. "I told you, Gus, you're not going up there. I can't have you fishing around like that. You're not a detective."

Gus stiffens, not knowing why that felt like a blow to the chest. "Look, Alex, I'm only trying to help where you can't."

"Fine. You get a vision or something, call me."

"What about that file I gave you?"

"I'll give it to Chase," Mills replies. "He's going to call you."

"What for?"

"I told him about the pickup, the license plate."

"Good."

"Anything else?" Alex asks.

"Sorry to bother you," Gus tells him.

"You're not bothering me. I just don't know how to convince you I'm off the case."

Gus shakes his head, completely bewildered, and then from his gut comes a sudden fire of words, like bullets, like warning shots, and he says, "I just don't know how to convince you to go to Prescott. She's waiting. She has something to say. She is the key to this. You must go. You must. If you don't the killing goes on."

"Parker. . . ."

"That's my vision. It's complete, Alex. You and her. That's the answer."

"I gotta go, man."

"And then you come home and you hand-feed the info to Chase and let him wrap the thing up. No one's the worse for it. That's it. That's how it'll come down."

The line goes dead.

Mills drives around the city as he has taken to do now, aimlessly searching for answers that he knows don't exist. He's accomplishing, in terms of the road, a circle of nothing; he does manage to indulge his boundless appreciation for the topography around him: South Mountain, Estrellas, Camelback. He hasn't been assigned a new case. He's been reading a lot in the down time. Thumbing through, actually, because the attention span isn't there. Enough, though, to feel for the poor, fictional, Irish farmer who's pissed off at God. He drives by the coach's house, then the high school. He doesn't expect to find anything, and he doesn't find anything. There's a game tonight; he sees it on the school marquee. A Friday night in early November. No surprise there. He thinks about his son, thinks about how if you remove God's beauty, the valley is as shitty as anywhere else to raise a kid, maybe shittier. Avenues to the west, streets to the right, a huge fucking grid of hopeless intersections and transplants looking for the sun. Cold weather dropouts and conmen and old people, all of them desperate. His hands are a little shaky. Too much caffeine. Kind of amplifies the frustration. Tweaks the anger.

Suddenly, he grips the wheel and turns it without compromise. He commits himself to the gas pedal and peels out. He needs no map. He looks at the file beside him on the seat. Just inside the cover flap he has written the address: *3589 N. Angel Gem Rd.* He's smiling, possessed by an affirmation or a conviction, or maybe a demon who gushes recklessness. The address is smack dab in the middle of an insignificant neighborhood of '50s-style ranch homes that fit perfectly into the flatness of the valley, or really any town, anywhere in the US where postwar families settled for a couple of generations until sprouting into the sprawl of suburbia's crappy subdivisions.

He turns off Thirty-Second and heads west and inches along until he finds North Angel Gem Road. He takes a left. The house is fourth from the corner. He parks across the street and watches. The stillness of the place challenges him to imagine a life inside, but he suspects from the drawn blinds in every window that there is no life inside. A few circulars litter the driveway. The yard is tended but unspectacular. A sliver of a window stands beside the front door; it's the only one without a blind, but there's darkness on the other side.

Mills gets out of his car and crosses the street. He traces the yard line back and forth, studying the house, inferring its emptiness, and then he figures what the hell and moves up the driveway to the one-car garage. He peers through the squares of glass and sees a white pickup. He can't fucking believe it. But he can. He stands there and sustains a kind of g-force between the two convictions. Again, he smiles, the hairs on his arms affirming his discovery in gentle ovation.

The vehicle has been backed in, so Mills can't read the plate, but he knows. He just does. He backs away and turns to the front door. He knocks and waits. Knocks again. Not a sound from the inside. He peers through the window and sees an empty hallway leading to an empty room.

"Can I help you?"

The voice is behind him and gives him a chill. He braces himself and turns around. "I was looking for someone," he says to the stranger.

It's a woman, probably in her thirties. She's wearing a gauzy skirt and a tank top, and she's lugging a huge Greyhound on a leash. Her hair is frizzy, falling just below her shoulders. "Nobody lives here," she tells Mills.

"And you are?"

"Just a neighbor. I live over there," she says, pointing to a house across the street, one door down.

"Oh. Well, maybe I have the wrong address."

"Nobody's lived here for a while," she says. "It's a rental."

"Where's the owner?" Mills asks. "I'm almost sure that's his truck in the garage."

She smiles. "You here to repossess it?"

He shakes his head. "Do you know who owns this place?"

"Not really. Some guy. He's never around."

"Even at night?"

"I'm not on neighborhood watch," she says smartly. "And I'm in bed by nine." The dog growls. She tugs at its leash. "He's a rescue. Abused at the track," she tells Mills as if she's seeking congratulations.

"Does the name Theodore Smith ring a bell?" Mills asks.

"No," she replies. "Who are you anyway?"

"I'm a cop."

She just looks at him. He's seen those eyes before. Those eyes are expecting to see a badge. Those eyes are waiting for the flash of a shiny something. Those eyes have watched a lot of TV, and Mills is happy to oblige. Yes, and now those eyes are satisfied, and the neighbor says, "Is there a problem here?"

"No. This is just a routine call. You know what the owner looks like?"

She shakes her head. "I don't really recall. I've only seen him once or twice. The house was abandoned for years. And then he showed up and stuck a For Rent sign in the yard."

"When's the last time he had tenants living here?"

"They moved out last month."

"I see," Mills says. "Now if your little puppy will let me pass, I should really be going."

The woman laughs and yanks the beast to back up. The dog utters a singular bark and lumbers away. Mills stops again at the garage door. He studies the pickup. The tires are coated in dirt, pebbles in the treads.

Not unusual for the dusty valley but, then again, maybe a match for the prints found at Camelback. There's a doorway that leads from the garage to the house. Below it rests a pair of work boots. For big feet. Huge feet. The garage is otherwise empty save for a calendar on the wall. The guy, if nothing else, is here often enough to care about the passing of time. But there's something not right about the long-hanging graph of days and weeks and months staring back at Mills. It's not the current calendar. He does a double take. The year printed across the top is 1973.

Mills is not back in his office for two seconds when Drennon busts through the door.

"Done and done," the guy from Narcotics says theatrically, his voice booming like a kettledrum.

Mills knows this has to be good news. But he fights back the smile. "Seriously? You found something?"

"We found a lot of somethings," Drennon says, taking a seat on the edge of the desk. "First we scared the shit out of some football players at Central High. Amazing how quickly these jocks melt down to pussies, you know?"

Mills does not know. So he doesn't answer.

"It was like Betty Crocker's finest cake, okay? They gave up the coach, and we didn't even have to promise leniency. Turns out if you promise them a little buggery in the county jail they say what you need them to say, and they said a lot, so much so that they'll get leniency after all because they turned state's evidence to the DA and now we know exactly where Coach Hadley got the shit and how he moved it, and it took like, what, a day for the DA's office to catch him in the act, and it's over, Mills. It's over."

"Well, not exactly," Mills says, thinking of his son.

As if reading his mind, the other cop says, "Yes, exactly, Mills.

Those jocks told the DA how Hadley had threatened them, including Trevor, with fucking torture if they talked to anyone, how some thugs from Sheriff Tarpo's office would use whatever show of force to keep them in line. Those assholes almost waterboarded one of the players. Can you fucking believe that? I think they'll drop the charges against your kid, Alex."

"Tarpo's office? What are you talking about?"

The guy belts out a laugh. A kind of hateful laugh. "Sorry," he says. "I know this isn't funny, but Hadley was getting the drugs from some rogue deputies, make that *moron* rogue deputies, who were out there seizing drugs across the valley and feeding it to Hadley for a cut of the proceeds."

"Jesus Christ."

"I know," Drennon wails, "classic, right? Like what kind of fucking idiot do you have to be?"

"What about an arrest?"

"Didn't you hear me when I said done and done?"

His whole body tremors, and he can't help it. There's a wave of relief rolling toward his chest, and he puts his hand there for an instant as if to stop the thing from crashing through. "When?"

"I just got confirmation that the DA's office brought Hadley in quietly," Drennon replies. "Tarpo's boys won't know what hit them."

"And Tarpo?"

"Uh, no," Drennon says. "Don't you wish. But there's no evidence that Sheriff Lardass had any knowledge. Kind of standard policy for Tarpo." Drennon leaps off the desk and extends a hand that Mills lamely shakes, still sort of shell-shocked by the news. "Gotta go. I think you owe me a drink."

Mills says, "I'm good for it, Drennon. And thanks. I'm, like, too stunned to even thank you enough." And as soon as the guy is out the door Mills lunges for his phone and calls his wife.

32

Beatrice Vossenheimer lifts the lid from the sterling silver serving dish. Steam rolls and evaporates, revealing a pile of browns and greens and a few stripes of black. Gus has never seen anything like it, and judging by the looks of the others at the table, neither have they. But they're all smiles. Of fear.

"Dig in," Beatrice says as she lowers the dish to the center of the table. She's invited her new beau from Safeway (Gus approves), Billie Welch (phase II of a master plan), and Billie's younger sister, Miranda (phase I of making phase II seem impromptu).

"It's basically tofu soaked in a cilantro lime sauce," Beatrice explains. "Then sautéed in basil and white wine. And the roots, of course. Roots from all over the desert."

Gus looks at Billie who offers him a girlish smile, a coy flirtation in her eyes. He volleys back a goofy grin, and then he says, "House of Dreams."

"What was that?" Beatrice asks.

But Gus is still looking at Billie and only at Billie. "House of Dreams," he repeats. "It's the title of your next album."

"Really?" Billie says.

"Really," Gus tells her. "It just came to me."

"It just came to you," she repeats. "How very intriguing. Would you like to do some of my songwriting for me?"

"No," he says. "From everything I know, you write your songs yourself. And you need no help."

"Okay," the singer says with hesitance. "But I'm not making another album now. I'm just starting to tour with the new one."

"I know," he says. "But when you do, you will name it for the song."

"The Native Americans call it *Ahwatukee*," she says.

"Doesn't have the same ring as House of Dreams," Miranda tells her sister.

"Isn't this so lovely?" Beatrice chirps. "Everyone connecting!"

"And the tofu's a hit," Gus assures her. "No curb appeal, but I've already cleaned my plate."

"Seconds?" she asks, ebullient with the flattery.

"No thanks," he replies, too abruptly to catch himself.

Later, during dessert (a simple, predictable, cactus mousse), Gus gets a text message. He pretends not to notice but peeks.

"Call me. 602-555-0109. Chase"

He feels a sort of satisfaction by proxy for Alex Mills. In the text he sees a desperation lingering in the characters; it's a vibe he's getting that Chase can't move forward without his help, that Chase knows that Gus is on to something. Oh, the gloating wrongness of it all.

"Is someone trying to reach you?" Billie asks.

He feels his face turn red. "Uh, no. I don't think so."

And then he sees her aura. It's as if there's a permanent spotlight on her, hovering, anointing her with this rare, timeless stardom.

He can't take his eyes off her.

Back in Phoenix, Alex Mills is sitting under the clear autumn night, under a canopy of stars, high up in the bleachers beside his son. This is where Trevor wanted to watch the game, away from the crowds, his shame unrecognized. After all, Trevor would be playing tonight if not for his arrest. Minutes away from halftime, the kid leans into his father and says, "I'm really sorry. Okay?"

Mills doesn't know exactly how to respond. He had been hoping for an apology. Probably best that it came out of the blue. But probably harder because it came out of the blue. He looks at his kid, and then looks away and says, "I know you are. How couldn't you be?"

"What is that supposed to mean?" the boy asks with a mild smirk in his voice.

"It means I'd be sorry, too," he replies.

"Jesus, Dad, I'm trying to apologize here."

Mills nods, thinks for a moment, clears a place in the harbor of his mind for reconciliation, and lets it sink in. Then, holding the boy's sturdy shoulders, he turns his son to him and says, "I know you are, Trevor. And I know I was really hard on you, but it was really hard on me. And your mother."

The kid lowers his head.

"Really," Mills continues, "how would you expect a father to react? You need to put yourself in my place for a second and think about that."

"Yeah, well, I wasn't able to do that, Dad, until they took you off the big case."

"No. It's not about what happened to me. It has nothing to do with the case or what you saw in the news. You just need to understand how important a son like you is to a father like me. You're everything your mother and I have. This hit us like a ton of bricks. We never saw it coming."

The crowd explodes in cheer. Touchdown. For one team. At this point, they're not following the game. They're following each other, watching intently, waiting for the next move.

"So, do you ever think you guys are going to forgive me?"

Alex smiles and offers a laugh. "Your grandfather used to say, 'The law punishes. People forgive.' He used to say that to make sure I knew the difference between a father and a prosecutor. He would reprimand me when I was wrong, and he would take away privileges when he thought I betrayed his trust, but forgiveness was in his heart the entire time. It was something I always knew. It's something I want you to always know."

Trevor nods and fidgets the way a teenager does when confronted with parental love. "Thanks, Dad. But I know you never screwed up as bad as me."

"That's irrelevant. I want you to think about what your grandfather said."

"Okay," Trevor says.

They turn back to the game and watch. Central is ahead by twenty. Despite the absence of their legendary coach.

Gus walks Billie and her sister to their car. Halfway down the path from Beatrice's house, Billie turns to him and grabs both his hands in hers, as if she's asking him to dance. "It was a great night," she says.

Gus nods shyly. "Yeah. We should do it again when you get back from LA."

Her eyes bounce as if she's seen an apparition. "How'd you know I was going to LA?"

"You mentioned it at dinner," he replies.

"No, I didn't."

He laughs. "Sorry. I guess I just got a feeling."

"Well, Mr. Parker, I'd be lying if I said I wasn't the least bit enchanted with your powers," Billie tells him.

"It's not a reliable power, I should warn you."

"It's just stunning," Miranda gushes.

He watches them drive away, Miranda behind the wheel, the rock and roll star in the passenger seat, her eyes gazing at him even as the car swings away from the end of the driveway.

On the way home he dials Chase.

The detective answers on the third ring and says he wants to meet with Gus to go over the Theodore Smith files.

"When?" Gus asks.

"Tomorrow."

He thinks for a moment. He doesn't want to meet with anyone tomorrow. He wants to take Ivy to the dog park. He wants to do laundry. He's thinking about taking a stealth mission to Prescott just to feel for vibes. "You know, I think Sunday would be better," he says to Chase. "Is that all right with you?"

Chase lowers his voice, as if conspiring with an informant, and says, "Yes. Sunday would be great. I'll call you at 0800."

33

Gus pulls into the cul-de-sac. There's a car parked in front of his house. It's not a white pickup. It's a white Mercedes. *Zen*, he tells himself. *Zen*. As he turns into the driveway he sees her. Bridget Mulroney is sitting on the small step to his front door. Her face is in her hands. He parks instead of pulling into the garage.

She looks up as he approaches. "I'm sorry, Gus."

Ivy is howling inside.

"You gotta stop showing up like this," he tells her.

"I didn't break in."

"That was considerate of you, Bridget."

"Can I come in?"

He folds his arms across his chest and studies her. He intuits a desperation, or maybe that's just the madness in her eyes. "It's late."

"I said I'm sorry," she begs. "I just don't know where else to go."

"Are you packing chopsticks tonight?"

She laughs, then bursts into tears. He watches her gulping nearly to the point of hyperventilation, and then he reaches to her and pulls her to her feet. "An hour," he tells her. "You can stay an hour."

They're in his office. Ivy's head is in Gus's lap. The dog is softly growling.

"She doesn't like me," Bridget says from the futon where she's sitting with her legs up, crossed.

"Would you like you if you were her?"

"I need help, Gus."

"I know."

"No," she says. "You don't. Mills is going to turn everything into the State. They're going to come after me and my dad and everyone. At this point I don't give a fuck about my dad. He can burn in hell with the rest of them. But why should I have to pay for his crimes?" Her speech is accelerating, like a child searching for an alibi. "I wasn't a willing participant. I wasn't. You've got to believe me, Gus. When this thing breaks open it will be the biggest scandal to hit the valley in years, maybe ever. And everyone will know my name. And I'll never work again. And who will ever love me? I might as well move to fucking Siberia." She rolls into the fetal position, fighting the mattress with repeated punches. A meltdown, a tantrum, and the woman is every bit as abandoned as she imagines.

"Bridget, stop," Gus says. "Catch your breath. And just sit there. Quietly."

She looks at him, dazed. The dog barks.

"And, you," he says to Ivy, "you hush! I mean it. Hush!"

The dog lowers herself to the floor and snorts. Gus lights a candle and then shuts off the lamp. "Stay quiet," he warns both of them. He closes his eyes. He falls easily into a trance, as if it's his only refuge. There he sits at the edge of the ocean thinking he can control the tides. He lifts his hand, and the waves roll backward toward a distant shore. The water peels away, exposing the sandy, rocky floor, and Gus watches a desert emerge. In that desert there are cacti blooming and flowering Ocotillo blowing in the brisk, dry wind. And there are no cops. And no bodies. And no blood. And there never has been anything here but life. Here the petroglyphs are masterpieces. They speak to him. They tell him stories of families and happiness, of love and protection. They also tell him of battles, and he can hear a distant war. Most of all, they tell him about survival, of people who lived to tell, who wrote down their notes, who could all teach us a lesson. Gus sees that this is the way it was meant to be, a kind of Eden; he sees this as a personal sanctuary, that everyone has his or her own sanctuary. This woman will find hers. He knows this intuitively. He opens his eyes.

She's looking right at him, a bird who's lost her way.

He doesn't blink. He hopes she can truly see the map of life in his eyes. Shadows of the candle flicker against the wall behind her. There's a code in those shadow flames, he believes.

"What are your choices, Bridget? Let's talk about those."

"My choices? Well, I can take off, but they'll come after me as a witness. Or I could cooperate right now and have Daddy's thugs at my doorstep."

"Or we could protect you," he says.

"Huh?"

"Alex will protect you. I'm sure he's told you so."

"But—"

"Let him protect you," Gus insists. "That is your sanctuary for now."

"I don't get it," she says.

"I'm telling you to trust him. In the end, it'll be worth it. In the end, you will stay here and live here and people will understand."

She stands up and extends a hand. Gus looks at it curiously. Suddenly, she's all business, and for that, Gus is glad, as well. He takes her hand and completes the gesture, and then, in a gust of a second, he feels as if he's hurling against the wall, but he's not; he just sees something that strikes him like a wallop against his chest. He rebounds from the surprise and says, without accusation, without judgment, "You're sleeping with Timothy Chase?"

Bridget gasps. "Oh my God," she whispers. "Oh my God. No one knows this."

Gus looks down and studies the floor. "I didn't either. Until now."

"Well now I know about *you*," she says with a lilt in her voice.

"Know what?"

"That you're for real." She turns to leave the room. Gus follows her to the front door.

"You're going to have to untangle yourself from him."

She laughs. "Oh, please, it's been less than a week. Hardly a tangle."

"I'm just saying you do not need the complications right now. You have to concentrate on other things. He's got a big case. And you have a big challenge. I don't see this going anywhere good."

"Neither do I," she says and walks out of the house.

"Seriously," he calls to her. "I don't really know the guy. But it's not about him. It's about you."

"I get it."

"Do you? Do you really believe me?"

She looks at him one more time before lowering herself to the car. "I do now. I absolutely do. And I think I know what I have to do."

"Do you?"

"Yeah. I'm going to Alex. This weekend."

Gus nods. "Good. I'm glad," he says. Then he raises a hand to wave good-bye.

A little later that evening—shit, it's almost midnight—Gus hears the chirp of a text message and grabs his phone reluctantly because he could use a little sanctuary of his own right now.

The message reads, "Detective Psycho closes the case! Trevor's coach arrested. You nailed it, Parker!"

He looks at the message about a dozen times, and later, a bit ashamed at the overt sense of vindication, he realizes he can't get to sleep because his smile hurts so much.

34

Saturday.

Ten thirty in the morning.

Kelly Mills looks at her husband with this beneficent smile; she's just beaming. Waving the newspaper and its giant headline about the arrest of Coach Hadley, she says, "There are no words for this relief."

"You can thank Gus Parker."

"All he did is tell you about his vibe or his vision, or whatever he calls it. But you took it from there. You went out on a limb."

Mills shrugs. They're sitting in the family room, their feet up on the coffee table. They're sipping coffee and watching CNN. They're not really watching; the TV is on, and they're in no hurry to move. Trevor is still asleep.

"I wouldn't call it a limb," Mills tells his wife.

"Whatever it was, I'm glad it's over," she says, her voice melodious, her exhale mighty.

Mills offers her forehead a kiss, but he's not thinking about the drugs, or the coach, or about Trevor, for that matter; he has a vague sense of something else that he needs to do. He senses some kind of slow, rising revelation, like an epiphany dragging itself out of bed in the morning. *All Gus did was tell him about his vibe. And Mills took it from there.*

"Honey, let's take a drive to Prescott tomorrow."

Sunday.

Two minutes past eight in the morning.

Gus Parker's phone erupts like a flock of birds startled from their nest. It's chirping, then shrieking as it dances across the surface of the nightstand. He groans and reaches for the device, doesn't recognize the caller, and rolls back over. Ivy licks his face. He's suddenly thinking about Billie Welch, the way he sometimes finds himself thinking in non sequiturs as he awakes. The phone rattles again.

"Yeah?" he says deep in the middle of a yawn.

"Wake up, Mr. Parker."

"Who is this?"

"This is Timothy Chase with your eight o'clock wake-up call."

"Oh."

"You don't remember?" the man asks.

Gus tosses in the bed, the phone cradled at his neck. "I remember you said you'd call."

"Great," the detective says. "I was beginning to wonder if psychics sacrifice their memories because they dwell so much in the future."

"That's very eloquent for eight o'clock in the morning," Gus tells the man, pulling himself up to lean on the headboard.

"I've been up since five."

"So, what's the plan?"

Chase tells him he's on the way over now. "I've got the file. Get your ass out of bed and let's go for breakfast."

Gus's first inclination is to negotiate for another thirty minutes, but before he can say anything the detective is gone. So he rushes Ivy out to the backyard where she can pee, poop, whatever, and then he drags her back inside where he leaps into the shower. He can't think straight. He forgot to put on the coffee. He scrubs his scalp with vigor. Still nothing. He towels off and heads naked, straight to the coffeemaker. "Hurry up," he tells it and then scavenges for clothes in the bedroom. There's a clean T-shirt, good. He pulls his last clean pair of shorts from a drawer, great. He eyes the flip-flops at the bottom of the closet, but a voice inside says, no, you need to be sturdier on your feet today, so he reluctantly grabs a pair of boots.

Ivy is all hyped up sensing the energy of her dad. She's bouncing everywhere.

"Oh, girl, I need to get out of here in a hurry," Gus tells her. "I'm so sorry."

Ten minutes later there's a knock on his door.

"I'll be right out," he calls.

He's dressed, and he grabs a mug, pours the coffee, opens the door, and almost runs down Timothy Chase who's hulking in the frame.

"I said I'd be right out," he tells the detective. "You're lucky I didn't spill hot coffee all over you."

"Smells like some fancy stuff."

Gus hadn't noticed, the aroma is routine to him, but he does, for an instant, smell something distant burning in the air.

They're in Chase's Jeep, now, making their way east. They drive in silence, just the way Gus would have the morning, the way the sky sneaks up on you on a golden desert day, unfolding at your window, offering you Zen that probably won't last through the day. But he'll take it. This is where he is. Riding east, with a man who seems difficult but determined, a quiet guy who sneaks up on you like a coworker to push you aside, a guy who gets results and who sleeps with a woman even though she's damaged. Or maybe because she's damaged. He studies Chase now, tries not to imagine him fucking Bridget Mulroney, and senses this guy, this so-called profiler, knows damage when he sees it.

Alex Mills and his wife are loading up the SUV with a cooler of drinks and sandwiches. Kelly grabs his arm. "Are you sure you want to leave him?" she asks.

"He's learned a lot this weekend, Kel."

"I know, but . . ."

"And he can have a day of freedom. We've got to show him there's a payoff."

She stares at him, and he can't look away. There is fear in her eyes, worry across her face. "I think we at least have to tell him to stay around the house," she says.

"He's earned some of our trust back."

"I don't want any of his friends to pick him up and take him driving all over making trouble."

Mills shakes his head and says, "What is it you're not seeing about this?"

"Huh?"

"This is a big deal for him, Kelly. This is huge."

She looks at him defiantly. "I *know* that, Alex. Don't condescend to me. Why don't you just ask to get back on the case so we don't have to go sneaking around? They have no reason to keep you off it now."

He shakes his head. "No. I'm not going to grovel at this point. But, fuck it, maybe we shouldn't go," he tells her with a sigh of disgust. "Not with all this drama."

Abruptly she turns away and walks toward the open garage.

"I'm sorry, Kelly," he calls to her. "Hey, I didn't mean that."

She's saying something from the dark box of the garage, but Mills can't hear her because a car is squealing down the street.

"What?" he yells to her.

She waves her hands and yells something back.

It looks as if they're fighting, but they're not. They're deafened by the hysteria of the approaching car. Mills is halfway up the driveway when he looks back and sees a white Mercedes barreling toward the curb in front of his house. The tires issue a final scream as one wheel slams into the sidewalk. From the driver's side door emerges Bridget Mulroney, her arms flailing.

"Where are you going?" she begs.

He might as well be scratching his head, but he just narrows his eyes and says, "Bridget?"

She races toward him. "Protect me please. Alex, please."

"Huh?"

"I'm cooperating!" she cries. Then she looks at the open hatch of his SUV. "Are you leaving town, Alex? Where are you going?"

He can't refrain from shaking his head, much the way people can't help but laugh at the absurd, the painfully absurd, and here it is, or rather here she is, and it bewilders him. "On a road trip," he replies. "To Prescott."

She starts to shake, addled on caffeine or panic, or both.

"Bridget, are you all right?" he asks, aware, of course, that she's not.

"Please don't leave," she says in a whisper. "I'm scared."

"There's nothing to be scared of," he assures her, though he knows he can't assure her. It's just what you do with crazy. He's done it before a million times with suspects, with victims, with whomever hits the curb of life and comes bouncing at him like a ball whacked out of bounds.

"You don't know," she says.

"I don't know everything. But I know you'll be safe. I'll be speaking to the sergeant tomorrow, and before we move forward there will be a plan for you."

She puts a hand to her chest. Her mouth opens, and from it comes a voice that's a roiling cauldron. "Don't leave me! Please, Alex. I'm begging you."

He's not sure if he buys her hysteria. Not sure if she's playing or suffering, if this is really Bridget or one of her many charades, but he doesn't have time to investigate her motive, so to speak, or the patience to think out the transaction, which is why he so quickly says, "Get in the car."

She doesn't hear him.

He says, "Get in the car, Bridget."

Still, she's possessed. And he can't indulge this. He has just fucking had it already. "Bridget, get in my freakin' car and close the door. You're coming with us. Day trip. We're packing lunch."

"Huh?"

"I said get in the car."

And suddenly she goes limp and obeys his order without saying a word.

In the kitchen Mills tells his wife about their guest.

"You're kidding me," is her first response.

"Wish I were," he concedes. "But, c'mon, we have to hit the road, babe, and I can't waste time sitting here and playing her shrink."

"Then call Timothy Chase. He's trained for that."

"Nice," he says with a puff of disgust. "Call Timothy Chase because he's the one to call when Alex fails."

"You know I didn't mean that."

One nod, and then he says, "Yeah. I know. But still."

"It was a stupid thing to say."

"Besides I think they're sleeping together," he says.

"Oh, God," she groans. "Of course they are. This just keeps getting better."

"Or worse."

"You can't ask me to sit in a car with her for almost two hours."

"I can make it in less."

She rolls her eyes, and then raises her hands in surrender. "This is completely not cool," she tells him. "But I don't have any better ideas."

"I wish you did."

She smiles. "You do?"

He reaches for her and pulls her close. "Yes," he says. "You're the smartest woman I know. Let's not argue."

Timothy Chase is chowing down on a cowboy's breakfast of steak and eggs and potatoes. He has a side of grits. Gus Parker on the other hand has ordered yogurt and fruit. With a side of granola. He can read Chase's mind and not in the psychic way: *Gus is a pussy.* That's how men like Timothy Chase think, and that's how they talk. Gus hates that word, but in order to eat healthy, if he had to stand up and say, *Yes, I am a pussy who eats yogurt,* he would do it. The reality is Chase is a man's man, with a huge body and practically no soul. In the limited exposure he's had with Chase he's picked up very little from the guy. Yes, he intuited Chase would elbow Mills out of the way, but that was probably obvious to the non-psychics in the room. And he intuited the sexual relationship between Chase and Bridget Mulroney, but that wasn't such a stretch either. The guy is a concrete wall, three cinderblocks deep. Gus assumes the interior is hollow, but now watching the guy eat, Chase unaware he's being watched, Gus acknowledges that maybe the interior is a black hole where stuff goes to die. Who doesn't have a black hole?

Gus asks for a refill of coffee.

Timothy Chase pulls the file out and smiles. "Good research," he says. "Now where do you see the connection to our killer?"

"Theodore Smith had a kid. The kid isn't a kid anymore. From what we know he lives in the valley. We got his license plate."

"So? That's not motive. Not physical evidence. We don't even know if the kid exists. Or whether he died in that fire."

"Maybe there's a connection to Willis," Gus suggests. "Maybe they're working together."

The waitress returns and fills Gus's cup.

"News flash," Chase says. "We have no fingerprints of Willis at Crystal Ledge. We tried for a match. It doesn't look like he ever entered that house where his wife was staying."

Gus sips then says, "Wait a minute. How did you try for a match? Did you have the guy's fingerprints on file or something?"

"Or something."

Chase dives into his plate again, carving up the meat.

"What do you need me for?" Gus asks.

Without looking up the detective, in mid-chew, says, "To trace back these murders with me. After breakfast we're going to South Mountain, then to Squaw Peak, then to Camelback, and so on. And I want you to concentrate, and I want you to focus, and I want you to lead me to evidence."

"Against Willis?"

"Against anyone at this point, Mr. Parker," Chase replies. "Look, between you and me, let's say Willis isn't behind this, then who is? This mystery man with the white pickup?"

"Yes," Gus says. "That's the vibe I get. You don't have to believe me, but if you believe that I can pick up evidence on a tour of the crime scenes, then surely you believe my hunches are reliable. Let's stop by the guy's house."

"Later," Chase says.

Gus has a hunch that it's going to be a long day.

Kelly tells the woman in the back seat to relax. "I love this drive," she says to Bridget. "It's so beautiful. You don't have to think of anything right now but the scenery."

Bridget smiles.

They're heading north out of Phoenix. Not north enough where the scenery truly inspires awe, but they're on their way, and Bridget is restless, fidgeting from one position to another. Kelly has already promised legal services to Bridget, but that hasn't pacified the woman; she needs medication, Mills suspects, and probably a new life. He can't give her either, but Kelly has insisted on taking Bridget to a doctor tomorrow morning, and Bridget has acquiesced, at least, to that.

Mills wants to let the women talk for a while so he can tune out. He'd like to drift off and imagine the journey north as a thrilling adventure upriver. He'd like to hear something like the howl of nature rushing by and feel the constant awakening of water dousing his face. That's his kind of therapy right now, but the car has fallen eerily silent, and he can hear the torture in the back seat, so much torture, and he looks to his wife beside him and sees a sort of helplessness on her face.

She's amazing, but she's not a magician.

She loves a challenge, but she also loves the harbor of a Sunday morning.

"Look," he says to the woman in the back seat, eyeing her in the rearview mirror, "I'm going to let you in on something."

She sits up and pokes her face between the front headrests. "Really?"

"Yeah," Mills says, aware of how easily he can manipulate her lucidity. "We're not going on a picnic."

Kelly gives him a look. He shrugs. The face between the headrests features two bulging eyeballs. "Are you kidnapping me?" Bridget asks.

What he wants to say: *No. You wouldn't last the ride. I'd throw you out before I'd get your ransom.*

What he says, instead: "No. We're sort of on an exploratory mission. Can you keep a secret?" He's fairly sure that she can't.

"Of course," she says. "I've been keeping secrets all my life."

He explains that she owes him the secret considering he has promised to protect her. He looks straight ahead, directing his explanation to the road in front of him. He says he's searching for a woman, a woman who might be the key to the murders. It's a gamble, he concedes, but in the face of an overwhelming lack of evidence, it's worth the trip.

"You think a woman did it?" Bridget asks, a lilt of excitement in her voice.

"No," Mills says. "I do not think a woman did it. But I think there's a woman in Prescott who might have some information about the killer."

"I'm intrigued," she says. "But you're off the case. Does Chase know?"

Mostly he continues to speak to the vista ahead, but occasionally he pivots and speaks to her profile, like he does now, to explain he is not on official business. He says he's simply doing some research, following up on a tip; he warns her that they may come home empty-handed. "And that's your part of the deal, Bridget. This is a secret mission. I don't want to interfere with Chase, but I also know I can't sit back and let more women get murdered in the desert."

"Wow, I applaud you, Detective. I really do," she says.

"No applause necessary," Kelly Mills tells Bridget. "If he weren't doing this, he'd be home climbing the walls."

Then Bridget announces that she's getting cramps. "I think I'm getting my period," she tells them. "Do you fucking believe this?"

Kelly asks her if she needs to stop.

"Well, yeah," Bridget says, "unless you'd like a bloodbath in your back seat."

Mills throws up a little in his mouth and says he'll get off at the next exit.

They're standing in the cave at South Mountain where the body of Elizabeth Spears was found just over two weeks ago. The trail has reopened, and a moderate stream of hikers passes by, crunching the ground beneath them, some of them stopping to point and whisper. Gus tunes out the curious humanity and tunes in, once again, to the artwork of the murderer. This place is dead; that much is obvious. And yet Gus senses that the crude petroglyph has life, as if it's crawling from the wall, to the floor, up his leg, etching itself into his skin. Gentle carvings, innocent droplets of blood. It advances to his torso. His first instinct is to swat it away as if it's a fly, but he lets it linger, feels it circle his neck. The petroglyph whispers into his ear; it recognizes Gus, recognizes Chase; it remembers all the cops. Then the whisper becomes a hiss, and it says, "He might be messing with you, Gus," and Gus stands there uncertain whether the voice is the voice of the artwork, or the voice of his uncle Ivan. And then the cave surrenders little else, except the suspicion that Gus has been brought here for entertainment and nothing more. And while it takes a lot to piss off Gus Parker, he's nobody's chump. If Chase is messing with him, then Gus, on an inconvenient Sunday morning, can certainly mess with Chase.

"Oh, God," he says, "the murderer has been back here. He comes to pay respects. He may be close right now."

Chase nods. "I wouldn't be surprised."

"Fits the profile?"

"Quite possibly. Anything else?"

Gus considers his fable and says, "Oh, yeah, much more. I know his footsteps now. His shoe size. Ten and a half D. No, make that C. He's married to an opera singer."

Chase steps forward. "Wow. This is getting interesting, Parker."

"He loves her very much. He wants to confess. Really he does. But he doesn't want to destroy her world, Detective. You see the jam he's in? How do you love and lie? This cave tells me so much. He's clean-shaven. Uses roll-on, occasionally a stick. Likes Mexican food, particularly fajitas."

Chase belts out a good laugh, then pulls Gus by the arm. "Enough," the detective says.

"No," Gus insists. "I've just started. You want to hear the rest, don't you?"

"Do I?"

He's messing with you. Remember that.

"Of course you do, Chase. You might want to know that our killer is on to you. He knows you're profiling him. He knows all about you. I wonder if he eluded you during your FBI days. Could this be personal?"

A thump in Gus's chest, a sudden tug between fact and fable, a discovery that the killer, indeed, knows all about Chase, knows all about both of them. He's about to say something when the detective grabs him by the shoulders and says, "Enough, Parker."

"No, wait. I think he's wearing a mask. Very hard to see the truth behind the mask."

"Not as hard as you think," Chase hisses, his face blistered with anger at Gus's subterfuge.

Their eyes are fixed. Neither flinches. The energy rises; there's fire and heat embedded in this ocular standoff. Each man quietly invades the other's brimming cosmos, their eyes like vortices of both mystery and revelation. Chase throws a cerebral punch; Gus hits back twice as hard.

Get the fuck out of there.

Unlock this.

Move.

Gus slowly inches backward, eyes still locked, and as he does he can feel the puzzle pieces disassembling on his face. This all could be over. He sees flashes of an apprehension, a fingerprint, a box of steel bars, and a sliding door.

"Something wrong?" Chase asks.

Gus takes a deep breath and exhales. He can't seem to find his compass, which is usually as instinctive, if not banal, as breath itself. Even the outline of the cave against the shockingly dependable sky is wary and unfamiliar.

"Do you already have another suspect?" he asks Chase.

"Of course not," Chase says defiantly. "Why would I be wasting my time with you if I did?"

He's fucking with you.

The look behind Chase's eyes, the one that only Gus can see, is a slow, emerging shadow of malevolence. The eyes won't let go, and Gus knows he's cornered. And, suddenly, he knows it's his fingerprint. He knows it's his prison cell.

"I'm your new suspect," he says. "Aren't I?"

Chase folds his arms across his chest. "Why would you say that?"

"Because you don't care about my research. This was just a ploy to get me out here and work me over."

Chase smiles. "Is that your psychic intuition speaking, or just your paranoia?"

Still fucking with you.

Gus shakes his head. "Seriously, Chase, you are dead wrong."

"But maybe all your 'research' about Theodore Smith was simply a ploy to distract us from the truth. . . ."

They're whispering now, gravely.

"You've got to be kidding me," Gus replies.

"Maybe you've been kidding us all along," Chase says, moving closer to Gus until their faces are mere inches apart. "You seem to know when these murders will happen. You seem to pick up these so-called vibes. Nice cover for a killer who isn't actually a psychic."

"That's crazy."

"Is it? You do know I'm a forensic psychologist, Gus. And it's not uncommon for killers, particularly serial killers, to come forward and in some way help the cops."

"Does Mills know about this?"

Chase shakes his head. "No," he says. "If he did, he'd be out here too."

"Then arrest me," Gus says flatly. "I'm not playing your game. We're done with the crime scene tour."

Chase spins Gus around and grabs his wrists together. Gus can hear the jangle of handcuffs, and he takes another deep breath. His visions, his memories, his psyche go dark. All he senses is the fragrance of a naked desert, that toasty, sunbaked emptiness of a valley. And fear. Not his fear alone, but the fear that resonates here, that will forever remain in this cave as an artifact of murder. Gus is waiting for the clasp of the handcuffs. But his wrists go free.

"Gus Parker," Chase says, "you are not under arrest for the murders of Elizabeth Spears, Lindsey Drake, Andrea Willis, Monica Banfield, or any other woman found dead around the valley. Anything you say can and will be used against you in the court of humiliation."

Then Chase cackles wildly. His shrilly laughter echoes from wall to wall of the cave. He's practically out of breath when Gus turns to him and says, "What the fuck?"

"I'm sorry, man. I couldn't resist. I'm so sorry," he begs, doubling over.

Gus bolts from the cave, stumbling into a trio of hikers.

"C'mon, Parker," Chase yells to him. "Can't you take a joke?"

Gus walks briskly back to the car. He can hear Chase advancing behind him, but he doesn't turn back once to look.

35

Bridget Mulroney hops into the back seat and says, "False alarm."

They're at a truck stop that sits right below the highway ramp. Kelly let Bridget use the bathroom first, then darted in to pee as Bridget returned to the car.

"I like your wife, Mills. She's a very good woman."

"I'm lucky," he says.

"She's lucky."

"We're all lucky," Mills tells her.

"I'm not," Bridget laments, flouncing back in the seat.

Mills can't engage. He's reaching a delicate breaking point with Bridget. He can reach out to help, so long as he doesn't get sucked into her vortex; crazy people are known for their vortices. Kelly returns.

"Anybody want something from the cooler while we're stopped?" she asks.

"No," Mills replies. "Let's hit the road."

Bridget leans across the seat holding a tampon. "No menses," she tells Kelly. "You want this back?"

Kelly shakes her head. "Oh, no, Bridget. You keep it. With my compliments."

They're back on the highway. Forty miles to Prescott.

"What's our first stop? The PD?" Bridget asks.

"No," Mills replies. "I'm not on official business, remember?"

"Right," she says. "So where then?"

"Don't worry about it," Mills replies. "Sometimes the best plan is no plan."

He tells her the news about Coach Hadley, that the rest of the charges against Trevor will likely be dropped, that everyone, at some point in life, needs protection. And then the car is quiet until they enter Prescott where Mills hears Bridget coming to life again with short, spastic fidgets of anticipation in the back seat. She's humming scales, as if she's scoring the music to intrigue, a kind of thrilling soundtrack that is probably just a beat or two from bursting out in song. As a pre-emptive strike, Mills swings the car into a diagonal parking space on the main drag, and the sudden motion evokes a "whoa" out of Bridget, and not an aria, which is good.

Perfect place. A craft show just across the street in a park. They wander over, Mills telling the women to stay close. It's turquoise and silver galore, the clichés of southwestern jewelry that every bored housewife believes will rocket her to gallery status, or QVC. There are all kinds of dream catchers and fake kachina dolls and belt buckles. In stall after stall are Santa Fe motifs, images of pueblos and horses and pottery. Once Mills has scoped the place out, he says they should split up, each of them taking a radius of ten booths in each direction.

"Just ask if they know Priscilla Smith. Nothing else," Mills says. "If they don't, move on. If they do, come get me."

Thirty booths later they come up empty-handed.

"You would think someone would have heard of her," Kelly says. "But maybe they're protecting her. Like people protect an old legend."

Bridget begins to hum again. She likes the sound of a legend.

"Maybe," Mills says.

They head back to the car and pile in. As Mills is pulling the door shut, he's startled by a rap at the window. He looks up at a young man, probably midtwenties with curly brown hair and Clark Kent eyeglasses.

"Sorry I scared you," the stranger says with a toothy grin. "I heard one of those ladies was looking for Priscilla Smith?"

"Yeah?" Mills says with hesitance.

"There's a Priscilla who works at the Mountain View Diner. I don't know her last name, but a lady named Priscilla waited on me yesterday."

"About how old? You remember?"

"I don't know," the guy says, shaking his head. "Older, I guess. I put you at forty-something. So I'd say she was maybe sixty."

Mills smiles. Always thought he looked younger. "You from out of town?" he asks.

"Yep," the guy says, extending a hand. "Joey Waters. I came up from Tucson to help my girlfriend sell some jewelry."

The men shake.

"Well, thank you, Joey. Mind pointing the way to this diner?"

Joey recites the directions.

It's almost noon. The diner is buzzing. The three of them stand in the doorway searching nametags for Priscilla Smith. People are staring at them. Mills can feel it. A waitress, Peggy, approaches. "How many?" she asks. Her brassy hair is piled on top of her head, a hairnet keeping the whole ordeal in place.

"Oh, um, we weren't really planning on eating," Mills says.

She puts her hands on her hips. "Then what are you planning on? Cabaret?"

She laughs and snorts.

Mills looks at his wife and shrugs. Then he turns back to the waitress and says, "I'm sorry. We were just looking for somebody. Priscilla Smith. She works here?"

Peggy backs up. "Priscilla Smith?" she asks, straining to get the words out of her contorted mouth.

The diner goes quiet.

A man steps out from behind the counter and comes forward. He's wearing a white shirt with a bolo tie. His pants stop just short of his ankles.

"Is there a problem here?" he asks.

Peggy steadies herself and says, "These people say they're looking for Priscilla Smith."

"Huh?" the man asks, turning to Mills. "We got ourselves a Priscilla Reynolds, but we don't got no Priscilla Smith. You looking for that Priscilla? That Priscilla don't go out much from what I hear. 'Cept to church. You wanna eat something?"

Mills smiles. "No, thanks. Sorry to bother you. We just really need to talk to Ms. Smith."

Another waitress, Jean, pops into the mix. "The talk of the town is that old Priscilla's turned to God now."

Mills notes the sarcasm in the waitress's voice.

"She in some kind of trouble again?" the man asks.

Mills says no, she's in no trouble. "Can you tell me which church?" he asks.

The man shakes his head. So does Peggy. But Jean leans forward and says, "They're all lined up next to each other. You might as well try 'em all. Go on over to Main Street. She'll be the one with the long white hair and the ugly scar on her neck."

Peggy laughs. "Jean, you're so crude."

"Oh, never mind that," Jean insists. "She's a good woman from what I hear. A little, I don't know, different. But she's old and sweet, I guess. I mean, despite what she's done."

The man orders them back to work, muttering something about hungry mouths to feed. As Mills ushers Kelly and Bridget from the diner, he's aware of a town council of eyes following their exit.

As soon as Chase drops into the car, Gus looks away. Chase apologizes again, but Gus won't acknowledge him. They're out on Forty-Eighth Street, turning right, and Gus, his head resting against the window, says, "I think you should take me home."

Chase laughs. "Aw, come on, Gus, man up, won't you?"

Gus takes a deep breath and exhales coolly. "You know, I think you sort of killed the vibe back there with that stupid stunt."

"Killed the vibe?" Chase snickers. "I guess I don't get all this New Age shit."

"No, I'm serious," Gus tells him. "There are many ways you can interrupt the flow of a psychic, you know. Masquerading is one."

Chase doesn't respond.

"Like doing something that isn't real," Gus explains. "Or being someone who isn't real. I work organically, Detective. When sources lie, misrepresent, distort, pretend, well, I can't go anywhere. It preempts the vibe."

Still, Chase says nothing.

"Bullshit distracts me," Gus simplifies.

"How many times do I need to apologize for you to get your vibe back?" Chase asks.

"Why don't we try another day?"

Chase slams the steering wheel. "No!"

Gus watches the man's face fill with the flush of red. Chase turns toward him, his jaw clenched. "No, Parker, we have to do this today. You need to focus today. I'm not going another week without a lead."

The man's desperation is palpable. The tires squeal as he rounds corners. He grips the wheel as if he's hanging on for dear life. Gus sees now the attraction between Chase and Bridget: craziness that creates chemistry. "Fine," Gus tells him. "But I'm not scaling down Squaw Peak to get to that cave."

Chase smiles. "Thatta boy! You don't have to scale. We'll just hike to the cliff above it."

And so they do.

The sky is boasting its eternity today, cloudless and impossible to fathom; it's a mirage without horizons, explored, but contemplating its infinity will make you crazy. Gus is in such a trance when Chase asks, "Do you sense anything from the cave down there?"

Gus looks briefly over the cliff and says, "No." And then, suddenly, he adds, "Oh, yes." And he sees the license plate. ILMD. And the white pickup in the parking lot. "Yes, he was here. He was definitely here."

"The killer?"

"Theodore Smith," Gus replies with a shudder. "That guy was here. I see his car."

Chase nods, encouraging Gus for more.

"And I know the license plate. I-L-M-D. And—"

"Can you see his face? Do you know when he was here?"

"Shh!" Gus tells him. "I see him talking to a woman. She's smiling. She's wearing hiking boots, and she has a ponytail. And they go off together up a trail. They've just met. He's asking her questions. Now they're laughing. She leans against that rock over there." Gus points. "And they're talking for like an hour. But, no, I really can't see their faces."

Chase looks at him in awe. "This is incredible, Gus. Absolutely incredible. You're seeing him in action."

"Oh my God," Gus whispers, sinking to his knees. He sifts dirt through his fingers.

Chase puts his hand on Gus's shoulder. "You all right?"

"Now they're right here. Right where we are. They're studying the view. And Smith tells the girl, 'You really are beautiful,' and the girl is all aglow. And then Smith says, 'How lucky am I to find you out here today,' and the girl looks down, shy, and demure, then reaches for Smith's hand. He's telling her about the cave, but she shakes her head, no, 'I won't go down there,' and he says, 'Trust me,' but she keeps shaking her head, and then he scrambles down the cliff to show her how easy it is and climbs back up and grabs her by the neck and kisses her."

Chase pulls him to his feet. "You think this is really how it went down?"

"I'm seeing it right now."

"Does she trust him?"

"She lets him kiss her, and she falls into him, and now he has her by the hand leading her slowly over the cliff. And now they're gone, and they're on the ledge, and he leads her into the cave, and he squeezes her tight and kisses her. And she starts to pull off her sweatshirt and then, Jesus Christ, he slams her head into the side of the cave, and she falls, and now he's on top of her, stuffing something in her mouth, and he pulls a knife out of his pocket. He just keeps knifing her. Oh, Jesus. She wants to scream, but she's gagging. She's sobbing. And she's wriggling beneath him. And then she stops moving."

"Stop," Chase says.

Gus feels his eyes bulge, tastes the sweat running down his face. Again, he shudders.

"Are you okay?" Chase asks.

"I don't know," Gus tells him. "But that's how it happened. It's Theodore Smith, and he's a big guy with a calm face. But his features are a blur. Everything happened so fast. I'm sorry."

"Sorry?" Chase begs. "Are you kidding me? You're brilliant. This is the best picture we have of how this killer operates. You need some water?"

Gus nods.

"I have some back in the car."

Gus follows.

The churches aren't exactly all on one street, but Mills figures the information was colloquial geography at best. Back on the main drag, they pass the First Congregational, and then a few blocks west they look down and see another church on South Marina. Up ahead there's a Methodist church and what looks like another church behind it. He parks outside the Methodist, and he tells the women to wait. He goes in, sees that the service is over, and drifts to a courtyard where a few women are cleaning up snack tables.

"I'm so sorry to barge in like this, but I'm looking for someone who may be a member of your church," Mills tells them.

One of the ladies wipes her hands clean and approaches him. "And you are?"

"Sorry. Alex Mills."

"Hello, Alex. I'm Cecilia—"

"You're not from around here," the other woman interrupts. They're probably sisters, with their dyed little bobs, their identical pearls, and their thin and spotted skin.

"I'm looking for Priscilla Smith."

"Are you from the media? She won't talk to the media," Cecilia says.

"Are you a friend of hers?" Mills ask.

"Please don't bother her," the woman insists.

"But I'm not a reporter," he explains. "Actually, I'm an off-duty detective."

The other woman comes forward and grabs Cecilia's elbow. "I'm sorry we can't help you," she says.

They're about to turn away, but Mills says, "She's not in any kind of trouble. I can assure you. I just need her help with something. Could you call her for me?"

Cecilia looks down at her feet, avoiding Mills's eyes. "I'm sorry. We're really not close friends. She's been keeping to herself mostly."

"And we don't have her phone number," the other woman adds.

"Okay, thank you," Mills says. "So sorry to bother you."

As he is walking from the courtyard, Cecilia's companion calls after him. "Priscilla is a Presbyterian. Maybe you should go look there."

When he's back in the car, Kelly is asking Bridget about drug and alcohol abuse. Bridget is saying she's never really had a problem with either.

"Maybe you're stronger than you think," Kelly tells her.

"No. I'm not stronger than I think. I'm a nutcase."

Mills lets them talk as he punches in "Presbyterian" and "Prescott" into Google Maps. The church is about seven miles to the south, a maze of surface roads to get there. "I found her church," he tells the women.

"I'm a total nutcase," Bridget says. "Aren't I, Alex?"

"Yes. You are."

"You see . . ." she says to Kelly. "Even your husband agrees."

"My husband is on a mission."

The mission takes about ten minutes and a mind-boggling series of lefts and rights and one U-turn because Mills missed a street. He looks in the rearview mirror and sees that Bridget is drifting off to sleep, and he's relaxed to know that even momentarily she's off the grid. Whether or not the woman is certifiably insane, she is a drain.

"Are you nervous?" Kelly whispers.

"Why would I be nervous?"

"Well I don't know. I guess the prospect of getting a good lead would be making you edgy."

"Not edgy," he says emphatically. "I'm stoked. I feel some of the mojo coming back."

She leans over and kisses him.

There are still a dozen cars or more in the parking lot of the Presbyterian church. It's a modest building surrounded by scattered pines. The climate here is different, cooler, crisper, Arizona's version of autumn. "Come with me," he tells his wife. "I think I upset the ladies at the other church. Maybe a woman's touch will help."

"What do we do about her?" Kelly asks, pointing to the sleeping cargo in the back seat.

"Let her rest," he says.

They hold hands and walk to the front of the church. Inside, the vestibule is quiet. They wander down a hallway to the left where sunlight is drenching the corridor through high-arched windows. They duck into the sanctuary, a plain, handsome room unencumbered by hefty religious ornaments. The service is over, but two middle-aged men remain, one collecting pamphlets, the other sweeping the floor.

"Can I help you?" the sweeper asks as he brings his broom to a stop.

"I hope so," Mills replies. "We're looking for Priscilla Smith."

The guy, bald and stocky, doesn't flinch. "Oh, I think she's back in the kitchen with the ladies. Would you like me to get her?"

"Please."

"Your name?"

"I'm sorry. It's Alex Mills. Detective Alex Mills."

The man nods politely and says, "It'll just be a minute." He then moves his broom to the front of the sanctuary where he disappears behind a side door.

Mills ushers his wife into a pew, and they sit and wait. She strokes his hand. Neither of them are churchgoers. Mills has always felt sufficiently blessed in his life. A minute has passed. And another. The silence rings in his ears.

Gus is not surprised to find the south side of Camelback, particularly the ledge and the cave where Lindsey Drake was murdered, abandoned on this Sunday at noon. The teenage vampires of the valley don't come out until nightfall, and he senses that even they have avoided the cave since the woman's body was discovered. Gus and Chase stand in the blinding sunlight; it's not fiercely hot, but there isn't a stir of wind.

"Quiet up here," Chase says.

"No distractions. And that's good, because I know we're on the trail of this killer," Gus replies. He looks away from Chase, to the ground, to the trail of a murder, to the invisible footprints of a psychopath. "He's been with us ever since I saw him at the Peak."

"What? Is he haunting you?"

Gus shakes his head. "No. But it's like he's hacked our GPS, spiritually speaking. He knew where we were heading."

Gus is sure of it. It's not a hunch. It's a fact. And it both emboldens Gus and scares him shitless because it means that Smith is close, and that he's a danger to both of them.

"Funny," Chase says and then follows Gus into the cave.

Gus leans on the wall opposite the murderer's petroglyph. He imagines himself in miniature, meandering through the grooves of the carving, following the trails, brushing up against the rough edges. He sees the artist's tools in a blue pouch. And then a big hand grasping a chisel, and the chisel is coming after Gus, just missing, going after him, chasing him down through the excavation of rock. Gus starts to swerve. But then he feels the ground below him, the real ground, the ground of the cave, and he catches his balance and says, "Much ado about nothing."

"Huh?" Chase asks.

"Just an expression," Gus says. "I was having a vision that was all about me and nothing about Lindsey Drake."

"What about you?"

Gus tosses his head. "I don't know for sure. But I think this confirms that Theodore Smith knows who I am and has, in fact, been following me, staking out my house."

"I don't get that," Chase says. "Why would he be following you?"

"If the guy's going to get caught, he wants to get caught on his own terms, not on mine. He's a control freak. You're the profiler. You should know that."

Chase clears his throat. "Of course I know that. There's nothing psychic about it. Murder very often is about control."

"Yeah, but this guy's an expert. He's orchestrating the beginning, the middle, and the end."

Chase kicks the dirt and says nothing.

Gus turns to the mouth of the cave and sees a broiling wave; it looks like a mushroom cloud of heat rising from a long desert roadway. And then comes a rush of cold air. The result is that he gets swept up in the suction of a cyclone, swirling above the crime scene, and from here he can see everything. He can see the man lead Lindsey Drake up onto the ledge. He can see him spanning his arms across the view. The woman smiles, admiring the scene, and she walks farther along the ledge where the view becomes even wider, grander; the man follows and says something, and she shakes her head. She snaps some pictures.

"They didn't meet here," he tells Chase.

"Right. We figured that."

Still, Gus is hovering, Chase's voice below him, and he watches as the suspect indicates the cave, as Lindsey Drake eagerly joins him for a look inside. And then that pouch of tools falls to the ground, the killer having removed a chisel. And he starts to carve into the rock. And he chisels feverishly. Then the woman says something. The man stops, turns around, and all Gus can see is the man's furious mouth, the teeth of a demon, and the woman shuddering, cowering.

"Wow," Gus says. "He starts carving this one before he's even attacked her."

"What?"

"The image is a blueprint of her death, not a remnant."

"You mean—"

"I mean, he carved his petroglyph, and then he killed her," Gus affirms. "I'm coming down now."

"Coming down?"

"Never mind," Gus says as he whirls back to the floor of the cave. Once he feels his feet on the ground again, he starts waving his hands. "She's in the corner over there begging him to stop, telling him he's defacing the mountain. And he's here right up against the wall carving like crazy. I see the back of his head. And I see his shoulders tighten up, and he tells her to shut the fuck up, and she says, 'I'm outta here,' and he says, 'No, you're not,' and as she moves to the front of the cave he spins around and slaps her in the face. Then, with one arm across her chest, he knocks her to the ground. He gags her, then plunges the knife into her chest. The rest is the same. The knife, the blade, the silent screaming, the same."

Chase shakes his head. "Damn," he says. "This is sort of freaking me out."

Gus is perspiring again, his muscles weak, his legs wobbly. "Okay," he says. "Is that enough for today?"

"Did you see their faces?"

Gus shrugs. "Not completely. But it doesn't matter. It was Theodore Smith at the Peak, and it was Theodore Smith here. Same man, same car."

"You look like you've been hit by a truck."

"I'm fine."

They're in Chase's car now, descending. Gus has an urge to call Beatrice and an urge to call Billie Welch. He understands the first urge, not the second. But he's come to realize that that which he doesn't understand is usually more meaningful. They turn on to Camelback. "You mind if I gas up before I take you home?" Chase asks.

Gus shrugs. "Whatever."

Three blocks later they pull into a Circle K, and Chase gets out to pump fuel. Gus listens to the chunk-chunk of the pump as it begins to release gasoline, and then the full gush when it starts to fill the tank. He just sits and listens, and he feels an affirmation coming. In his state, he knows he can't really handle a full head-on affirmation at high speed, so he braces himself. And then it hits, more gently than he would have expected: this is the gas station where Lindsey Drake met Theodore Smith. This is where she asked him for directions. Of course.

Chase pokes his head in the car. "She's all filled up. You want something from inside? I'm all out of water."

"You know this is where Lindsey met Smith."

"Yeah. That's the theory. Not exactly psychic. We have the receipt from her car."

"No. I realize that. But it just occurred to me that we're at the same place. I've just confirmed it."

"You still think Smith is still following you?" Chase asks with a smile.

"Probably."

"Water?"

"Yeah."

Chase is in no hurry walking into the store. He strides like a man who's done his day at work. So it's surprising that he's in such a hurry coming out. He's thundering toward the car, juggling the water, his face seething with urgency.

"What is it?" Gus asks when Chase jumps in.

"We have a body," Chase says, flinging the bottles to the floor. "Some hikers found a body this morning at the Superstitions. The crime scene's a match!"

"Jesus. . . ."

"No shit. I get a call from headquarters while I'm standing in line with the water." He starts the car. "I don't even know if I paid, 'cause all I could hear was there's a body and a carving and we've got crews on the way."

Chase pulls out to Camelback, nearly hitting a pedestrian. In an instant, they're going fifty-five and climbing.

"My house is the other way," Gus says gently.

Chase turns to him suddenly. "Are you kidding? Are you freaking kidding? You don't want to come along? Especially now?"

"Well, it's just that I think I've nailed Theodore Smith about as good as I'm going to nail him."

Chase grips the steering wheel. "Fine," he says. "Then I'm going to have to let you out here. Call a cab or something. I don't have time to take you home."

They're at Hayden Road. Beatrice could come get him. But Chase shows no sign of slowing down.

"Hey, if you need me out there, I'll ride. Okay?"

Chase accelerates. "It would be helpful to know if this is the real thing or not. Could be a copycat now that the trails are open and the story of the petroglyphs has all but gone public."

"I was worried about that," Gus says. "But, honestly, I think this is Theodore Smith taunting us. It's just a vibe I get."

Chase nods. He obviously thinks so, too. He swings onto Route 60. And it's the Superstition Freeway all the way from here.

A door creaks open, and through it a petite woman passes. She stops for a moment, looks across the sanctuary, and sees them. Their eyes meet. Hers are wide with anticipation, and she approaches them. She's wearing a cardigan sweater and a denim skirt. Her hair is white, pulled back tight, clenched in a ponytail that drapes down her back. There's a scar on her neck, just above the jugular, like a warning. Her walk is steady, but she walks slowly, guiding herself by clutching the end of the pews until she reaches theirs. She's a bird, tentative, but curious. "Can I help you?" she asks them.

"I'm Alex Mills," he says, rising, extending a hand. She gives him hers, and they don't shake but rather stand there holding the introduction tenderly.

"What can I do for you, Mr. Mills?"

"This is my wife, Kelly," he says. The older woman offers his wife a tiny blossom of a smile that fades almost as quickly. "I'm a detective with the Phoenix Police Department."

"So I'm told," she says. "What could you possibly want with me?"

"It's about your son," Mills replies. "I have some questions."

He feels her hand tremble in his; she pulls it free and places it to her chest. "My son?"

"Theodore Smith," Mills says. "Junior."

Her eyes are brimming. But she steels herself. Her posture goes stiff. "What about him?"

Mills assures her that he is not on duty, that they can talk off the record, that this is not entirely official business.

"Not in here," she says. "Please follow me outside."

The older woman leads them to a picnic table at the side of the church, at the edge of a pine grove. Mills and Kelly sit on one side, Priscilla Smith opposite them. The trees towering above them whisper in the breeze, and for a moment that's all they hear. The crackling defense of branches and the faint whimpers of a woman who, in her wild eyes, is begging them to go away.

"My son is dead," she finally says.

36

About ten minutes into their speedy ride on the freeway, Gus's phone rings.

"Where are you?"

It's Beatrice.

"Hey, Bea. I'm on my way to the Superstitions."

"There's another murder, right?" she asks.

"Wow. You must be psychic."

"Seriously, Gus. That's what I'm seeing. That's why I'm calling."

"You're calling about the murder?" He turns to Chase who shakes his head and puts his hand up like a stop sign.

"I just woke up feeling like today's the day," she sings into the phone.

"For a murder?"

"Maybe," she says. "You're getting closer."

"We're on the trail of Theodore Smith, if that's what you mean. I'm feeling him every step of the way."

"Hmm. Right. As you should," she whispers. And then she disconnects.

Gus rolls his eyes. "My friend Beatrice Vossenheimer is a trip," he tells Chase. "I think you've met her."

"I'd appreciate a little discretion here, Gus. You can't just go telling everyone about the murder. It's not public information yet."

Gus shrugs. "It's just Beatrice—"

"I don't care who it is."

Duly reprimanded, Gus shuts up. The reprimand reminds him in a way of his father, and he closes his eyes and imagines his father standing over the hospital bed of Meg Parker. His father stands there stiffly, holding his wife's hands, looking brave in his misery, in his fear. His eyes are wet with tears that won't let go. Gus looks at his helpless mother. Her skin is mustard-colored, and her hair is flat and gray and matted against the pillow.

He leans against the car window, his eyes still shut. And he begins to survey the landscape of regrets. What they couldn't have known. What he should have told them. If only he could have explained it better. Or shut up altogether. If only he had decided not to pursue this gift. What, then? There was really no decision. Had they been looking for a reason to let him go? Or did he legitimately frighten them? He was frightened, too, he remembers. And exhilarated. And exhilaration won. He feels the rush now.

There's the rush of knowing something that few others know. There's the rush of exploring where no other has explored before. There's the rush of chasing down an apparition who is out of reach but not unreachable. And now he's speeding down the highway, and that's a rush, too.

He opens his eyes and looks to the detective who has gone into his own sort of trance, as well. There's a guy sitting there who might as well be driving alone. Chase's eyes are glazed over, and his lips are forming microscopic words. Timothy Chase is on a mission, and Gus respects the mission. Chase seems to have forgotten his passenger, and that's okay by Gus; he understands more now than ever that a detective is not so much what he does but how he thinks. It's that zone of crime calculus that Gus has never understood, has never had to understand, but he sees the pieces coming together on Chase's face. Those lips moving so subtly. Spelling out the story of Theodore Smith, not rushing to a conclusion but fig-uring out where one sentence ends and another one begins. Now Gus is a lip-reader. He hyper-focuses on the words until, like the occupants in this speeding car, the words are trapped in inertia. One word, really.

"I sense you're thinking about a fire," Gus says.

The man snaps to attention, his eyes bulging. "As a matter of fact, I am. That's remarkable," Chase tells him.

"What about the fire?"

"How it all makes sense."

Gus nods. Then suddenly bristles at a ghostly chill.

Kelly clutches Mills's hand and says, "I'm so sorry," to the older woman.

Priscilla Smith nods, like a woman truly accepting condolence. She's bereaved, and yet she's placid, as if her loss was processed long ago. Mills listens to his thoughts fidget. He knows he must tell her.

"Look," he says. "We have reason to believe that he didn't die in the fire."

She studies the picnic table, tracing a groove with her delicate finger. She doesn't look up when she says, "I know he didn't die in the fire, Mr. Mills."

"You do?"

"Oh, yes. I do."

"But you just said he's dead."

"To me. He's dead to me. Hardest thing I ever had to do was to let go."

"What happened?" Mills asks.

"Please. Can't we just leave it at that? I can't relive the heartache. Please," she begs.

Her eyes begin to fill. Kelly reaches to her, but the woman stiffens.

"I'm sorry, Mrs. Smith," Mills tells her. "But your son may be linked to some horrible crimes."

Then she just stares at him hard, and now he sees all the years of prison written across her face, a kind of inevitable indifference in her eyes. "I don't want to know," she says.

"I understand," Mills assures her. "I'll keep it as simple as I can. I just want to ask you some questions."

She says nothing.

"Mrs. Smith?"

Still nothing.

Mills removes a notepad from his front pocket and flips through it. "Thirty-five eighty-nine North Angel Gem Road," he reads. He looks up at Priscilla Smith. He sees a woman braced.

"That's my house," she tells him. "That's where we raised him."

"Except for the summers," Mills says. "That's when your family would go to the ocean. To Cape Cod."

"Correct."

"We tracked a pickup truck in his name to the Angel Gem Road address," he says. "We think he's living there now."

"Wouldn't surprise me."

"So, it's common knowledge he didn't die in the fire."

She shakes her head. "No," she corrects him. "It's not. But I have a feeling it will be."

"Tell me what happened to your son, Mrs. Smith," he says. "Legally I can't make you answer any questions. And I'll remind you I'm not on official business, but I'm asking you to please help me."

She leans in close. "You know I killed my husband in that fire?"

Mills nods.

"It's all public record now. I had to kill him. He had been terrorizing me and Teddy for years."

Mills takes a deep breath, then exhales. "So I've read."

"He was a good artist," she says. "But he was crazy. He went off the deep end. He had no idea. No idea who he was."

"Sounds like you were living in fear," Kelly says.

"Of course I was. He knocked me unconscious so many times I didn't recognize myself in the mirror. I'd stand there and look and say, 'Who is she?'"

"Oh my God," Kelly says, reaching again to the older woman. Priscilla Smith takes her hand.

"It's okay," she says. "I'm better now. I haven't had a nightmare in years. And yet, I . . ."

She hesitates and shakes her head.

"Go on," Kelly tells her.

"And yet I knew I wasn't finished with Teddy."

"How so?" Mills asks.

"Well, he never forgave me. Not even after all the abuse he suffered at the hands of his father. Ted had indoctrinated him into his madness. It was ritualistic and scary," she says.

"What did your husband do to him?" Mills asks, meeting her eyes, trying to project warmth from his.

"He would beat him, but while he was beating he would say, 'I love you, Teddy. I love you. You're the best boy in the world.' It was very sick, and I couldn't stop it. And then Ted got all obsessed with symbols and started making them up, though I don't think he knew he made them up. . . . I think he thought they were real. And then one day I walk into the garage and he has Teddy splayed across a workbench, and he's carving symbols into his skin."

Kelly takes a sharp, audible breath. Mills puts his arm around his wife's shoulder and squeezes. "What kind of symbols?" he asks.

"The kind from his book," she says. "Supposedly old Indian symbols."

"And your son? He didn't try to get away from his father?"

"Yes. He did at first. There was a lot of screaming and fighting. And I tried to call the police, but then I'd end up unconscious. After a while, it became a ritual, like I told you, and Teddy thought it was something special, very special between the two of them. Like some kind of magical secret. I couldn't take Teddy to a pool or a lake or anywhere to swim because everyone would see what Ted had done. When we were at the ocean I made him wear a T-shirt in the water."

"He must have those scars today," Mills says.

"I would imagine so," Priscilla answers. "I'm sure he wears those wounds like some kind of tribute to his father."

"He knew you killed Theodore Senior?" Mills asks.

"Yes. I told you. He never forgave me," she replies. "He didn't know at first. I sent him to live with my sister and brother-in-law. He wasn't even on the Cape when it happened. He was here in Prescott with them. But obviously the case made the news, and as much as they tried to shield him, eventually Teddy figured it out. I mean, it was in the newspapers everywhere."

Mills says, "I have a son."

"Everything that's wrong with Teddy is my fault," Priscilla says. "Had I known the depth of my husband's madness I would have moved my child out of harm from the very beginning. Lord, if I knew anything, I never would have had a child."

This is when Mills expects her to weep. But she doesn't. She's stone-faced.

"Everything that's wrong with *my* son is not my fault," Kelly tells her.

"Amen," says Mills.

Priscilla looks right through them. "Once he figured it out," she says, talking deep down from the pocket of a memory, "he started sending me notes in prison. Notes meant to torment me. All they said was, 'I love my daddy,' just like the words across his back. Nothing else."

"What words?"

"Ted Senior carved those words across his back. 'I love my daddy.' And, again, in very small script, on each of Teddy's shoulders. He made me stitch up the wounds myself."

"That's sick," Kelly says. "I'm sorry, but that's evil."

"I know," Priscilla says. And now she begins to weep.

They watch her cry. Mills and Kelly steal a haunted look at one another, but they watch Priscilla Smith cry her eyes out.

Mills hears a car door. He turns and sees Bridget Mulroney stumbling out of the SUV, like a drunken coed. He waves her back. She doesn't notice. He flails his arms at her until, as she's moving toward them, she stops in her tracks. She puts her hands on her hips. Her mouth makes the words, *what the fuck*. He points to the SUV. She shrugs and turns around.

"Would you like to come to the house?" Priscilla suddenly asks.

"If you think that would be helpful," Mills replies.

"I do," she sniffles. "I still have those awful notes. I want you to see them."

Mills tells her he'd like to see the notes and anything else about Teddy Jr.

"You can bring your friend," Priscilla says, pointing to the SUV where Bridget waits.

"Good," he says. "She's a colleague. We're stuck with her."

Priscilla says she'll pull her truck around so they can follow her home. "But tell me, first, what is my son accused of?"

Mills feels his jaw tighten like a vise. He gets up and says, "He's not accused of anything at this point. But surely you've heard about the cave murders around Phoenix."

She starts to swoon, like a branch floating to the ground. He rushes to her side and grabs her. "Mrs. Smith?"

"Please," she insists as she steadies herself. "I'm fine."

But she's not fine. Mills can tell. She's a petrified woman who has just seen a ghost on fire.

In the distance Gus can see the Superstitions. On a clear day, from the right vantage point, you can see them from Phoenix. They rise red from the horizon, like walls of a fortress, elusive but enchanted. He figures they're still about thirty minutes away.

"You said the fire makes sense?"

"Yup."

"How so?"

"An absolutely traumatic event like that can stay with you forever," Chase replies. "That's Forensic Psychology 101. We see it all the time, especially with serial killers. Sure, some of them are just mentally deranged, but most seem to have been influenced by something very disturbing in life."

"You're right. It's textbook," Gus says. "How about you trade me some of your forensic psychology for some of my parapsychology?"

Chase laughs. "I'm good," he replies. "But thanks."

"Can I ask your advice about something?" Gus asks.

"Advice? I don't know that I give good advice."

"Well, it's just that I find myself thinking about something we might have in common."

Chase turns to him and smirks. "You and me? I doubt it."

"My mother's dying, I think."

The guy doesn't register anything on his face. "I'm sorry. That's sad to hear."

"Thanks. But we don't speak really. I'm kind of having a hard time deciding if I should go see her."

Chase doesn't alter his connection to the horizon. He doesn't turn back to Gus. He doesn't move his eyes. "You should. I did."

"Yeah. I heard. You moved your life here to be with her."

"I did."

"It was the right decision. . . ."

"It was."

"Were you close to her?"

Chase's face turns red. His eyes begin to brim. "Very," he says. "I held her while she died."

Gus nods, then feels himself nodding repeatedly. "Wow," he finally says. "I don't have that kind of relationship with my family."

"It's never too late."

This is a side of Timothy Chase that most people never see, Gus assumes. He sees that the detective has an archeology like everyone else, but he's also sure that he's unwelcome at the site. He can't even fathom the tools he'd use to dig. Instead, he refocuses on the crime scene at the Superstitions, and he thinks of the tools used by the killer. A knife. A chisel. He concentrates, really squeezes the muscles of his brain until he can conjure up a vision. At first it's a house. Then an empty room. The place is dimly lit. He sees a bench. With an assortment of knives and chisels. He knows exactly what to tell Chase.

"You'll find evidence at the Angel Gem Road house associated with Theodore Smith," he says. "I just saw it."

Chase offers a shrug. "I assumed we would. If he's our man. No-brainer, really."

Mildly offended, Gus says, "What I mean is that I actually saw it just now. A room with a bench and all these tools. And the knives he's used to kill these women."

"You think he's used more than one?"

"I do." Gus studies the room for another moment. "I see several. Two on the bench, three on the shelf below it. Identical knives, I think."

"Like some kind of trophies."

"I have no idea, Chase. That's your department."

Chase tells him he's an asset. He looks at Gus warmly and says, "You're the first psychic I've worked with who seems like a real person. The rest of them act like they're from another planet." Then he goes for his front pocket and practically tears it off. "Damn it!" he cries. "Un. Fucking. Believable."

"What?"

"I must have left my phone at the Circle K."

"Seriously?"

"Shit. Yes. I got the call about the Superstitions, bought the water, and ran out of there. I think I left it on the counter."

"You think we can turn back?"

"Of course we can't turn back," Chase snaps. "I was wondering why nobody was calling me with an update. What a fucking nightmare."

Gus offers his phone, and Chase grabs it, dials a frenzy of numbers, and apologizes breathlessly to whoever answers. Gus tries to listen but doesn't hear anything specific. Mostly a chain of "yes, yes, yes," and "no, no, no," from Chase's end. Then he hears Chase mumble "twenty minutes," and he assumes that's their ETA. The detective hands him back the phone.

"Anything new?"

"I guess the locals hesitated when our officers got there, but that's all been settled. They don't get a lot of action out there," he says and laughs.

"Stranded hikers is all, I suppose."

"Yeah," Chase says as he accelerates.

Priscilla Smith contemplated the ground below her, in front of her, as if she truly did not know how to move or where to go. Kelly offered her arm, and the older woman took it absently. Mills suspected that the years in prison had cured Priscilla Smith of the need to lean on anyone, and yet, he knew nothing about being a victim incarcerated, of being revictimized by flashbacks of a life that had just taken too many unfortunate turns. "The cave murders? Please, I can't, I can't," Priscilla said to them, or to herself; Mills wasn't sure. Then the woman put a hand to her heart and shook her head. "No, no, no," she chanted. "No this can't be. If I had thought it was Teddy, I would have done something, said something. But I didn't pay enough attention."

Mills took her other arm, and he and his wife started to coax her toward her truck, but as they got close Priscilla just stopped, gripped both of them tightly, and said, "If he did this, I did this."

"I don't understand," Mills told her.

"My hands are as bloodied as his," she said. "I created that monster. I'm responsible for all those women dying. All those young women. And look at me, so old, with a life that has caused nothing but grief."

"You didn't cause any of this," Kelly replied, her voice crisp, insistent, like the lawyer that she is, closing an argument.

"Why don't you drive with Mrs. Smith," Mills said to his wife. "And we'll follow."

On the ride over, Mills offered details to Bridget.

"Classic abuse," Bridget said. "Typical battered woman's syndrome."

"Interesting how we see in others what we can't see in ourselves."

"I'm not a battered woman," she seethed.

"No. Not in the 'classic' sense."

"Mills, you can go fuck yourself."

"You wanna hear something totally messed up?" he asked.

"I already have."

"No. You haven't." And then he described the carvings on Teddy

Smith's body. "Not just the symbols," he told her. "But those words, 'I love my daddy.' Sick, huh?"

Bridget said nothing. He watched as her face went white and turned to stone. He saw a butterfly of red break out across her chest and crawl upward, spreading to her neck. "You okay?" he asked. "Looks like a rash."

"I'm fine," she whispered. "Keep your eyes on the road."

Now they're sitting in a modest ranch house. From the outside it looks more mountain cabin than home, with log accents and pine green trim, but inside it's a typical family layout: a sparkling kitchen that opens to a family room, and a hallway off to the bedrooms. Big windows in the back look out to a small creek. A stone fireplace rises in the family room. That's where they are as Priscilla offers them something cold to drink. Mills and Kelly decline. Bridget asks for water and pops a pill when Priscilla brings her a bottle. "Cramps," Bridget shares.

"I've been staying here with my sister, Patty, and her husband since I got out of prison," she tells them. She points to a counter and a table. "You'll have to excuse the mess. They're on vacation. That's all their mail piling up."

"No problem," Mills assures her.

She's sitting now in a rocking chair opposite them. "I couldn't go back to that house in Phoenix," she says. "Never will."

"But it's still in the family."

"I never sold it. I guess I figured the city would eventually take it."

"But your son is maintaining it."

"If you say so. I guess he's paying the taxes. I'm really not sure." She looks out the window as though she'd like to escape.

"Any idea what he does for work? How he supports himself?"

"I have no idea."

Priscilla leaves them for a few moments, and Mills and Kelly say nothing, staring at each other, communicating their anticipation with their eyes only. When Priscilla reappears she is holding a stack of envelopes. They're five-by-seven manila mailers, and she hands them to Mills. He inspects them, and the notes confirm exactly what Priscilla had said. Her son had been in touch with her throughout her prison stay; he had reached out to torment her. Note after note:

I love my daddy.
I love my daddy.
I love my daddy.
I love my daddy, and if you ever get out I'll prove it, Mommy.

Mills holds up that one. "What does he mean?"

Priscilla shakes her head. "I have no idea. I think he was threatening me. If you keep reading you'll see more like that."

Dear Mommy, you'll be sorry if you ever leave that prison.

Mills puts the notes aside. "He wanted revenge. Clearly."

"Right," Priscilla says. "Proving to me how much he loved his father meant killing me."

"Or making an even bigger statement."

The remains at Squaw Peak, he thinks. *And her release from prison. Her freedom was his trigger. And the killing began.*

Mills sorts through another pile of notes; there are about fifty cards, and all they say is "Dear Mommy" followed by a random collection of symbols. Mills studies the envelopes, the postmarks.

"So, for about eight years the letters came from this address here in Prescott," Mills says.

Priscilla nods. "Yes. He lived here with my sister and her husband. It was a formal adoption. Name change and everything. But look at the other postmarks, Mr. Mills; he was writing these notes to me well into his thirties and still signing them 'Teddy.'"

"You changed his name?"

She hugs herself, sitting there in the rocking chair. "We thought we were making it easier on him by changing his name. I mean, the story was all over the news. When we moved him here with Patty, we gave him a whole new identity," she explains. "Not that he wouldn't figure out what happened. But he was a kid, and we didn't want him to be stigmatized, you know, especially when you consider he was a namesake."

"The last envelopes are postmarked from Phoenix," Mills says. "He wasn't necessarily hiding from you."

She opens her hands. "Apparently he has a life for himself in Phoenix. With the house. And the truck you're telling me about. He's officially Patty and William's son, and the name they gave him should be on everything else, far as I know. Social security card, bank accounts. But maybe not the truck."

"Damn," Mills says as a piece falls into place. "The license plate . . . it makes sense. ILMD. 'I love my daddy.'"

"My son hasn't forgotten who he is," Priscilla says as she rises from the rocking chair. "I'm going to get something from Patty's room that I never, ever look at. Not anymore. If you'll excuse me."

Mills stands and holds his palms out. "Wait. Tell me what they called your son. What did they name him?"

She looks back and smiles. "Patty and I renamed him after our father, Timothy. A strong, decent man," she says. "If my dad had been alive he would have intervened. He would have stood up to my husband. That's how he was. Kind of a savior to anyone in need. My Teddy became the fourth Timothy in a line of Timothys."

She disappears down the hallway. Mills glances at his wife who nods and smiles, dispatching silently that her husband has done good. Then he looks at Bridget who abruptly looks away. Suddenly he feels a rising warmth. It's moving up his arms, across his chest, spreading to his face. It's a crawling, tingly recognition that makes him leap to the counter and riffle through the mail there. It's all addressed to William Chase. And Patricia Chase.

"Please have a look at my son," Priscilla says as she returns to the room and crosses to the fireplace where she holds up an eight-by-ten photograph. "Timothy Chase at his high school graduation."

The boy looks like the man he'll become. Unmistakably.

Bridget erupts from the chair and races from the house. Kelly goes after her.

Mills stands there detonating.

37

One strip of cloud, like a contrail, hovers over the Superstitions. It's a bright white puffy line; the rest of the sky is clear and unbreakable.

"Beautiful," Gus says.

Chase says, "What?"

"The view."

"Hmm. You know it's federal land up there."

"So?"

"So that means my friends at the FBI will probably be very interested."

"Yeah, but, this is your case."

"Of course, of course," he says. "And it's a good thing it's my case. I'm just saying that they will look at this with a vested interest. There will be another layer."

"I get it," Gus tells him.

"And, hey, there might be some good connections out there for you. The bureau can always use a good psychic."

Gus can't remember the last time he was this far east on Route 60. He's hiked the Superstitions, but that was ages ago, when he first got to Phoenix. He and Ivy have their favorite trails now, some at South Mountain, some at Dreamy Draw and White Tanks. He watches as signs for Apache Junction and Globe blow by. They still have a ways to go but not as far as Globe. He recognizes the signs for Lost Dutchman State Park; that's probably where they'll get off. He should get out here more often, for no other reason than to hide behind the huge walls and detach.

"If you need to get home, Parker, I'm sure someone at the scene can give you a ride back. I think I'll be out here for a while."

Gus leans his head on the window. "No problem," he says. "No plans tonight, so I'm good."

"No big date?"

"Uh, no."

"You don't have a woman?"

"Not at the moment."

"Maybe you should cut your hair," Chase says.

"Huh? Cut my hair?"

Smiling, perhaps even measuring the rise he'll get out of Gus, Chase says, "Well, I'm just saying, that shaggy look from the seventies doesn't exactly say, 'Serious guy, here.'"

"What does it say?"

"Kid. You look like a kid. Like a surfer boy who doesn't want to grow up."

Gus shakes his head. "I haven't surfed in years," he says.

"I can cut it if you want," Chase says. "I have scissors in the trunk."

Gus laughs. "That's okay. This is a classic look for me."

Chase rolls his eyes. Then he points out a sign: Lost Dutchman State Park—Exit 6 miles. "Remember I have water if you're thirsty."

"I'm fine," Gus says.

"Been meaning to offer it to you."

"I'm fine."

His phone rings. He recognizes Mills's number and picks up.

"Hey, man, what's up?"

"All I can say is wow," Mills tells him.

"Really? That's all you can say. What an odd thing to call about."

Mills doesn't laugh. He pauses, and Gus tries to intuit the pause but cannot. He senses women, though, women in the presence of Alex Mills. And then Mills says, "We have our man, Gus Parker. I'm on the way back from Prescott now."

Gus gets all chilly. "Seriously? I'm, like, all goose bumps."

"Are you sitting down?"

"I'm in a car. So yes. . . ."

"Timothy Chase," Mills says.

"What about him?"

"Timothy Chase," Mills repeats.

Gus can't speak, but he understands. He can't move, but he feels a head rush; he doesn't breathe, but he feels a flash flood of blood in his veins. There's a free fall in his belly, as if the pieces are actually plummeting into place. "Really?" is all he says. He feigns a calmness, a composure of indifference, but the news doesn't sit well with his sphincter. His skin truly turns goosey. He wonders if the elevator of red is showing up on his face.

"You don't sound surprised," Mills says. "Don't tell me you knew all along."

"Not exactly. But I think it kind of makes sense."

"Makes sense? You're damned right it makes sense."

Mills quickly narrates the story of Priscilla Smith. "Chase made up the whole thing about his dying mother," he says. "Priscilla Smith is alive and well and in my back seat, right now. We're going to search the house in Phoenix. Tonight. The department's all over it."

"I imagine," is all Gus can say, his mouth as dry as tumbleweed.

"No, you can't," Mills tells him and then describes cards and notes Priscilla Smith received in prison and what they reveal about the license plate. "'I love my daddy.' Can you fucking believe that? Dozens of cards, he sent her. That shit all over his body. Man, this is crazy. And I've seen crazy."

"Well, then, I should probably go," Gus says.

"What's with you, Parker?" Mills asks. "Something wrong?"

"I'm just kind of busy, that's all."

"No shit, you've been busy, my friend. Did you get my text the other night about the coach? If it weren't for your hunches I'm sure my kid would be headed for jail."

Gus feels himself nodding, affirmed, amused, and scared shitless.

"Parker?"

"Okay, then. Call you when I get back."

"From?"

"The Superstitions."

"What the heck you doing out there?"

"I'm with Chase. There's been a murder."

Gus hears Chase's neck snap and can see without looking that the man is simmering.

"You're with Chase? Right now?"

"Yep."

"Oh. Jesus Christ." Gus hears Mills fidget over the phone, hears the spasms of a flummoxed man. "Jesus Christ," he repeats.

"How about we call you from the scene?" Gus asks.

"How about you stay in the car," Mills tells him. "Hang up now very calmly but keep your phone on."

"Right," Gus says. "Good advice." Then he hangs up. His stomach is in the basement. His hands are cold and sweaty. Again, the sphincter.

"Dammit, Parker," Chase says, and Gus jumps in his seat.

"What?"

"I told you not to run your mouth off about the Superstitions."

"It was Mills. That's all."

"What did he want?"

Gus tells Chase about the drug ring at Central High. "I guess my visions paid off."

Chase turns to him, and the killer's fiendish smile is like the penciled-in hyperbole of a suffering clown. The slit of Chase's mouth might as well be carved from ear to ear with one slash of a knife. Gus sees the knife. One is missing from the bench. He feels the knife against his back, slitting through the fabric, ripping through his flesh and digging at his vertebrae. He settles into the cradle of the seat. Chase is still smiling. "Look at you," the man says. "All proud of yourself."

"Well, it was nothing, really. Just a hint."

Chase slaps him on the knee. "No way! You solved the case, Parker! Good job. Really, I mean it."

"That means a lot coming from you."

"Does it?" Chase asks, the grin suddenly collapsing.

"Yeah," Gus tells him. "Of course."

Chase steers the car to the right-hand lane, then down an exit ramp. "Almost there," he says. The signs, indeed, are pointing to Lost

Dutchman. Gus leans again on the window and closes his eyes. Yes, he sees Teddy Smith in the cave with Elizabeth Spears, in the cave with Lindsey Drake, in the cave with the others, in the room with Andrea Willis, and he sees the man wild with rage then gently carving, then wild with rage and then gently carving again. And over the dying bodies, Teddy Smith is chanting, "I love my daddy. I love my daddy. I love my daddy."

The ding of his cell phone startles him. It's a text message from Mills.

> AM: There's no murder
> GP: Huh?
> AM: There's no murder at the Superstitions
> GP: There are cops out there already
> AM: Just called into HQ. No one working a murder. Are you there yet?
> GP: About five minutes

"Who are you texting, Gus?" the killer asks.

"Beatrice," he says instinctively. "She thinks she can guide me to the murder, and maybe the murderer."

"I told you to keep your mouth shut about this. At least 'til we get there, dude."

"Technically my mouth is shut. I'm texting."

"Technically I'll throw that damn phone out the window," the killer warns him. "I don't mean to be a dick about this, but nothing can compromise the investigation. Not at this point. Woods already pulled Mills from the case. I'm next."

"Fine. I'll just call her and tell her to stop. Okay?"

"One call."

"Like I've just been arrested. . . ."

"Don't tempt me."

He calls Mills. "Hey, Beatrice, dear—"

"Who? What the fuck?"

"Look, Bea, I'm not supposed to be saying anything about the case right now. I mean, we're not even sure it's, you know, linked to the other murders. And Chase is getting pissed."

Chase laughs a crazy, startled laugh beside him.

"Don't get out of that car," Mills tells him.

"Not sure I can refuse. Dinner sounds great, Bea."

"Well, do what he says then," Mills instructs. "But don't do anything stupid. The guy's got weapons, you know."

"Right."

"We're alerting everyone. An army's heading that way, but in the meantime the best you can do is stall him. If you try to get away chances are you'll end up dead."

"I think that might happen anyway, Bea."

"Do not hang up. I want to hear every move he makes."

"Okay," Gus says tentatively.

"I'm telling you, put the phone down like we're done. But don't hang up."

Gus complies, but, despite the warning from Alex Mills, he considers jumping from the moving car. He imagines the velocity of his escape, his head cracking open on the pavement, a limb or two severed by an oncoming vehicle. He figures it's probably safer and less bloody to simply bolt once the lunatic parks the car.

38

They enter a parking lot. The place is empty. Not a sign of life.

"Where are all the cops?" Gus asks. "You said they were already out here."

"They went in at another trailhead. At least that's what they told me when I called in. My job is to look for evidence coming in this way."

"All by yourself? That's a lot of ground to cover."

"You're coming with me."

Chase parks the car.

Gus points to a sign. "Now I see why no one's out here. 'Spirit Rock Trail Closed for Maintenance,'" he reads.

"Lucky for us," Chase says, "or else we'd be turning away hundreds of hikers on a day like this."

"Yeah. Lucky." Gus starts to unbuckle but then pauses. "You know, why don't you go ahead of me? When the techs are finished with the scene, have them send me in."

Chase laughs. "You scared? You've seen a dead body before, Gus Parker."

Gus tries an ambivalent chuckle. "Of course I'm not scared. I'm good. Just don't want to get in the way."

"Come on," Chase says. "It's a ways in, I'm told. Easier if we go together."

Gus doesn't budge.

Chase grabs the keys, jumps out, and heads to the trunk. Gus eyes him in the side-view mirror. He's no match. The brawny Teddy Smith could flatten him like a warm tortilla. But Gus bets he could outrun the psychopath. What he lacks in mass he makes up for in agility, dexterity, and speed. That's it, he'll scramble away, hide behind boulders if need be. He grits his teeth, tries to speak without moving his lips, and says, "Mills, if you can hear me I'm at the Spirit Rock Trail. I assume we're heading in. That's all I know."

Suddenly Chase is at the window, rapping hard.

"You coming?" His smile is almost gleeful. He's thrown on one of those khaki jackets with all the pockets, the kind TV correspondents and photographers sometimes wear to blend into a war zone, an earthquake, or the migration of wildebeest.

Gus has given up on his bowels; they're either with him or they're not. He tries to go Zen and usurp the cramping inevitable with a dream or a meditation or a vision. And he sees an empty cave.

The door opens beside him. "You know, we're sort of in a hurry," Chase says. "I'm afraid we're keeping a dead body waiting."

"Right. Sorry," Gus says, surreptitiously sliding the phone into a pocket as he climbs out.

When they reach the trailhead, Chase pivots toward Gus and says, "You thirsty?"

Gus shakes his head.

"You sure? By the time you're thirsty you'll already be dehydrated."

"Yeah. I've heard that line a hundred times, Chase."

The killer moves toward him with that strange, exalted smile on his face.

Gus retreats a few steps, wishing there were hikers out here he could call for help, or mountain bikers, a fucking goat herder, anybody. Thinking Mills might not be able to hear the muffled conversation, he slides his hand in his pocket and tries to lift his phone higher. But it's no use. The phone keeps slipping back down, and it just looks like Gus is standing there playing with his dick.

"I brought some water just in case," Chase says. "Love this jacket. Lots of pockets. I'm like a boy scout. Always prepared."

"That's comforting," Gus tells him.

They walk. The trail is gentle at first, and it doesn't feel like a climb at all. Gus remembers this hike and the bounty that awaits: about a mile into this trail is a gallery of petroglyphs. Hikers make this pilgrimage with almost religious piety, practically genuflecting at the sight of the legendary etchings. It's the perfect place for a man obsessed with ancient artwork, even more so when it's abandoned without a soul around to come to Gus's aid.

The climb becomes slightly more strenuous, but, as they reach an apex, Gus can see a boulder-filled canyon in the distance.

Gus scans the horizon, takes in the sun, and lets it land on his face. He closes his eyes and disappears for a moment in a square of white, listening to the crunch of the psychopath's footsteps ahead of him, and he sees the simple radiance of God. In this square there is nothing but peace and light, not a murmur, not a scuffle, nothing. He assumes that this is how it will end. Not necessarily here and now, for he still believes that he has much work to do, that he is not destined for a final bow at the Superstitions. But he assumes that this is how it ends for everyone: a white square of nothing blessed with everything.

"Keep up, dude," Chase barks.

Gus's eyes pop open. He smiles. "Sorry."

The man looks back at him with an empty face; there's nothing there but a wall of flesh and ageless secrets. Gus sidles up beside the killer, and they continue their hike like old buddies on a break from the stewing madness of married life, kids, and relentlessly mediocre careers. They're the kind of friends who will plan a guys-only weekend at Lake Havasu or maybe Vegas but never go. They're the kind of friends who won't slay each other. The pretense is all Gus has to work with—and he has no faith at all that it's working.

"You feel anything yet?" Chase asks.

"Feel anything?"

"You know, Parker, you getting one of your vibes out here?"

Gus stops and feigns an inward search. Chase moves in close. Gus sees nothing except a certain disappointment, a frozen frame of the view ahead where nothing happens and no one knows what to do. It's like a test. Here's a sentence; fill in the blank. Gus is about to emerge from the view when he sees a flash of something, an object dangling, here then gone, then back, dangling. A rope. He reports that to Chase.

"Interesting," Chase says. "What do you think it means?"

"I have no idea," Gus replies.

They walk in silence for about another ten minutes. The whole way Gus feels himself short-circuiting, as if his vibe gets no signal out here.

Chase stops and points. "Down there," he says, indicating a rocky area near the trail's end. "Blessed with petroglyphs."

Interesting choice of words, Gus thinks. "Yeah. I've been out here before."

"One of the best collections in the Southwest. This killer has chosen the ultimate sanctuary for death."

"Eloquently put. You must know him well," Gus says, trying to taunt the man out of his lunacy. "A very complex profile, I'm sure."

But Chase is unfazed. "It's my job," is all he says.

Gus understands Chase's mission now and can't think of how to distract him. It's psychic versus psychopath.

"I don't know, Chase. I'm not getting any more vibes about this place."

The man is breathing heavier now. He puts one foot up on a rock and leans there. "You will. I have faith you will."

You're faithless, Gus thinks. *Your soul is on empty.*

"We're going down to the scene," Chase tells him. "I've been told exactly where it is. It's just beyond the petroglyphs. Our killer's consistent."

Gus follows. The trek is steep. Their footsteps release a landslide of pebbles. Chase stops at a ledge.

"We stuck?" Gus asks.

"Hell no," the man says. "Just hang and drop."

Chase goes first.

"Hang and drop," Gus repeats. He lowers himself to the ledge, then over the side, his hands gripping the edge. There is a bump of land right below, not much more than two feet of air between his feet and another solid surface, but still Gus's blood stirs. He hangs. Wishes that if he did fall he'd fall forever. The sun is beating at his neck. The man below grunts and spits and grabs his leg.

"I got you," Chase says. "Just drop yourself slowly."

Gus complies. The man takes his arm and guides him down. Gus follows him to a lower path that meanders between walls of rock. They turn a corner, and a stony wash comes into view. "There," Chase says, pointing across the dry riverbed. On the face of a boulder, pointing a bit to the east, is the ancient artwork of a lost people. The crude rendering has eyes, and teeth, sharp teeth, like a reptile's. "He wants the bodies to be found," the detective says. "It's his fingerprint."

Chase is awestruck and almost giddy.

"That's not the way all murderers work," he continues. "I mean, if I were a killer and, say, I wanted to kill you, I'd make it so your body was never found."

"That's a comforting thought, Chase."

"You know what I mean," the man says with a bold laugh. "I'd put you way out in the desert. Like in the middle of nowhere."

"Well, this is kind of in the middle of nowhere."

"No," Chase insists. "This is the perfect gallery for him."

Of course it is. The walls around them are all adorned with petroglyphs, an exhibit of tribal art in 360 degrees. The portraits could be alive—they feel alive—whispering to each other about the two visitors below. Gus truly senses that these etchings have voices; he has a primal sense of spirits dwelling in the rock, behind those masks. There is water here, too. Of all places. As if to support these cliff dwellers.

Gus looks at Chase who is similarly transfixed, only deeper, in worship, and he realizes this is his opportunity to get away.

And so he backs up a few steps, then a few more, pretending to admire the artwork as he retreats. He steps gingerly over a pool of water, then another. Then the way back to the trailhead opens in front of him and he takes off running upward out of the canyon.

At first his strides are as quiet as a whisper. He's slithering, like a snake.

He has no sense of time. It feels as if he's been running forever, but he knows desperation never runs as swiftly as it needs to. Thirty seconds feel like five minutes. A minute feels like an hour.

And desperation rarely remains quiet. Desperation has a sound. And now he hears it, how his feet are kicking stones, loosening rock as he flees. The tiny avalanche betrays him now, and he can absolutely sense the moment Chase emerges from worship and notices him gone—he knows this without looking back. And then he can hear the man coming after him, another rush of footsteps against the hardscrabble of earth.

Chase is yelling, "Stop, Gus Parker. Stop right there."

But Gus keeps running.

He doesn't turn around, even as he hears the voice coming closer, even as he feels the vibration of the killer's feet ripping up the dirt behind him. He pulls the phone from his pocket and, in a staggering voice, yells for Mills. There's no answer. Of course there's no answer.

No signal.

No shit. The phone is useless. He has only his feet. And he's pounding the rock, the dirt, more rock, nearly tripping, nearly spinning out of control. There's a breeze at his neck that might as well be Chase's breath.

At the ledge he reaches. He jumps, and his hands land on sharp stones, the pain jolting through him. He loses his grip and slides down, then jumps again. He holds himself up, clutching the ledge and pulling his body upward. A simple push-up, but he stops to catch his breath.

Okay. Stop.

His heart is exploding. His hands are bleeding. One more contraction of his shoulders and he'll be up and over, and so he exerts those muscles and begins to rise. He clears his torso and is about to lift a knee when there is a distinct seizure of his legs.

And Gus knows it's over.

Chase has him in the vise of his hands. The vise might as well be cuffs, otherwise Gus would try to kick. But there is no kicking. Chase has immobilized his prey. And the predator begins to pull slowly. Inch by inch Gus comes down, his face scraping against a wall of rock. Then

Chase grabs him by the stomach, spins him around, and Gus's feet hit the earth.

The man is smiling again. "Perhaps you believe there's no body out here after all," Chase says. "Well, there isn't. Not yet."

"But what do you want with me, Teddy?"

The man's face turns purple. "What did you call me?"

"Teddy. Teddy Smith."

Chase lunges. His hands make swift and forceful contact with Gus's chest, and Gus feels himself falling to the ground. His head hits a rock. "What the fuck?" he says, his brain a scrambled egg as he tries to reassemble the image of the man towering above him.

"Hi, Gus Parker," Chase says.

Gus's eyes are foggy.

"I said hello, Gus."

"Yeah. Hi, Detective."

"You having fun yet?"

"Loads."

The fog clears, and now Gus is blinded by the sun. The silhouette of Timothy Chase bends to him, hoists him by the back of his collar, and then suddenly he's airborne. Chase has lifted him from the ground in one swoop and thrown him over his back. It's the firefighter's carry, and Gus tries to appreciate the irony, but his head is throbbing and the world is upside down, maybe inside out, from this position. The man rushes back down the trail, jumping from rock to rock in a manic zigzag as if he's traversing a minefield.

Gus, bouncing around up there, tries reaching into one of Chase's pockets, thinking maybe he can grab the guy's gun. He figures it's his only option at this point, but he doesn't find a gun. He tries another pocket. Again, nothing. He's only riding Chase's back for maybe a minute before the killer throws him to the ground and his whole body lands in a thud. The thud echoes everywhere.

Gus listens as his body is dragged along the hardscrabble. Every inch is a bruise to a bone. He can't tell how far he's combed the surface of the earth (it feels like the beginning of forever), but he's guessing thirty feet, maybe less. And then, inch by inch, the light recedes, as they disappear into a black hole.

The cave offers a stingy entrance, tight walls of rock, a slash in the monolith. Gus blinks repeatedly, trying to adjust to the light, but only a sliver of day creeps into the cave. "You'll feel better in a sec," the man says, leaving Gus on the ground.

Gus lets out a deep breath. As he does this, Chase spins around and unleashes a bottle of water into his face. Gus spits and wipes his eyes. Chase throws him a towel. "Told you," the psychopath says. "Refreshing, huh?"

"What are we doing here, Teddy?"

The man lowers himself to his knees and smiles. His squat is rugged. His stare explosive. "You and I could be the best of friends, Gus Parker. And only the best of friends get to see how I work. I hope you don't mind."

"I don't, Teddy. This is fine," Gus tells him.

"I mean, I hope you don't mind this," Chase says, reaching into another pocket. He pulls out a three-foot section of rope and yanks it taut as if to make a point. "I'm sorry, Gus Parker. But I want you to sit still. I can't have you leaving until I'm done."

Timothy Chase coils the rope around Gus's wrists and tightens it.

39

Alex Mills is afraid that if he grips the steering wheel any tighter he'll pull it loose from the column. He's plowing down the highway, probably averaging ninety. Priscilla Smith is quiet, nearly catatonic in the back seat. Next to her is Bridget Mulroney, eyes closed, but awake, groaning now and then as if the truth is hitting her like contractions.

"You ran out of that house for a reason," he says to her.

She opens her eyes and nods slowly. "Yeah."

"You and Chase?"

"Now and then. . . ." She tries to clear her throat. "I knew it was him as soon as you told me about those carvings on his body. But I was hoping against hope."

"Did you ever ask him where they came from?"

"All he said is they were relics. And personal. In other words, none of my business. I was okay with the mystery."

Mills nods and says no more about it.

He had called everybody before they left Prescott. And then again, after talking to Gus, using Kelly's phone so he could keep his own line open to monitor the man's whereabouts. And then once more, frantically, after Gus located himself at the Spirit Rock Trail. The department is mobilized. A team is waiting at the North Angel Gem Road address. Others are racing toward the Superstitions. His sergeant notified Pinal County and the feds to let them know what was going down. Mills also got a call from Ken Preston who confirmed that Chase had been living in a downtown condo all along, corresponding to the address on file with the department, leaving the house on Angel Gem vacant or in the hands of renters. He has two addresses, two cars, but the two identities have rarely intersected. *That poor woman*, Mills thinks to himself, eyeing Priscilla Smith in the rearview mirror. Or maybe, he wonders, she might just be happy to have this whole thing over.

He heard a scuffle, he thinks, between Chase and Gus. He's tried calling twice, but Gus hasn't answered. But he dials again. Still nothing.

Kelly reaches for his hand. "Hon, stop," she says. "You've done all you can do from here."

Logically, he knows that. Gus's phone is dead.

Kelly's hand is resting on his leg now, radiating warmth. "Hon, are you listening to me?"

"Yeah," he says. "Done all I can do from here." And then he adds, "But if he's such a fucking psychic, why did he get in the car with him in the first place?"

Kelly gives him an ironic laugh. "I don't think it works that way, but you can ask him when you see him."

"Ask him when I see him?" Somewhere a fat lady sings, a camel collapses, a pot boils over; it's obviously too late to choose the right metaphor when his thoughts are already roiling in doom. "Don't you get it, Kelly? Gus Parker is in serious fucking danger. If that lunatic has his way we'll never see Gus Parker again. How come nobody in this car fucking gets that?"

Kelly recoils. "Jesus, Alex," she whispers.

"He's as good as dead," Mills shouts. At her. At Bridget. At everybody. At the world. "Chase didn't take him on a joy ride. He didn't take him for a picnic. They did not go bowling. I haven't been a detective all these years not to know what the plan is."

Kelly doesn't look at him but says, "Gus is a smart guy. Psychic or not, he can handle himself."

Yeah right, Mills thinks, *intelligence is really going to save his life.*

40

Intuitively, Gus knows the rope around his wrists is from the same coil of rope that killed Andrea Willis. To confirm he closes his eyes, and the vision comes to him immediately: she, struggling in the hallway, knocking pictures out of place, kicking at the man's shins; he, dragging her by the waist, lumbering toward the bedroom; they, rolling on the floor, cracking a closet mirror.

She's clutching the carpet, holding on for dear life.

He's clutching her neck, beginning to wind the rope.

When Gus opens his eyes the cave is aglow. On the floor of the cave, a small army of flickering candles. And there on the wall is a portrait. The beginning of a portrait. A carving in progress. Gus's orientation comes together. He's inside an arched monolith; it's like an ancient tomb excavated from the earth beneath Jerusalem. Or maybe his imagination is hyped up on adrenaline. He knows this: Chase has been here before, has set his stage, and has thought through this whole piece of theater. There are provisions on the floor against another wall. Tools. A few jugs, contents unknown. A blanket. Gus takes this all in as if he's a visitor to another world.

"Snap out of it, Parker," Chase tells him. He hands Gus a bottle of water. "Stay hydrated. You'll be here a while."

Gus begins to sip. The killer removes his jacket and then reaches for the tools.

"Going to do some art today, Teddy?"

"It's excellent to have an audience."

"So you made the women watch you first? You made them see their own murders?"

Chase spins around and thrusts the chisel into the rock. "Some of them. It's only fair. Don't you think?"

"You've been camping out here?"

"Sort of."

His back is to Gus, and he begins to carve. Gus strains to see but can't see the man's progress. The sound of metal hitting rock continues, gashing, chipping, ringing in a way that, like the days when you actually love your mother and she's banging pots and pans in the kitchen, is surprisingly soothing, settling to Gus; in fact, he's feeling calmed, sleepy. He doesn't understand, but he feels himself drifting to the insane lullaby of the artist's work. The sounds are getting distant, first like echoes, then like receding surf, then an empty hallway. He's about to take another sip from the bottle when he startles himself with a discovery, one that sort of leaps from his chest.

"Did you drug all the others?" he asks Chase.

Chase doesn't answer.

"I said did you drug all the others?"

The man turns. "No. Just you."

"Why?"

"Because you're bigger and stronger. Because it was easier just to gag them."

"What's in here?" Gus asks, struggling to hold the bottle in front of him.

"Don't worry. It's very mild. I'll wake you when I'm ready."

"Don't you want me to watch?"

"Close your eyes, Gus Parker. You can surely conjure a vision of your own demise."

Gus's head, heavy like a bowling ball, collapses against his chest. He's a marionette, a rag doll, a charm on his mother's bracelet. But he won't let this happen. He won't surrender to the potion. He's fighting back, kicking at the ground beneath him; he's riding a recumbent bike, and it's getting him nowhere, but it's keeping him awake.

"Finish the water, Gus Parker," Chase insists. "Finish it now."

Gus clumsily empties the bottle on the dirt. "Sorry," he says.

"There's more." Then the man comes over and whacks him across the face.

"A knife is missing from your garage," Gus says.

"Of course it is. It's here with me."

Gus sees his body parts scattered across the floor of the cave; the vision is too dreamy to be frightening or to be real. There's his arm. A severed hand, and its dripping tendrils. There's his leg, more muscular than he's given himself credit for. Oh, Jesus, there's his head. His smiling face. Oceans of thrilling waves in his eyes. *Holy shit! Jesus Christ, make this stop. Jesus, Jesus, make this stop. Our Father who art in heaven, Hail Mary, and all the other shit I forgot to pray about, stop!*

And it does stop. All he has to do is ask. All he really has to do is seize the moment in all of its brilliant and microscopic brevity and consider it done. "The knife," he says. "You're not going to use it on me, are you?" He hears a slow laziness in his own voice.

"I brought it just in case," Chase says. "You could have put up a fight. But you didn't. I have other plans for you. You're a good boy. Your daddy loves you."

"He loved you too, Teddy Junior. He did."

Again, a whack to the face. "Don't you say a word about him, Gus Parker. Now, open up and drink."

With one hand holding Gus's jaw, the man forces a bottle into Gus's mouth. "Told you I had plenty of fluids. Fluids are so important."

Gus can't speak. He's trying to reject the malevolent cocktail in violent spits and coughs, but he's choking and gulping and choking again, and most of it goes down his throat, the rest down his windpipe, and he thinks this must be what it's like to drown.

"Sure, I added something to it when you weren't looking," Chase says.

Gus watches the cave spin in circles, or maybe that's his head rolling, or maybe he's at the bottom of the ocean, flailing for life. His mouth is open, but he can't say a word. All he can do is listen—to a rumbling, to words creeping up from the bottom of a stairwell, to words of a man escalating as they surround him. I love my daddy. I. Love. My. Daddy.

Gus feels himself falling asleep, not to a gentle melody but to the thunderous cries of a grown man.

By the time they get to the North Angel Gem Road house, the place is crawling with cops. Priscilla Smith shields her eyes as if she is shielding them from a blinding sun. Kelly helps her from the car. Bridget follows. She's shivering and begging Mills not to leave her. "I can't be alone," she cries. "I'm freaking out, totally freaking out."

He nods to Kelly, and Kelly understands. "I'll take her, Alex."

Woods approaches. "You and I will have a long talk later," the sergeant tells Mills. "A good talk. But right now I need you and Myers to hustle out to the Superstitions. Like yesterday. I got a crew over at Chase's condo. Preston and I will handle stuff here. We'll need Mrs. Smith to stay with us."

Mills nods. His pulse is banging in his ears. He pulls his wife close and whispers, "Thank you," then, "I love you." Then he's off. The road, the sky, the residue of the sun, everything is in front of him as he hurtles down the highway. Myers, who's monitoring the chatter, says there are six cruisers ahead by twenty-five minutes or so. A chopper is up. Myers's voice is calm. Extra calm, the way cops sometimes talk to a hostage taker. *Got to give the guy some credit.* He's good, Myers, way smarter than he looks, the way he senses the silent howl climbing up from Mills's diaphragm, the way he overcompensates so maybe the windows won't bust out of the car with a sonic boom.

He's going ninety, but he can't get there fast enough.

Eighteen miles to the exit.

"Everything is going on at once, and I know that Chase knows he's fucked," Mills says breathlessly. "People who know they're fucked are dangerous."

Myers won't really indulge him. He says, "The rangers have cleared all the trails, and they're searching all of them in case Chase detours."

"Good."

They ride in silence for a few moments, and then Myers says, "I guess I'm off the hook."

"What do you mean?"

"I mean it was obviously Chase who made that call to lure Bobby Willis out to White Tanks," Myers replies. "Not me."

"I never really thought it was you."

Twelve miles to the exit. Twelve *fucking* miles.

Timothy Chase is going to kill Gus Parker. Mills knows it. He feels it in his gut, and he sees it all go down: the torture, the blood, the garden of death.

That wall of rock is taunting him. It looks much closer than it is.

Seven miles.

The chatter has ceased.

"Get someone on the radio, Myers. Now!"

An officer responds and tells them patrols have already hit the trails. "No contact yet. What's your ETA?"

"Five minutes," Myers says.

Three minutes later, Mills's car screeches to a stop in the parking lot. It shudders, and he flies out. Myers follows, trudging behind. Mills sees the first piece of evidence and points. "Chase is here. That fucking Jeep is his."

A ranger greets them. "You've got guys out on the trail already," the man says. "I put some of my men on some surrounding trails just in case your suspect didn't stick to the Spirit Rock."

Mills raises his radio and calls to his search party.

"We found footprints going both ways," someone tells him. "No real caves to speak of. No blood. We're heading back."

"Go meet them up there," the ranger suggests, pointing to a rocky bluff where the trail descends.

They climb in that direction, shuffling through stones, pounding the earth, boots on the ground, like a drill. As they reach the bluff Mills sees a head popping up over a ledge, then another. The officers, three men and a woman, dusted up and sweating, climb toward him. He recognizes the young patrolman, Hall, and Jan Powell, the officer who worked the Squaw Peak detail. The other two have faces he knows, but the names are unfamiliar.

"Sorry, Alex," Powell says. "I think we lost him."

"We didn't lose him," Mills tells the officers. "He's out there."

The ranger steps into the circle of Phoenix cops and says, "Detective, why don't I take you up the trail so you can have a look for yourself? The rest of you can go off to the east. There are plenty of caves out there, a few random petroglyphs."

"Let's do it," Mills says. He climbs down the ledge, followed by the ranger.

Myers hesitates, then dumps himself over.

They zip up the Spirit Rock Trail, pushing ahead as if they have to diffuse a ticking bomb. Yes, the trail yields plenty of petroglyphs but few openings in the rock.

Mills stops by a pool of water and turns to the ranger. "No caves out here?"

"Lots," he replies. "But they're mostly off-trail."

"I don't think Chase goes far off-trail. He's efficient."

"But if he's looking for a cave, most likely he's left the trail. And not necessarily far."

Mills nods. "Fine. Lead the way."

They march onward into an open canyon, which, itself, yields nothing but sky. The ranger points out a petroglyph bearing a half moon and a collection of stars on a slate towering above them, and as they approach Mills narrows his eyes and makes out a series of holes at the base of the rock, mini caves that look like a neighborhood.

There are no footprints. No signs of residents. No evidence of visitors. But the ground is more stone than dirt, so it's plausible people come and go without leaving a trace.

He tells Myers and the ranger to scatter, one to each side of the monolith.

"Check out every one," he orders. "Meet me in the middle."

In aggressive strides, Mills makes a straight line to the center caves, draws his gun, and slides quietly into each. They turn out to be more dents than caves, and each one of them is empty. He hears Myers coming closer, the ranger, too, shouting out in intervals of two minutes, maybe shorter, "Clear."

Fuck clear.

Fuck this. Fuck the fucking symbols.

Mills, with the other two in his wake, heads back to the trail. He gets on the radio, asks for Powell and Hall to meet him on the bluff, and then in silence, he retraces every step back down the Spirit Rock in case he's missed something. Of course he's missed something. He's missed everything. How did he not see that the man he worked with so closely was homicidal? He doesn't even want to wrestle with that right now because he knows there's no good answer.

"He has to be here," he shouts once they've all climbed the ledge. "Chase planned this. And he found the perfect killing ground. Think about his MO."

"Good profile of the profiler," Myers tells him.

Several cops, hearing Mills's booming voice at the bluff, have gathered. Among them are Powell, Hall, and a few deputies from Pinal County.

"Nothing out there," Powell reports. "I've been on the radio, and we've got nothing coming in."

"We're going back up the trail," Mills insists. "Chase is here. His car is here. He can only get so far with a victim in tow."

They approach the ledge again. The uniforms go down, several of them. Mills follows. Myers is next, this time a bit like Humpty Dumpty—but, hell, the man is as dedicated as anyone else, and he won't be deterred, proving himself clumsy but loyal. Clearly overexerted and drenched in sweat, Myers loses his footing and rolls to the ground. With him comes a shower of pebbles. They land at Mills's feet, and Mills immediately sees the stark contrast between clay and blood. He kneels to the ground and, indeed, sees traces of blood, fresh blood, on the shreds of rock. He looks to Myers; the man is not bleeding.

He tells three of the uniforms to stay on the Spirit Rock, directing them off to the right. He tells the other one, Powell, to stay with him and

Myers. "Something happened here. Could've diverted Chase." He points off to the left where no one has searched. "We're going down there."

"Off the trail again?" Myers asks.

"Yeah."

Within twenty feet or so there's a disturbance in the dirt, maybe animals, maybe Chase. One crude set of footprints. They follow the prints through restricted areas for less than a quarter mile until the footprints stop at a bony riverbed. "Perfect," Mills says. "It's all rock from here."

No one answers him. He looks back and sees Myers doubled over, the other officer trying to help.

"I think I need to stop," Myers says. "I'm sorry."

"Stop?" Mills barks.

"Just for a minute. I need water."

Mills shuffles impatiently in the dirt. Of course. Water. He needs some, too. He's a shower of perspiration, but it's dry as fuck out here. In a moment they're all sucking on their water bladders as if it's the last drink of life.

He knows they're running out of time.

He wanders, surveys the area, and scans the walls of rock rising from the riverbed. A hawk soars across the sky, banks sharply, and circles. Then he feels a tap on his shoulder and nearly jumps out of his skin. "Turn around, Mills," Powell tells him. When he does, she points to a stack of boulders about ten degrees to the right, maybe thirty yards away. Something giant is etched into the rock. The three of them rush in that direction, dodging prickly pears and other thorny cacti, and as they get closer the image becomes clearer. Rising high above them, etched across the face of the steepest, most improbable cliff like an ancient logo, a creature is pleased with itself as it looks upward to the sky. Maybe God, maybe man, maybe animal; who the fuck knows? And the artist isn't telling.

The outline of the creature's face is faded, a dusty blemish where the mouth should be. But those eyes. Those eyes, with their huge pupils, have survived centuries out here and have seen enough to stop visitors dead in their tracks.

Myers calls out for Gus. The name echoes off the canyon walls, then tapers like a dying pulse.

"No," Mills tells him. "The plan is not to alert Chase."

"But what if he dumped Gus out here and Gus can hear us?"

Mills ignores his colleague because there, far below the eyes of the creature, at the base of the cliff, there's a pathway into the rock. "Look," he says.

Very quietly, like a tiny pilgrimage, they approach.

They find a single set of footprints ahead of them. They track the prints without disturbing them, and then, about twenty feet before the opening in the rock, Mills points to a sweep of sand where a predator has dragged its prey—dead or alive. Mills reaches for his radio.

Gus has no idea how long he's been out. When he opens his eyes everything is sideways. He doesn't know where he is, so he feels around him; the surfaces are hard, and he tastes dirt in his mouth. Then he remembers, vaguely, the cave. The right side of his face is against the ground. He tries to twist his neck around, can barely see the opening of the cave, but sees enough to know it's still daylight out there; he's not sure what day, but the sun is shining.

He lifts his head, but he's woozy. He stares at the wall, but he can't decipher the killer's artwork. "What is it?" he asks. But he realizes his voice is but a whisper. He clears his throat.

"Wakey?" Chase asks.

"I think so," Gus replies. "Are you done chiseling?"

"Yes. You like?"

"I'm not quite sure what I'm looking at."

Chase lunges at him, pulls him by the collar, and sits him in the middle of the cave. "What do you think you're looking at? You're looking at death. Your death. You should know me by now."

"But that's not death, Teddy," Gus says with the sourness of sympathy. "That looks more abstract."

"Look closer," Chase says. "There's nothing abstract about it. I've been working on it even before I brought you out here."

"But there's no body. I don't see me."

"Look closer."

Gus squints if for no other reason than to appease the killer. "Yeah, still nothing. I'm sorry, Teddy."

"You've been seeing it all along, Gus Parker. Your visions have not deceived you. Look closer. Look and you'll see the fire."

Gus follows the etchings from floor to ceiling and sees in the manic and desperate exhibit the imagination of a child. From a child's hand comes the rendition of flames, monstrous and cartoonish, at once. The cave is intensely silent.

Gus says, "Your fire, Teddy. Your house in flames."

Chase says, "I never saw the fire."

"Right. Then I don't get it."

And Chase says, "Of course you do. It's your fire."

"My fire?"

"You're going to burn to death, Gus Parker. I'm going to light you on fire."

Gus looks up at the man. Chase is covered in sweat. His huge shadow is lumbering behind him across the wall.

"Light me on fire?" Gus asks evenly.

Chase paces. "What am I supposed to do? You saw the house burning down. So fucking psychic of you. But you wouldn't shut up about it. Why didn't you shut up? You should have shut up."

"It's not like I leaked it to the media, Teddy."

"You shouldn't have told a soul. That was a sacred fire."

"It led us to you. And so you lured me out here."

"I've been scouring the valley for the perfect opportunity," he says, still pacing. "It's not hard to find a trail closed for maintenance, but not every trail is surrounded by so many beautiful symbols."

"The symbols mean everything to you."

Chase comes toward him. Circles him.

"And now they mean everything to you, Gus Parker. Because now they symbolize your demise. How did you not see this coming if you're so psychic?"

"I rarely have visions about myself. Or maybe I just wasn't concentrating. I don't know."

Gus doesn't like the taste in his mouth. He spits something out, but the taste doesn't change. He's hyper-salivating. The drug is wearing off. He knows if he tries to speak again he'll find himself with a black hole of a mouth and no words, like a scream in the night that doesn't make a sound. His face is cold, then hot, then cold again. He tries to anchor his breath somewhere deep in the basement of his gut, but he can feel his breath is actually shallow and fleeting. There's a tightening in his throat, like a noose around his neck, but the only thing gripping Gus is the ending he never saw coming.

There's a flame in his face.

The killer is kneeling behind him, reaching around with one of those wand-like lighters that people sometimes use to light charcoal grills. It occurs to Gus that he's about to be charcoaled.

"I'm going to light you on fire," the man says. "I think I'll start with this ridiculous head of hair."

The flame gets closer, close enough for Gus to feel heat on his skin. Chase laughs.

"Are you scared, Mr. Parker?"

Gus nods.

"I was never scared," Chase says. "Never scared. Never scared. Never scared...."

Chase goes on like that, chanting his mantra, but the flame goes out.

"Never scared ... never scared...."

Chanting like that as he backs away.

The words descending to a whisper, then silence.

In this protracted stillness, Gus hears the flutter of something at the opening of the cave, like the unwinding of a snake, and Gus turns to the light but sees nothing. The gash of light at the entrance disappears halfway, and Gus senses the presence of a creature there, an animal with its prey, perhaps, but Gus smells nothing wild, hears the panting of nothing, hears nothing at all, save for the percussion of his heartbeat ringing in his ears.

It's at least another five minutes before Chase emerges from the dark corner of the cave. He's shirtless, muscles bulging. He turns his back to Gus, as if to strike a bodybuilder's pose. But there's no bend to his arms, no roll of the shoulders, nothing. Just the landscape of torture, an arbitrary collection of symbols carved into the man's skin. Gus recognizes none of them. And there are words. Burned into the skin, it seems, as if Teddy Smith had been branded like cattle.

"What does it say, Gus Parker?" the man asks.

"'I love my daddy.'"

"Come again?"

"'I love my daddy.'"

Then Chase turns around. "Now we're speaking the same language." The man reaches to the floor of the cave and retrieves the lighter wand and one of the jugs. He staggers toward Gus. His shadow follows, larger than life against the wall. "I wanted you to see the real vision, Gus Parker, before we put an end to this. Any final thoughts?"

Gus hesitates then says, "I'm sorry this happened to you."

The man laughs. "Don't be," he says. Then he pours liquid from the jug. Instantly Gus knows it's gasoline or kerosene as Chase draws a circle of the accelerant around him.

The fumes almost knock Gus out. They're so potent that he can taste them on his tongue. He tries to spit the rising vapors from his mouth.

"I want you to look at my artwork as you go up in flames. You're going to look at it as you burn to death. Ashes to ashes. It will be your final vision. Ashes to ashes, Gus Parker. And you're going to behave like a very, very good boy. Do you understand that?"

Chase crouches and pours the liquid over Gus's clothing.

Then he douses his own.

"Do you understand that, Gus Parker?"

Gus doesn't answer.

"You will fucking answer me, young man!"

Gus kicks his feet out, hoping to knock Chase off-balance, but

Chase is already behind him. With one hand, the killer grabs the rope that binds Gus's wrists. Gus tries not to resist, but resistance is instinctive. The rage in Gus comes defensively. He listens to it, doesn't recognize it; it's the rage of a stranger, and it beats like the heart of a stranger. He has a sort of revelation: somewhere in all of us there it is. Hot, blinding rage. Somehow life either works it out or hires an undertaker. Maybe it emerges as art, or a great game, a world record, or a scorching song. Maybe the only way out is by camouflage, or, more likely, through a transformation that no one, not even the self, will recognize.

Then Gus hears a shuffle of footsteps and wonders if this is what it sounds like to dance with your killer, to waltz your way to your grave.

"Freeze, Timothy Chase! Just fucking freeze!"

Gus spins around, breaking free, and sees a man on his knees about ten feet inside the cave aiming a gun at the killer's chest. "Mills?"

Alex doesn't move, doesn't take an eye off Chase. "Can you move, Gus?"

Gus regards his own wrists. They're still tied, but Chase has stumbled backward. "I think so," Gus replies.

"If you can move, Gus, I need you to get out of the cave."

Gus turns back to Chase, and the choreography becomes clear; Gus is dead center between the killer and the detective. He moves an inch, then another, as if he can escape in unnoticed increments. But he's making no progress, and he panics for a moment, like a spider trapped in its own web. His eyes can't seem to focus now. He hesitates. "Hey, Alex, I think I'm disoriented," he calls.

"Listen to my voice. And try to get behind me," Alex instructs him. "I'm over here, Gus. Right here."

"Okay. That's better."

"No. It's not better," Chase says.

Then the killer bends forward as if he might suddenly charge at Gus. But he stops, ignites the lighter, and just as he aims it at himself a shot rings out.

There's a spark, then a flame.

Someone grabs Gus by the armpits and pulls. All at once, there's sunlight.

41

They questioned Gus for days. He wasn't surprised with the FBI involved now. He gave his story to at least six different agents. "Take all the time you need," they told him.

They would call him back hours later with more questions.

It was like a shower. Lather. Rinse. Repeat. But only now, two weeks later, is he finally feeling clean.

He couldn't get away from the story. It was everywhere. On TV, online, in the newspaper. Magazines, like *Time*. He couldn't get away, and he couldn't look away, like driving by the scene of your own accident, not quite recognizing that that's your car and that's your life.

He saved the newspaper from the first morning.

PHOENIX DETECTIVE ARRESTED
FOR CAVE MURDERS
Cop Worked Under Pseudonym, Fooled Colleagues

(That was just the headline. There were four more stories that morning alone.)

CHASE, FORMER FBI PROFILER, CAUGHT UP IN
CYCLE OF DOMESTIC VIOLENCE, MOTHER SAYS

(Priscilla Smith gave a lengthy interview.)

POLICE REPORT: SUSPECT TRIED TO KILL HIMSELF

(But failed.)

CHASE ARREST BLACK EYE FOR CITY

(The chief and the mayor made short, dueling statements. Let the spin begin!)

FBI JOINS INVESTIGATION,
MOST DETAILS WITHHELD

(Ironic.)

Amazing how a story with few details could yield five separate headlines and five separate reports in one newspaper. But it did. The media exploded. To reporters, the story was better than sex, and they were having newsgasms everywhere. The arrest report had been heavily redacted, but they milked it and milked it and milked it, splattering their stories above the fold, below the fold, across the TV screen, extended newscasts, special editions, late-breaking developments, blogs, tweets, posts, #cavemurder, @cavemurder, #phxkiller, and every which way up and down the hyperbole highway.

No one knows about his involvement yet (one of those details that, so far, has been withheld).

The last thing he really remembers about the cave is Alex Mills rushing to the killer's side. And then Gus was out, looking up at the sky, into the barrels of a SWAT team perched on the surrounding cliffs, and the droning sound of a chopper, undoubtedly sent from heaven, its blades slicing the sky, speaking the language of a savior.

Mills's hands are calloused and knotty. They look old and arthritic. Stress, he tells himself. Too many clenched fists. And yet he's okay with the FBI stepping in.

"They're not taking over," his sergeant, Woods, told him. "But this is as much their case as ours."

"I understand," Mills said.

"You're technically the case agent."

"As far as the department's role is concerned."

"Right."

"Okay then," Mills said. "I'm good."

And that was it. There was no rancor or dissent. It just was. Mills is done with the hard part. He's done mining for truth. Let the FBI turn it into gold.

His desk is a mess. There are files everywhere. And newspapers. They all basically say the same thing. Serial killer caught. Bad man arrested. Cave murders solved. Police department in hot water. What the fuck and who gives a shit what the media reports? He doesn't. But still he saves the newspapers, all of them, from the first report of Elizabeth Spears's murder to the report of Chase's arrest. So many reporters and so many headlines squeezed out of their asses after a shockingly limited diet of facts.

And this one is his favorite:

COACH, DEPUTY CHARGED IN HIGH SCHOOL DRUG RING

Alex was with him for most of the questioning. That made the whole ordeal, even the redundancy, easier. But Gus didn't learn until two days after Chase's arrest how Alex had found him. It was the first time the two of them were alone together away from the friendly interrogators. They were walking back to their cars after a meeting with the FBI. The air was crisp for the desert, a kind of clear. wintry night that is met by the aroma of mesquite as thin-blooded Phoenicians flock to their fireplaces to escape the downright frosty sixty degrees. Even Alex rubbed his hands together briskly to ward off the chill.

"You okay?" he asked Gus.

"Yeah. Fine."

The detective looked at him as if he didn't believe him.

"What?" Gus asked.

"Just making sure. Not every day a serial killer threatens to burn you alive."

"How'd you find the cave?" Gus asked.

Alex described the frantic search at the Superstitions. "But when I saw that something had been dragged into that cave, I knew we found you. Took me a few minutes to get my bearings in there. I didn't know what the fuck was going on."

"Well, I was mighty glad when you showed up," Gus confessed.

"It was nothing."

"Maybe for you."

Alex laughed. "Actually I was kind of freaking out. Thought we got there too late."

"So, how did Chase make it out without burning to death?"

"It was the flash of the gunshot that started the fire, not his lighter," Alex replied. "Then Powell tackled him, smothered the flames before they spread. You probably owe her your life."

"I think I owe you both," Gus said.

"Yeah, well, I probably shouldn't have fired that shot, Gus. Not smart," the detective admitted. "Could have blown us all up. I'm in a little bit of trouble for it."

Gus winced. "Sorry to hear," he said, and then added, "What do you think? Chase wanted to get caught? I mean, he lured me to a rather obvious place with all those symbols."

"What we think is a clue or a symbol is not always a clue or a symbol to the killer."

"Of course it was. Did you see his back?"

Alex snickered and rolled his eyes. "Oh, yes. I did. But you can't assume Chase was working on a conscious level. He's had two identities in a lifetime. Who knows how much the two were really allowed to know about each other?"

"That explains why my intuition was right and wrong," Gus said.

"How so?"

"A while back, I sensed Chase would crack the case, that somehow he'd upstage you, but it turned out he cracked the case because he *was* the case."

"You could have warned me."

"Like I said, my intuition was right and wrong. And I knew how important the case was to you. I didn't want to mess with your mojo."

Mills laughed. "My mojo," he repeated. "Yeah. There's that."

The two men shook hands. "You need me again tomorrow?" Gus asked.

"I do. Sorry."

"No problem. Just call. Let me know where and when," Gus told him. "And when you're all done with this, I think you should take your family away."

"Is that a vision you're getting?"

"No," Gus replied. "It's just a suggestion. A nice vacation somewhere far away."

"I hear England is very nice in the winter," Alex said.

"I hear it's rather bleak."

"How about you?"

Gus stood there considering the options. He thought about spinning the globe, pointing arbitrarily. He thought about surfing at Puerto Viejo or maybe hiking the Inca Trail and meeting with a shaman in Peru. Then he thought about Wales. He got an instant and fleeting vibe that something or someone was waiting for him in Wales. "Seattle," he replied. "I think I'll head up to Seattle."

"Seattle? Talk about bleak."

Gus shrugged and laughed. Then he got in his car and drove home to take Ivy out for a winter stroll.

42

Gus stayed for three days. He couldn't tell how much Seattle had changed, because the big things about Seattle hadn't changed and those big things tended to upstage the little things.

She looked yellow to him and bruised. She acknowledged him with a thin smile then closed her eyes and slept.

There was not a lot of Meg Parker left in the Meg Parker in the bed. Every time he came into the room he looked for her. Sometimes she'd stare back at him with glassy eyes and, again, that thin smile. She said very little. And she answered questions with a yes or a no.

His father said that she'd been getting sick for a couple of months before the diagnosis. He said that the cancer was already taking a toll. He said other things, too, mostly clinical things, and he did go to work half days.

One morning Gus went with them to the hospital and watched his mother undergo chemo. She brought a book. The place smelled of astringent and the rotting, dying organs that the astringent was meant to mask. He asked to speak to her doctor who could not be found until they were all just about ready to leave.

"My father's been cagey about the prognosis," Gus said. "I'd really like to know."

The doctor did a doctor thing (Gus had seen the expression among the radiologists who soberly ponder bad news) and tilted his head back and forth, not a nod, not a shake, a metronome of thought, and said, dispassionately, "We're looking at a year, maybe eighteen months. Are you here for a while?"

"No," Gus said. "I'm leaving tomorrow afternoon."

"Oh."

"But I'd like your number. I'd like to call and check in," Gus told the man. "If that's okay."

"Sure."

Meals were quiet but respectful. There was a din of inevitability that lightly hummed throughout the house, like the running of the refrigerator when everything else goes quiet. Gus didn't want to flash back, but he flashed back. And he saw her in a bathrobe, then a business suit, then an evening gown. He saw her at the grocery store with flawless skin. He saw himself running down the street. An eight-year-old being chased by his uncle. He saw his mother's heart break looking from the window even though Ivan was still alive. He saw a piece of her disappear. He wondered who was estranged from whom. He thought about forgiveness not as a debt but as an act of grace, but he lingered there until he realized that forgiveness often flows both ways, in two directions, often mutual, often magnetic, taking a distinct charge out of the atmosphere.

When Gus left Seattle, when he waved good-bye as he closed the door of the taxi cab, he took with him a visceral distinction between life and death, almost a physical line that split something inside him into two parts.

On descent now, he sees the antennas poking out of the Estrella Mountains, a cluster of alien eyes blinking in the night, and then the more barren outline of South Mountain. The aircraft dips and turns, a precarious bird in a dive home, and Gus sees the muscular ridges of Camelback, blacker than the sky. There's a heartbeat in these monoliths of the valley. There are vibrations that will never die.

And now here is Beatrice Vossenheimer waiting for him as he emerges from the shuffle of arriving passengers. She gives him a big, breathtaking hug. Then kisses him three times. She is gushing. "Gus, Gus, Gus, I'm glad you're home," she sings. "I'm glad you went, but I'm glad you're back."

"You're a sight for sore eyes," he tells her.

She drives him home, and they're greeted by a frenzied Ivy. The dog charges at Gus, slobbering, yipping, and wrestling him to the ground.

"Thanks for dog sitting," he cries from the floor. "What did you feed her? Red Bull?"

Beatrice ignores him and moves into the kitchen. "I hope you don't mind," she calls to him. "I took the liberty of whipping up a salad."

"How great," he says.

He showers while Beatrice puts the food out. He's in sweatpants and a T-shirt when he enters the kitchen. "Looks like you need to hang out for a few days just as you are," she tells him. "Decompress from your trip."

"I'm back to work the day after tomorrow."

They sit. Gus forks through the salad and munches a crouton. The air is easier to breathe here. When they finish eating, Gus clears the dishes and Beatrice curls up on the couch. "There's mail for you," she tells him. "Elsa dropped it off along with the papers."

The pile contains mostly bills and one actual piece of mail. Not much has changed in the newspapers. The arrest of Timothy Chase is still making headlines. Chase has been formally charged and will likely face the death penalty if found guilty. He remains under psychiatric observation at the state prison. According to public records, Chase has been placing calls every day to his mother, Priscilla, who has declined to talk to her son. Everything else about the case continues to be speculation and carrion.

"You weren't following the news during your trip?" Beatrice asks him.

"Not at all."

Gus turns to today's morning paper that, finally, offers up an original headline, one that sends a full recognition to his face:

VALLEY CONTRACTOR INVESTIGATED
IN BRIBERY SEX SCANDAL
Case Could Implicate Local Officials,
May Reveal Forced Prostitution

He is, at once, relieved and terrified for Bridget Mulroney. He wonders if she has the true grit to survive this. Not the affectation of grit with which she has lived from day to day. Vindication isn't always a Hollywood ending. More often it's a maelstrom. He knows this.

"Did you open the card in the mail?" Beatrice calls to him.

"No," he says. "I didn't."

"Open it," she tells him.

He reaches for the pile again and finds a card with no return address, a Paradise Valley postmark. "Are you inviting me to a wedding?"

"Open it."

Inside, Billie Welch's signature lightning bolt adorns the cover of the card:

I'm playing Phoenix Sky Pavilion on the 18th. I'd like to put you on the guest list. Hope we can spend some time. Peace, love, Billie

He smiles. He can't help himself.

"Geez, who writes letters anymore?" he wonders aloud.

"She says she doesn't own a computer," Beatrice says. "Doesn't have an e-mail address."

"Did you know about this?" he asks her as he approaches the couch.

"Like, psychically?"

"No. Like, did she tell you?"

"Yes. She invited me as well, with Max."

"The dude from Safeway?"

"His name is Max," she chirps.

He sinks into the couch beside her. Ivy hops into his lap. "Are you going?"

She smiles impishly. "No, no, Gus. Time for you and Billie to be alone."

"Alone with her band, her road crew, her hair and makeup entourage?"

She raises her head. "Gus. It's time for you to be alone with that woman."

"Okay," he says. "Cool."

She snorts and falls back into the pillow. "Cool? Is that all you can say?"

He nods. That's all he can say. But that's not all he can see.

ACKNOWLEDGMENTS

Thank you for everything, everything, and everything, Paul Milliken. Without you I never would have come back to the velvet underground. I certainly never would have stayed. It doesn't matter if no one else understands what that means. You do. Your faith in me is relentless. You've given me incredible support. To my sister, Nancy Sciore, for calling me every morning and not asking if I'm writing. For just calling and, every so often, saving my life. I'm enormously grateful to my parents for a lot of things, but when it comes to the work I'm doing now, for understanding I am too old to have a fallback position. Thanks for the support, Mom and Dad. My beautiful nieces, Chloe and Marielle: You promised to take care of me when I'm old and senile if I mention you here. I love you like crazy. You amaze me. I mentioned you here. To David O'Leary and Jean Stone, for being the dearest, oldest friends. Billy, Greg, Beth, Nate, Ivette, Mia, and Ethan—I did really well in the in-law department.

I'm grateful to my agent, Ann Collette, for being such a great advocate for this book. She's also an enthusiastic coach, and I hope she doesn't mind if I call her the "Queen of Revisions." She expects you to work. And you're always the better for it. I want to thank my editor at Seventh Street, Dan Mayer, for welcoming *Desert Remains* with such open arms and grooming it with such a keen eye to final publication. I appreciate all the hard work the people at Seventh Street and Prometheus Books do to bring books like this one to life. And thanks, as well, to the team at Penguin Random House for getting *Desert Remains* to booksellers everywhere.

Prior to becoming Maricopa County sheriff, Paul Penzone helped